Sins as Scarlet

NICOLÁS OBREGÓN

PENGUIN BOOKS

PENGUIN BOOKS

UK | USA | Canada | Ireland | Australia
India | New Zealand | South Africa

Penguin Books is part of the Penguin Random House group of companies
whose addresses can be found at global.penguinrandomhouse.com

First published by Michael Joseph 2018
Published in Penguin Books 2018

001

Amexica: War Along the Borderline by Ed Vulliamy. Copyright © 2010,
Ed Vulliamy, used by permission of The Wylie Agency (UK) Limited

Set in 12.46/14.70 pt Garamond MT Std
Typeset by Jouve (UK), Milton Keynes
Printed and bound in Great Britain by Clays Ltd, Elcograf S.p.A.

A CIP catalogue record for this book is available from the British Library

ISBN: 978–1–405–92693–5

www.greenpenguin.co.uk

To Camille

'For where the river runs through,
people will drink.'

– Ed Vulliamy

Mexico–United States Border

The woman was running – half naked, one shoe missing, blood slick down her thighs. She was going as fast as she could, wheezing on the cold air, but the baby inside her weighed so much now. The truck was gaining on her, the sound of the engine deafening.

There was meant to be a river, that's what Adelmo had said. *When we cross it, we'll be safer.* She begged the desert for water, for higher ground, for anything that would stop the truck. She saw only emptiness.

The woman couldn't stop herself from looking over her shoulder. Her foot snagged between two rocks, her ankle twisted, she landed hard on her side. In that moment she knew it was over. All she could do was lie there, trembling.

There was dogbane and Indian paintbrush on the wind, the smells no different than in her own country, less than a mile away. But in her fear it was as if she were smelling them for the first time, a perfume she realized now she had always taken for granted.

The truck was almost on her, dust billowing out behind it like a coming tornado. She knew she had to get up but her body simply wouldn't respond – there was too much pain, too much cold, too much exhaustion. It was numb except for a torn burning in her vagina and a disturbing pain in her ankle.

Headlights blanched the earth white. The little stones around her looked like eyes unblinking. With a quivering whisper, the woman closed her eyes and began to pray in Spanish. 'Most sacred heart of Jesus, I accept from your hands whatever death may please you to send me this night –'

The truck stopped at her feet, the engine still snarling. A door opened and footsteps crunched towards her.

'– with all its pains, penalties and sorrows, in reparation for all my sins, for the souls in Purgatory, for all those who will die today, and your greater glory. Amen.'

'A–*men*!' The man was tall, his voice jolly, an ordinary face beneath his cap. The patch on his shirt read: COUSINS. He smiled. 'You thought you got away, huh?'

A second man got out of the truck. He was short and, despite the thinning black hair and sparse moustache, he had a baby face. His patch read: ORTEGA. Ignoring the woman, he shone his flashlight into the darkness. 'Can't see shit out there.' He smoothed down his moustache. 'Ask her.'

Cousins crouched down beside the woman. 'Okay, honey: husband, boyfriend, Mr Invisible. *¿Dónde está?*'

The woman kept her eyes on the dirt with petrified defiance.

'You know, I don't believe she likes me,' said Cousins.

'Yeah, well.' Ortega scanned the shadows irately. 'I wouldn't like you either.'

Cousins flipped her over and laughed as he batted away the rock she was trying, weakly, to hit him with. 'Aw, now come on, pumpkin. Y'all ran away before our business was concluded.' He ripped off her jacket and flung it away.

'Cousins, we're going to lose him.'

'Okay – *okay*. You're in some mood tonight, you know that?' He gave the woman's breasts a squeeze but stopped when he felt wetness. 'The fuck is this . . . ?'

Ortega shone his flashlight down at the woman's massive belly. 'Pregnant.'

Cousins got up and brushed himself off. 'Didn't notice.'

'Quit fucking around and ask her.'

'You know what your problem is, Theo? You got no sense of serenity.' Cousins gently patted the woman's shoulder, as if it had just been a misunderstanding. 'Ma'am? I'm sorry about before, all right? I didn't realize your, ah, condition. Now, my name is Agent Craig Cousins and that feller right over there is Supervisory Agent Ortega. We're with the United States Border Patrol. You understand that?'

The woman didn't reply. She was crying.

'I want you to know that you're not in any trouble, okay? We just wanna let you go on your way. We have the authority to do that. But listen, we do need to find the man you were with. So come on now, pumpkin. Help us help you. Which way'd he go?'

The woman's eyes were closed in shivering repugnance, tears slicing through her dust-coated cheeks like oil, her teeth chattering.

Sighing, Ortega picked up her jacket from the sand and took out a Top Cat wallet from the pocket. The ID card told him her name was Evelyn Olivera. She was twenty-three years old. He tossed it over.

'Evelyn? That's a pretty name you got there.' Cousins smiled approvingly. 'Lemme ask you something, Evelyn. Is this man the daddy of your baby? I'm asking cos it's colder than shit out here. If you *do* care about him, you gotta tell us which way he went. Else he's in big trouble, pumpkin. Look *around* you.'

Evelyn looked. There were only miles of empty desert, the wind roving through its silent cambers. She wondered if Adelmo Contreras was still out there, if he could see her. She hoped not. She hoped he was miles away.

And then she saw it. In the distance, between her tears, the river. It glittered silver like an arcade coin-pusher. She chose to believe Adelmo had crossed it. He'd made it.

The sky above yawed between black and purple, galaxies long extinguished. Evelyn Olivera knew she was going to die. She wondered if she could adjust to death. Maybe it would be like eyes getting used to the dark. And if God was there, maybe He would be able to forgive her.

'Last chance, *chiquita*.' Cousins patted her on the calf.

She looked both men in the eye, then spat. 'Fuck you.'

'Well, that sure is a shame.' Cousins tutted then turned to his partner. 'Come on, man. It's not my turn.'

Ortega shrugged. He took out his gun, pointed it at Evelyn's face and fired twice.

She made small sounds, like a broken radio trying to find a frequency. When that stopped, her leg twitched several times, then she was still.

A few hundred feet away there was a scream – a figure standing next to a mesquite tree.

4

'Ah, there you are.' Ortega licked his lips, took aim and fired.

The figure broke into a run towards the river.

Another three shots hit nothing. 'Fuck, I'm out. Cousins, give me yours.'

'My gun's still in the truck.'

'Then go fucking get it!'

'Theo, he's running north. He's finished.'

'We can't afford any stragglers.'

'Partner, he's *gone*. He's got no drinking water. Look at him, he's running for the river and it's already freezing. The fucker's heading straight into a black hole.'

Ortega re-holstered. He squinted into the distance and saw the figure running – almost at the river now – tiny in the darkness.

Supervisory Border Patrol Agent Theodore Ortega spoke in a whisper. 'Welcome to America.'

PART ONE
Four Years Later

1. Gold Coins to a Cat

Kosuke Iwata was pushing a shopping trolley along the aisles of Mitsuwa Marketplace. It was busy for a Monday. Akiko Nakamura was singing 'San Francisco (Be Sure to Wear Some Flowers in Your Hair)', the verses in Japanese, the chorus in English.

Iwata passed by Cosmetics and the woman behind the counter waved. They made small talk and she told him his mother seemed to be doing well. He knew the woman didn't mean anything by it, but the implication was that he wouldn't know how his own mother was. He thanked her and pushed his cart towards the pickle aisle, where he picked up ginger, daikon and plums.

For the better part of an hour Iwata deliberated over baby abalone, their shells pearlescent in the bright lights. He weighed up fresh yellowtail steaks, gleaming ballet-pink against the dark, woody flesh of bluefin tuna. There was no shopping list; the tradition had always been that he would buy ingredients that jumped out at him and his mother would interpret them as she saw fit.

When his cart was finally full Iwata made his way to the checkout. The cashier bagged his goods, gave him his change on a plastic platter and bowed. Outside, he loaded his shopping into the trunk of a moss-green Ford Bronco almost as old as he was. As he did so he listened to two elderly Japanese men chatting about the coming snow – *the kind that really accumulates.*

Iwata looked up. The sky was sharp blue, the sun tingling on his shoulders. Palm trees shushed in the breeze. Across the road, McDonald's was open twenty-four hours a day, the American flag flying outside it. An inactive neon sign above the parking lot read:

BILLIONS SERVED

It was still winter, but there would be no snow here. This was Torrance. Yet the old men were not discussing the weather in California. Iwata took them for *nisei*, second generation, born in a new land to Japanese immigrants – *issei*, first generation. He listened to the way they spoke about America, as though their lives here were temporary, little more than a quaint reverie. For them, it was Japan where the weather mattered; the Torrance palm trees merely likable props.

Iwata understood the importance of heritage, he just didn't much care about home or where it could be found; he'd done without for the better part of forty years. Here in California he was Japanese. In Japan, he was an outsider. And so, for him, the weather was simply whatever was happening over his head.

Kosuke Iwata's mother, Nozomi, had abandoned him in a rural bus station when he was a child. Down the years, there had been the odd phone call and a few strangely worded letters, as though Iwata were on some well-planned journey, but he did not see his mother for the better part of a decade.

The summer before she came back for him had been a torrid one for Iwata. His only friend, Kei, had disappeared from the orphanage, the police able to do little more than shrug shoulders. After that he had become lost in a silent, miserable rage, expecting nothing from anyone.

And so, although Nozomi had repeatedly promised that she would collect him, he was shocked to see her standing at the gates one day. By then, he was a head taller than her. To his surprise, there was a man by her side, a tall American in military uniform. Gerry Kaminsky, his new father, clapped him on the back. *Let's get you out of here, pal.*

Iwata remembered the flight clearly. Gerry explained that, due to the time zones, their arrival at LAX would be earlier than their departure from Narita. *Like travelling back in time.*

Seeing Los Angeles for the first time, he thought it looked like a city trying to disguise itself as a greener place, the scorched browns and greys in some kind of tropical drag. Within a few days, Iwata was enrolled in a new school and speaking a new language. Almost immediately, Japan and the orphanage faded away, as though none of it had ever happened.

Gerry thought Torrance would be perfect for his new wife and son. There had been a large Japanese community there for decades. It was home to major Japanese corporations, Japanese schools, Japanese restaurants, Japanese banks. Some even called it 'Japan's 48th Prefecture'. Gerry put down the deposit on a house and booked the Toyota Meeting Hall for his wedding to Nozomi. He figured the Japanese hotels would come in handy for relatives visiting from Japan. None ever came.

As he grew up Iwata understood the logic in his stepfather's choice. But to him, Torrance would only ever feel like a place he happened to be staying in – never home. As soon as he was able to he escaped to Los Angeles.

917 Beech Avenue was an agreeable ranch-style house, dappled in the shade of a tall sycamore. Iwata parked outside and crossed the lawn, seeds crunching underfoot, the glass wind chimes tinkling in welcome. The TV was loud. He opened the door and took off his shoes in the *genkan*. Some of Gerry's were still there.

Iwata sighed and drank in the smell of the house, a mess of sweetness that had never changed – clove with star anise. He paused to look at the photos hanging on the wall, something he rarely did.

Iwata saw himself as a teenager, in his school's baseball uniform, a grudge match against North Torrance. Though he was pale with fear, he was expressionless, looking to camera, the bat hanging by his side. He remembered that day. He had struck out.

The choice of high school for her son had been a no-brainer for Nozomi. Almost half of the students enrolled were of Asian descent. She had seen no reason why her son wouldn't be able to make friends, get good grades and fit in. In the end, she had been right about the grades.

In the next photograph Iwata was holding his college diploma, a half-smile on his skinny face. In the dim hallway he saw his reflection. It was still a slender face, his stubble darker. His hair was longer and greying, a stubborn clump of frozen grass on some tundra. His skin was a mellow tan with some small wrinkles at the eyes. Cleo had once compared him to Hiroyuki Sanada, though he hadn't seen it himself.

And there she was in the final photograph, grinning to camera. *Cleo*. Her hair was dark blonde – she wore it in a pageboy style back then – her dusky blue eyes narrowed, as if suspicious at happiness itself. She was wearing one of Iwata's shirts over paint-spattered dungarees and covering her smile with a hand. Iwata was next to her, caught mid-blink, holding Nina. Her little eyes were closed, one fist clenched as if about to choose rock, paper or scissors. On her pudgy forearm there was a chestnut of a birthmark. Iwata was smiling too, facing the horizon, not realizing the picture was being taken.

Only their upper halves were visible. He wondered whether there were any photographs in the world left of Cleo's feet. Seeing them for the first time, large and monkeyish, he had laughed, and Cleo had swatted his arm. When Nina was born, scarcely able to take in her face, he had looked at her feet instead. They were pink and chalky, but tiny replicas of his wife's.

In the photograph there were mountains, a hazy Californian sunset beyond them. Somewhere in the Angeles Forest, he thought. Pacifico Mountain, maybe. Or was it Mount Williamson? Either way, it would have been Cleo's idea; the hike would have been a homage to one of their early dates, as if returning victoriously to an old battlefield, now with a husband and an infant to show for it.

Cleo always spoke of their early days with a zealous passion. It was an intensity Iwata was never able to outwardly match. Something had always hindered him, some numb embarrassment. Even on their first meeting Iwata had known they were very different people. Cleo always found great significance in small details – weather, dates, names; he found significance in very little. Iwata labelled things coincidence while Cleo would smile with enigmatic satisfaction, as though the cosmic designer had just tipped its hand and she'd been quick enough to glimpse it.

For Iwata, those differences had not seemed so significant. He asked her out on their second meeting, some pretext about listening to a record she had coming into her shop. They had gone for a picnic, he was almost certain, and there were *absolutely* strawberries, that was inarguable. But much else was gone. He wondered how strawberries could be clearer than entire conversations. Perhaps their simple red flesh was easier to grasp than the tide of inflections and subtleties that constituted human interaction.

Or else the mind was, Kosuke Iwata concluded, an unsentimental curator. It clutched stubbornly to the insignificant yet dispensed with the meaningful in great clods.

He consoled himself with the fact that details were less important than feelings. Up in those hills, high above Los Angeles and feeling much further away from the city than they were, they *had* walked together. Through a never-ending parade of Californian walnut trees, along dusty ridges enveloped in chaparral and succulents, he half expected to see cowboys galloping over the horizon.

Long after the sun had set, in the true dark of mountains, she had lain on his chest, the feel of her like warm lead. Though they were less than an hour's drive from the city, hidden deep in their swale, the small fire had been the only light either could see.

For Iwata, the sound of that fire was categorically clear to this day. It was a soft rustling. It was Christmas wrapping paper. It was a quiet snapping, like dreams. It was the singing of his ghosts.

He opened his eyes. Cleo and Nina were both gone. Iwata wondered if he could ask his mother to take the photographs down. She had only met his wife and child on a few occasions and never once displayed any kind of approval. She had been affectionate with the baby and sent gifts through the mail but he had sensed her discomfort even in her brief letters. And she had barely spoken to him as his life disintegrated through the winter of 2009, as though it were better to let him spiral than try to pilot the crash landing.

Yet here the photographs of Cleo and Nina still hung, proudly welcoming the gaze of any visitor, the first impression of the house. It was as if they were souvenirs from a country Nozomi Iwata had never been to. Iwata wanted them gone, but that would take talking. He couldn't even begin to find the words for such a request. The time for talking with his mother was long gone.

'Kosuke?' Nozomi called out.

'Yes,' Iwata called back.

'I thought I heard something.'

In the kitchen Iwata kissed his mother of the top of her head, the sound of her voice softening his disposition. 'That perfume smells nice.'

'It's nothing.' She blew her fringe out of her face. It was a fine face, pouty lips, big, beseeching eyes and a thick head of black hair – little of which she had passed on to her son.

'Nothing, huh? The cosmetics girl said you looked well.'

Nozomi rolled her eyes, one of their few shared gestures. 'Stop being a detective for five minutes and help me clean the fish.' Iwata laid the shopping bags on the table and his mother inspected the haul. 'You spent a lot. Work must be good.'

'What are you watching?'

'*The Wendy Williams Show*. I hate her, but I watch.'

'That'll rot your brain.'

'What makes you think it's so fresh to begin with?'

Iwata wondered why they only ever really conversed in English. It was true that his own was flawless and his mother's had little wrong with it beyond an accent and the odd slip-up. Yet it was not their language. Gerry was no longer here. For whose benefit was it? Perhaps, he thought, it was easier to separate their past from when their new life in America had started. Japanese, then, represented the *before* – Iwata's childhood in the orphanage, before Nozomi had come back for him. She never spoke of those years and Iwata had never asked. He knew enough. She had been in a bad place and had left him at the bus station.

He never asked her reasons for leaving him there, whether out of pride or fear, he didn't know. She certainly never offered any. That was the *before*; that was Japan. It hardly seemed to make sense to dredge it up here in America. So it came to be that English overtook Japanese, although silence, more often than not, was their lingua franca.

'Is everything okay, Mom?'

She looked at him. 'Everything is fine.'

'Good.'

In the small kitchen, they prepared lunch, Nozomi occasionally giving directions and pausing as celebrities cried, Iwata just shaking his head.

After lunch they sat out on the porch, drinking coffee. The sky was turning amber in the dusk, warblers singing in the branches above them. A Van Morrison album was playing in the lounge, Iwata's mother's favourite song – 'Beside You'. Van Morrison was one of the few things they agreed on absolutely. Nozomi was wearing sunglasses and reading the *Torrance Tribune*. She would read every word of it, even the sports and adverts, as though one day someone were going to come and test her on her American knowledge. It was also her usual prop for conversing with her son.

Iwata sipped his coffee and waved hello to a passing couple he didn't recognize. 'Who are they?' he asked when they had passed.

'I don't know, but they argue.' Nozomi peered at him over the top of the paper. 'Then again, at least they have somebody to argue with.'

'Not this again. You're wasting your breath.'

'Why, have you already met someone? Is she Japanese?'

'I don't understand why you're so obsessed with Japanese women.'

'Where you're from is important.'

'Yet you haven't been back there in years.'

'My reasons are my own. Now listen, does she know what you do for a living? This matters. Women prefer dumplings over flowers.'

'What does that even mean? You always talk at me in aphorisms.'

'What?'

'Aphorisms. They're like a –'

'Kosuke, you know *I* don't feel this way but men in your profession are seen as losers.'

'By who?'

'*People*. People around here whisper about you. They call you a *debagame*.'

'Well, believe it or not, I'm not too concerned with supermarket gossip. I'm a professional investigator. If they want to call me a peeping Tom, it's no skin off my nose.'

'I'm just saying.' Nozomi dropped her paper and

spoke into her coffee. 'You're forty. You follow married women around all day and take photographs. A nice girlfriend won't like that.'

Iwata laughed. 'Maybe I'm not looking for a nice woman. Or any woman at all. But that's not the point. The point is, if the biddies at Mitsuwa disapprove of what I do, too bad. But if it's you that disapproves of what I do, just say it out loud.'

Nozomi put down her cup and took off her sunglasses. Sometimes months would go by without Iwata seeing her eyes and every so often her elderly appearance would startle him.

'Kosuke, listen. It's your life. I never pressured you to make me proud. I just don't want you to be alone –'

'I don't think either one of us has ever been very proud of the other, Mom.'

She looked up at the sky and put her sunglasses back on. 'Maybe not.'

'Look, I know you don't like what I do with my life. It doesn't reflect well on you, pillar of the community that you are. But understand this: I'm not marrying again. I did it once. And look how that turned out.'

Nozomi exhaled slowly. 'You hardly come to see me and every time you do you argue with me. I'm not disappointed in you. I never will be. I just want you to be happy.'

'Okay.'

'Kosuke, one day I want to talk to you. Explain. I think we could –'

'Not today, Mom.'

She nodded once and they sat in silence until it was dark. Then Iwata checked his watch and kissed his mother on the top of her head. From that angle, he could see the tears in her eyes. Pain and guilt tumbled through his gut. He wanted to say something but he just didn't know where to find those words.

'Take some of the food with you.'

'No, you have it tomorrow.'

'I always tell you to buy less.'

'Next time I will.'

'Gold coins to a cat, son. That's what my words are to you.'

2. A Sad Business

Driving east on Sunset Boulevard, Iwata decided to treat himself. He stopped at his favourite walk-up spot, Tacos Delta, and went for a plate of steak picado, rice, beans and an iced Jamaica. He sat near the open kitchen door, enjoying the sound of the laughter and the Spanish over the hiss of the cooking. Iwata liked the smell of the warm spices mixing in with the smoky tang of the parking lot.

The cooks doubled as waiters, wearing hairnets and neat moustaches, addressing customers in English or Spanish, depending on their skin colour. They would manage to fire off several wisecracks as they wheeled out of the kitchen, dropped off dishes and scrambled back in.

Iwata's food arrived and he slathered it in the spiciest salsa they had. He ate under the coloured bulbs, amid grinning families and day-labourers swatting away moths.

3375 Descanso Drive was a small ten-unit condo complex with butterscotch-stucco exterior walls veiled in bougainvillea. To the south, there was a sudden and beautiful vista of Downtown LA. This neighbourhood had once belonged to the poor, the sex workers, the junkies. Later came the artists, the hipsters, the hopeful actors. Now, like many once-diverse slices of the city, it made developers hot under the collar, ripe for reinvention in luxury, highly vendible to wealthy white folk looking to buy in 'edgy' areas.

Iwata opened his front door and smelled the usual mix of laundry and dashi stock. He silently greeted the sweet bay plant in the corner that was starting to make its case as a small tree. He'd been meaning to organize the place ever since he'd moved in, but that had been three years ago. He owned little beyond books and records anyhow.

Iwata picked out two letters from his mailbox, one from his internet provider, the other a clipping from the *Torrance Tribune* regarding a Japanese singles night on Sawtelle Boulevard next week. A Post-It note in his mother's awkward little handwriting was attached: *Go. x*

Sighing, Iwata took an alcohol-free beer from the fridge, sat at the coffee table and fished out his advanced-Spanish CDs. He took a swig and pressed Play on his CD.

'Hello, again! *¡Hola amigos!*'

Iwata raised his beer.

'*¿Cómo están todos?* Today we'll be looking at the preterite versus the imperfect. So let's get started! *¡Empezamos! ¿Estás listo?* Then let's try: Ramón spoke for two hours. I'll repeat. Ramón spoke for two hours.'

Iwata cleared his voice. '*Ramón habló dos horas.* Preterite.'

'. . . did you say "preterite"? *¡Bien hecho!* Well done! Okay, let's try another one: The girls were speaking in English. The girls were speaking in English.'

'*Las chicas hablaban en inglés.* Imperfect.'

'. . . did you say "imperfect"? I bet you did! *Aplausos, amigo.*'

Iwata went through the exercises on autopilot. He'd never really thought too much about learning Spanish but when he had found himself colliding with it on an almost daily basis in his work, he had decided to take classes. Now he was more or less confident in his conversation and his vocabulary was solid. He enjoyed being able to use interesting sentence structures, arriving at a destination along differing routes. It gave him pleasure to think how far he'd come.

When the CD was over Iwata went into the spare room, took off his shirt and sized up his heavy bag. Iwata threw fast, snapping punches, his feet always moving between shots, his hands never dropping. He'd joined the boxing class on a whim, drawn in by the stupid neon bicep outside; it was something to fill empty hours. Pleased with the lack of chat and posturing, he'd stayed with it.

As he worked out, he thought about apologizing to his mother. He knew he should. But then, it was always so easy to do in theory.

Hearing a noise, Iwata embraced the punchbag. The phone was ringing. He wiped his brow and picked up. 'Hello?'

'Kosuke . . . it's me.'

'Kate? Is everything all right?'

'Actually, it's not.'

'How can I help?'

'God, I don't know how to say this.' She took a shaky breath. 'It's my husband. Kosuke, I need you to follow him . . . I'm going crazy. I need to know.'

Iwata had known Kate Floccari for over a year, having met her at a convention. When he had told her what he did for a living she had given him her card – as a prosecutor, she was in need of someone in his line of work. Since then, they had worked together on dozens of occasions. Iwata helped her prep for cross-examination, spending long hours going over weaknesses in witnesses, or an opponent's background and how they might react under pressure. He had located assets for her, everything from stolen artwork to offshore accounts – even industrial designs. And, their bread and butter – he had located people: reluctant witnesses, secret mistresses, employees with knowledge of corporate misconduct; on and on it went . . . But it had never been personal. Until now.

'Meet me at my office at 9 a.m. We'll talk then.'

Anthony Floccari was miles away from campus. Even if anyone saw him, it could surely be written off as coincidence. Professors bumped into their students all the time. He sat on a bench reading *Malina* by Ingeborg Bachmann and told himself that he was doing nothing wrong. Then, biting his nails, he contradicted himself. *Maybe, sooner or later, forbidden acts are just inevitable.*

Distant drilling reverberated through the afternoon.

Soft currents rattled the cherry blossoms into pink wedding send-offs. The brunch crowd grinned over iced coffee and eggs.

Anthony had wanted Anya since the first time she walked into his class. That was not particularly surprising; he frequently found himself fantasizing about his students. He'd just never done anything more than fantasize.

It would have been nice for him, as a sort of moral black box, to be able to point to a startling aptitude with sentence structure, or even just a splash of originality in her work. But the truth was Anthony just liked the way she looked.

'Hey, Prof.'

He turned, feigning surprise. The straps of her tank top and bra were misaligned. She had three freckles beneath her collarbone, as if indicating her rank in an army of women he wanted to fuck.

'Anya,' he purred. 'Sit down.'

'Thanks.' She sat and rolled her tongue across her teeth. 'So I checked, and the line in there is, like, crazy long.'

She's cancelling. Anthony felt both disappointed and relieved.

'Well, it's no big –'

'But, uh, I live close by,' she blurted. 'We could just have coffee at my place?'

He glanced at her mouth. Her lipstick was almost black. She tossed her hair, apricot shampoo drifting under his nostrils. They hadn't even agreed on a pretext for meeting.

Just have coffee at my place, he repeated in his head. *Just. Just. Just. How many shipwrecks had come from* just *a few grey clouds.*

'Or not!' Anya laughed. 'It's okay. I get it if it's, like, you know, *weird*.'

Anthony stood and grinned. He knew it was a formidable grin.

'No. It's not weird at all.'

When Anthony got home he felt both exhilarated and terrified. For some reason he thought he was going to burst out laughing as he opened the front door. Then he heard his wife's voice. Kate was muffled, speaking over the sound of running water.

'What did you say?' he called out, trying to sound the way he always did.

'*Ants*. They're back.'

'Ants?'

'You know: tiny, six legs, unwelcome.'

'They're back?'

'Yes. They're back . . . As are you' – she glanced up at the clock – 'at a quarter to ten.'

Kate was drowning the ants with torrents of hot water, like some small offended god.

'I lost track of time at the gym.'

'For *three* hours? I called the college; they said you'd left early.'

'You called?' He used his smile, hoping it looked unthreatened. 'Since when do we call?'

She was still holding his gaze.

'Kate, what is this? I left early to beat traffic, which

obviously I didn't do, then there's parking, there's changing, there's showering, there's getting gas, then there's more traffic. Come on, it's LA – you know this.'

It sounded solid, but he reminded himself to fill the tank first thing tomorrow.

'I'm sorry.' She shook her head. 'I just – I don't know . . .'

Anthony turned off the tap and hugged her. 'It's okay. The pregnancy is just playing hell with you, that's all. I love you, Kate.'

'I love you,' she murmured into his chest.

He stroked her hair, knowing there was no way he could smell of anything but soap. They took two alcohol-free beers out to the balcony, him on the right, her on the left. That's how they slept, how they fucked these days, and how they usually posed in photographs.

Kate reached out and pinched his bicep. 'That gym is paying off.'

The far-off whoosh of the freeway was soothing, the lukewarm night ruffling their hair paternally. Anthony's return smile was wan. 'Gotta keep tight for my girl.'

She stroked the rim of her bottle with her bottom lip and looked at the ocean beyond the freeway. He knew he was the only one to see these childlike gestures. As one of the most feared prosecutors in the city, every daytime gesture, every word, would convey purpose. But these throwaway mannerisms that only came out at night were the real her – like gentle, reclusive nocturnal creatures. He used to love these gestures. Now, he just knew them.

'Hey,' Anthony spoke brightly, despite his thoughts. 'You okay?'

27

'Mm.'

'What's up?'

'Nothing.'

'*Kate.*'

'I just had this dumb feeling earlier.' She whispered it. 'Like maybe the idea of the baby had freaked you out and you were going AWOL on us.'

Anthony met her eyes. Sometimes she looked like a kid. He felt disgusted with himself.

'I know,' she laughed. 'I know. It's dumb.'

'It *is* dumb.' He regained himself in that winning grin and curled a hand around the nape of her neck. 'I'm not going anywhere, Kiki.'

They held hands in silence.

She's going to be the mother of my child. I'm happy with my life.

But as the traffic lights far below changed he asked himself the obvious: *Then why Anya?*

Anthony Floccari was respected for his writing, in his work. Money had ceased to be a real concern some time ago. He had a beautiful wife. But none of it was enough. It never was.

Once, as a small child, he had met his great-grandmother in Bologna. His Italian was sparse but he had understood her judgement of him. *He's a looker but careful with him, that boy has a hole in his basket.* For a few years Kate seemed to have filled him in, like concrete. But she lived her life by a certain code, which, after such a long time, he had grown weary of. With her rules and expectations, she felt like a beautiful little prison.

Anya, however, had no rules. She was absolutely his.

She would do anything he wanted and would knit her brow in concentration to get it done well. She would laugh at his jokes, gag on his cock and *learn* from his anecdotes. In the afternoon sun, naked in her bed, she had shrieked with laughter at his impressions of her classmates. Closing his eyes, he could still see her tits jiggling, still hear the lilt of her giggles as she begged him to stop. To his alarm, Anthony realized he was getting an erection. He folded his legs.

'I need a shower,' Kate said.

They kissed. When she was gone, Anthony went downstairs and grilled some asparagus. As he ate, he watched a documentary about Mayan culture. At 10.30 p.m. he deleted the text message that read: *I'm still sore. I love the feeling.* x

One week later Anthony took Anya away for the weekend to San Diego. He kept his cap on during the day, feeling more relaxed after sunset. At the hotel, he liked that she would take hours perfecting her make-up and evening dress – as though her entire life had been leading up to this long weekend. They ate prawns grilled by barefoot men in white jackets, wooden torches illuminating the private beach. In that light, he thought Anya could pass for a tanned Jane Russell.

On their last day they went for a stroll through Balboa Park. At the outdoor theatre her delighted squeal when he revealed tickets for *King Lear* scared the birds from the trees. During the performance Anya whispered along with Cordelia and Anthony tried to hide his irritation.

The sunset was perfect against the flowering jacaranda trees, the girl next to him was beautiful, his life was inarguably a good one. Yet he could almost taste his dissatisfaction. Everything was annoying to him now. He regretted coming to San Diego. The risk of running into an acquaintance was foolish and, on reflection, four days with the girl had been way too long. Once he had come her repertoire of charms greatly diminished, while his list of irritations had grown to a point where none of it made sense anymore.

As Edmund plotted to depose his brother, Anthony decided he had to get rid of her. *Soon as I'm back, I'll talk to her. She'll understand. How could she not understand? I'll cut her loose and then it'll be as if nothing ever happened. Kate won't know a thing and I'll work hard to make her happy. Happiest she's been. This was all just a freak-out before fatherhood.*

Anthony looked up and a deafening rumble grew closer.

On stage, the actors froze.

Amiable laughter rippled through the amphitheatre as the passenger jet passed overhead, making its final descent to nearby Lindbergh Field. When the sound had passed, the actors sprang back into life as if un-Paused.

'"The art of our necessities is strange."' The king shook his head gently. '"That can make vile things precious."'

Anthony distantly registered a flash somewhere behind him. He turned to search the audience but recognized no one. Even so, he pulled the brim of his cap lower.

'You okay?' Anya whispered, her smile glittering in the dusky shadow.

'Sure. Why?'

'You just seem, like, kinda far away.'

He slipped his hand around the nape of her neck and grinned. 'I'm right here.'

'Good.' She rested her head on his outstretched arm and kissed it.

A dozen rows behind, up in the balcony, Kosuke Iwata unscrewed his telescopic lens. He put the camera back in its case, as if placing the murder weapon in an evidence bag. Packing up the rest of his equipment, he put on his tea-shade sunglasses and quietly left the theatre.

In the end, it had taken Iwata just a few days to catch his mark. The Floccari house was in Pacific Palisades, on a pretty cul-de-sac with a handsome ocean view. Hopping out of the Bronco, Iwata drank in the beauty of Coperto Drive – single-storey houses, cached in ceanothus lilac, bougainvillea and flowering palms. Clients came in all shapes and sizes but just as often than not they led enviable lives, full of wealth and pleasure. Yet these were lives they risked throwing away, seemingly as extreme sport. Iwata didn't judge; there were always reasons and he had been there himself.

Iwata let himself in using the spare keys Kate had given him. First, he checked the browsing history on Floccari's computer then combed his study for the better part of an hour, but he found nothing relevant. He searched the house for a hidden phone: no dice. He riffled through clothes, shoes and gym gear. The laundry told him nothing either. Outside, he upended the garbage and there, in amongst the scraps, Iwata found a piece of paper ripped into six pieces. They formed a jigsaw of hasty blue letters:

S DIEGO HOTEL. CHECK IN AFTER 12.
PROMO CODE: THURS25.

Iwata googled 'THURS25 San Diego hotel' and struck gold. Taking out his phone, he dialled.

'Hotel del Coronado, how may I help you?'

'Hi there, my name is Anthony Floccari and I checked in a few days ago. I just wanted to see if there were any messages left for me? F-L-O-C-C-A-R-I.'

'Absolutely, sir. Let me just check that real quick . . . No, doesn't seem to be anything for you Mr Floccari. Is there anything else I can help you with –'

Iwata hung up.

The drive from Pacific Palisades to San Diego had taken just over three hours. With his brightest smile, Iwata approached the hotel reception and asked after his dear colleague, Tony Floccari. The receptionist, clearly new to the job, cheerily confirmed the reservation.

'Is he in now? I'd love to surprise him.'

'He left a little while ago with his partner.'

'Shoot.' Iwata snapped his fingers ruefully. 'Any idea where they went?'

'Matter of fact, I do, sir,' she beamed. '*King Lear.* Sold him the tickets myself.'

*

In the consultation room of Iwata's rented unit, Iwata Investigations LLC, Kate Floccari held a glossy photograph with quivering hands. The lighting in the image was unintentionally gorgeous, the golden hour catching the girl's beauty with devastating clarity. She was closing her eyes in pleasure as Floccari held the nape of her neck. They looked stock-photo happy.

Iwata supposed Kate recognized the gesture. In his experience people were capable of inhabiting various sexual personas, depending on what they were hiding, or what they were trying to be. But when it came to intimacy, people only ever knew one way of loving, a solitary assemblage of gestures and murmurings.

'I'm very sorry, Kate.'

No speeches were needed. The wounded were barely listening anyhow. They were living in a new reality.

'You were fast.' She spoke without looking up. 'Thank you for being fast.'

'Do you have any questions?'

'She's young. A student?'

'Yes. I have her name. If you wanted to know. Other details . . .'

Kate shook her head. 'They look good together.'

'Do you want some water? Or maybe . . .'

She broke down. Iwata stayed in his seat. It wasn't that he felt nothing and it wasn't that he had no wish to comfort her. He just knew that sitting in silence was the best response. The only response. All else was useless.

As Kate sobbed, she held her stomach. She was already showing.

33

Iwata looked out of the window. Wilshire Boulevard was clogged with afternoon traffic. Roadworks had dragged on for weeks and the heat shimmered between stationary cars. A homeless man in flip-flops pushed his cart of blackened teddy bears and knick-knacks slowly along the sidewalk, stopping to address injustice wherever he saw it. Iwata saw him most days. He would rail against the system or, if he was in a good mood, he would revert to his catchphrase. *The best of luck. The BEST of luck!* A grubby American flag fluttered in his cart.

Kate stood up and placed the photograph face down on the desk. She never needed to see it again. Her eyes were red and her lips trembling but her expression was resolute.

'Thank you, Kosuke. I mean it. I'm in your debt.'

'Not at all.'

'You'll have payment by tomorrow afternoon.'

'Please, none necessary.'

'You'll have payment by tomorrow afternoon.'

She left the room and Iwata waited a few minutes before filing away the photograph. Anthony Floccari disappeared into the folders of the unfaithful, the missing, the liars. They were the unwitting clientele in Iwata's trade, one half of an equation of human doubt and vulnerability.

Iwata looked at the framed cityscapes of Downtown LA on the wall. They had been left by the unit's previous occupants, an accounting venture run by Armenian brothers. The print on the wall behind him showed Angels Flight in black and white, full of passengers, in all its glory. Beneath it, the words of Norman Mailer ran in Didot font:

LOS ANGELES IS A CONSTELLATION OF PLASTIC

Iwata closed the blinds and left the consultation room. In the elevator he tapped his foot along with a bossa nova version of 'Hotel California'. Though he usually had no feelings about the cases he took on, he was glad this one was closed.

Iwata did not particularly enjoy his job, but he did like solving puzzles, even rudimentary ones. His was the business of lives changing, the cataclysm of the truth for money. But it was never personal. Kosuke Iwata didn't do personal.

Back on Descanso Drive, Iwata picked up the sweet bay plant and went outside. He sat with his back to the front door, gently inspecting the leaves. They gave off a fragrance only when touched. It was the closest he was ever going to get to having a pet.

Iwata felt serene, more or less. He scanned the black-orange tinsel of the cityscape and wondered what it meant to him. LA wasn't home, but it was something. Japan was behind him and there was little that he missed.

In its place, Iwata had gotten used to the palm trees and the blue skies. He'd gotten used to the February summers and the June gloom. To the swarm of helicopters that criss-crossed the skyline at any one time. The toy-sized subway system and one-minute waits at pedestrian crossings. Mothers walking children to school under parasols and dark Mexican men in high-vis fixing what needed fixing.

He'd gotten used to crammed freeways named after dead police officers and a half-empty Downtown in the evenings. The lines for sushi in Little Tokyo nearby, its businesses largely operated by Koreans now. The loquacious Hollywood touts that pounced on tourists gazing down at the sidewalk stars. The smell of baking wafting through Little Armenia and the distant barbecue aroma of wildfires devouring cypress, mesquite and pine trees.

He had gotten used to the officer-involved shootings in Vermont Vista, in Crenshaw. The police car chases every other night. The addiction treatment centres flecked along the Pacific Coast Highway. The near-dead trickle of the Los Angeles River. Little speakeasies in Silver Lake where wannabes tried to flog screenplays to executives only interested in lines young and curved, or white and straight.

He'd gotten used to the smiling Scientologists south of Los Feliz wearing waistcoats and slacks like an army of flight attendants with nowhere to fly to. The infinite homeless camps over intersections, under bridges, in doorways. The convertibles revving along Rodeo Drive.

He'd gotten used to the countless glowing yard shrines to the Virgin of Guadalupe in East LA. The hopeful singers in Mariachi Plaza and the downhearted drunks that looked on. The million aspiring actresses lining up for work, paid or unpaid. And the men who would make promises to them. The brief celebrity sighting under the hotel portico and the blood drying in the alleyway behind it. The little clouds of jasmine perfume that turned dark street corners into wedding arbours. And the Santa Ana winds, blown in from the Great Basin by the devil himself, leaving fire in their wake.

Kosuke Iwata had gotten used to the staggered pockets of city that made up Los Angeles.

He showered, brushed his teeth and got into bed. He figured tomorrow would be just another day, another case.

3. The Best of Luck

As usual, Iwata woke at dawn. He opened the bedroom window and breathed in the chilly air as he listened to the groundswell of distant traffic. He dressed in an old T-shirt and went outside to stretch under the bougainvillea. The cityscape was still black, but the sky beyond it was turning musk melon. As Iwata clutched his kneecaps to his stomach he had a vague feeling it was going to be a productive day.

It took him half an hour, running through the near-empty streets, to reach Downtown. As he ran he thought about his life, though he stayed in the shallows.

In 2011 Iwata had left Japan blindly, arriving back in California with nothing. A few days later he passed a private investigations agency in Hollywood. There was a sign in the window:

WE'RE HIRING

Iwata already had the requisite six thousand hours of paid investigative experience and he figured he was too old to hone another skill-set anyhow. He aced the two-hour multiple-choice exam on laws and regulation, and learned the Private Investigator Act by heart. He paid his $175 to the Bureau of Security and Investigative

Services and applied for his licence. $32 went to the Department of Justice for a fingerprint-processing fee and $19 to the FBI for the same. Within a month Iwata was officially a private eye, though he preferred the term 'professional investigator'.

Originally assuming it to be a simple pay cheque, Iwata quickly learned what a competitive industry private investigation was. But he had pedigree. Languages. He had cleared major cases. Back in Tokyo, his last homicide investigation had become a national media event.

Those that knew him wondered openly why he didn't apply for LAPD, reasoning that he could waltz his way to a detective's desk in a few years. After all, he'd already graduated from the academy. Peers would laugh at him, seeing a Michelin-star chef working at a Taco Bell. But it didn't bother Iwata.

After a year at the Hollywood agency and a quietly solid reputation he took out a loan and set up his own firm. The work poured in and the months floated by. For the first time he could remember Iwata felt a mild contentment with his life. His stint with the Tokyo Metropolitan Police and the Shibuya Homicide Division felt like another Iwata – a strange, grey golem of himself.

Of course, leaving Japan behind had come at a cost. On a superficial level there was the relinquishment of his police career. Iwata had not only brought the killer to justice in the infamous Black Sun Murders, he'd also exposed deeply entrenched corruption in the Tokyo Metropolitan Police and beyond. His name had been in all the papers. Now he was riffling through Anthony Floccari's rubbish.

But he'd walked away from the TMPD in a heartbeat. Homicide demanded its disciples to live in death and Iwata had lost his stomach for death a long time ago, if he'd ever had one in the first place.

Leaving Japan also meant abandoning Cleo. Not that she knew much about it; his wife had been in a persistent vegetative state, or unresponsive wakefulness syndrome, or whatever the neurologists were calling it now, for several years. He hated the idea of leaving her at the sanatorium; the guilt of it was all he could taste for months. But he knew he couldn't stay in Japan any longer.

Cleo died in her sleep two years later. In a broken relief, he had her ashes split between their daughter's urn and another one he sent to her family. Even before her death he knew his guilt would never truly leave him. Like the scars on his body, Cleo would always be there inside him.

But realizing that meant accepting it. He no longer went to bed with vodka on the bedside table. He craved the chalky crunch of sedatives less frequently. No more did he wake up sobbing. Iwata had started a new life and though he didn't feel he deserved it he had found something approximating peace.

Stopping behind the opera pavilion, he bought a bag of diced mango, cucumber and jícama. He heaped on the tajín powder and added extra lime juice. The old lady behind the cart, her grey hair up in a bun, her golden crucifix gleaming in the morning sun, told him to go with God.

Iwata headed for Pershing Square subway station at a stroll. There was plenty of time to get home and shower before work. Downtown rose up all around him, abandoned grandeur slowly being gentrified, the homeless, for so long left in peace, now being moved along, out of the gaze of the open-top tour buses.

The smell of garbage and exhaust stung Iwata's throat; the spicy fruit burned his tongue deliciously. The sun refracted through skyscraper glass, overlaying glinting rectilineals and curlicues on the streets below. The homeless sat in clusters, coughing, glad for the warmth.

Soon they would curse it.

Patience was the cornerstone of Kosuke Iwata's job. An impatient private eye was a used-car salesman without the blarney. But patience came easy on billable hours. *Not so much on the free consultations*, Iwata thought, tapping his foot under the old metal bureau.

It was a bright, broiling afternoon and the walls of the small unit were too narrow for the huge redheaded man before him. Ninety thousand people went missing each year in LA County and the man was convinced his wife was one of them.

Iwata asked if any clothes had been packed, if her job had been vacated, if there had been any problems in the relationship. When the man confirmed all three, Iwata politely turned him away.

Next up was a college student who suspected her boyfriend of infidelity, though she did not have the means to meet Iwata's rates for a single day, let alone the several he required as policy. After her, it was the unwanted regular – an elderly man who claimed to know the whereabouts of Osama bin-laden, who, of course, was not really dead. Last week, it had been Jack the Ripper. Iwata told the man, as he told him almost every week, that it probably wasn't the case for him.

The sun was setting and Iwata was about to close up for the day when the door opened one last time. A small woman walked in. Iwata was debating whether or not to accept her consultation when he realized he recognized her. He stood on reflex, unable to speak.

'We need to talk,' she said.

Iwata nodded at the black-and-white floor tiles as though he were a chess piece with nobody to move him. Heart thudding, he led her into the consultation room. The woman sat on the end of her chair and declined water. Iwata sat across from her, unable to meet her eyes. Instead, he gazed at her wrinkled hands, the veins beneath them sea-green. She was in her early sixties, fair skin, with short blonde-grey hair and dark blue eyes. People might have assumed her to be beautiful in her youth but Iwata had seen old photos of her – she'd always looked severe.

'You can't look at me, can you?'

Iwata remembered her voice as accusatory. Now it was just drained.

'No,' he replied. He was sweating, his voice feeble. 'You look too alike.'

Charlotte Nichol was gripping her handbag so tightly her knuckles had blanched. 'People always told me Cleo was the spit of me.' She nodded vigorously, as if someone had questioned the point.

They sat in funereal silence for a long while, Iwata's eyes not leaving the woman's hands. The ceiling fan quietly rattled and car horns could be heard distantly.

Finally, Charlotte opened her bag and took out a photograph. With a liver-spotted hand, she slid it across the table. Iwata turned it over to see a woman – familiar somehow.

'My boy,' was all the woman said.

Iwata realized it was Cleo's younger brother. Julian had transitioned gender years ago, though Iwata had never been close with the Nichol family and did not know much beyond the fact that Julian was now Meredith.

'Look at that face,' Charlotte said, her bag pulled tight against her chest. Iwata already knew where this was going. The woman wouldn't have ventured a thousand miles south from the Nichol home in Kennewick for anything other than calamity. With a bellyful of dread, he returned his gaze to the photograph.

'Mrs Nichol –'

'*Look* at it.'

Iwata looked. Meredith was looking to camera, maybe in a restaurant somewhere. Her mouth was open, she was speaking – telling a joke, he guessed from her expression. A gold hoop earring peeked out behind brown, pampered hair. Though her forehead was broad and her jaw had some heaviness, her eyes were vivid blue and her lips had been rouged perfectly.

When Iwata looked back up Charlotte Nichol was crying. He was used to that in this space, but the sight of his dead wife's mother's tears was unbearable.

'Mrs Nichol . . .' He shifted in his seat but she flung up a hand.

'Don't touch me.'

'Okay.'

'Don't you ever touch me.'

'No.'

'You're a son of a bitch.'

'I know.'

'Good,' she wept. 'Good.'

Taking back the photograph, Charlotte Nichol caressed it. 'My boy was murdered two weeks ago.' She looked up at the ceiling fan and tears dropped on her lap. 'The police have done nothing.'

'I'm sorry. I –'

'No.' She shook her head angrily. 'I don't want that. Not from you. I've come here because Meredith was murdered and you're going to do your work for me. Do you understand? You're going to find the fucking *person* who did this. You owe me that much for Cleo.'

Iwata looked at the floor. She was right. Charlotte Nichol had lost one daughter to him, and now another child to murder. The inequity of it was almost preposterous. A normal person might have felt sympathy for this woman, but Iwata's overriding emotion was fear. A clear, crystalline terror at having to care once again. Apathy was all that could be contained within him now; anything more would cause him to split open. Iwata had surrounded himself with misery. He had cauterized his own wounds with the tears of this city. Tears that were real to Angelenos but, to Iwata, just business. Maybe it was an ugly way to get by in life but he didn't know many better ones.

Charlotte stood up. 'You're going to do this for me.' It was decided.

Iwata thought about his empty apartment. His Spanish classes. The quiet streets on his morning runs. Existing was simple these days. But now Cleo's mother had come for him, like a faded ghost.

Iwata closed his eyes. All he would ever be was a hunter of bad men.

'All right.' It was the only thing he could say.

'I won't ever forgive you for what you did to Cleo. But maybe you can still do some good in this world.' Charlotte Nichol stood and placed two items on the desk. One was a large envelope. The other was a business card:

LOS ANGELES POLICE DEPARTMENT
Joseph Avery Silke
Detective II
Robbery / Homicide Division

'That's the detective. He's useless. The police have said some cruel things about my boy. All lies, of course. Julian was confused, that's all. He was a good Christian who made mistakes in his lifestyle. But we all have our sins.'

Iwata nodded.

'Kosuke, you find the man that did this. If you can't have him arrested, ruin him.' She paused at the door. 'That much I know you have a talent for.'

Then she was gone.

Iwata opened the envelope. It contained ten thousand dollars. He swivelled in his chair to look down on Wilshire Boulevard, which crept all the way to the Pacific Ocean. In the winter, it was a corridor for the cold to drift along, deep into the city. But today, the street was bleached white in the heat, the palm trees parched brown.

Iwata saw a familiar face, caked in grime. He could read the man's lips as he trundled along the street. '*The best of luck! The BEST of luck!*'

Iwata couldn't help but feel he was talking to him.

It was 2 a.m. These were the good hours, mostly just drifters left. Benedict Novacek sat at the bar of Club Noir drinking a Rum Swizzle. He wore a black leather flat cap and, tight on his bearish frame, a blue Hawaiian shirt – a big jungle canvas of parrots and plumeria flowers. He was in his late forties, with short black hair, a greying box beard and, despite his size, an osseous face. He wore silver rings and tattoos on his hairy arms. On his forearm, in Latin, the words 'Only God forgives' were inked. Between sips of his Swizzle he nibbled on his fingernails, wide and circular, like old nickels he was testing for authenticity.

Novacek liked this seat. The mirrored bar afforded him a perfect view of the dance floor without giving away the fact that he was looking. Under the brim of his flat cap, he could watch to his heart's content, his raw-oyster eyes freely grubbing through the bodies. Sometimes he would sit here for hours, drinking slowly, saying nothing. He would stay until he found the right one. And Benedict Novacek usually did.

It was a noir theme night, an entire room in mimesis of an ersatz era, a hundred femmes fatales and desperate dicks recreating a long-held fabrication – that there ever was a glorious age in the City of Angels. On the wall there was a framed print of Marilyn Monroe beneath which ran her words:

HOLLYWOOD IS A PLACE WHERE THEY'LL PAY YOU A THOUSAND DOLLARS FOR A KISS AND 50 CENTS FOR YOUR SOUL

Novacek whispered the words to himself as the woman sat down in the chair next to him. There were other seats free. She didn't need to choose this one. He listened to her order a Sazerac. It was a good voice.

Novacek looked her over in the mirror. The make-up was a little too heavy and he preferred ones that didn't have so much mileage, but she was in good shape. It was a decent waist, and the tit-work obviously hadn't been scrimped on. The package wasn't thrilling, but she had, in a way, offered herself to him. That made things easier.

Benedict Novacek took a sip of his Swizzle, padded his mouth dry with a napkin and pointed his cocktail cherry at the woman. Then he uttered the only sentence he ever needed.

'How would you like to make a lot of money?'

Tokyo – 1975

Every year around Nozomi's birthday there were meteor showers called the Perseids, or the Tears of St Lawrence to Catholics. She didn't know who he was or why he cried, and she didn't care all that much. She just wanted to get out of Tokyo, climb the nearest mountain and watch St Lawrence weep. Maybe she'd drink a beer and try not to get too big-headed that the universe was celebrating her existence once again.

Sometimes, especially on her birthday, Nozomi had gloomy thoughts about death. In the newspaper recently she'd read about a company offering a space burial service, their client's ashes blasted up into orbit. She imagined herself buried across the galaxy, circling the Earth for all time but for ever outside it. With no stones or relics left behind, it was nicer to imagine simply leaving the Earth, as if she had never been there.

But Nozomi wasn't feeling blue tonight. Even though she was working she was in a decidedly good mood – the kind that can only be brought on by clarity. She stopped sweeping now and blew her fringe out of her face.

It was a warm, sticky night. The red paper lanterns bobbed in the soft, summer eddies. Neon signs fizzed. Three homeless men in the empty lot at the end of the street were debating the advantages and disadvantages of the seventies as a decade. It sounded like the latter was winning out, as their conversation took in the Japanese Red Army, the Lod Airport massacre and the hijacking of Flight 351. Nozomi didn't think the calendar itself could be blamed for any of those.

Her father's place was just a shabby little watering hole in the brick arches beneath the train tracks near Yūrakuchō Station, but it was always busy. The beer was cheap, the snacks were passable, and her father always had a funny line for regulars and new faces alike. *Good with jokes, bad with life* – that's what Nozomi said to him. Her father, no matter what the customer was saying, would make it seem like they were always in the right.

That's the secret, Nozomi-chan. They might be morons everywhere else, but not here. Here they can do no wrong. That's why they come back.

In the summers they laid out plastic tables and overturned beer crates. The punters would cram in to complain about their wives or husbands before finally resigning themselves to the train home. Treachery, bad blood, deep love – growing up, Nozomi had heard it all. She had never been in love herself but it occurred to her that there were as many different types of it as there were routes home from Yūrakuchō.

Yūrakuchō was wedged in between Ginza and Hibiya Park. Less flashy than its neighbours, it still offered a window into the old way. This little district contained countless izakaya and the prices ensured that salarymen would always find their way to Yūrakuchō, every night, like the migration of little black birds seeking winter sun.

49

Her father was usually the last to close up. That meant Nozomi was usually the last person out on the street, sweeping up cigarette butts. She'd seen a few things in her time holding that broom.

The Yamanote Line train passed by overhead now, the little bars beneath its girders trembling, as they always did. The electric lights from the train lit up a puddle by her feet, her reflection suddenly revealed to her. She thought of what her mother used to say before she left: *How can you look so miserable, Nozomi? You're just a child.*

But she wasn't a child anymore. Today she was twenty-six: Christmas-cake age – nobody wanted one after the 25th. Well, that was fine by her. In truth, there was very little that bothered Nozomi. Very little except the idea of living out the life she was expected to live.

There was no way she was going to take over the bar for a start. Nozomi liked people but had no interest in the business and certainly no interest in inheriting its debt. It wasn't that she *hated* the bar, and she loved her father, though he could be stern and forgetful. She simply yearned for more. Or, perhaps 'more' wasn't the right word. Just something *else*.

On the TV lately there had been talk of traditional values and time-honoured characteristics but she could feel a change in the air the way you could tell rain was coming. That very morning she had heard on the radio that in just fifteen years the percentage of people who worked in agriculture in Japan had decreased from 40 per cent to 15 per cent. *For better or worse*, she thought, *Japan is doing new things.*

And Nozomi had decided to do something new with her life too. Which was why, even sweeping up cigarette butts at 2 a.m., she was in such a good mood. She had decided to become a writer of horror fiction.

Nozomi had always loved authors like Edogawa Ranpo and Yumeno Kyūsaku. Why couldn't she do what they did? People often asked her if she was planning to go into modelling or perhaps air-hostessing. Yet Nozomi couldn't imagine anything more boring. Being posed and positioned and pawed at by some creep, or serving box meals in a metal tube, day in, day out. No, she had decided she would be a slave only to inspiration.

And as she sat at her little desk after work each night inspiration is what flowed through her – same as the dark freight trains whooshing past her bedroom window, her thoughts full of precious cargo, hurtling towards their destination.

Nozomi loved the sounds of those tracks. To her, the trains were like pets, making the apartment shake all day and all night, like nervous little embraces. The noise didn't bother her. Not usually. Though sometimes it reminded her of life passing by, just out of reach. Vendettas, job interviews, perversions, presents, poetry – all of it flowing under her window like a river of possibilities, and none of them belonging to her.

Nozomi put away the broom now, locked up and switched off the lights. She went upstairs and carried out her nightly ablutions. Then, although exhausted, she sat at her desk, took out her writing book and flipped to the right page.

A train thundered past, the rails screeching goodbye in the distance. Downstairs, the television was blaring. By the music, Nozomi could tell it was the cologne advert with Charles Bronson in it. At first he appeared in a desert, riding a horse. Then, magically, he was transported to a boardroom overlooking the Tokyo skyscraper-skyline – as if he worked there. Now, wearing a jacket and tie, he slapped the cologne on and growled: 'Mmmmm, *Mandom*.'

After that, it was a rerun of her father's favourite show, *Robot Detective K*. Even for him, Nozomi thought it was ridiculous – a robot with eyes that changed colour according to its mood and which would often make deep, philosophical statements. Though its clothes were a little eccentric (yellow Gatsby cap, red blazer and white slacks), it fought crime as valiantly as any of the detectives in Tokyo's Metropolitan Police Department. The thing her father liked best about the show was K's car, a red Nissan Fairlady Z (which could fly). He usually fell asleep around the final act of the show, remote control in hand, mouth open, legs under the *kotatsu*. Often, she would have to tell him how the show had ended in the morning, or at least how she thought it had ended.

The TV was the only thing that really brought them together these days. Sometimes, if he had been drinking, her father would point out women onscreen that looked like her mother. This was strange to Nozomi because it wasn't as if she didn't have her own memories. Even so, he would jut his chin at some model or news anchor and say, 'Just like your mother.' Nozomi's mother had left when she was just a little girl and nobody had heard from her since. Some months were easier than others, but Nozomi and her father got along fine.

Stretching, she looked down at her writing book. Nozomi had been playing around with her novella, *The Mannequins*, for the last month or so. Although she knew that there was a tendency for people to overestimate the quality of their own writing, she truly believed it had potential.

The inspiration for it had come from a strange place. Last spring there had been a terrible fire in a department store, one of the worst in Japan's history: over one hundred people had died. Inside the building there were various other businesses, including a haunted house and a cabaret. It was thought that a cigarette butt had caused the blaze and within ten minutes of the fire starting thick black smoke was seen pouring out of the entire third and fourth floors – the dresses in the ladies' clothing departments helping it spread. It had taken firefighters three days to put it out. There had been no survivors. Many had died inside the cabaret; its fire escape had been locked. Those who had not burned to death, died from smoke inhalation or been trampled in the panic, had jumped out of the windows.

Nozomi had followed all the news coverage closely and had bought three or four different newspapers each morning. She didn't know what it was that fascinated her so much, but something about the fire had gripped her.

Then she came across the picture. Inside the department store, in a charred corner, stood four mannequins, their kimonos singed by the heat, their fingers melted and drooping down to their waists. Their wigs had been scorched away, leaving only burnt scalps, and their heads were inclined, as if just noticing the photographer. Smiling demurely, their blackened, lidless eyes stared down the lens. The image took Nozomi's breath away.

What if they had caused the fire somehow? Scolding herself for such a ridiculous thought, she turned the page and tried to read what Osaka's mayor had to say about the tragedy. But she quickly flipped back to the image.

What if they had *cursed that place?*

Nozomi imagined the mannequins silently whispering incantations, their lips unmoving, their eyes unblinking as the fire-escape bolt fell into place. As the smoke started to creep into the cabaret, she imagined background music playing through the empty, shining halls of the building. She imagined the muffled screams and desperate thudding at the cabaret doors.

Nozomi returned her gaze to the mannequins. Looking over her shoulder, she tore out the image with quick, precise rips then stuck it on the first page of a new notebook. She looked at them. They looked back at her. What Nozomi Iwata could not have known was that this tiny little whim would change her life.

4. Thirty-Five Thousand Choices

Arriving at LAPD headquarters, Iwata asked for Detective Silke. After many wrong turns and terse referrals, he found him. He was a tall white man, the colour of sour milk, his fingernails dirty. His mouth was open wide in sleep, his head arched back, his hand still clutching a can of breakfast Red Bull. Iwata cleared his throat and Silke's red eyes opened, his dark pupils jittery as they took the visitor in. 'What?'

Iwata held up his investigator's licence. 'Detective, can I talk with you for two minutes?'

Silke spat into his wastepaper basket and necked the last of his Red Bull. 'Men of few words are the best men.'

Iwata sat across from Silke. 'Detective, I'm here about Meredith Nichol. I know she was murdered a few –'

'*Woah*, papa-san. Let me stop you right there. That's an open case. You a reporter?'

'No.'

'Show me that card again.'

Iwata passed it over.

'Professional investigator?' Silke laughed. 'That's cute. Tell me something, if you're a *professional*, what does that make me?'

There was a short, caustic silence between them.

'Sir, I know you don't know me, but Meredith Nichol

55

was family. My wife's sister. If I could just briefly see the case file —'

'That's your play, huh? Sister-in-law. I say "sister" . . .'

'It's no play. Meredith's mother came to my office earlier and asked me to look into it.'

'Mama Bear had concerns, I see.' Silke popped open another Red Bull. 'Do you see a sticker on this desk that says "How's My Investigating?" Every *single* vic's family doesn't think I'm doing enough. They think it until I clear the case. Or not. That's just how it is. But then again, I do this for a living; they don't. And you don't neither.'

The two men considered one another. Iwata stood. A dead end was a dead end. Silke opened a PayDay bar and bit half off. When Iwata was ten paces away he shouted after him with a full mouth. 'Hey, papa-san!'

'What?'

'Sorry for your loss.'

The Records and Identification Division offered support and information to LAPD investigators 24/7. It was responsible for compiling and maintaining records – everything from runaways to stolen boats and pawned shotguns. Positive identification was carried out here, and the automated fingerprint identification system was also monitored by the division.

Earnell McCrae was a bison of a man – in his early forties, black, crew cut and bright brown eyes. His hands barely fitted in his pockets and his lavender shirt was tight around his chest, his cornsilk tie nowhere near his belt. McCrae had been one of the most prominent and respected men in the force, but an exchange of gunfire in a parking lot six years ago had resulted in substantial nerve damage and a change of department. Some strings had been pulled and a good position in R&I had been found.

Though the shooting manifested itself outwardly only in odd blinking, almost everybody saw the change in McCrae. He still smiled and cracked jokes, but his poise was gone. Every day he longed for the street, the freedom of unpredictability, but he knew those days were over. He was left with a desk, underneath which he kept his resentment. McCrae had also, for the first time in his life, started to fear things. He flinched at loud noises. He avoided steep staircases. The future filled him with a quiet, unspecified dread.

It was when his eldest daughter started seeing someone at college and using the L-word that McCrae came to Iwata out of the blue. There were slapped biceps and talk of old times at the LAPD academy before McCrae lumberingly arrived at the point: *I need you to look into him, Kos. It's my little girl, I can't take any chances*. It wasn't the sort of the undertaking that Iwata habitually accepted, but McCrae was an old friend. He agreed, refusing any payment. And now, a year later, as Iwata stood before him, McCrae realized the private eye had come to collect.

'I need to ask you a favour,' was all he said.

McCrae searched his old friend's face for a moment.

Iwata wondered what he read there. *An angle? Loneliness?*

Desperation? He didn't suppose he could argue with any of them.

Less than a mile from LAPD HQ, Iwata and McCrae were drinking coffee in a twenty-four-hour donut shop in Chinatown. There was a detective show on the TV, *Magnum, P.I.*, or maybe it was *Moonlighting*. Nobody was watching. The polystyrene coffee cups carried a slogan in a jaunty font:

DONUTS MAKE KIDS SMILE
AND ADULTS KIDS AGAIN

They discussed families and careers, though, in Iwata's case, he left out much regarding the former. He tried to enquire after academy acquaintances but those he could recall had quit long ago, or died. They soon hit a silence, a small boat running into predictable bad weather.

'Sorry about this place,' Iwata offered.

'Nah, I like it. We go back. Years ago, I busted a guy here in front of my little girl. Been looking for him for months and then just bumped into the asshole. He tells her, "Kid, your dad's a worker, he'll die with his boots on." And she adopted it. To this day, she gives me a hard time with that – "Daddy, you'll die with your boots on."'

Iwata smiled. 'Not any time soon, from the looks of you.'

'It's the diet my wife has me on. I shit infrequently and, when I do, it's green.'

They laughed and raised their cups. 'To shitting green.'

McCrae's donuts arrived and he tossed his tie over his

shoulder. The tiny pink sprinkles sparked a memory in him. 'Hey, you remember –? Never mind.'

'What?'

McCrae looked around, then leaned forward in conspiracy. 'You remember the graduation prank you got me with?'

Bemused, Iwata shook his head.

'*Seriously?* Come on, man. Graduation day? Hottest day of the year, and I'm a bag of nerves. You filled my car's air-con fans with glitter. Of course, I crank it up and *kaboom*. Half an hour later I'm shaking hands with the chief of police looking like a fucking drag queen. For years people called me Glitter McCrae.'

Iwata laughed now, a long-forgotten life suddenly resurrected. He wondered who he was back then. Someone who played jokes, someone who had friends.

'Yeah,' he said quietly. 'I remember.'

McCrae shook his head with a grin, then wiped it off along with the sugar. 'I couldn't believe it when I heard you left, Kos.'

Iwata simply nodded.

'So where'd you go?'

'Back to Japan. Ended up in Homicide. First out in the sticks then, later, Tokyo. My wife and I figured more money, better healthcare for our kid, less chance of me getting a bullet in the . . .' He trailed off.

McCrae nodded. In his line of work offence wasn't a package he would sign for unless it was marked 'priority'. 'So why'd you come back to California? Your wife missed home?'

Iwata tried to find an abridged answer but fell short.

He didn't feel like telling this man his story, his truth. He was barely comfortable telling himself.

'My marriage . . . didn't work out. I ended up here.'

'Sorry to hear that.' His tired eyes drifted up to the screen. Tom Selleck was radioing for a helicopter. McCrae had read Iwata's pain and his heart was big enough to offer a defeat of his own. 'I love Loraine, I love the kids, it's me I'm sick of. Or of me *like this*. Every day I wake up thinking today should be my last day. Thinking I should just leave. Old Homicide buddies come looking for records, guys who were half of what I was. Worst thing is, they feel sorry for me. I can see it in their eyes.'

'So what keeps you?'

'I don't know, man,' McCrae laughed the way he would at a child's question – simple and yet impossible all at once. 'Some people are just born to be insect-killer. Even if I'm not out there, at least I'm part of it. And yeah, I'm not what I used to be, but I guess that's life.' McCrae looked down at his empty plate now, embarrassed by the admission.

'Maybe it's better this way, Mac. Maybe what you're cut out for isn't necessarily what you should be surrounded by every day.'

'Is that what you tell yourself?'

'I don't tell myself much.'

Irritated, McCrae took a sip of coffee, as if the scalding might mollify his tone. 'Kos, you were the biggest brain in the room back in the academy. You had the eyes, you had the ears, your questions sliced through. And you're gonna sit here and tell me that you're not cut out to be a detective? That's horse shit, whichever way you pile it up. Okay, you're not with your wife anymore, I get that, but for you to just quit? And I'm stuck filing god *damn* cabinets for the rest of my life.' He shook his head. 'I'm sorry, but you're a born cop. And what are you doing with it? Following cheaters with your binoculars.'

Another man's pride might have stung. 'I understand your point, but you're wrong, Mac. I'm not who I was. Not anymore.'

They both looked out of the window for a while. Chinese lanterns swayed in the breeze kicked up by a trundling orange bus. Lines formed outside banks with stone dragon ornaments, money flowing out to Asia, money flowing back in again.

'I'm sorry, Kos. I shouldn't have . . .'

'Don't be.' Iwata knew it was easier for most men to trail off than it was to complete phrases – of love, of apology, of contrition. 'You know what my mother tells me? *Don't ask for pears from an elm.*'

McCrae smiled. They looked at the sticky surface of the table between them, sugar granules constellating on the pink Formica.

'Mac, I know you don't have much time. And you already figured I didn't ask you here for the coffee, so I'll just say it. Meredith Nichol. Murder victim a few weeks back.'

'Yeah, trans woman living on Skid Row. She was strangled out by the train tracks. But what's any of that to you?'

'Meredith was my wife's sister. Her mother asked me to look into it.'

Iwata watched McCrae putting the pieces together to form a disagreeable jigsaw. It was true that Iwata had helped him all those years ago in the academy, and again, recently, in the matter relating to his daughter. But now Iwata was pointing to an open murder case.

'What exactly are you asking for?'

'A copy of Meredith's case file.'

McCrae puffed out his cheeks and looked up at the TV. Iwata guessed he was balancing accounts – an old friend that had done him favours versus protocol and the risks of defying it. In this city, like most, that meant not hanging your balls out the window. Especially not for nostalgia.

McCrae sighed. 'I have a pension, man. If I get found out passing you files . . .'

'Just the officer's initial report, then. A few photographs. It'd never get back to you.'

'I'm sorry, Kos. I can't –'

Iwata wanted to leave it at that but he knew he was going to have to be honest. 'Mac, listen to me. My wife killed herself. I failed her. Meredith was her sister. The mother came to me and told me I owed it to her. And I can't say no, Mac. Not after Cleo. You told me I belong in Homicide, and I'm asking you to let me back in.' Iwata stopped himself from saying anything more. On the screen Tom Selleck was smiling, hands behind his head, feet up on his desk – another case closed.

McCrae looked at his plate. He crushed a sprinkle with his enormous little finger and then considered its guts. 'I didn't know that . . . I'll have to think about it.'

Earnell McCrae stood, hesitated for a moment then patted Iwata on the shoulder. Then he was gone, striding back towards 1st Street. On the TV the narrator was bringing down the curtain on the episode: 'Every day we make thirty-five thousand choices. And every single one of them we expect to walk away from.'

*

LOS ANGELES POLICE DEPARTMENT
CENTRAL COMMUNITY POLICE 251 E 6TH ST

INCIDENT REPORT #900691Q2 | **OFFENCE:** HOMICIDE
REPORTING OFFICER: Bergin, James.
APPROVING OFFICER: Lauber, Joel C.

NAME: Julian Nichol (alias: Meredith) | AGE AT TIME OF DEATH: 29 | PLACE OF BIRTH: Kennewick, WA | PHYSICAL: Male, 5 ft 8, 140lbs, hair dark, eyes blue. DISTINGUISHING MARKS: Deceased had undergone plastic surgery for breasts. ADDRESS: Boarding house on E 6th / Ceres Ave. INVESTIGATING DETECTIVE: Silke, Joseph A.

Body was found at 4 a.m. on the morning of 24 February near the train tracks running alongside N Myers St – approx. 100 yards from E 1st St Bridge. Victim was discovered by a homeless man named Joseph Clemente residing under said bridge. Clemente claims he witnessed an unidentified male in the immediate vicinity. Clemente observed this unidentified male 'messing around with a body until the train came along and he ran away'. Witness can only describe the suspect as 'male, around five nine, wearing a hooded sweatshirt'.

63

Additional notes: Relatives identified the deceased as Julian Nichol, a white transgender individual and a known prostitute and drug-user. Nichol was widely recognized in certain exotic dancing clubs and Latino bars in the Santa Monica Boulevard / Lexington Avenue area. No motive is as yet established. The victim had $62 on their person at the time of discovery. One possibility is a violent reaction to the discovery of the individual's genitalia. Forensic analysis of the crime scene and the victim's body have so far failed to yield results. No tire tracks were found in the immediate vicinity. Cause of death is strangulation with an as yet unidentified wire, cord or rope. No traces of sexual assault, though victim does appear to have sustained damage to the anus from prior sexual encounters.

Iwata put down the copy of the file McCrae had couriered over. Attached to it were three photographs scanned on to paper.

The first was of a starkly lit body near some train tracks. Meredith had died wearing jeans with a diamante star pattern and a yellow tri-cities charity-run T-shirt. In death, her body had lost its humanity, like a cheap mannequin. Whoever had killed her had kicked away their shoe prints in the dust.

The second photograph was an extreme close-up of her throttled neck, the ligature marks clear in the shredded, mangled flesh.

The last photograph was of Meredith looking to camera, the same one he had seen before. She was out somewhere, with friends most likely. She wore a vintage black dress with a red floral print. This Meredith, out in the world and happy, or in love, perhaps, had been recorded eighteen months ago. Yet the face in the previous photograph was gaunt, the ageing in the skin far exceeding the normal effects of such a quantity of time. Something had happened to her.

Rereading her last known address, Iwata picked up his sunglasses and left.

5. The Shrimp that Sleeps

On the eastern fringes of Skid Row, Iwata parked in front of Meredith's apartment block. The Wanderlust was a shabby four-storey flophouse with dirty white stucco walls and mint-green trim. On one side there was an abandoned factory; on the other a preschool for low-income parents to get free daycare, a place for the children of those who broke concrete, tended lonely parking lots and cleaned toilets.

Iwata got out of the Bronco and took off his sunglasses. It had been cloudy recently, an oppressive heat that sat jealously over the city, but this afternoon the sky was a clear, scorching blue.

He entered the building. The corridor was gloomy and hot, leading to a metal security door. He pressed the buzzer.

'Yeah?' The man on the intercom had a foreign accent but it dripped with the mistrust of a born-and-bred Angeleno.

'LAPD business,' Iwata replied tersely.

'Business?'

'I need you to open the door, sir.'

It buzzed open. Iwata knew America was a country where immigrants tended to relent in face of a certain autocratic tone of voice. He had seen it many times, not least in his own mother. Often Gerry had reminded her: 'You're American now, Nozomi. Don't let anybody give you shit.'

The sorry little lobby smelled of vomit and sandalwood incense. There was a repining female voice on the radio, accompanied by the beat of a dhol. The man behind the counter was short with a neatly trimmed moustache. He twirled a small banana leaf cigar between his thumb and forefinger. 'Business?'

Iwata held up his investigator's licence. 'Are you the owner?'

He shook his head.

Iwata took out the photograph of Meredith Nichol. 'Recognize her?'

He shook his head again.

'Show me your guest register, please.'

The man took a long drag and watched Iwata through the thick smoke. Then he placed the register on the counter and Iwata flipped back to 23 February, the day before Meredith Nichol's body had been found.

'Here she is. Room 12. Was her rent paid?'

The man checked a booklet in his breast pocket. 'Until end of month.'

'The rent here, is it monthly?'

'Most pay week to week. Most late.'

'I'm going up to look.'

He shrugged, and Iwata stepped into a dim, tilted stairway. The vomit stench had a more acrid quality here. The stairs had been painted red and the walls were the same mint green as the exterior. Up on the second floor a TV documentary about the universe was blaring through a thin wall. There were occasional high-pitched chirps of a lovebird somewhere nearby.

At the end of the corridor, next to the fire escape, Meredith's room was small, the wingspan of three children. The cheap, peeling wallpaper was a faded green. Two plywood cabinets took up one corner, one on top of the other, above which an old family photograph was framed. Iwata was shocked to see a young Cleo looking back at him.

He composed himself and put it in his pocket.

The broken sink was surrounded by mangy make-up products and knock-off celebrity-endorsed perfume. A microwave sat on top of a mini fridge, both of them plugged into a fizzing wall socket. The single bed was made. In a box in the corner there were clothes, a counterfeit Louis Vuitton handbag containing a Washington driver's licence, Big Red chewing gum and two clean syringes.

Iwata spent an hour in the room but found nothing beyond tokens of a simple, squalid existence. What he learned was that Meredith was not one for schedules or personal items beyond the sole family photograph.

Iwata left the room and knocked on the door opposite. A short Bolivian woman answered. Iwata handed her a twenty and she told him she hardly knew Meredith except for the fact that she was a working girl too. The woman didn't know of any boyfriends or regulars and she rarely heard Meredith come or go. Iwata gave her his business card and she promised she would call if anyone came looking for Meredith.

He left by the fire escape and hopped down into the

alleyway, wall to wall with garbage. An old piano had been shunted into the corner, its sostenuto pedal broken off, the fallboard left open. On a whim, Iwata ran his finger down the keys. The sound was discordant, something missing in the sour notes.

A mile south-west of the Wanderlust, Iwata turned off Maple and parked behind a slaughterhouse. The main road was mobbed, the whole neighbourhood turned into one teeming flea market, a circus without the roof. The Spanish language, in all its variegation, could be heard – haggling, joking, promising. These exchanges competed with car horns, electronic toy dogs yapping and a blind man playing *De Colores* on his keyboard.

Santee Alley catered to any low-cost whim: novelty contact lenses, plastic aquariums containing hatchling turtles, baby onesies with madcap slogans:

MY MOM IS TAKEN BUT MY
AUNTIE IS HOT AND SINGLE

Iwata made his way through the bustle, soapy bubbles swirling through the air around him. Men with flags coaxed cars into overpriced valet lots. On every other street corner hucksters carrying more balloons than seemed possible resembled giant multicoloured raspberries. Ground-floor living rooms had been turned into makeshift taquerias with cubbyhole toilets that charged seventy-five cents to shit. A fast-food truck doled out huaraches, quesadillas and tlacoyos, dishes that

69

pre-dated Christopher Columbus. On the other hand, portable grills sizzled with avocado hot dogs.

In the shop windows, dresses for all occasions were on display, gaudy little numbers encrusted with fugazi frills and gems, flamboyant head-turners for proms, weddings or quinceañeras. Another food truck, specializing in honeyed camotes, advertised for staff in Spanish on a piece of card. There was a single requisite:

MUST BE VERY EAGER TO WORK

Iwata turned into a gloomy rialto, ignoring the emoji T-shirts and fake eyelashes made of '100% human hair'. He passed rabbits in cages, far older, he presumed, than the ages listed on their cards. Beneath the age was a name, short and punchy for the males, princess-like for the females. Every cage was sitting in bin bags, spread out by the pet-pedlars to facilitate quick getaways.

At the back of the building, obscured by arcade machines that hadn't worked for decades, Iwata stopped at a stall. It held bongs, spices, cellphone charms and legal highs. Behind the stall stood a man about Iwata's age, a Mexican Elvis in *Jailhouse Rock* denim and a striped shirt. It was too warm for the outfit, but Mingo Palacio was too cool for caring. His hair was blue-black and greased tall. On the back of his hand there was a small tattoo of an oak and two wolves, the symbol of the Mexican state of Durango. Around his neck hung a battered old guitar.

'Mingo!' Iwata called. 'Need to talk.'

He hoisted his lip on one side and answered in a

Mississippi drawl, 'Ain't nobody talkin' *to* The King, meng'. The King be talkin' to *you*.'

Iwata handed over a fifty. 'Then let me hear you sing.'

He gave a sonorous strum of his guitar and beckoned him into the alleyway. They sat on some crates and Mingo hid the money in his leather shoes. His socks were stained black with polish but he wiggled his toes as if in the comfort of his own living room. Iwata watched him build a roll-up and thought how stupid it was to have soft spots for hard people.

'So, then.' Mingo had a clement, unhurried voice that many had misread for friendly. 'How's my second favourite dick in the world?'

'Surviving,' Iwata answered in Spanish. 'How's business?'

'My stall is full, my pockets are empty.'

'But not your shoes.'

Mingo Palacio grinned like the born operator he was – a handsome shyster that, one way or another, had fucked more people than all the Nigerian princes of the world combined.

'So tell me. What kind of song does Yojimbo want to hear?'

Iwata took out the photograph of Meredith.

'A love song, huh?' Mingo gazed it. 'As my old man used to say: "There's always a girl." '

'This one's personal to me.' Iwata switched to English. 'Police just assumed she worked Santa Monica and Lexington. But I'm betting you know more.'

'Cops don't see different types of trees. They just see forest, man.'

An old lady was standing at the stall, but he poked his head around to tell her he'd just closed up for the day. Iwata, like most around here, knew the wares on Mingo Palacio's stall were nothing more than a charade, a pretext to arrive at his only true commodity. And that was contained beneath his neat, inky pompadour.

Returning to the alleyway, Mingo apologized and looked at the photograph once again. He mulled Meredith over for a few moments, then nodded.

'Okay, yeah. I seen her a couple of times. Pretty sure she used to be a dancer up at Club Noir. That would have been months ago, though. Maybe longer. Then a second time, not so long ago, around Skid Row. She wasn't in good shape. Doubt there would have been much work for her in the clubs like that. But that's not information, that's just logic, man.'

He lit his roll-up and took a languid drag.

'But if she was such a junkie, why was her rent paid up a month in advance?'

Mingo shrugged. 'I guess that'd be Talky.'

'Boyfriend?'

'If you want to call it that. Guy's a gorilla. Mute, but lets his hands do the talking.'

'Where do I find him?'

'You wanna find a lion, you go look where the wildebeest drink.'

'A bar.'

'Of the titty variety – the Happy Gopher. But I ain't seen Talky for a while.'

'I know the place. Let's go back to Meredith. What else have you got for me?'

Mingo squinted one eye, as though it hurt to go back through a memory the size of his. 'Maybe she was tight with a girl called Jen? Or Jenny? That mean anything to you?'

'No.'

'Geneviève, that was it. Pretty little black girl. Pana-manian, I think. Worked at Club Noir too. You should swing by. Bouncer there has got a tongue on him.'

Mingo tried to return the photograph.

'Keep it. I want you to show it around your sleazy friends. Anybody knew her, anybody paid her, anybody that ever bought her a drink.' Iwata handed over another fifty.

'All my friends are angels.' Mingo took the money. 'Now you get going, Yojimbo. The shrimp that sleeps is taken by the tide.'

'Mingo of Santee, you're too good for this town.'

'Yeah, who ain't?' Mingo stuffed the money in his shoe once again, put his sunglasses on and strummed his old guitar. 'Thank yuh, thank yuh very much.'

Downtown LA was heart-shaped. And like any real broken heart, it was mostly empty, one of the least populated city centres in the world. Gentrification had eventually descended, but it wasn't in a hurry, the streets still brimming with rubbish and broken glass. The wrong side of town in many a movie had been filmed here, Downtown's stark concrete drags good for car chases, its doorways fitting for voyeurism, its dark alleyways perfect for double-crosses.

The Jewelry District verged on Hill Street, which ran through Downtown's core. Its grand old buildings once housed grand old functions, but no one could remember what those were anymore. Seedy little boutiques and long-distance-call shops had sprouted up in their place. Neon signs above cinemas that had died long ago were still present on the skyline, like extravagant headstones. Pawn-shop windows displayed gold chains and diamond-encrusted dollar-sign medallions hocked by failed rappers.

Iwata turned right on 8th Street and California's tall-est building rose up out of the blue distance, the US Bank Tower. He took a left on Grand Avenue and stopped outside the Happy Gopher. The neon sign was off; the door had been left open for deliveries. Inside, the bar was dim and hot. There were dancing poles, private booths, well-stocked shelves. Though the bar had been recently cleaned, the smell of sweat and money grease wasn't going anywhere.

'We don't open till eight.' A large man came out of the office door. He was wearing a red sateen shirt. The amount of gold rings told Iwata a fifty-dollar bribe wouldn't go far here.

'Afternoon, sir.' Iwata held up his ID. 'I'm hoping you can help me. I'm looking for someone.'

'Not a lot of people use their real names around here, pal.'

'That works out, actually. The person I'm looking for goes by Talky. You know him?'

The man bristled. 'You police?'

'Private investigator.'

At this, he seemed to soften. 'Talky used to work the door for me.'

'Any idea where he is?'

'He's not any place.' The man smiled wryly. 'He was found dead, needle hanging out of his arm. His real name was Lyle Babich, by the way. Personally, I didn't mind the guy. Never spoke too much. That's the advantage of working with mutes.'

Iwata thanked the man and left.

As Iwata drove he snatched glimpses at the sun setting behind pylons and palm trees. Los Angeles was a city of new starts, of mixture, of diverse blood. He understood why Meredith Nichol would come here. But this was also a city of despair, a city that never tired of rejecting those within it, a city of unclaimed dead.

The coroner's office was on Mission Road, just a few miles from the train tracks where Meredith had been murdered. It was a handsome red-brick building, death's own lost-property office, the only medical examiner's in the world with a gift shop. Iwata had been here many times; in cases of missing persons, it was his first port of call – to search the unclaimed, the unidentified.

Lily Trimble was sitting outside the Jack in the Box across the road, nursing a vanilla shake and her vape pen. She was tall, her skin the same colour as her shake. Her red hair was up in a topknot today, her pale eyes on the distance. Beneath her white coat she wore a black T-shirt adorned with a cartoon chalk outline that read:

OUR BODIES OF WORK
SPEAK FOR THEMSELVES

'Lily.'

She smiled up at Iwata, not for his company but for what he represented – a pay day. Lily Trimble was forensic tech support at the medical examiner's office. In a factory of death, she was quality control. But she was also a student with fees to pay.

'Evening, Inspector.' Her voice was small, as though heard across a body of water.

'How's the milkshake?'

'These tastebuds died a long time ago.'

'And the studies?'

'Fine.' Trimble was like Iwata had been once – she dealt only in death. Speaking with people was peripheral to her day. She liked her small talk microscopic. 'You waiting for a friend?'

Iwata nodded. 'He's a little late. Maybe you've seen him pass through?'

'How late?'

'Just a few days. Lyle Babich was the name. Big guy, I think. And mute.'

'Give me a while.'

She stood, crossed the road and disappeared inside the coroner's office. Twenty minutes later she reappeared and placed a Polaroid of the dead man on the table. As billed, Talky was big. Even in death he looked hardnosed, a big Ikea cabinet pissed off that it had been assembled wonkily.

'What are you thinking, Lily?'

'Put simply? Your friend died of massive heroin overdose. Signs of long-term usage.'

Iwata mulled this over. If Meredith's pimp had died within a few days of her murder, it was no surprise that the police weren't exactly kicking down any doors. Dead pimps made good culprits.

He passed her a napkin with a hundred-dollar bill folded inside and stood. 'Thanks for your help.'

'Hold on, there's something else. Now what I said was true: he died of an overdose.'

'I'm sensing a but.'

'*But* his body also displays some pretty textbook defensive wounds.'

'You're saying somebody could have done it to him?' Iwata felt an old, long-buried sensation – the genuine buzz of a potential lead – unearthed like a white truffle.

'I'm saying maybe someone did it to him. Or maybe it was occupational. I guess that's where you come in, Inspector.' She took a final toke on her vape pen and stood. 'Better get back to my clients.'

'Don't keep them waiting on my account.'

With a pale hand, Lily Trimble gave a dispassionate wave.

6. To the Pure, All Things Pure

On Hollywood Boulevard, a few yards away from what used to be called Grauman's Chinese Theatre, a bored Superman waited for tourists to take his photo. He could charge more to pose with kids, though he preferred solo photos, for hygiene reasons. Meantime, he was swiping through the profiles of men on a dating app, though nobody was taking his fancy today.

By the subway station, Darth Vader duelled with a young Chinese child, the hollow plastic clashing of their lightsabers drawing laughter from the crowd. Marilyn Monroe squeezed her tits together for a Frenchman, while an HIV-positive Batman jumped out of the shadows at passing tourists, less a crusader against injustice and more a darkly dressed prankster. Along the boulevard, sitting on the stars of Errol Flynn, Jean Harlow, and Groucho Marx, runaways and junkies turned pink behind cardboard signs.

Hollywood was a lie believed only by tourists. Its realities were smaller, sharper, more pungent. In place of heroes on white horses at sunset, there were only hungry scavengers here after nightfall. The very word promised glamour, excitement, people. Yet behind it, beneath it and all around it there was only a drab, perfunctory emptiness. In the early hours the eyes of coyotes were illuminated by passing headlights, brilliant green marbles rolling only and forever towards flesh.

Iwata too was searching, but Club Noir was hidden away like a schoolboy's porn stash. He had traipsed up and down Hollywood Boulevard. On Vine he passed the star of Sessue Hayakawa, leading man and heart-throb of Hollywood's silent era, as popular as Charlie Chaplin in his day. A celebrity bus droned past, its chassis painted purple, its slogan gold:

YOU'VE SEEN THEM IN ACTION. NOW
SEE WHERE THEY LIVE

Iwata's job was much the same, sitting in vehicles and looking at houses across the street. The only difference was that who and what went on inside provoked no curiosity in him beyond the requisite amount his work demanded.

On McCadden, at last he found Club Noir. Its entrance was in an alleyway between an old coffee house and an electrical repair shop. Latin-techno beats reverberated like a muffled tommy gun and the line was growing. Iwata picked up a flyer from the floor. It depicted a buxom trans woman in a spangly red dress, with auburn hair, and heavy make-up: Jessica Rabbit made flesh. In golden cursive, words were embossed over her torso:

TRANSFIX – EVERY GIRL HAS SECRETS

The bouncer was a well-upholstered Mexican wearing

black, his tattoo-green hands clasped over his belly. He spoke with a dusty voice and a grin that would never be anything other than threatening. 'Welcome to Noir, sir.'

'I'm looking for someone.' Iwata flashed his ID.

'In an hour, there'll be about three hundred people in here looking for someone too. Join the line. Our bar boys smile and don't water down.'

'I'm looking for Geneviève.'

'She don't work here no more, güey. Just up and left.'

'Any idea why?'

He shrugged a shoulder the size of a chain wrench. 'People don't always leave a note here.'

'What about her friend Meredith Nichol?'

'I knew her a little more. Nice girl. What happened to her is . . .' He shook his head.

'Yeah. So who did it?'

'Guessing that's your job, no?' He grinned. 'I don't know who, but I can tell you *how*.'

'Okay. How?'

'Same as the rest of 'em. They hop the bus in from Buttfuck, Tennessee, with those big, wide eyes that only see palm trees and auditions. And this city eats them alive. *Puris omnia pura*, güey.'

'To the pure, all things pure?'

'If this city could speak, that's what she'd whisper.'

The bouncer received a message on his earpiece and turned away from Iwata to check a few more IDs. The line shuffled forward. As Mingo had suggested, the man seemed happy to talk. More importantly, he also seemed to have been paying attention. After all, he worked the door to a secret grotto. It made sense that eyes would go with a tongue.

'So,' the bouncer turned back. 'You're a sneaker, huh?'

'I prefer "professional investigator".'

'Yeah.' He laughed. 'And I prefer "ingress executive".'

'And what are the chances of my ingress to Club Noir's employee records?'

'I'd say slim to deceased. The privacy and security of the girls is taken seriously here.'

'Point taken.' Iwata held up the Polaroid he'd bought from Lily Trimble. 'Did you ever see Meredith with this guy? Name was Talky. He was mute.'

With a slight smile on his lips, the bouncer gave a theatrical shrug. It might as well have been a hotel porter's cough. A private investigator couldn't knock down doors and throw threats around. Door hinges had to be greased; tongues did too. Most of the time, the only lubricant was money. Iwata knew it. The Mexican bouncer knew it too. Iwata handed over a fifty and the bouncer took it in one smooth motion before gazing down at the Polaroid.

'Saw him a couple of times, yeah. He used to wait for Meredith right over there. But if you're thinking it was him that killed her, I'd tell you it was unlikely. She spoke about him a lot. Their future, you know, all the shit you hear a fly say from a spiderweb.'

'Well, from what I've heard, he didn't exactly sound like the romantic type.'

'Maybe not, but one thing was clear. She made him money. That guy had a temper, sure. But you could tell he was too much of a cheap fuck to lose out.'

Iwata contemplated this before changing tack. 'How about friends? Did Meredith or Geneviève have any here?'

'Think there was a skinny tattooed girl. Real pretty. Don't know her but she comes in from time to time.'

Iwata handed over his business card. 'If you see her, I'd really appreciate a call.'

The bouncer winked.

Back in the Bronco, Iwata chewed over the information. The picture made more sense now. At least, Detective Silke's angle was clear enough. *Pimp kills his girl, pimp ends up ODing, end of story.* There was no evidence tying A to B, so he would simply leave Meredith in cold cases and move on. Iwata wasn't surprised; A to B thinking saved a lot of people a lot of trouble. It was as old as villagers blaming wolves for the disappeared girl. In truth, he too wanted to leave Meredith in cold cases. But Lily Trimble's words were like tiny fishbones in Iwata's gums. *The body also displays some pretty textbook defensive wounds.*

The Bronco was dark. It smelled of old leather, old metal, old parts long since discontinued. He couldn't help but think about Charlotte Nichol, her hands gripping her bag tightly. There was no way he could tell her no. Sighing, Iwata dialled Kate Floccari's number.

She answered almost immediately. 'Kosuke?'

'Sorry to call so late. I thought I'd go to voicemail.'

'It's fine. I was up.'

'How are you, uh, dealing?'

The question was almost offensively simplistic. Up until now their relationship had been black and white.

Work, nothing more. Now they were obliged to acknowledge humanity. Down the years Iwata had taught himself to restrict his own feelings as best he could. But in trying to negotiate the emotions of other people, he was a badger at a chessboard.

'I'm . . .' She laughed softly at the pointlessness of the answer.

'Listen, Kate. If you need anything.'

'How about you tell me what you need?'

'I know you're going through a lot at the moment. I wouldn't ask if it wasn't important.' Iwata bit the insides of his cheeks and said it. 'I need your help.'

'Of course. With what?'

Iwata had been thinking about it all day, the small, nagging worry at the back of his mind. No clues had been left behind by Meredith's killer. An enraged john was unlikely to have the presence of mind to remove every trace from both the crime scene and the body. The same went for Talky. And Iwata was troubled by something else. Meredith had been murdered in a dark, desolate place but more or less out in the open. Of course, the smart money was on Talky being the murderer. But there was the matter of his defensive wounds. And now Talky was gone.

Either way, Iwata had to be sure. 'Kate, I need you to look into something for me.'

Just before midnight, at a back table at Tacos Delta, Iwata leaned back in his chair and puffed out his cheeks. He had just finished going through the stack of papers Kate Floccari had brought him.

'Five trans women in LA County in the last year.' Iwata looked up from the pages. 'Only one case solved.'

'Five that were *reported*,' Floccari corrected.

'All except one of them were strangled.'

'Kosuke, I dragged the chief coroner out of bed and he told me they've had at least twice that many unclaimed bodies of trans women in the last year. Mostly women of colour. Their murder rate is disproportionately high anyway, but that's a huge spike. Then there's also the fact that police are misgendering in their reports. Meredith, for starters, was listed as male.'

'So if we put it all together . . .'

'Who knows what the true figure is.'

Iwata looked gravely into the distance. 'There's a club in Hollywood where Meredith used to work. A friend of hers, Geneviève, worked there too. Apparently, she just up and vanished. Now, the bouncer told me girls come and go and that might be true, but I don't like coincidences. Five women in twelve months. Add Meredith, that's six. And Geneviève is missing.'

Far above the huffing night buses and the sagging telephone cables, up in the chalky hills, the little white stain of the Hollywood sign was illuminated.

'Iwata, you think there's someone out there, don't you? Someone murdering trans women.'

'I don't know.' Iwata rubbed his eyes. 'But if there is, nobody has caught his scent yet.'

'I think you just did.' She balled up her napkin. 'If he exists.'

Iwata thanked Kate Floccari for the favour and walked her back to the car. Though it had no reason to be, their goodbye felt final somehow. As he watched her tail lights dwindle, Iwata felt the weight of the box she had brought him – the paperwork left by hatred and death.

Walking up the stairs to his apartment, Iwata saw the faint green blinking of his microwave's unset clock. Another city, another kitchen, another unused appliance. He reached the stairs with his eyes already closed, the only sound on Descanso Drive the jangling of his keys.

Distracted by the usual metronome of self-pity and guilt, he missed it. The absence of cricket noise, the dead lightbulb and, beneath them, the innominate disquiet that intruders always secreted, no matter how silent they were.

Before Iwata could turn he felt the arm around his neck, the hard object in the small of his back, then words in his ear. 'Your money or your life, motherfucker.'

'You're a real barrel of laughs, you know that?'

Grinning, Mingo Palacio released him with a pat on the shoulder and handed him the lightbulb he'd unscrewed. 'Ah, come on, don't be like that. Dangerous days call for a sense of humour, Yojimbo.'

'I'm laughing inside. Coffee?'

'Wish I could. But I'm here on business.' He handed over what seemed to be a rolled-up magazine. 'A little light reading courtesy of my sleazy friends.'

Iwata unrolled it – it was a sex catalogue of some kind. 'Could they tell you anything about Meredith?'

'A lot of not much. Nobody really remembers her, doesn't seem like she was in the game for long. One or two recalled a quiet girl with Talky. Didn't sound like it was long term, though.' He shrugged. 'The flame that burns twice as bright burns half as long, huh.'

'So what is this?' Iwata held up the catalogue.

'Page fourteen and eighteen. Enjoy your night.' Mingo descended the stairs, into the street dark.

Back inside his apartment Iwata grabbed a zero per cent beer from the fridge and sat cross-legged at his coffee table with a groan. Taking a long swig, he scanned the catalogue's offers. Some were circumlocutory, others a little blunter. Then he came to page fourteen.

It was Meredith Nichol.

She had a good half-page spread to herself: no words, just a phone number. The photograph of her was beautiful; someone had clearly put effort into their work. She was naked, her back to the camera, standing against a tremendous blue. She was looking at a night ocean somewhere, anywhere, and the shadows between her shoulder blades, her buttocks, and her inner knees recalled Colville's *Pacific*.

Iwata looked at her for a long time.

On page eighteen he found an almost identical photo of an attractive black woman. It was Geneviève. The same phone number was listed beneath. In this image, she was facing the camera, folding her hands across her breasts, looking off to one side. It was the same profound navy-blue ocean, the same essence of night, clear and obfuscated all at once.

Chest prickling, Iwata dialled the number. He licked his lips.

It rang twice. Then the automated woman spoke. The line had been disconnected.

Iwata flipped restlessly through the rest of the catalogue. There was no information on where it had been printed, nor when, nor who by, as though it had simply come to be – a multitude of women, all with numbers on them, like they had been tagged by safari-keepers.

Returning to Geneviève, Iwata looked again. Beyond the hint of shutters to one side there were no details in the room, no landmarks, nothing that said anything beyond: *ocean*. Meredith's scene was identical, the shutter slightly more visible. It was as though they had both been photographed in a glass box over the blue.

Iwata dropped the magazine on to the coffee table. Another door opened to another door that led nowhere. He told himself he needed sleep; there was nothing more he could do tonight.

He looked at the magazine on the coffee table again. Seen upside down, he realized there was something there. A white speck.

Iwata fetched his pocket-sized square magnifying glass and peered through it. And now the speck became a white biplane, an advertising banner flying behind it:

FAT FILIPPO'S – WHERE THE EATING TAKES BEATING

Exhilarated, Iwata leapt over the table to his laptop

and googled Fat Filippo's. It was a chintzy all-you-can eat grill on the Pacific Coast Highway, a few miles east of Malibu Pier. He looked again at the image. Assuming the banner-towing plane was advertising locally, it had to have been flying west. Iwata guessed it had flown a loop over Santa Monica at sunset and was heading back to some small landing strip up in Simi Valley. He couldn't be certain, but it made sense. Santa Monica was where the tourists were and Fat Fillipo would know that a drive out to Malibu was on the cards for many of them.

Taking out his map, Iwata calculated the distance between Santa Monica and Malibu Pier to be about twelve miles. The total area of Malibu was some twenty square miles and that didn't take into account the canyons and mountains to its north.

Iwata's excitement faded. He had narrowed down the place where the photographs of Meredith and Geneviève had been taken to a fixed area. He didn't need a cartographer to tell him he had done little more than find the haystack he'd lost his needle in. Thousands of houses, thousands of windows, thousands of ocean views.

Dejected, Iwata took the catalogue, the box of papers Kate Floccari had given him and his sweet bay plant outside. He sat on the balcony and went through the images, the pages, the details. Nobody else seemed to be looking for a pattern in these trans women, but Iwata couldn't help but see one. Names, ages, birthplaces, physical descriptions, aliases, causes of death – Iwata soaked himself in them.

Benedict Novacek pressed Play on his sound system and John Martyn's 'Man in the Station' submerged the room in the right emotion. The girl stood with her back to him. He knew she was drinking, he could hear the ice moving in her glass. Everything was as it should be.

'It's a little dark in here,' she said. He could almost taste her nervousness.

Novacek pressed the button under the counter and the blinds quietly hummed open. The ocean view revealed itself and, as usual, the girl gasped. The moon on the water rippled like mother of pearl in lacquer. It was his knockout punch. Something about moonbeams on a dark ocean made women take the plunge.

'How can someone live in such a beautiful place?' she said, more to herself than to him.

Novacek reached for her name, but names to him were mayflies; they didn't live long enough to matter. What mattered was keeping the girl pliant, keeping the mood serene, keeping up the hocus-pocus of free choice. 'Honey, you can come here any time you want.'

She laughed softly at that, then downed her drink. The swiftness of it didn't communicate any relish, merely that it was time to get this over with.

'Where do we do it?'

He licked his lips. This one wasn't perfect but she wasn't too far off. Benedict Novacek pointed to the room at the back. The door was slightly ajar.

The girl took one last look at the ocean.

7. City Beautiful

Iwata woke up cold. He drank old coffee and left the apartment. Not wanting to face the freeways today, he took the backstreets. As the sun rose it turned the clouds sashimi pink. On empty roads, Iwata glided, first through Silver Lake, skirting Dodger Stadium and Elysian Park, then finally cutting through Montecito Heights.

Our Lady of Solitude was on East Cesar E Chavez Avenue, a little jewel box of a church built in the Spanish Colonial Revival style. It was a small funeral, just Charlotte Nichol and a few relatives sitting at the front, the devout giving them a few pews of distance.

The priest spoke both in English and in Spanish. Iwata stood at the back, his attention drifting in and out of the homily. The light through the tall stained-glass windows was so glorious it scarcely felt real. Motes in the sun looked like sand grains settling through shallow water.

'. . . Our emotions are God-given, they are a part of who we are. Our hearts rightfully ache over the passing of such a good young man.' The priest looked around, as though his congregation were much larger than it was. 'Yet we are not too proud to seek God's soothing touch, trusting in Him to give us the strength to continue in His path. Loss can cloud us, drag us into questioning what we know in our hearts to be true. So then let us recall Job. "For I know that my Redeemer liveth, and that He shall stand at the latter day upon the earth."'

When the service was over Charlotte Nichol saw Iwata but said nothing to him. There was just a dumb pause between them, two people seeing each other through prison visitation glass. Then she was led away by a woman Iwata recognized as Cleo's aunt.

When the church had emptied out Iwata sat in a pew. He watched the funeral men prepare the casket to be moved. Fresh flowers and fairy lights were strewn throughout the nave, little Mexican touches here and there. The sunlight was even brighter now, chiffon totems of colour. In other circumstances, Iwata would have thought it was a beautiful day.

As he stood to leave he became aware of whispering. Soft 'k' sounds, soft 's' sounds, both airy and sticky. Then she emerged from the confessional – a beautiful woman with tattoos, her dark hair up in a ponytail. He caught part of a tattoo beneath her collarbone:

1:1–

She smiled as she passed him.

Getting out of the Bronco, Iwata turned up the collar of his linen shirt against the searing midday sun. He was standing in front of the train tracks on which Meredith Nichol's body had been found. Beyond them there was a fence blocking off the Los Angeles River below. Iwata could see a man hunched over the thin stream, washing his shoes. On either side of the water the concrete was criss-crossed with the tyre marks of bored young bikers.

To the east and south only warehouses, factories and pylons were visible. Industrial LA rarely saw pedestrians. Beyond through traffic, its streets contained little more than grey dust and coyote tracks – both lifelong Angelenos, present well before fruit, gas and movies had conspired to fabricate a city in the desert.

To the west the sparkling skyscrapers of the financial district shot up into the fierce blue. To the north, the denticulate verge of the San Gabriel Mountains, a hazy indigo in this light.

Iwata had parked on a dusty fringe along the train tracks, behind a Korean wholesaler and a tomato-soup factory. Between them, a large billboard showed two men embracing:

BLACK GAY MEN MATTER TO GOD

Iwata was standing a few hundred yards north of 1st Street Bridge. He crouched over the tracks and inspected the ground. No trains were coming in either direction. There was nothing but dirt and grease in the air. He didn't know what he had come here for, but he certainly hadn't found it yet.

Iwata walked along the tracks until he reached the ramp that led up to 1st Street Bridge. A sign told him it had been built in the early 1900s, swept up in the City Beautiful movement. Its neo-classical design was trying to call to mind Paris or Budapest, but it didn't fit – as if a piece of some belle époque city had been stolen and arbitrarily implanted into this stark industrial district.

Beneath the bridge ran Myers Street, the eastern set of tracks used for freight, the Los Angeles River and the western set of tracks used for passenger rail. On the bridge itself there were four traffic lanes. The tracks for the Metro Gold Line light rail ran between them.

Iwata surveyed the area, the bridge, the tracks, the river, the grey, dead earth. Even at 4 a.m., killing a person out here would have carried the obvious risk of exposure. Whoever had murdered Meredith, whether it was Talky or someone else, had done so out in the open. Iwata had thought this before, but now, seeing the area, it struck him how brazen the killer must have been. Or desperate.

Iwata went back down under the bridge. Huddling in the darkness was a small community of tents and shopping trolleys. The smell of bodily waste clung to the graffiti-laden walls and some kind of fluid leaked down the columns, already encrusted with pigeon droppings. Three rats, as if motivated by an opportunity, scurried along the kerb, dodging cigarette butts and broken glass.

'Joseph Clemente?' Iwata called after the single witness in the police report McCrae had given him. He heard back only an echo and the sound of traffic whooshing by overhead. 'Joseph Clemente, are you there?'

'He ain't here,' an irate voice answered from somewhere. 'He showers on Wednesdays.'

'Where?'

'Where else? The Sanctuary.'

Iwata thanked the voice and left it to its darkness.

Skid Row, blooming out over fifty blocks, was a city of the destitute, the American capital of homelessness. Thousands lived in these streets, or perhaps 'existed' was a better word. Many were disabled, many were mentally ill, many were undocumented, many were too young, many were too old. Few had any hope of accessing what little support there was to begin with. They were the marginalized, the vulnerable, the undesirable, and this was their kingdom.

Missing-persons cases had brought Iwata into Skid Row many times – usually the second place he looked after the coroner's – and each time he entered he was shocked at the human squalor. The smell of piss and gastric juices commingled for blocks. In every slit, in every cranny, the stink of bodies dying, some fast, some slow. The heat could be savage and the street bone dry, yet Skid Row always had a sticky wetness to it, an infinite effluvium. Grimy tents lined the streets like a colourful brigade, an encampment of recruits ready for shipping, though there was only ever one destination. Alleyways trapped warmth like narrow jungle gullies and in them, at night, little nebulas of crack smoke distorted coyote shadows.

A fleet of people in wheelchairs inched along the sidewalks. A laughing man lying under a blanket masturbated furiously, his eyes closed, tears running down his cheeks. A young black woman crouched over a gutter to shit, pages of the morning paper scrunched up in one hand, ignoring the honking of passing cars. Across the road, a man wearing a baggy red T-shirt and a gold chain watched the woman while he sipped from his orange Slurpee. The drug dealers were out in numbers today, joking about their favourite fiends and making amicable conversation. *Not so long till Mother's Day now.* Mother's Day, the 3rd of the month, when mothers had been visited and government cheques had been obtained – market day for the dealers.

On the sidewalk another homeless man was probably dead, his mouth open, one shoe missing. His toes were very brown. His head was resting against a bent street sign which read:

NO LOITERING

A man with a coiled silver beard was weeping over him. A pink blonde woman with a black eye was trying to console him and keep her jeans from falling down at the same time. She reached out and rubbed the tip of his nose with her thumb. 'Come on, baby. You know you did your best. You did your best.'

Iwata just kept on walking.

At the end of the street a group of pale-faced volunteers were bringing hot dogs and prayer. As they jumped out of their new vans Iwata could hear the group leader warning them to keep their gloves on at all times and to be extremely careful about physical contact.

'Hepatitis, typhus, lice, scabies, HIV – remember,

guys, it's all here. You've come to help, but you always, always, always look after yourself first. Okay?'

There was a murmur of orison before the volunteers donned colourful T-shirts and turned on their Christian smiles. Buns were slit open and cups of lemonade poured.

On Crocker Street Iwata reached his destination. The Sanctuary was a modernist structure with pale salmon-coloured walls, corrugated-metal panels and a copper chapel. The line snaked around the block, a sinfonietta of coughing, swearing and trembling. Iwata joined it. Nobody looked at him twice.

An hour later he reached the front. Those without ID were being turned away by a burly man with Virgin Mary tattoos on his forearms. Those that got through were given bed tickets for five nights on the proviso that all bags were to be checked in. One hygiene bag was allowed in, as was one book.

Once inside Iwata was sent down a corridor lined with framed photographs of celebrity volunteers. Miss America 2011 was serving teriyaki chicken, Harrison Ford was shaking hands with a homeless woman, Mayor Villaraigosa was slicing Christmas turkey.

Iwata joined another line into a side room. There, his scalp was checked thoroughly for lice by a Filipino woman listening to jazz on the radio.

'Go with God,' she said, almost angrily, before signing off on his bed ticket.

Iwata was then ushered into a large chapel. A Brazilian man with a thick moustache was instructing those in the pews to remove hats and earphones. Then the sermon began. A small white man in his sixties with a yellowish beard looked around the room. He could barely disguise his disgust as he spoke, for the next hour, of the fire that awaited the addicted – far beyond any cold turkey or suffering found on the streets of Skid Row. He barked and snarled, the chains of darkness, the second death, the weeping and the gnashing of teeth.

After the sermon, it was lunch. The pews were called forward, starting at the front, and Iwata realized now why there was practically nobody sitting in the back rows. When it was his turn he surreptitiously shared out his sticky rice, fish stew and pomegranate juice to those around him. It was taken without question or comment.

Iwata tried to ask around for Joseph Clemente, but there was no time; the volunteers were rounding everyone up for the mandatory shower. Thirty or so men, some still chewing their food, were marched into a changing room, where they were told to undress. They complied, automatically, many wincing as they peeled off blackened socks or pulled away dirty denim from their bloodied kneecaps. Clothes and bed tickets were put in small plastic bins and soap was handed out.

Iwata followed the men into a long shower room with slimy walls. As the torrents of hot water came on, groans could be heard. The warm human stench was almost overwhelming. Like the others, eyes on the floor, Iwata began to lather his body. As if reading his shame, the elderly man behind him began to weep.

'Mom,' he mewled, his long grey hair plastered over his eyes. 'I miss you. I miss you. I miss you.'

97

Tokyo – 1975

Nozomi woke early to a perfect blue sky. Getting out of bed and stretching in the warm sunlight, she decided that today would be the day – no more waiting. Once showered, she put on her indigo blouse with the fashionably large collar, her yellow tartan dress and her brown sailing shoes. She cleaned the sunglasses which best matched her short bob, then telephoned Hisakawa.

Faithful Hisakawa. Loyal Hisakawa. But dull dull dull Hisakawa. Poor boy. Some people are born into so much wealth they'll never know which way is up. Still, Ryoma Hisakawa knew a thing or two about literature, particularly western literature, and given who his father was, it could hardly be a bad thing to show her face around Jinbōchō with him in tow.

Feeling bad, Nozomi reminded herself that Hisakawa was her friend. A *good* friend, even if he had made that one clunky marriage proposal at university. Within half an hour Hisakawa was outside, leaning on the bonnet of a brand-new white Mazda Cosmo. As she opened the front door his face spread out into a wide grin.

'What do you think of her?' he asked, adjusting his white leather driving gloves. He was a tall but chubby man with sparse eyebrows and full lips which he had a habit of chewing. Though he had gone grey early, he looked younger than his thirty years.

'It's beautiful,' Nozomi replied, though secretly she was disappointed they wouldn't be walking in the sunshine.

It was a short drive to Jinbōchō, an area north of the palace known for its myriad bookstores and publishing houses. Its alleys teemed with students, intellectuals, liberals and curio-hunters. Nozomi loved the smells and sounds of Jinbōchō: the roasting coffee, musty old pages, megaphones blaring with earnest political appeals.

As he drove Hisakawa talked about the pressures of work now he was a director in his father's company, how hard it was to stay interested in the same girl. It was the usual ground that Hisakawa would traipse over, eager as he was to impress upon her the evidence of his life as a big shot. Nozomi listened intently as ever, like a babysitter indulging tall tales.

Arriving at the print shop, Hisakawa insisted on paying for the eight copies of her novella and made a big show of demanding that the employees bind the pages carefully. When they had finished, he told them to put the books in the trunk of his car.

Getting back into the Cosmo, Hisakawa finally asked what *The Mannequins* was all about anyway. Nozomi's cheeks burned as she opened up to him. It was something she had never really done before, but she felt she couldn't be cagey, considering the trouble he was going to.

Abruptly, he pulled over. Before going any further he insisted on hearing the rest over coffee. Embarrassed, Nozomi agreed. Hisakawa listened to her eagerly as he chewed on baby sardines, little scales falling between the folds of his red Argyle pullover. When she was finished he shrugged, as though she had been talking backwards. 'Well, way over my head, but sounds interesting nonetheless!'

Hisakawa then drove them from publisher to publisher, demanding that *The Mannequins* be delivered directly to the senior editor. Most of those he addressed seemed to recognize him or, if they didn't, they at least recognized the air he had about him. Nobody argued with Hisakawa, though Nozomi worried that the minute they left, her manuscript would be going straight in the bin. Still, she couldn't very well ask him to leave her to it at this stage.

After a few hours of delivering copies they returned to the car and he slapped his stomach.

'Okay, I'm starved. Let's eat.'

'I'm not sure I can, Ryoma.'

'The nerves, eh? No need, no need at all.' He winked. 'I bet you'll have messages waiting for you when you get home. I have a good feeling about this.'

Two months went by and Nozomi heard nothing back. She printed off more copies of *The Mannequins* and tried the smaller publishers. When that failed, she delivered them by hand at the third-rate places. Nozomi was thrown out on several occasions. None of the magazines wanted to know, not even the student titles.

And it was on one simmering afternoon towards the end of summer as she was turned away by a tiny pulp publisher with the circulation of a corpse that Nozomi decided she had had enough. Though she was never one to express her emotions freely, she found herself standing in the doorway, crying.

She couldn't have been there for more than half a minute when someone tapped her on the shoulder. She turned to see a man, a slight smile on his lips conveying a cocky embarrassment that she couldn't quite read. He was young, probably not even her age, and good-looking. He had sideburns, long hair, a roguish quality about his face, yet he wore tasteful clothes: a chocolate-coloured suit, an olive tie.

'Are you all right?'

'I'm fine,' she snapped.

'Why are you crying?'

'It's nothing.'

He nodded at the building behind her. 'Have they fired you?'

'No. I don't work here.'

'Then where do you work?'

'Not that it's any of your business, but at a bar.'

'Which bar? I know all the good bars in Tokyo.'

'Well, you don't know this one.' She pulled herself together. 'I have to go.'

'Come for a drink with me. We'll have fun. Dance a bit. Laugh. You need happiness.'

'I *am* happy,' she answered, trying not to sound offended, though she was.

'Why don't you start living your life, Nozomi?'

'What? How do you know my name?'

He nodded down at her unwanted manuscript. 'Meet me tonight at ten.'

'You're crazy. I don't even know you.'

'Well, I know your name. And I'm Kimura. We can work the rest out tonight.' He handed her something. Nozomi looked down and saw a little matchbook from Club Hedonia in Akasaka. When she looked back up Kimura was walking away, hands in his pockets.

Back at home, Nozomi dropped her manuscript on the bedroom floor and opened a beer. She drank it in silence and looked out of the window. Not even the passing trains could lift her spirits. The grey, rainy evening depressed her even more.

Later, when the phone rang, Nozomi expected it to be her father. His simple, unflustered way of talking would make her feel better, she knew it. But it was Hisakawa.

'Nozomi, darling. How are you? I was wondering if you felt like going to see a movie.'

She let herself drop back against the wall and closed her eyes. For some reason Hisakawa was the last person she felt like talking to. 'That's . . . nice of you, but I'm not really in the mood.'

'Are you sure? It's a James Caan sci-fi movie. Meant to be good.'

'Maybe another night.'

'Well, how about something to eat? I know you're always in the mood for –'

'Ryoma, I said no.'

'Oh.' She could hear the hurt in his voice. 'Okay, sorry. I guess.'

'No, it's fine. Don't be sorry.' She sighed with guilt she was too tired for. 'Look, I'll call you in the morning or something, all right? I'm just – I don't know. I'll call you.' Hanging up, Nozomi felt utterly inert. Not so long ago, she had felt that her life was on the precipice of something exciting, something wonderful. Now she felt absolutely sedentary.

Fed up, she decided to steal one of her father's cigarettes. He didn't smoke but he kept a few American packs and sold them under the table for a reasonable price. Nozomi figured he wouldn't miss one. Fumbling around for a light, she took out from her pocket the matchbook the strange Kimura had given her. Nozomi Iwata struck the match and, as she looked at the little flame, decided to do something reckless.

Club Hedonia had only opened a few months ago yet long lines snaked around the block every night of the week. Inside, great clouds of cigarette smoke swirled pink. Glimmering disco balls, strobes and mirrors made it seem as if the room itself was spinning, while the dance floor throbbed like a school of fish changing direction.

Kimura smoked languidly and poured them champagne. From their table they had a great view. 'See him over there? That's Pierre Cardin.'

'Who?'

'He's a fashion designer. That's the Gabonese ambassador next to him. And those guys over there making all the noise? That's Bad Company. You know Bad Company?'

Nozomi shook her head.

'They're from England.'

She nodded like that meant something. 'You never told me what you do.'

He sipped his champagne before answering, 'I'm in the commodities business. Mainly diamonds. People in Japan know very little about diamonds.'

'I actually happen to have some expertise in diamonds.'

'You said you work in a bar.'

'Well, what do you think I studied at university? Some of my papers were widely praised.'

He frowned. 'Well, I've never heard of you.'

'I'm kidding, I don't know anything about diamonds.'

He laughed. It was a nice laugh. 'I was going to say.'

'So tell me something about diamonds, Mr Kimura.'

'Well, uh, they're very, very old. Sometimes, three billion years old.'

'Go on.'

'The ancient Greeks believed they were tears cried by the gods.'

'I see.'

'That's not that interesting, huh?'

'Not *that* interesting, no.' She laughed.

'Okay, how about this? Scientists have discovered a planet that they believe is composed mostly of carbon – it's one third pure diamond.'

'Okay, that's a tiny bit interesting.'

He grinned. 'Next time a pretty girl asks me about diamonds, that's the fact I'll use.'

She sipped her champagne. 'Do you often do this type of thing?'

'What?'

'Pick up girls in the street. Bring them to fashionable clubs.'

'I've tried once or twice. They usually tell me to piss off.'

'I don't believe you.'

'They do!'

'No, I mean about the once or twice.' She smiled and Kimura felt like he too had discovered a diamond planet.

Nozomi and Kimura were walking along the Sumida River. It was almost 1 a.m. The smoky perfume of fireworks drifted along the black water. People had tossed empty beer cans into the flowerbeds. Kimura had given Nozomi his jacket, which hung loosely from her shoulders; she liked the faint citrus of his aftershave. She was eating a chocolate banana while he chomped on a tomorokoshi stick – corncob grilled with miso, butter and soy sauce. As they ate they discussed his poor school record, travel, music.

Nozomi was pretty sure that he wasn't in the diamond trade; the scuffed knuckles and bruises on his forearms suggested another trade altogether. But he was nice and he was funny without trying too hard – nobody said they had to get married. Besides, she enjoyed chocolate bananas and wearing nice warm jackets.

When they had finished their food they bought two cans from a man selling beer from a cart, then sat down on the quay to watch the river boats slip by. They leaned against the metal railings, their legs dangling over the water, and spoke about their families. It turned out that Kimura didn't have much of one either, having grown up between his seafaring father and an uncle who barely said a word to him. Nozomi in turn told him about her own mother leaving, the bar in Yūrakuchō, the degree she had no use for.

When another beer cart passed they bought two more cans.

'*Kampai!*' Kimura said, grinning at her.

'*Kampai!*' she smiled down at the little black ripples. 'So, then. How did you end up in the diamond business?'

'It's a long story.' Kimura lost his smile.

'I like stories.'

'Long and boring.'

'Try me.'

'I have a better idea.'

'Mm?'

'You think you'll let me read *your* story? I love ghosts.'

She looked at Kimura like he had lost his mind. 'Maybe some other time.'

They fell quiet for a while.

'What's wrong?' he asked.

'Kimura, are you really in the diamond trade?'

He looked at the river and shook his head.

'What do you really do?'

'I work the door at a bar.'

'Explains the bruises.'

He looked down at his forearms. 'I just wanted to impress you, I'm sorry. It was stupid.'

106

'Why diamonds, of all things?'

He laughed. 'I really don't know. I tried to think of something glamorous.'

'But you knew those facts.'

'I met a guy at my bar who told me.'

She nodded.

'I'm sorry I lied to you.'

'It's okay.' Nozomi reached over and took his hand. His knuckles were healing. 'Listen, Kimura. I can tell you like me, and I like you back. I had a lovely evening, but I just don't want to get into anything with you. I hope you understand. I'm just not really . . .'

Kimura's smile was pained but he nodded anyway. 'I understand. Yeah. I wouldn't want to go out with me either.'

She laughed. 'Shall we be friends?'

'Okay, but be careful because, once I'm your friend, I'm your friend for evermore.'

Nozomi squeezed his hand. 'Okay. Just no more lies.'

'I swear it.'

The Tokyo skyline rose high above them, an electric parade of neon branding, watches, cameras, electronic keyboards. The moon was hard to spot at first, just another bright logotype. The Sumida River curved into the distance. All along it, where before there were squat huddles of shacks and wooden houses, now there were gleaming skyscrapers to accommodate the progress, the growth, the money.

From where she was sitting Nozomi could see the evening paper. Its headline was announcing that Japan's per capita income had now comfortably surpassed the United Kingdom's.

'But if we are friends,' Kimura said, 'you have to let me read your story one day.'

'Okay.' Nozomi began to laugh.

Kimura threw the ring-pull from his beer can at her. 'What's so funny?'

'Nothing, it's stupid.'

'Come on, what?'

'It's just that in my story the main character meets a strange man by chance. And I just realized that here I am, the very same thing happening to me.'

'Well, if you won't let me read it, tell me about it. All you said was it was about ghosts. What do these ghosts do, fall in love?'

'No. The opposite, actually.'

Nozomi proceeded to tell Kimura the story, how it began, why she loved horror fiction so much, the thrill of being creeped out. They spoke until Tokyo's half-dark began to lose its fuzzy pitch and the seguro-sekirei birds began to call out.

When they were tired of talking they just watched the glassy river change colour. Nozomi laid her head against Kimura's shoulder. After a long silence he told her in a whisper how beautiful she was. 'It makes me sad,' he added. 'Your decision.'

'Yeah. Same for me.'

Over the next few weeks, as summer turned to autumn, Nozomi and Kimura began to see more and more of each other. He lived in an old apartment block in Ike-bukuro and she would frequently go over after work to listen to records and cook with him. The leaves of a tall beech tree tapped the windows whenever a breeze blew. Nozomi thought it was an even more beautiful sound than the trains passing her bedroom window. Kimura's single room looked out over a neighbourhood park and they enjoyed making up stories about the locals: their infidelities, their resentments, their silly little lives.

As autumn deepened an unsophisticated courtship played out, an efflorescence of intimacies and secrets culminating in an awkward dinner and bunglesome first sex. Afterwards, in that chilly dark, sure as they were both breathing, Nozomi and Kimura knew they were in love.

'Tell me something, Nozomi.'

'Mm?'

'How many publishers are left in Tokyo that you haven't tried yet?'

Her laugh was a tired croak. 'A few, probably.'

'Well, I think it's time for you to start trying again.'

8. Sorry

Iwata finally found the witness from Meredith's case file, an enfeebled Puerto Rican man, sitting in the shade by the window of the common room. He was freshly shaved and wearing the pyjamas he had been issued earlier that day.

'Joseph Clemente?'

'Who are you?' He spoke softly.

Iwata reached for his ID but he had already checked it in. 'Sir, I'm a professional investigator and I'm looking into the incident you witnessed. I'd really appreciate a few minutes of your time.'

'You faked your way in here just to talk to me?' Clemente hoisted a bushy grey eyebrow.

'Someone was murdered, sir.'

'*I* know that. I saw it.'

'That's what I want to go over. Exactly what you saw. I'll pay you, of course.'

'How much?'

'Let's start at twenty and see how much you know.'

Clemente shrugged. 'I couldn't sleep so I went for a walk. A little ways out towards the tracks, I seen two figures. At first I thought it was a couple fooling around. Figured they were probably in a good mood so I went to ask for change. But then I saw it. The train headlights showed me everything.'

'What was that?'

'He had just dropped her. I could see right away she was dead. I've seen my share of bodies. I shouted out and he just split. Just as the train came, he disappeared on the other side of it. By the time it passed he was gone.'

'You didn't see a car in the area?'

'Nope.'

'What did he look like?'

'Like I told the cops, I didn't really see his face.'

'About five nine, wearing a hooded sweatshirt.'

'Yeah. That's all.'

'Was he big? Muscles?'

'He looked strong but he wasn't big. More like, slim, you know?'

'Can you remember anything else? At all?'

'Look, pal. It happened fast and it was dark. Then he was gone. I didn't see anything more than that and it's been a while since.' Clemente looked up at the clock. 'It's almost time for afternoon sermon.'

'Last question. You say you shouted out. Did this man say anything back?'

Clemente frowned now. 'You know what, maybe he did.'

'To you?'

'No. It was like . . . he was talking to the girl after he dropped her.'

'Go on.' Iwata grappled with his excitement.

'I didn't hear him too good but he had kind of a strange voice.'

'Strange how?'

'Just, like, *strange*. Almost soft.'

'Softly spoken or quiet?'

'Both. At first I thought he was praying. I didn't hear that part clearly, but it had the rhythm, you know? But when he dropped her there was something else. Something clearer.'

'What was it?'

'"Sorry." He said, "Sorry."'

Iwata reclaimed his clothes, put two twenty-dollar bills in Joseph Clemente's plastic tray and left the Sanctuary. He gave his bed ticket to a woman who had been turned away for lack of ID. Then he walked the dusky mile and a half back to the train tracks. It was chillier now, the breeze around his body bringing out gooseflesh. On the one hand, Iwata felt the old buzz of a hunt taking shape. If there was a murderer out there, he would find his scent. At the same time, in the pit of his stomach, he couldn't ignore the sinking dread of a fear confirmed.

In the Bronco he dialled Kate Floccari's number. When she picked up Iwata spoke without greeting. 'It wasn't Talky who killed Meredith. It had to be someone else.'

'How do you know?'

'I just spoke to the witness. He told me the killer said something to the body as he dumped it. If he said something, then it can't have been Talky.'

'Shit. Are you going to call Detective Silke?'

'Going by our introduction, I don't think there'd be much point. I have zero proof of anything. But I know whoever killed Meredith is still out there. And I don't think he's finished.'

Floccari inhaled quietly. 'Listen, Kosuke . . .'

'I know. You can't help me. You've already stuck your neck out far enough and you've got things in your own life to deal with. I just didn't want to be the only one in this city to know about him.'

They were silent for a moment.

'Well, then. Good luck, Inspector Iwata.'

Iwata thanked her and hung up. Kate Floccari had never used his old title before. He watched a freight train lumbering past. He too, now, was alone, fixed to the track. He didn't know where it would take him. The only thing he knew for certain was that Meredith's murderer had said, 'Sorry,' after he killed her.

Why? Why did you say, 'Sorry'?

Iwata realized he was sweating. He was trembling. From nowhere, he felt an urgent, disastrous terror, like he was hurtling down to a depth at speed. Gasping, he tried to free himself from the seatbelt he didn't have on, pawing at his own chest. He was hyperventilating, punching the dashboard to regain control. Iwata saw the murder victims from his past, their bodies ribboned and riven, their intestines slopping out. He tried to scream.

And then it was over.

The train was already dwindling in the distance.

Panting, he told himself it was just a panic attack. That it was just his body's resistance to returning to its old function. Yet Iwata knew it was more. He knew the feelings intimately. They were the ones he had tried to self-medicate his way out of for such a long time. It was a fear that used to draw him into the foetal position in police station toilets, a fear that would force him to pull over to the side of the road to vomit.

And now here he was again, with a boxful of murder – a headful of memories he could no longer pretend away. No matter how much he hoped he was wrong, he knew that, somewhere out there, there was a man with a garrotte and a taste for transgender women.

And it fell to Iwata to find him.

When his breathing had normalized he started the car and drove to the hardware store as though he were a normal person doing normal things.

Back at home, Iwata showered, then made himself yellowtail with ponzu citrus sauce. He put his Spanish CD on and tried to relax. But he couldn't stop himself gazing at the photographs of Meredith, the police report and the papers that Kate had given him on the missing and murdered trans women.

Iwata shuffled through Meredith's smile, her death, her neck. Though it was clearly the same person, the difference between the photograph of her in the restaurant and the photograph of her by the train tracks was vast. It was like seeing a real-life, normal person, and then, smiling and lit by candle, the movie version, played by a younger, far more beautiful actress.

Iwata had met Meredith as Julian several times in the past, but they'd never shared more than pleasantries. Charlotte Nichol and her husband were stern, exacting parents. But Cleo and her sibling had always been close, that much Iwata knew.

Iwata had spent his life trying to abscond from who he really was. Yet Meredith had moved a thousand miles to be herself. He wondered if she had died for it too.

Iwata put the photograph from the restaurant to one side and peered closely at the second, which clearly showed Meredith's garrotted neck. Her blue eyes were half open. Her hair, raven black, was a drab brown at the roots, a few greys here and there. One of her hands had fallen across her chest. Her fingernails had not been cared for, and her skin, particularly for someone who had lived in Southern California for several years, was very pale.

Nobody raped you, nobody stole from you, nobody beat you. But somebody wanted you dead. Was this hatred? Did someone hate who you were? It didn't seem likely to him, somehow. Whoever had murdered Meredith had done so with precision, with economy, almost impersonally. There had even been compunction, according to Joseph Clemente.

Sorry.

Iwata turned the photographs face down, cleared away his dishes and took out two old mugs. He poured two fluid ounces of multipurpose glue into the first mug, the same again of water, added a little pink food dye, then mixed thoroughly. He dissolved a tablespoon of borax into the second mug, this one with a fluid ounce of water. When he combined the two mixtures, the pink liquid began to congeal. Iwata stirred the mixture thoroughly then kneaded it with his hands for ten minutes until it became a flesh-like putty. He took the putty to the coffee table, laying it on top of a few sheets of kitchen towel. Then he opened the bag from the hardware store and took out his purchases.

First, Iwata pulled some fishing wire taut across the putty in mimicry of the possible murder weapon. He garrotted the pink substance for two minutes, enough time to end a life, then took away the wire. He held a lamp over the ligature mark. It was straight and unforgiving, and did not resemble the marks on Meredith's neck at all.

Iwata moved on to a variety of ropes, a scarf, a small chain – he even tried his telephone cord. But the ligature pattern in the photograph wasn't close to matching any of these things. It was a distinct, wavy imprint in angry pink around the throat. Iwata fell asleep trying to imagine what, and who, had caused it.

Iwata spent much of the next morning trawling through the Casual Encounters page of Craigslist in search of some kind of link between the catalogue Mingo had given him and the images of Meredith and Geneviève against the ocean. He narrowed his search to *trans4m*. Most of the ads were composed using oblique, almost adolescent vernacular, seemingly from people seeking mundane activities:

◆◆◆ DDF Chocolate Beauty in town to see fireworks ◆◆◆
Cute blonde looking for movie nite
+ maybe nite cap ⁑ lol xxx

Others were less twee:

Hung? Gorgeous Tgirl in Bellflower waiting to suck you –
just unload + leave

In most of the ads a cellphone number had been pasted
across the images of the girls themselves to circumnavi-
gate the rules against solicitation. Practically all of them
were written in the parlance of the internet hook-up
world. Some were easy enough for Iwata to decipher: a
prostitute called Molly was seeking an encounter involving MDMA; another named Poppy was after heroin; a
'night on the ski slopes' meant cocaine. But he had to
look up countless apparently innocuous words or acro-
nyms for their hidden meaning: ABR, *adult breastfeeding
relationship*; Roses, *financial recompense for sex*; GHM ISO
HWP TOP, *gay Hispanic male in search of height-weight pro-
portionate male to be penetrated by* . . . on and on it went. Any
mention of *generosity*, *kindness* or posts with dollar signs
in them – *Lookin 4 nice guy$* – again related to a financial
exchange.

By midday Iwata had sent dozens of messages to trans
women asking for information about Meredith or Geneviève in exchange for cash. He was met with silence.

One subject did, however, keep on cropping up. They
called him John Smith – a trick killing transgender prostitutes. On the sleuth forums some speculated that he
liked black women, others said only white. Many believed
he'd been going for several years, his murders falling
beyond the gaze of the police. On the trans message

boards there were countless warnings, suggested precautions, advice on where to find economical self-defence classes.

To Iwata, John Smith felt like an urban legend, a spook story. But he knew that even in the outlandish, fragments of truth could sometimes be found. He also knew that bodies were turning up, spook story or no. And if John Smith *did* exist, then Iwata saw him as a manifestation of silent loathing, obsession, desire, all wrapped up in the costume of a normal man. The sort of man Meredith might have invited into her room or gotten into a car with.

Iwata turned away from his laptop and thought about coffee. In doing so, he noticed something. He had two supposedly identical photographs of Meredith in the restaurant, one from Charlotte, the other from the police report McCrae had sent him. But they were different. The larger one – the police copy – had been blown up somewhat. But the other had a few more inches of detail. And right at the fringe of the photograph a hand had been caught in frame. It was holding a credit card. And on it, a name: Joyce Carbone.

Iwata returned to his laptop and logged into MARPLExp – a data-fusion search tool he spent a small fortune on in monthly fees. Though he preferred the old-fashioned low-tech brand of investigating – shoes slapping concrete, fingers on doorbells – the technology was undoubtedly useful. Were it not for the cost, he thought, similar technology would likely be rolled out throughout every police station in the land.

Logged in, Iwata could now link a name with criminal histories, employment records, addresses, bankruptcies, vehicles, phones, utilities – and so on. It needed something tangible, ideally a social security number or a driver's licence, but a full name was better than nothing.

Iwata typed in the name Joyce Carbone along with the visible details of her credit card. Immediately a little constellation of data appeared before him. Joyce Carbone lived in Highland Park and had worked at Club Noir for a period.

Iwata wrote down her address and left his apartment.

9. Hope Heaven Feels Good

Although only five miles from Downtown, East LA felt like another city. Once home to many of LA's ethno burbs – Japanese, Jewish, Italian and Eastern European – today it was overwhelmingly Latina, the largest Hispanic community in the country. It was home to fresh arrivals from all over South and Central America, home to the multigenerational residents whose foremothers dated back to the original ranchos.

As Iwata drove along Whittier Boulevard he took in East LA's version of the Walk of Fame, the late-afternoon light glinting on its stones. He passed mariachis eating outside taquerias that seemed always to have been there, old ladies lining up outside money-transfer shops and young women in coffee shops studying for college entrance. Poets wrote on typewriters. Glass Coke bottles full of flowers were left beneath murals of the Virgin. Gang members in baggy T-shirts chatted buoyantly on corners, their eyes constantly darting up and down the road.

5520 Amalia Avenue was a plain house with white stucco walls. A German Shepherd lifted its head from the porch as Iwata opened the gate. He let it smell his hand, then rang the doorbell. A few seconds later the door opened a crack.

Iwata held up his ID. 'Joyce Carbone? We spoke on the phone.'

She had silent-movie looks: dark features, almond-shaped eyes, a well-defined nose. Carbone checked for prying neighbours before letting him in. The house smelled faintly of bleach and dog. She led him into a kitchen of granite counters and dull mosaic tiles. 'Go ahead, sit down,' she said, her voice softer now.

'Thank you.'

'Coffee?'

'Black, please.'

She leaned against the counter and looked at Iwata with a mixture of annoyance and faint-heartedness, as though his presence were a burden she was obliged to bear.

'You're not a cop.'

'No.'

'So what are you, Robin Hood?'

'I'm helping with Meredith's murder.'

'Nobody just helps. Not for free.'

'Meredith's sister was my wife.'

Carbone said nothing. The coffee-maker flicked off. She brought over two cups and sat warily across from Iwata, her fatigue clear. 'How'd you find me?'

'You used to work at Club Noir.'

She shrugged as though that time in her life were a mistake. 'Look, I'd like to help. But I don't know anything about what happened to Meredith.' She looked up at the clock. 'And Michael will be home from work soon. Will this take long?'

'Just a few minutes.'

Carbone sipped her coffee in consent.

'I assume the police already talked to you about Meredith?'

'Mm. Briefly.'

'What did they ask?'

'"Most murders are personal, blah blah blah, can you think of anyone who wanted to hurt Meredith?" And I couldn't. She was just a wonderful person, no enemies.'

'Boyfriends?'

'Nothing serious.'

'What about Talky?'

'Who?'

Iwata took out the Polaroid. Although shocked at sight of a dead body, Carbone shook her head. He could tell genuine mystification from feigned.

'When did you last see Meredith?'

'It's been a while. Michael prefers I don't mix with the old crowd.'

'Police were thinking her murder could have come about due to a violent reaction –'

'To finding out she was pre-op, yeah, they made that much clear with their line of questioning. But like I told them, that'd be surprising to me. So far as I know, she was always upfront with the johns.'

'What about a hate crime?'

'It's possible. You just have to look at the statistics for that to be obvious. But if you're asking me if I can think of anyone specifically, then no. There was nobody in my time at the club, no creep, angry ex, whatever. I'll be honest with you, it was probably more likely to do with something she did.'

Iwata looked up. 'You said she was a wonderful person.'

'She was also a junkie and a pickpocket.'

He looked out of the window. The branches of a lime tree wavered in the breeze.

'Tell me about the last time you saw her.'

'It was about six months ago, maybe more. She came by looking for money and I gave her what I had. She accused me of holding out on her so we argued. More than anything, I think she was angry at me for meeting Michael, for leaving her alone. She kept calling me fake, I lost my temper, I called her a fucking hophead and I didn't see her after that. I tried calling but got nothing back. I figured I'd lost a friend and hoped that one day we'd reconnect.'

'And when she came asking for money, that was out of the blue?'

'Kind of. It was after she quit Noir.'

'Why did she quit?'

'She met someone.'

Iwata looked up. 'You said you couldn't think of any boyfriends.'

'Not a love interest. More like a talent scout for a VIP. That was the sense I got. After that, she left the club and was throwing money around for a while. She bought me some earrings. I still have them.'

'So how did she end up on Skid Row?'

'Mr VIP dropped her and things changed. She tried to get her old job back at Noir but the manager told her to stick it. She lost her apartment. Things fell apart for her. She came to me for money but, after that, she just sailed off the end of the earth.'

Iwata sipped his coffee in thought. He was familiar with the lacunae in the lives of the dead he was tasked with understanding – secrets held, decisions made, always hidden from him, always buried. Carbone looked around her kitchen, as though it were the first time she was seeing it. Iwata read loneliness in that face.

'What about this?' He took out the sex catalogue. 'Do you know anything about it?' He tapped Meredith's photograph on page fourteen.

Carbone shook her head.

Iwata flipped ahead to page eighteen. 'What about Geneviève, did you know her?'

'I knew her, sure. She was more Meredith's friend, though.'

'Any idea where she is?'

'We were never close.'

'Do you know her full name? Address?'

'It's Darlington, I think. She lived somewhere near MacArthur Park.'

Iwata pocketed the catalogue. 'Thank you for your time.'

'There's something else.' Carbone closed her eyes. 'It won't help you but I just have to tell somebody. That day . . . When Meredith came round . . . She was just so outside of herself. I'd never seen her so angry, so desperate. After we argued, she seemed sad, even. Almost like she knew we wouldn't see each other again. As she left, she said something. It was throwaway, but I haven't been able to get it out of my head.

'I was trying to talk to her about getting clean. I know it's stupid, it's not like a pep talk is going to drag anyone out of that. But she just looked at me and said: "Joycie, no matter how hard I try, nothing feels good to me. Not anymore . . ."' Carbone bit her lip and looked up at the ceiling, eyes brimming. 'So, if it's up there, I just sure hope heaven feels good.'

Returning home, Iwata logged on to MARPLE and found Geneviève. She was not listed on any missing-persons database. She had been born Jeremy Domínguez in Nuevo Laredo almost twenty-six years ago to the day. There was a cellphone number and several addresses for her around Texas and California, but only one in Los Angeles: Bonnie Brae Street near MacArthur Park.

He called her home phone but received no answer. The listing for Geneviève's parents was a Texas number. Iwata dialled and eventually an old man answered.

'Mr Domínguez?'

He grunted.

'Mr Domínguez, my name is Kosuke Iwata. I'm a professional investigator and I'm calling about Geneviève. Is she at home with you?'

'She?' There was a harsh hackle of laughter. 'No, mister. *She* ain't here. 'Cos the person you're talking about? Ain't ever welcome in ma' house ever again.'

'Mr Dom—'

'Don't call here again.' The line went dead.

*

Iwata emerged on to South Alvarado across from the old Westlake Theater. He passed the Japanese beef bowl drive-thru next door, which did not make him think of Japan, and crossed the road, passing the 99¢ Only Store. Here the sidewalk was packed, restless preachers and hustlers in amongst the workers, the mothers, the wasted.

It was all for sale: calling cards, fake IDs, salvation itself. From under rainbow parasols small women hawked snacks – sugary churros, pork tamales, langoustines out of a repurposed potty. Working girls and boys looked into car windows, Jehovah's Witnesses smiled. A cop was questioning the crowd about the stone that had been thrown at his car. His partner was scanning the fringes of the park hoping for any bagman dumb enough not to have taken a coffee break.

Iwata turned on Bonnie Brae and stopped outside a dilapidated apartment block next to an old convalescents' hospital. He pressed the grubby buzzer and waited. Receiving no answer, he tried the building supervisor.

'Yeah?'

'I'm looking for Geneviève Darlington.'

'She's not answering? Hey, it's a free country.'

'Did she say she was going away?'

'No, but it's not my business until pay day.'

'It could be pay day today.'

There was the drag of a cigarette, then a crackling silence. 'I'd lose my job.'

'We're talking. Nobody is going to lose –'

'Just get out of here, pal.'

*

Back on Descanso Drive, the palm fronds against the sunset moved like flies drowning in honey. Iwata climbed the steps to his apartment slowly, as though the conflicting doubt and certainty in him had a physical weight. Usually he was glad to be on these stairs, glad for the silence of home. But that feeling didn't come now. Or it didn't seem to matter anymore.

Opening the door, Iwata smelled garlic. Orchestra Baobab's 'Utru Horas' was playing. Callie Mendoza wore a blue polka-dot wrap dress tonight, her coiled, dark hair much shorter than usual. Having never seen it before, Iwata couldn't resist kissing the nape of her neck.

'Hey,' she said, turning to kiss him. Her voice was warm like strong rum.

On the stove, swordfish steaks were cooking in vinegar and olive oil, the ingredients for escabeche sauce – yellow onions, bell peppers, carrots and bay leaves – neatly prepared to one side.

'That looks incredible,' he said.

Callie smiled. She was the spitting image of a Cuban actress he had once seen in a movie about a family who inherited treasure. It hadn't ended happily.

He stole a carrot and crunched into it joyfully.

'You'll ruin your appetite.'

'Around you, all I *am* is appetite.' His orange grin was cheesy.

Callie shook her head. 'How's your mother?'

'She's fine,' Iwata answered, while flipping through his LPs. He chose an old Detroit Soul compilation. 'She wants me to meet a nice woman.'

'And how's that going?'

Iwata laughed. They hadn't met each other's parents. That wasn't the kind of liaison they shared. Their meetings depended mostly on Callie's husband's work schedule.

As they ate they discussed Anthony Floccari. Iwata didn't mention Meredith Nichol or the murderer the message boards had labelled John Smith. Callie spoke about her own cases – she too was a private eye, though she worked mainly in the corporate sector.

Getting up, Callie changed records and served two bowls of lemon sorbet with mint coulis. They ate on the sofa, feet touching.

'Who is this playing?' Iwata asked.

'It's your record – you don't know?'

'Half of these boxes I haven't opened.'

'The Joe Tatton Trio. "Sunday Shade".'

'I like it.'

'That doesn't surprise me, it's very you.'

He laughed. 'And what is "very me"?'

'Cool, baby.' She kissed his forearm and his skin hardened. 'Very cool.'

In the sticky small hours the street glow through the blinds turned the bedroom wall into blotting paper for the shadows. Far away, a man screamed out, in pain, in jest, in madness – nobody was interested except for the neighbourhood dogs. The distant heckle of a helicopter could be heard. Traffic lights clunked loudly as they changed colour.

Iwata and Callie had been this way for almost a year now but still deep sleep wouldn't come easily when they were together. To Iwata, these hours felt like the only time he said anything real to anyone. He became aware music was still playing in the other room – Julie London's 'Don't Worry' 'Bout Me'.

'I'll go switch it off,' he said.

Callie shook her head, her hair susurrant on the pillow. 'Leave it on.'

She would always face the window and he would always lie behind her.

'I used to listen to this in college,' she whispered.

'I can't imagine what you were like back then.'

She smiled. 'I had clearer ideas about things.'

'In what way?'

'Well, I had rules.'

'Rules?'

'For example, I would only ever sleep with someone if I could happily switch lives with them. You know what I mean? Like trade lives and be okay about it.'

'My schedule is a nightmare, you'd hate it.'

She leaned her head back towards his mouth. It meant she wanted to be kissed there. Iwata closed his eyes and complied. Some time passed. Maybe just a few moments, or maybe hours; it was hard to judge time with her.

When he opened his eyes again Callie had her head on his chest. She was tracing his scars with a finger.

'Kosuke?'

'Yes?'

'Who could a hurt a man like you?'

'Maybe you could.'

She lifted her head to look at him. 'Is that one of those jokes that means something?'

'Jokes should never mean anything. Otherwise they're not jokes.'

'You think I'm a terrible person, don't you?'

'Of course I don't.'

She put her head back on his chest. 'Then why do I do this? I'm no different from all those people you follow every day.'

He stroked her hair. 'I'm in this too.'

'Hm.' Her tone told Iwata his answer hadn't been enough.

'Look, Callie, I think you love him. I really do. But I also think that maybe he just isn't enough for you. And I'm not sure that's anybody's fault.'

She thought about this for a long time and then bundled her face into his chest hair. 'You make me happy, that's all. It washes away the guilt.'

Iwata did the sign of the cross over her face. '*Ego te absolvo.*'

'You're a dick.' She slapped his stomach.

'Cal, listen.' Their noses were touching now. She could feel the breath of his words on her lips. 'You are *not* a bad person. And you don't hurt me. All you do is make me feel good. That's all you do.'

'Okay.' She kissed him on the eyebrow. 'So.'

'So.'

'Who *did* hurt you?'

'Just a crazy man, a long time ago.'

'Where is he now?'

'In jail. He's never coming out.'

'Good.'

'Good.'

'Kosuke?'

'Mm.'

'If I ask you something, will you be honest?'

'Probably.'

Her gaze flicked from one eye to the other as if undecided where the truth might be found. 'Do you love me?'

'I . . . I love this.'

Callie Mendoza laughed. 'You really are a dick.'

'Speaking of which . . .'

She was shrieking now as he tickled her, his fingers digging into her ribs. The dirty windowpane was iridescent in the pre-dawn, a square puddle of gasoline. Iwata knew that sharing a darkened bedroom with someone that liked you while everybody else was dead to the world was the closest thing to fairy tales life had to offer. It wasn't the sex, it wasn't the talking. It was the tan line of a watch, it was the space in between toes, it was sweat on a forehead turned silver by the moon.

It was the smallness of two existences taking refuge from the world.

At 3.35 a.m. Iwata's cellphone rang. It didn't seem possible that there should be anything beyond warm limbs in darkness, yet the noise wouldn't stop. He answered with his eyes closed.

'Yeah?'

'I'm calling from Club Noir, you gave me your card.'

It was the Mexican bouncer. Iwata was awake. Reality returned. 'The tattooed woman?'

'Just walked straight past me.'

10. Same Circles

The air was thick, sliced by strobes. Red laser and purple light alloyed through the smoke. Chic's 'I Want Your Love' was blaring. Go-go dancers were up on podiums, the dance floor was packed. The blonde was sitting at the end of the bar, drinking alone. Her tattoos were hidden by a plum-coloured romper. Her hair looked recently dyed, her leather boots gleamed. Most people wouldn't be able to pull off that much make-up.

As he sat down next to her Iwata realized he had seen her before – coming out of the confessional after Meredith's funeral. She had been beautiful then, in the morning sun, but in this smoky half-dark, dressed the way she was, Iwata found himself taken aback by his own attraction. Beneath it there was also a vague fear he did not understand. Distantly he recalled Rilke's words: 'Every angel terrifies.' Iwata felt the urge to turn around and leave, but that was impossible now.

'Hello again.' He spoke over the music.

She looked up. Dark, hooded eyes, curious, free of apprehension. 'Have we met?'

'I saw you at Our Lady of Solitude.'

'Ah, you know what, you *are* familiar.' Her smile was beautiful, her jaw firm, her voice carried a soft Mexican inflection. 'You're a man of faith, then?'

'I wouldn't go that far.' Iwata laughed. 'How about you, did you get things off your chest?'

'I wouldn't go that far.'

It was the moment where they had to decide, either chalk the meeting up to coincidence or introduce themselves. The woman made the choice. She held out her hand, her arm strong, wiry, deeply tanned. Iwata shook it.

'Mara,' she said.

'Kosuke.' He nodded at her blonde hair. 'You dyed it.'

She touched it lightly, as if calming its nerves. 'I'm still not sure about it.'

'Suits you.'

They both looked at themselves in the mirror behind the bar. 'So,' she said. 'Is this your usual kind of place, Kosuke?'

'I don't have a usual kind of place.'

'Maybe you just haven't found it yet.'

'Maybe.'

'Kosuke is Japanese, huh? What does it mean?'

'Clear. How about Mara?'

She stuck out a fatalistic bottom lip. 'Bitterness.'

'Now that doesn't suit you.'

'Not like my hair?'

'Not even close.' He smiled and looked around the club. 'Are you waiting for someone?'

'I was. Looks like I've been stood up. You?'

'I'm alone.'

They fell quiet and observed each other daringly until Mara looked away with a half-smile. 'You know, Kosuke, when a man wants something from a beautiful woman, he usually starts by offering her a drink.'

'Does that usually get the man the thing he wants?'

'Depends on the woman.'

'Not on what he wants?'

'The list is usually pretty short.'

Iwata laughed and ordered her a margarita. 'Well, you're not wrong. I do want something.'

'I'm listening.'

'I'm actually looking for someone. You might know her. Geneviève?'

The drink arrived. Mara sipped it, then twirled the cocktail umbrella between her fingers. 'Yeah, pretty girl. Is that why you're looking for her?'

'It's to do with my work.' Iwata took out his investigator's ID and Mara inspected it.

'Is she in trouble?'

'I just want to ask a few questions about a friend of hers. Meredith Nichol. You know her?'

Mara looked at him, her gold hoop earrings glinting green in the red light. 'I don't know any Meredith. And I haven't seen Geneviève in a while.'

'You're sure?'

'You have to ask?' Mara looked playfully hurt and crossed her heart with the cocktail stick.

'When was the last time you saw Geneviève?'

'A while is a while.' She downed her margarita.

'Where?'

'Around. I don't recall.'

'I'd really appreciate it if you could take a stab.'

'I better go.' She slipped off her barstool. 'But thanks for the drink.'

'Sure.' Iwata nodded. 'Maybe I'll see you again.'

'It's possible.' Smiling, she reached down for her handbag. Iwata caught sight of her tattoo along her collarbone again. This time, he was able to make out letters after the numbers:

1:18 IS—

The date of birth of a child or sibling? Anniversary?

'After all,' she shouted over the music now, a few paces away, 'seems to me like we move in the same circles!'

Then she was gone.

Iwata stopped at the twenty-four-hour truck across the road from the Mexican Consulate, ordered two fish tacos and a kiwi licuado and sat on a bench at the park entrance. As he ate, he listened to a group of men discussing job opportunities. One had decided to leave the city to work as a field hand, another was going to wait in the Home Depot parking lot tomorrow in the hope of odd jobs. They shared around cans of Tecate and discussed football, children, immigration crackdowns.

As the men talked about their lives Iwata mulled over Meredith's death.

The accepted wisdom was that motives for murder rarely extended beyond money, sex or revenge. The first was unlikely, given that the killer had left behind her money. The second was possible, but there had been no rape, no injury to her genitals.

This left Iwata with revenge. So far, it seemed the least implausible. It could have been rudimentary in nature; Joyce Carbone had mentioned Meredith had been a pickpocket, for instance. Perhaps it was a more intimate reprisal, some kind of deep-rooted bitterness. But then he recalled Joseph Clemente's words. The killer had said, 'Sorry.'

Or, if it didn't fit in to any of these categories at all, was there a fourth element hiding here?

It was gone 5 a.m. by the time Iwata had finished eating. He knew it didn't look good to be ringing doorbells at this hour, but he had little choice – there was a killer out there, and Geneviève was missing.

Iwata cut through MacArthur Park, seeing the figures sleeping on dead grass, hearing their grumbling dreams. Beyond Wilshire Boulevard, which cut MacArthur Park in two, he could see the lake glittering, as though it weren't filthy.

When he reached Bonnie Brae Iwata stood under the fig trees opposite Geneviève's apartment. In the alley next door the shiny hoods of cockroaches glimmered like lost sapphires. An old man in the empty parking lot was muttering to himself. There was a new moon. Somewhere nearby Iwata could hear a gameshow host asking the audience a question:

¿Quién quiere ser millonario?

Iwata crossed the road, hands in his pockets, and pressed Geneviève's buzzer once. He scanned the street as he waited. After half a minute he buzzed again. Knowing he should just go home, he went to the side of the building and climbed over the fence. He dragged a large dumpster until it was sitting beneath the fire-escape ladder.

'Forty years old,' he hissed, then jumped as high as he could.

He grabbed the lowest rung, dangled awkwardly for a second, then got his knee on to it. From there he was able to heft himself up. He climbed the fire-escape stairs as quietly as possible. Up on the roof he skirted broken satellite dishes and coils of cable. The door into the building was, unsurprisingly, locked.

Iwata took out his pocket-sized lock-picking set. He had been police long enough to know that with a pinch of determination and a few cheaply acquired tools most doors were nothing more than an illusion of security. Inserting the tension wrench and applying gentle pressure, he pushed the pick in and began to rake it back and forth. The pins lined up in seconds. There was a quiet clunk, then a release.

Inside, the stairway was dark and echoey. Iwata descended cautiously. Two floors down, he stopped at number 52. The door was ajar. That was never good.

Instinctively, he reached for a gun he didn't have. With no choice, he entered.

The apartment was still and murky in the weak moonlight.

'Geneviève?'

There was no reply. Holding his breath, Iwata scanned the gloom and took out his canister of tear gas from his pocket. With the other hand he picked up a heavy glass ashtray.

'Geneviève?' Louder now.

Still nothing.

Iwata flipped the light switch but no light came. Just a few soft footsteps.

Someone filled the bedroom doorway.

In the dark, it was only a figure.

Iwata looked at it. 'Geneviève? Is that you?'

There was no response.

They rushed each other.

Iwata cleaved the ashtray down but it was blocked, thunking away in the darkness. The squirt of tear gas missed completely. And then it was fists. The man hit hard – ribs, solar plexus, anywhere he found meat – his blows voracious. Iwata landed his own, muscle memory kicking in, but there was no light, too many objects in the way. With no space to back into their bodies locked together, all desperate grunts, bunched clothes, skin under nails. Iwata was aware of the pain but felt only the rushing nausea of fear, his blood flooded with adrenaline, his ears pounding with the breathlessness.

He threw a lead hook, praying for the sweet spot behind the ear, but the man was too fast, too strong, his movements frantic. Iwata reached out; he wanted hair, an eye, an ear. Instead he got a forearm smash flush in the face. There was a pop, like an eardrum on a night-flight landing, then warm blood was gushing out of his nose.

With that, Iwata's legs were gone. He fell to the floor and saw the ceiling fan like a wooden flower. Iwata felt him from behind, legs slipping around his ribs. Then the cushion was over his face, the man squeezing ruthlessly. The pressure in Iwata's head sounded like a train coming, his throat sucking for something, anything.

The man said something, something Iwata couldn't hear. His hands fumbled for help. He felt a magazine. A broken candle. His canister of tear gas. Clutching it, Iwata pointed it over his head and pulled the trigger. A loud hiss resounded, then a yelp. The pressure vanished.

Iwata forced himself on to all fours, wheezing hard. The man that had tried to kill him was retching somewhere behind him, stumbling into furniture, clawing at his eyes. Iwata picked up the ashtray. He wouldn't have long; he had to end this now.

The man opened the window. Then he was gone.

Trembling, Iwata crawled to the bathroom, locked the door and closed his eyes. He could hear the breeze outside, the fig branches rasping at the glass. He could hear gameshow applause, as though the audience had appreciated the fight. He could hear his own whistling breath.

Iwata had not seen the man's face. He had barely heard his voice. It was as if he had just been attacked by the wind itself. Battered and exhausted, he closed his eyes.

11. Home

The smell of warm bread and honey is strong. Iwata is trying to feed his daughter small chunks of carrot but she is shaking her head and screaming. There is a variety show on the TV, the delighted audience applauding. Rain is pounding the windows hard, their little apartment over the café shuddering in the building typhoon.

Cleo is ironing yen bills to make them crisp for the condolence envelope – a colleague in Chōshi PD has died suddenly.

She pauses. 'Kosuke, don't you think this is a bit –'

'If you're going to say it's too much money, don't bother. He was my superior. I can't have his family thinking we're cheap.'

'We're not cheap, we're struggling.'

'What do you want me to tell his wife, "Sorry, there's a recession"?'

'No, it's just that you barely knew the guy.'

'Clee, just trust me. You don't understand how things work here.' Iwata closes his eyes. He lets the plate of carrot clatter on to the table. 'She won't have any of this.'

Nina is still screaming, her face now a deep pink. She smells of almond oils and the scent has always turned Iwata's stomach. Outside, Toriakeura Bay is churning, a convulsion of verdigris waves and black clouds.

Cleo looks through the window and knows that beyond Inubōsaki Lighthouse there is only the nothingness of the North Pacific – nothing all the way to San Francisco. She breathes in the warm steam and feels desolate anguish. 'Kosuke, can we talk for a second?'

'What is it?'

'Okay, don't worry.'

'Just say it.'

'No, it's nothing.'

'Cleo. For fuck's sake.'

'All right. I don't want this life.' She bites her lip, then looks at the floor. He hasn't responded and she can't tell if he's heard her. 'Kosuke, I know you don't want this life either.'

Iwata looks up at her for a moment, shakes his head then points at the baby with the pink spoon. 'How does *want* come into it?'

'Don't shout, I'm just telling you what I'm feeling.'

'What you feel?' He closes his eyes, red splotches teeming over his vision. Voices are ringing in his ears, voices that he has not heard for a long time. He finds himself back in that mountain bus station where his mother left him. *Do good things, boy. Good things.* He clutches his face and groans. He doesn't understand how they can still be speaking to him, after all this time.

Iwata hurls the plastic spoon at the window and it smacks sharply on the glass. Cleo flinches and Nina stops crying for a moment, stunned. A small chunk of carrot has stuck to the window. Now the baby is howling. Iwata strides over so close that Cleo is leaning back against the counter. She is confounded. She has never been scared of him before.

'What *you* feel?' He grips the iron. The steam drifts between their faces.

'Kosuke? The baby is crying. She's going to hurt herself.' Cleo takes the iron from his hand, pushes past him and pulls the plug out.

'The baby the baby the baby.' He spits the words. 'Look at her, she's already hurt. She wasn't born right. What, you think she'll grow up normal?'

'And you'd know about that?'

He hisses insults in Japanese. Cleo knows these words. Something like 'coward', 'clueless'.

'I think you call me those names ' – she is trembling as she picks up Nina, her voice whiffling – 'because that's how you feel about yourself.'

'Feel feel feel. All you do is feel and talk.'

'At least I'm not running away.'

'What does that mean?'

'It means Solanax. Cipralex. Zoloft. Or did you think I didn't know?'

'*Fuck* you.' He picks up the envelope and rips his keys from the peg. 'Both of you.'

'Kosuke, one day you're going to have to accept who you are.'

The door slams and Cleo is left alone with the screaming child. They are both shaking. She throws away the carrots and calls her mother. Her mother tells her what she always has. *He's bad news.* Well, that isn't news anymore, Cleo thinks. She packs a suitcase and looks up flights. It's only nine hours from Tokyo to Seattle. Then a drive over the Cascade Mountains, through the Snoqualmie Pass, and on to Kennewick – home.

She thinks of the smell of the hallways of her high school, the slogan on the walls: BE THE BEST YOU CAN BE. She remembers arguments with her mother, some benignant, others noxious. She remembers Julian bringing her Almond Joys afterwards to cheer her up, his only ally in the world. She remembers hitchhiking with friends to see Yes play Spokane. She remembers walking along the Columbia River with her first boyfriend. She wonders what might have happened if she had stayed with him. Maybe she never would have moved to California. Never met Kosuke. Never come here.

Beyond the baby and Kosuke, Cleo has nothing in Japan. She misses having friends. She cannot abide the deferential tone she is met with wherever she goes. She has tried to meet people but quickly becomes exasperated by the non-committal doublespeak. Frustrated, she has often retorted: 'You are as slippery as an eel.'

If she is not being kept at an amicable distance by the people of Chōshi, then she is being stared at. Kosuke used to glare back at them, ask them what they thought they were looking at. Though Cleo would make a show of being embarrassed, she secretly loved that protective side of him. Now he tells her to ignore them. And it's easy for him to say that. She's the one with the blonde hair, the different body, holding the mixed-race baby.

Cleo has overheard Kosuke and his mother arguing about this, whispered phone calls from the kitchen, pleading with him to come back to the US. *Cleo would find work that way. Your father and I could help. We'd find a way to pay for the treatment. If you stay there, Nina will grow up different. Not just her looks but the neurodevelopmental thing. The nail that stands up will be hammered down, Kosuke. Come home.*

And where would 'home' be for me, Mother? With you?

Cleo knows that Nozomi just wants to atone. She just wants the best for her son and his family. But Kosuke lurches between being patient with her and exploding with rage. He'd live in an igloo if his mother told him not to. Cleo wonders how she could have married a man before ever discovering the gorge of anger hidden inside him. She wonders how long it is until she is swallowed by it. And Nina? Would she be sucked into the whirlpool too? Maybe they already had been. Maybe everything inside the smiling, contemplative man that made up Kosuke Iwata was, if you inspected it closely, stitched out of hate.

Cleo wipes away her tears and opens the front door. A desperate wind buffets her. Lanterns thrash from side to side. The waves smash themselves against the cliffs, foam spraying high up into the air. The hateful storm batters the row of souvenir shops and apartments. Cleo sees the lighthouse, its Fresnel lens piercing the gloom. Like her, it's from a faraway place, designed by a Scotsman.

Cleo closes the door, pads into the bedroom and looks down at Nina, sleeping at last, a pained expression on her face. She looks at her small mono-lid eyes, her miniature eyelashes so dark. 'But you are.' She kisses Nina's foot. 'You are from here.'

Cleo begins to unpack the bag.

That night Iwata is back, crying for forgiveness, the gentlest kisses of apology on his daughter's putty-like crown. *That's not who I am*, he murmurs. *That's not who I am.*

Cleo says she knows. She knows. She says this as she kisses Iwata's head, his scalp smelling of beer and smoke. He is on his knees, his arms wrapped around her stomach. *I'll be the best man I can be. The best father I can be.* Cleo says she knows. As she looks out at the rabid Japanese sea she also knows that on this day they have lost something. Something that can never be retrieved.

Iwata gasped awake, soaked in sweat. He ripped open drawers and cabinets, searching for a gun, searching for a bottle, but this wasn't his apartment. It took a long time for his breathing to even out. It took a little longer to remember whose bathroom this was. Outside, the dawn light was navy blue. It had rained during the night.

Iwata forced himself up, pain filling his face. He stood, doubled over, the blood from his nose painting little patterns on the tiles. Head pounding, he blinked away tears and stuffed cotton balls into his nostrils. Then, at a slow pace, he searched the apartment.

In the living room he found only evidence of a struggle. In the kitchen he learned nothing beyond the fact that someone had eaten a reduced-guilt mac n' cheese from Trader Joe's recently. In the bathroom he found toiletries, oestrogen pills, anti-androgens; nothing unexpected.

The bedroom was small, the futon taking up most of it. Iwata searched through Geneviève's clothes but found nothing remarkable. The bedside table contained nothing significant either: some pills, books, condoms, family photographs. They were old and it took a moment for Iwata to realize that Geneviève appeared in them. There she was, an unsmiling young boy, not yet twelve he guessed. Iwata tried not to think about the phone call he'd had with Mr Domínguez. That there were no recent photos did not surprise him.

Iwata sat at the small desk by the window. There was a pile of books, mostly plane-crash thrillers, and Portuguese language texts. In the drawers Iwata found only natural clutter: airline earphones, a manual for a rice cooker, hair bands, Wite-Out correction fluid. The bottom drawer contained the important stuff: social security, medical papers, tax returns, bank statements going back roughly twelve months. Most of the payments seemed regular but there were a few outliers.

Geneviève had received large sums of money from an unknown source twice in the last year. She had also paid a plastic-surgery centre several times – Fox Hills Feminization. Iwata took pictures with his phone, then returned the papers. It was time to go.

At the front door he paused. There was something sticking out from under the sofa – a strap. Iwata pulled it and out came a grubby sports bag. Inside it there was money, there were dirty clothes and, at the bottom, a California driver's licence. Iwata turned it over and recognized the name: Zambrano, Mara.

Her hair was the wrong colour in the photograph and she looked different – softer, somehow – but it was her.

Iwata hoped there was an innocent reason for her things to be here. Maybe she had lied to him last night and had been staying in Geneviève's apartment. Maybe Geneviève was just holding on to some stuff for her. But then he thought back to what she had said.

Looks like I've been stood up.

Iwata's stomach dropped. What if it was John Smith who had arranged to meet her at Club Noir and, for whatever reason, hadn't shown up? And if John Smith was the man who attacked him last night, what if he had his eyes on Mara?

Pocketing the driver's licence, Iwata was out the door before he could consider a single alternative.

12. The Real You

Having tried in vain all morning to find Mara Zam-brano, Iwata managed to secure an appointment with a facial-trauma specialist in Little Tokyo. It was almost midday and he was in the waiting room looking at the framed watercolour Kyoto landscapes on the walls. There was also a map of California. It was a similar shape to Japan – only inverted. *Maybe I am too.*

The receptionist offered Iwata tea, which he accepted. It arrived on a saucer loaded with butter biscuits. 'Looks like you could do with something sweet,' she said to his injuries.

Iwata smiled, though he felt a hollow loss. They were Noriko Sakai's favourite – his old partner. They had not had long together but she had been one of the few people he had ever really known. It was not so much that they understood each other; they were from very differ-ent rat's nests after all. But they had respected each other's silences. Strengths. Weaknesses. They had accepted one another. Cherished one another. Someone equally fucked up to cling to out of the blue.

Four years after her murder Iwata now understood that what they had shared had been true, had been real. He wished he could have known her in other circumstances, in another time. Instead, he found her at his nethermost, lost in the labyrinth of grief, surrounded on all sides by enemies. But just as gold is known in fire, she had given him her friendship – Iwata would never forget it.

The specialist turned out to be of Japanese heritage, though she did not speak the language. It occurred to him that, except for that detail, his mother would have approved of her. As she worked she asked Iwata questions about Japan, speaking of it with the dreamy reverence of a little girl bound for Disneyland. His answers were short and vague. Being from two places meant he had languages, perception, experience. Being from two places also meant he was from nowhere. The differences and similarities of shared homelands couldn't be addressed with words. Especially not with a numb mouth.

In the end she was able to restore the position of Iwata's nasal bones, telling him that this would allow for proper healing. He left with his nose bandaged, the bruises under his eyes already turning blue.

Iwata arrived back at his apartment at 2 p.m. He was too wired for rest, his mind going over the pieces. Meredith, Talky, Geneviève, Mara, John Smith. Two were dead, one was missing, one in danger.

Iwata couldn't prove that the man who had attacked him was the murderer but he had been in Geneviève's house. He had Mara's driver's licence. If it wasn't the murderer, then what was he doing there? Iwata had too many questions for a head too full of agonies.

Rubbing his sore eyes, he typed the name 'Mara Zambrano' into MARPLE. Eleven names appeared, but only one matched the exact name. But that woman was in her mid-fifties and lived in Nevada. There was a *Maya* Zambrano, there was a *Mayra* Zambrano and there were eight *Maria* Zambranos. Only two were in the right age range and neither of them lived in California. If it was her real name, MARPLE was telling him Mara was a ghost. Yet he'd seen her at Noir. Heard her laughter. Felt her hand. Smelled her.

Iwata typed in the address from her driver's licence. It corresponded to a real road but a bogus house number and zip code. *Could it be a fake licence?* Iwata tapped it against his lips in thought. *Mara. Mara. Mara. Who are you?*

From the Santa Monica Freeway, Iwata could see Vermont Avenue, home to the city's Salvadoran diaspora. A quarter of the country had fled the civil war in the eighties, many arriving in LA. Since then, Vermont had become a long corridor of strife and redemption, home to whole generations with stories to tell. But to many Angelenos today, Vermont Avenue just meant good pupusas.

Iwata overtook an orange-and-grey bus. Rush hour had no clearly defined shape or schedule. Down at street level, he saw Spanglish signs advertising cleaning, childcare and income-tax services. An entire life could be lived out in Los Angeles without a word of English: slimming classes in Spanish, Ponzi schemes in Pashto, Tarot readings in Tagalog. There were a million Mitsuwas, havens where the mother tongue could be heard and compatriots conversed with. This city was a never-ending jacket of innumerable pockets, pockets that contained foreign cultures to slip into and forget the outside, forget America, whatever that was meant to be.

Iwata exited the freeway and headed south through arid hills and factories. In the shimmering distance oil derricks pecked at the land like drunken vultures. As he drove he felt the blows from last night hardening into bruises, the pain embedded deep in the muscle. The cool air rushing through the windows was pleasant against his busted nose, his closing eye.

At a red light he relived the sensation of being smothered by the cushion, the closeness to death. In that surreal haze he remembered that his attacker had said something. Iwata tried to distil it, closing his eyes. The driver behind hit his horn and the word became clear.

He said, 'Sorry.' The man had said, 'Sorry.'

'You're the one that killed Meredith,' Iwata whispered.

He turned on to Sepulveda, then Slauson, then Bristol Parkway, finally stopping outside a business park on Green Valley Circle. Iwata got out, crossed the parking lot, and entered Suite G. Inside there was a sleek reception of dark wood surfaces, neutral carpets and black ceramic figurines. There were gold letters on the wall:

Fox Hills Feminization – *The Real You*
Dr Aidan Van Coeszvelt, MD, FACS

Iwata walked in with one aubergine-coloured eye and a nose guard that gave him the look of a graceless bird, but the receptionist beamed at him like he was all tuxes and roses.

'I need to speak with Dr Van Coeszvelt.' He flashed his ID.

'Oh. I'll check if he's available.'

A minute later Dr Van Coeszvelt emerged. He was a tall man – balding, with small eyes and large spectacles perched on a long, pink nose. He spoke in low tones with the receptionist, his eyes on her breasts. Pretending not to notice, she pointed at Iwata, who stood now.

'Dr Van Coeszvelt.' They shook hands. 'A pleasure. I'm Inspector Iwata.'

Though the man smiled with the control of a surgeon, Iwata also saw concern in his brow. People tended not to like the word 'inspector'.

'Inspector . . . ?'

'Iwata.' Again he showed his ID.

'What's this about?'

'A client of yours.'

'Will this take long?'

'Shouldn't take more than a minute.'

Van Coeszvelt led the way into a lavish side office and offered Iwata a seat. His tone was warm enough but it was clear he was unaccustomed to being the one without the answers in this room.

'So.' He linked his fingers on the bureau. 'How can I help you?'

'First, could you tell me a little bit about your practice?'

Van Coeszvelt sat back in his chair. He liked this territory. 'We offer an extensive range of cosmetic-surgery procedures across the male-to-female panorama while avoiding cookie-cutter outcomes. Ultimately, we deliver bespoke results to bring forth the client's most feminine beauty.'

Iwata nodded. It was a nice pitch. 'Procedures – could you give me specifics?'

'Breast augmentation, chin reduction, fillers and inject-ables, tracheal shave, endocrinology – everything the client needs.'

'And Geneviève Darlington. A patient of yours, correct?'

'The name doesn't ring a bell.'

Iwata brought up the photo of Geneviève's credit-card statement on his phone. The surgeon peered at it. 'Then I suppose she is a client. Though I wouldn't be able to disclose any personal information, of course.'

'She's missing.'

'I'm sorry to hear that. Now I suppose I know why you're here . . .'

'Did she ever mention anyone or anything, even in passing, that gave you concern for her wellbeing?'

'We only ever discussed medical matters.'

'So you do remember her, then?'

'You jogged my memory.' The surgeon glanced sharply down to his watch. 'Now, I'm sorry, but I do have an appointment coming up.'

'Last question. Did you know Meredith Nichol?' Iwata took out the photograph of her.

'No, I don't think so,' Van Coeszvelt answered coolly, but Iwata caught the twitch in his face.

'She was murdered, Doctor.'

'That's terrible.'

'It doesn't jog your memory?'

'I've answered your questions. You'll appreciate I have work.'

Iwata stood. On the way out he paid particular attention to the locks and security.

That afternoon Iwata watched the business park from across the road. As he listened to the radio he thought about the ocean and the man that had photographed Meredith and Geneviève against it. Did he live there? Did he rise in the mornings marvelling at his view? Did he buy the house for it? Did seawater run in his veins? Was that why he had to be close to the waves?

Iwata imagined John Smith taking the photographs. On the one hand, it wouldn't make much sense for him to be advertising the sexual services of his murder victims. On the other, perhaps it gave him some kind of kick. Posing as a photographer would also be a good pretext to get his victims into his home. Either way, if Iwata could find that ocean view, he'd find answers.

It was gone 6 p.m. when the receptionist and Van Coeszvelt left the building. Over the sharp tips of the ghost pines the sunset was melted neapolitan. A security guard made an uninterested loop around the grounds every twenty minutes or so. Iwata opened his glovebox and shuffled through his collection of expired IDs and lanyards he'd bought from flea markets, all of them belonging to Asian men of varying ages and professions.

Nobody ever scrutinized the photograph itself too much and he was always ready to palm them off with a joke about weight loss or going grey. The crucial thing was the lanyard itself. People wanted to believe Iwata had a reason to be there. Wanted to believe that he was legitimate. It was an easier world to live in.

Iwata picked some techie that had been made redundant, looped it around his neck and got out of the Bronco. From the trunk, he took out his more heavy-duty lock picks.

Ninety minutes later, Iwata was back in his office, going over Van Coeszvelt's records. It didn't take long to see that the surgeon had lied – Meredith had been his client. The pages showed that she'd had regular blood work to ensure her hormones weren't putting her in any danger. Her anti-androgen had been causing a slightly increased level of potassium in her body, which increased the risk of heart attack

Since then, Meredith had undergone breast-implant procedures and consulted with Van Coeszvelt over sex realignment. There had also been minor rhinoplasty and a lip lift noted in her records. But Meredith's last appointment had been over a year ago.

Why lie about her? He tried to picture the surgeon being John Smith. But it didn't stick. Van Coeszvelt was too tall for the man he had fought with, his voice all wrong, his posture off. Then again, there was a murder victim and a missing person sitting in his filing cabinet. Two trans women, two patients, two employees, two friends.

Iwata supposed those kinds of connections were worth lying about.

In financial matters there were further oddities. Both Meredith and Geneviève had been billed by the clinic, but the paperwork showed they weren't the ones paying. Nor, seemingly, was any individual. Instead, an entity was settling the bill: Grupo Valle Dorado.

Iwata learned it was a real-estate investment fund, its glossy little website full of smiling stock models and shiny new homes but no addresses, no names, no official business registration number. *Why the hell would an investment fund in Mexico be paying for Meredith's and Geneviève's procedures?*

Iwata span in his chair and looked out of the window. The Best of Luck was gone today.

'Where are you when I need you?'

He picked up the sex catalogue Mingo had given him and left the office.

It was 11 p.m. After touring every sex shop in Hollywood, Iwata stopped in a small, dull lot on Vanowen. Hollywood Zest was above a cheque-casher and a chicken rotisserie, its windows blacked out. On the door, there were two words:

ADULTS ONLY

An electronic chime resounded as Iwata entered, as though a game were beginning. The shop was much bigger than was apparent from the outside. It smelled of artificial citrus and used socks. The shelves were stacked with dusty

DVDs, a zoo of colour, flesh, penchants. Each shelf was ordered according to genre: creampies, bondage, amateur, squirting, gangbangs ... on and on it went. An inflatable sex doll in the corner was wearing a T-shirt that read:

YOU DON'T HAVE TO BE CRAZY
TO WORK HERE BUT IT HELPS

For some reason John Mellencamp's 'Jack & Diane' was playing.

There were four customers but the shop still felt empty. They all kept their eyes on the porn and off each other. The small man behind the counter gave Iwata a brief nod – *welcome, pervert*. He was bearded and seemed tired, a young Kubrick lookalike wearing a teriyaki-stained 'This Guy Needs a Beer' T-shirt. The book in his hands was *Getting Things Done: The Art of Stress-free Productivity*, a middle finger bulging a nostril as he read.

'Welcome to Hollywood Zest,' he droned. 'We've got a promotion going. Any six movies for four.'

'I'm looking for something else.'

'Speciality stuff is through that purple drape.'

Iwata placed the sex catalogue on the counter. Kubrick looked at it like it was a dead fish. 'You're in the wrong place, Jack.'

'If you know the wrong place from the right place' – Iwata placed a fifty-dollar bill next to the catalogue – 'then you can help point me in the right direction.'

Kubrick chewed his lips for a moment, then picked up the money. 'Follow me.'

The back room was wall to wall with metal shelves supporting cardboard boxes of DVDs, sex toys, lubricants, butt plugs, whips, tingle-inducing liquids. Posters of nineties porn stars lined the walls, broken price-tag guns and bottles of air freshener were strewn about the floor.

'I can give you five minutes, or until a customer is ready to pay.' He nodded at the CCTV screen. 'Whichever comes first.'

Iwata nodded.

'You wanna know what that thing is.' Kubrick jutted his chin at the catalogue. 'And you already figured it's not the regular kind, huh?'

'It has no contact information, no names, no back matter or legal stuff.'

'Think of it like an artist who wants to paint family portraits for the wealthy. He needs somewhere to advertise, right?'

'Advertise what?'

'Content on commission – movies or images.'

'So why hide that in some catalogue?'

'Okay, let's take the zeroes that come in here every day. They're dinosaurs. Maybe they're technophobes, maybe their probation doesn't allow an internet connection. Whatever, point is, they don't get we live in a porno Promised Land, Jack.'

'I don't follow.'

Kubrick picked up a green rubber cock and waggled it around as he spoke. 'Half the world is pleasuring itself to tits and ass online, right? So what does that lead to?'

'Blindness?'

'*Normalization.* Thirty years ago half the adult male population of middle America didn't know what the fuck an orgasm was. Now ten-year-olds know what ass-to-mouth is. So what do you think that leads to? It leads to people needing bigger, badder, harder to get off. And *that* leads to a market for niche content.'

'Hasn't that always been there? You've got a room behind a purple drape right here.'

'I'm talking stuff you can't buy legally. People being hurt. And I mean hurt. Real people being abused. Kids. Animals. People dying of fucking cancer. Trust me, amigo. It's easier not to know you live in a world where hospice fetishes exist. Take my word for it, anything you think people can't whack off to? You're dead wrong.'

'That still doesn't answer my question about the catalogue. And why go through print? Why not online?'

'The internet used to be the Wild West. But more and more these days it's getting to be a tricky racket.' Kubrick nodded at the catalogue. 'These folks are going retro to stay under the radar. There's no information in there other than phone numbers and bodies, right? That's no accident. Encrypted communications lead to product agreement. Let's say I want a transvestite to be tied up to a palm tree, whipped with belts by Cuban midgets, and I want her to use my Christian name as she looks to camera. Once that's thrashed out, money is transferred abroad to a dummy account and the movie gets made absolutely to specification. Everyone gets off or gets paid, everyone walks away.'

Iwata flipped to pages fourteen and eighteen. 'I need

specifics – these two girls. I need to know who photo-graphed them.'

Kubrick peered at them. 'Easy enough. That's Nova's work.'

'Who?'

'Nova Entertainment. One of the more respected names. Boutique stuff. High-end commissions from clients with tendencies that run to . . . let's say the *exotic*. Exotic prices too.'

'So he advertises the girls he's working with in this and the commissions come in?'

'Exactamundo.'

'Does the client only ever want movies?'

'Sometimes images. Sometimes they even want to meet the girl or the boy in question.'

'Who owns Nova Entertainment?'

'No idea. That's the point. Neither do the clients. It's not a cake-decoration business.'

Iwata thought about this. 'Do you have any other copies of this catalogue?'

Kubrick shrugged. 'You're free to look around.' He glanced up at the CCTV screen. A bookish man wearing sunglasses had just come up to the counter. 'Break's over, Jack.' He tossed Iwata the rubber cock. 'Hope you find your happy ending.'

By midnight, Iwata was back in his apartment. Before leaving Hollywood Zest he had found more nameless sex catalogues going back a few years, all of them featuring Nova's work. And on those pages he had found a connection: three more trans women – all of them in the box of missing persons Kate Floccari had given him.

Iwata cross-checked them with the files he had copied from Fox Hills Feminization. Another connection: all of the three missing women were also past clients of Van Coeszvelt. Again, their bills were all paid for by the Mexican investment fund Valle Dorado.

'A surgery, a Mexican investment fund and a sex-salesman photographer,' Iwata

looked at his plant. 'Any ideas?'

MARPLE told him Nova Entertainment was a small business connected to an address in Beverly Hills and registered to one Benedict Novacek.

Iwata did not know if he was John Smith. He did not know if he was the man that had tried to kill him the other night. But whoever he was, Benedict Novacek was connected to a lot of missing women. One, at least, was dead.

Porno Kubrick had said Nova was not in the cake-decoration business and Iwata found it unlikely he would be forthcoming. Iwata unlocked the bottom drawer of his bureau and took out the gun. It had no bullets but it looked the part.

Sunset Boulevard was a never-ending serpent known for its scales of neon, its alleyways like venom glands, its diet strictly composed of dreamers and wannabes. This far west, however, Sunset was a pampered-domesticated pet – all old-world mansions and pruned hedges, strip clubs replaced by country clubs, the wannabes replaced by those who wanted for nothing. Tudor manors had tennis courts, French Regency villas were gussied up with infinity pools – everywhere Iwata looked he saw the aping of long-dead epochs.

Delfern Drive was a quiet, silk-stocking street of loud hedges and missionary-style houses the size of holiday resorts. The only sound was the whistling of Mexican gardeners mixing in with the birdsong. At the top of the street Iwata stopped outside a large Craftsman home surrounded by white walls and Jeffrey pines. He got out and buzzed the intercom.

A raspy, dispassionate female voice answered.

'Good morning. I'm looking for Mr Novacek.'

'I'm Mrs Novacek. Who is this?'

'Ma'am, my name is Kosuke Iwata. I'm a professional investigator.'

'I see. Well, he's not home.'

'I really need to speak with him. Do you know when he'll be back?'

'Hard to say. Is this serious?'

'It is.'

'Then you'd better come in.'

The gate clanked open and Iwata crossed the brown lawn. The house was not as handsome as it had seemed from the outside – windows rimy with dust, a large rubber plant growing over the balcony above like a suicidal housewife.

Iwata climbed the steps to the cankering porch and found the door open. The hallway smelled faintly of cat urine. He stopped as he heard music he recognized – Nina Simone's 'I Got It Bad (and That Ain't Good)'. The song was like a kick in the gut.

Iwata wanted to turn and walk straight out. But he'd been given an envelope full of money, there was a gun in his pocket and women were missing. He'd already walked out on walking out.

The living room could have been plush but its owner had gone for expressive – dove-white walls, thick rugs, marble pyramids, framed feathers belonging to birds of paradise, ugly paintings, a jade chandelier in need of dusting.

Mrs Novacek was splayed out on a large green leather couch. She ran a slow hand through her roaring copper hair and sipped a tumbler full of something similar in colour, the lemon rind pushing against her lips as she did. The brass side table held a bottle of good bourbon. She looked up at him like she had forgotten his call.

'Mrs Novacek,' he said. 'Thank you for seeing me.'

'It's Dana.' She pointed to the armchair opposite, the ice cubes tinkling like some little charm. Iwata thanked her for the seat, unable to decide if her black crêpe dress was especially for the morning drinking session or a leftover from the night before. She tossed French *Vogue* from her lap and watched him.

'You have a beautiful home,' Iwata offered.

'No, you hate it.' She leaned forward and curled a bare toe into the telephone wire, the receiver lying off the hook. 'Don't you?'

'No.'

'A little bit?'

'I'm not the right person to ask.'

'Why?'

'I think maybe I hate everything a little bit.'

She laughed now, taking her time about it, as if tasting a wine she was unsure about. She had green eyes and her face had a sulky beauty, but her real allure, Iwata thought, was the warm apathy in her voice. 'Well, then,' she said, 'you have good taste.'

'So, Mrs . . . Dana –'

'You want to ask about my Benny. What's he done?'

'Well. Nothing.'

'Then let's gab a little while longer. We can talk about him after.'

'All right.'

Silence passed between them until she grinned. 'You're not very good at this, are you?'

'At what?'

'*This.*'

'I guess not.'

'Ask me something, then.'

'What are you drinking?'

'A Horse's Neck. Would you like one?'

'No, thank you.'

'Why'd you ask about it if you didn't want one?'

'Wanting is different from asking.'

She took a long swallow then slowly tilted her head from side to side. Though the music was still playing, her movements followed no rhythm that Iwata could discern. He looked past her at the turntable in the corner. It cost more than he made in a steady month.

'So, Mr Investigator Iwata, you don't like my house. Do you like my music at least?'

'No.'

'I can tell. It looks like it pains you.'

'I just prefer other things.'

'Who doesn't like Nina Simone?'

'Me.'

'Why?'

'Because.'

'Because it's personal? Does it make you think of a girl?'

Iwata saw Cleo, dejectedly thumbing through a baby name book. *We need something that makes sense in both languages, but there's nothing in here.* Nina Simone's 'Do What You Gotta Do' had been playing at the time – Cleo's favourite. *How about Nina?* he had said. *Nina works.*

Dana Novacek tinkled her ice cubes like a bell. 'Cat got your tongue?'

'I don't have a lot of time, Mrs Novacek. I'd really appreciate your help.'

'Shouldn't you share with me first? To establish trust?'

'If you won't tell me, you won't.'

'I'm curious about you. Aren't you curious about me?'

'I just need to find your husband.'

'What a cruel thing to say.'

She downed her drink and poured herself another few fingers, though fingers thicker than any of those on her own hands. Iwata imagined how the coldness of the ice might feel, the flavour of the bourbon seeping down his gullet. He couldn't stay in this place. Iwata stood.

'Okay, okay. I can tell you where he *might* be. But first you have to tell me something.'

'About what? The song?'

'You already pretty much told me about *that* by getting so sore. No, I want to know why you're after my Benny.'

'I think he could have information I need. That's all.'

'If I asked you to find out if he's fucking someone else, would you do that for me?' Her face retained the same unwavering expression as she asked this – hazy eyes and a Xanax smile.

'That isn't my business.'

'Yet your business brought you here, didn't it?' She chewed her lips. 'What happened to your face, anyway?'

'I'm not the right person to ask.'

She scolded Iwata with her forefinger and mouthed two words: *Bad boy*.

'Mrs Novacek, if you want me to look into the possibility of your husband having an affair, we could talk about that another time. But frankly, you don't seem to give too much of a shit.'

'Knowledge is not made for understanding; it is for cutting.'

'That Nietzsche?'

'Foucault.' She downed her second Horse's Neck and grimaced. 'Though I like Nietzsche too. I've always had a thing for melancholy men. *Is man one of God's blunders, or is God one of man's?* Well *somebody* messed up, right?' Dana threw back her red hair and laughed. 'Jesus, look at us. Philosophy, violence and infidelity. If you'd have worn a jacket, I'd call this one of my better dates.'

'Mrs Nov—'

'All right, all right. So pushy.' She tore out a fragrant page from her magazine and wrote down an address. 'Benny'll most likely be at his little studio. It's not too far from here — horrible little soulless place. Benny, of course, thinks it's the cat's meow.' She handed over the page but held on to Iwata's hand. 'One last thing, buster.'

His heart had been thudding since the word 'studio'.

'Come back and visit me sometime?'

Iwata took the page and left.

Tokyo – 1975

Dear Mr Kuroki,

My name is Nozomi Iwata. I'm 26 years of age, a graduate of Sophia University, currently working as a waitress. Please forgive my presumptuousness but enclosed you will find the first few pages of my novel in progress, The Mannequins. I know your highly successful weekly magazines serialize genre novellas and I believe my own sits within the horror fiction you have published recently. My sincere thanks for your time, I can only imagine how many submissions an esteemed editor such as yourself must receive.

Once again, please forgive the trouble.

The Mannequins

Yoko Maeda was twenty-one years old. People said she was very beautiful and she was fine with that. Being so attractive wasn't always a picnic but, undoubtedly, it had some benefits. It certainly hadn't hurt her chances when applying for the job at Department Store Q; the manager was salivating as he listened to her answers.

She had been at Q for a month now, in ladies' fashion, and she excelled in her work. It wasn't rocket science, murmuring approval when women tried on blouses or silk scarves they couldn't afford. But even so, Yoko had a talent for making people feel good about themselves. This was no simple task, given her beauty. Most people felt threatened by it, so immediately she adopted her silly-girl routine, pretending to forget her train of thought, or that the customer had illuminated her with some perfunctory statement. This way she invited them to judge her for being an idiot. And an idiot who told you that the scarf suited you was probably telling the truth. After all, idiots tended to be guileless.

The manager let Yoko keep her commission on the designer items, which, at the brand-new Department Store Q, housed in Osaka's premier shopping complex, accounted for most things on sale. She worked on the sixth floor, a clean, windowless expanse of fabrics, heels and curvy white mannequins. Tinny music played discreetly over the speakers, and the mirrors, which gleamed, were everywhere, making it seem like there were more people present than there actually were.

Yoko worked with a team of eight girls, though she hadn't made any friends. That suited her fine; they seemed boring in any case, spending most of their time in the back room, whispering amongst themselves. Yoko didn't feel left out at all. If anything, it boosted her ability to rake in commission.

No, nothing bothered her at Q. Well, except for the one small, trivial matter. It would have been invisible to anyone passing through, but after a few weeks Yoko had caught glimpses of prayer beads being worn by the girls. Here and there around the store, almost hidden, she had come across *yakuyoke* talismans to ward away evil. When she asked the security guard about it, he just laughed it off.

'Those girls are all as superstitious as each other.'

But it wasn't long afterwards that she noticed he too wore the prayer beads. Yoko didn't care if her foolish colleagues wanted to waste their money on trinkets. She put it to the back of her mind and went about her work.

Yoko was in charge of four mannequins at the back of the floor. They were very tall, practically six feet, and a pure, eggshell-white colour. Though they had no hair and no eyes, their full lips came together in a slight smile.

It was Yoko's responsibility to ensure that the mannequins were the very embodiment of elegance and she took it seriously. She changed their clothes every other day and slowly developed what she supposed one could call a fondness for them.

Sometimes she even got the funny feeling they were smiling at her, as if they enjoyed her fussing. Frankly, Yoko quite enjoyed this part of her job. It reminded her of being a little girl – posing and dressing them. She didn't care if her colleagues called her 'The Puppet Master'.

After all, it was an almost daily occurrence that a customer would ask her where they could find the exact outfit that mannequin was wearing. More often than not, that meant raking in commission.

People could say what they wanted, Yoko didn't mind. It wouldn't be long until her credit-card debt was completely paid off. At least, that's what she told herself. She often told herself this, though deep down she knew it was untrue.

She was not the sort of person to change her spending habits. No, what she bought was an expression of her desires. Suppressing them was out of the question. Besides, Yoko loved to look good. What was so terrible about that? Not to mention the fact that she had an in-store discount.

On her free days, it was her favourite thing to sit outside the cafés of Ginza wearing the latest French label, just smoking and watching the people pass, rebuffing men loudly if they dared to approach. They mostly stared at her from a distance, though. And this, for much of her life, was the only kind of relationship Yoko had been comfortable with.

It was true that she could turn on the charm to make a sale: she was an expert in that sort of interaction, one with a clear narrative and outcome. But when it came to the free-hand of socializing, she often felt lost and irritated. All through university she had tried, but it had been exhausting. Vagueness and subtlety drained her. Men never said what they meant, and women could do nothing else.

Afterwards Yoko groped around for purpose like a child reaching for a medicine they do not particularly want to take. Though they said nothing, she knew her parents had expected her to take a job more deserving of her expensive education. But Yoko had no real drive, no genuine ambition.

Sometimes she daydreamed about being noticed by a talent scout or a famous photographer, but even then she had no desire for fame. No, Yoko just liked to be looked at from afar. That was probably the reason why a job in a department store appealed to her so much. She was an ambassador for the things that would turn heads. A peacock to sell peacock feathers. Yes, Yoko would work extra hard, clear her debt and live out the next decade experiencing only simple, empty pleasures. What else were her twenties for?

*

Yoko had been working at Q for four months when her manager asked her to dinner. She knew he was married and she had no intention of it going anywhere, but she also happened to love grilled eel and this is precisely what the manager was offering – dinner at the best eel spot in Osaka. When he suggested sake, Yoko agreed. What he didn't know was that her family was in the sake trade and she could handle her drink better than most. But Yoko had not just agreed to dinner for the free food.

After she had had her fill of eel and once her manager was slurring his words, she seized her opportunity.

'Sir . . .' She looked at the floor. 'I was wondering something.'

'Anything, Yoko,' he purred. 'You just have to ask.'

'I hope you know how much I think of my colleagues. You should be praised for your acumen in selecting such fine employees.'

'Thank you, dear.' He took a languid sip. 'I hope you include yourself in that.'

'You flatter me!'

'But what did you want to know? Don't be shy. I'm your manager, you should trust me. I have your best interests at heart, Yoko.'

'Well . . .' She bit her lip and glanced out of the window. 'I don't mean to pry. But do you know why all the girls wear prayer beads? Even the security guard wears them.'

The manager lost his smile.

Undeterred, Yoko kept on driving at her point. 'It just seems so odd for a group of such smart girls to act so skittishly.'

He licked his lips before answering. 'Yoko, there are certain things which happen in life . . . And people don't always respond logically.'

'I'm not sure I follow.'

'I suppose you have a right to know.'

Yoko wondered if he was realizing now that it was not *he* who had lured *her* here under false pretences. Perhaps he was accepting the fact that there was no way someone like Yoko would ever do anything more than drink his sake and eat his unagi.

He sighed. 'Years ago, before the renovation, there was an incident on the sixth floor.'

'Incident?'

'There was an employee, Kameko. Now, she was a plain-looking girl, maybe even ugly. Even so, she worked in fashion, just like you. She was, by all accounts, gifted in sales. She would take little extra steps to ensure the customer would feel valued, wrap the purchases beautifully, even trivial items, offer refreshments, that sort of thing.

'Anyway, the story goes that there was one particular customer. He came in one day looking for a gift for his wife. He seemed the wealthy type so, of course, Kameko pounced on him. He obviously liked the service he received because he came back the next day. And the day after. After a while he started pestering the girl to come out with him. Nobody could understand it; the man was, apparently, quite handsome and clearly rich. Why was he so taken with plain old Kameko?

'Even so, it got to the point where he would buy things he didn't need, just so the security guard couldn't say anything to him. You know, sunglasses in December. Or an atlas of the world. Anyway, eventually Kameko requested a transfer to another store, but her boss was loath to lose her. Instead, he proposed a holiday. She hadn't taken any in three years and he thought it might convince her admirer to fixate on someone else.'

The manager ordered more sake, as if he required Dutch courage to continue. Yoko was enraptured by the story; she realized her back was arched and her toes were curled in her shoes. She exhaled, trying to disguise the shuddering in her breath. 'Did the man come back?'

'Kameko took the time off and after that the man stayed away for a month or two. She thought things had gone back to normal and she was beginning to flourish again. Now, as you know, winter is a fruitful season, given the demand for good jackets. She was doing very well, always ready to take a second shift straight after her first if someone was sick. It so happened that this is what she did on the night in question.'

'What happened?' Yoko could barely breathe.

'The man came back, of course. He waited until closing time and must have slipped into the bathrooms to hide. The security guard had left early that day. Kameko was alone and tidying up when the man attacked her.'

'What did he do?' she whispered.

'He dragged her into the changing room, raped her and beat her to death. Her colleagues found her the next morning with her neck broken. Well, some say it was a broken neck, others say she was stabbed.

'Now this alone, though obviously deeply unpleasant, wasn't enough to make people say the sixth floor was haunted. But a few weeks after the murder the boss who had convinced

Kameko to stay on died in a traffic accident. A little later the security guard who forgot to check the toilets died of a heart attack. He wasn't that old. After that, some odd things were apparently seen around the store.'

'Like what?'

The manager finished his sake and considered the empty cup. 'It's just stupid talk, Yoko. People say the sixth floor is haunted by Kameko's ghost, angry that she was talked into staying and ultimately murdered. But it's just a silly story. A girl did die in the store, it's true. Honestly, I'm not even sure if she was called Kameko. Then again, it was just as likely that she had an aneurysm as that she was murdered. Before the renovation, all the old staff were laid off, so nobody can corroborate. And, of course, people prefer to cling to the ridiculous than hear the truth. Reality is boring.'

'What about the rich man?'

'I'm not sure there ever was any man, Yoko. And if there was, they probably caught him. Who knows? Who cares?' He seemed to get an optimistic second wind. 'Come on, let's discuss something nicer over a nightcap. I happen to know a little –'

Yoko thanked him and rushed out of the restaurant. She was so taken with the story, ridiculous though it was, that she took a taxi home, not trusting herself to navigate the multiple changeovers on the subway.

Back in her shoebox apartment she found several final demands from her creditors in the mailbox. They agitated her even more. She spent all night worrying about her debt and thinking about the ghost of the murdered girl.

Normally, Yoko would sleep like a log. But she woke in the

middle of the night when she heard a loud thud. Sitting up, she saw it was just a book that had fallen from the shelf. It was normal for things to fall over in her little apartment overlooking the railway. Or perhaps it had just been a baby earthquake.

In the morning Yoko picked up the book and put it back on the shelf. She did not notice it was an atlas.

13. Los Angeles Dreams

At the end of Sunset Boulevard, Iwata turned right on the Pacific Coast Highway – scorched cliffs, shimmering blues, chocolate-box houses hugging the shoreline. He could see Santa Monica in the rear-view mirror. Tanned roller skaters would be gliding along Ocean Avenue, dogs exploring trimmed lawns beneath tall palm trees.

In the distance, where the sky met the sea, there was only a silvery morning haze. Sheaves of cirrus clouds scattered across the blue. To the south, the horizontal circus of Santa Monica Pier. Beyond it, Muscle Beach, Venice, eventually Torrance. Cleo had owned her record shop – Vinyl Notice Records – on a Venice backstreet; it was where they had first met.

Iwata rarely allowed himself these memories, painful revisitations slowly losing clarity. Entire months with her had started to become mere sentiments, distilled into moods. Days of sex had been crystallized into a single sigh. Bitter arguments compressed into a few cutting phrases, like calcium in hard water.

Yet though these memories faded, there were also constants. There would always be those Santa Monica sunsets – vivid blues and oranges – and there would always be Cleo set against them, turning to look at him, her skin washed rosé, her hair molten.

Santa Monica. This had been the home Cleo had made for herself. It had been here where she had carved out a life. And when the time came to leave it for Japan, he'd always sensed she'd left some part of herself behind.

Of course, they had talked everything through. As a couple. As man and wife. As parents to be. But he had been so determined. That resolution was absolutely clear to him back then, though now he couldn't for the life of him remember why. Perhaps some small part of him had wanted to prove that he could make it in Japan. That he could disprove his mother's warnings.

Don't go back there. There's nothing for you.

Iwata had become determined to leave America, to start a new life. He had showed photographs to Cleo. Told her about little traditions, dialects and cuisines. Left articles on the table for her.

When had been the moment she had agreed? At the red light, Iwata closed his eyes to remember.

Where you go, I go. That was it. That was what she had said.

'Where you go, I go.' He repeated it out loud, a line from a script delivered without passion. But Santa Monica was behind him. The lights turned green. Iwata drove.

A few miles east of Malibu he took a right up towards Tuna Canyon. There, on a dusty road of switchbacks and sagebrush, he saw the turn-off. It was little more than a dirt road curving up a tall hillock and he would have missed it were it not for his directions.

Iwata stopped a few hundred yards short of the end of

the track and got out, the Bronco wheezing. When the dust cleared he saw an old red barn up ahead, the only remnant of the ranch that must once have stood here. He walked the rest of the way until he was standing outside it. There was a racing-red vintage Jaguar parked outside. Behind the barn there was only a squat forest of chaparral running downhill, all the way to the Pacific Ocean.

The door opened and a large man emerged. He had a leather flat cap, facial hair, tattoos, a Hawaiian shirt. Despite a bulky frame, he was hatchet-faced, his expression stranded somewhere between irritation and curiosity.

'Afternoon,' Iwata said.

The man appraised him for a moment before speaking. 'Road accident?' His voice was soft, almost amicable.

'No.'

'You're lost.'

'I hope not.' Iwata took out his investigator's licence. 'My name is Iwata, I'm a professional investigator. You're Benedict Novacek?'

A nod.

'Then maybe we can talk inside.'

'Here's fine. Talk about what?'

'This.' Iwata held up the sex catalogue.

Novacek's deep-set eyes took it in. The ocean couldn't be heard from up here, but it smelled like last night's lovemaking. 'No, I think I'm good.'

'Mr Novacek, it would be better for you to talk to me. A few things require clarification.'

'Is that so?'

Iwata could see past him into the barn. It had been completely refurbished, though sparsely furnished – a white couch and some stools by the breakfast bar to give it the appearance of a normal room. But no TV, no books, no personal touches. None of that interested Iwata. He could see the window with the ocean vista – the spot where Meredith and Geneviève had stood.

Novacek stalked his eyes. 'Do you like the view?'

'There's no denying it.'

The two men looked at each other. After a few swampy seconds, they offered one another thin smiles. 'Probably best if you left now, Mr Iwata. I'm busy. You understand.'

'Mm. I understand.' Iwata took one last look at the ocean view, then walked back to the Bronco. Benedict Novacek watched him all the way.

Murky grey night had ensconced the city. Los Angeles dreams could flower in this half-dark, ambitions and desires still attainable, yet to be burned away by tomorrow's disbelieving sun. This was a town of red-carpet applause and shell casings tinkling on concrete. Parched hills aflame with pink checkermallows, interrupted only by occasional mansions custom built for leeches in suits. Normal little lives ran into subplots like raindrops into raindrops on dirty glass.

Iwata thought about what Frank Lloyd Wright had once said: 'Tip the world over and everything loose will land in Los Angeles.' He figured that had to be true. For

Meredith Nichol and Geneviève Darlington it had been, anyhow. *Same for me*, he supposed.

The 110 Freeway was lit by rusted floodlights, racemes of chemical amber intersecting the smoggy darkness. Iwata didn't know where he was going, but he didn't need to. He was following. He had been following ever since Benedict Novacek had set off from his studio up in Tuna Canyon forty minutes ago.

As Iwata drove he thought about Benedict Novacek. Could he be Meredith's murderer? Could he be John Smith? Could he be the man who had attacked him the night before? He was more of a match physically, but the voice was wrong.

Iwata had no answers and the clock was ticking – a killer was out there. Geneviève was missing. Mara Zambrano was nowhere to be found.

Shaking his head at all the unknowns, he took the 4th Street Exit for Downtown and stayed two cars behind Novacek's old Jaguar. Sleek black skyscrapers mushroomed up around him, dwarfing the Bronco. Iwata glanced up through the sunroof and saw the countless windows of Bunker Hill, a commercial hive of electric honeycombs in the night.

Novacek turned on Hope Street, then right on Grand all the way to the Happy Gopher. He got out of his car and tossed the valet his keys.

Iwata overshot and parked a few blocks away in the darkness. Nocturnal figures stood like black flamingos on a murky river here. In the shadowy doorway of an abandoned hotel a homeless woman was talking to Los

Angeles itself: 'I know how it is. You ain't foolin' me. That's all you got – lies. But I see you, clear as day. Clear clear clear. Yes, sir.'

Iwata hurried back to the Gopher. It was busy tonight, the clientele mixed like a cheap drink – bankers who had ventured down from Bunker Hill and girlfriends celebrating a thirtieth. The dancers were on break and the majority of the Gopher's patrons – lone, horny men – nursed drinks like they'd been left at a party by the only person they knew. The little line for the staircase at the back told Iwata the private rooms upstairs were doing good business.

Benedict Novacek was alone at the bar, hunched forward, peering into a Rum Swizzle. Iwata took the stool next to him and ordered an alcohol-free beer. 'Small world.'

'You're following me.' Novacek took an irritated sip.

Iwata put the sex catalogue on the bar top. 'Just came to do a little light reading.'

'There's a nice library nearby.'

'I know the one. Don't think it'll open till the morning, though.'

'Why don't you go elsewhere? Have fun. Make some money. A man with your persistence could do well in this town.'

Iwata puffed up his chest for the quote. '"Ah, Misha, he is haunted by a great, unsolved doubt. He is one of those who don't want millions, but an answer to their questions."'

'You know' – Novacek smiled, calm as a frozen lake – 'you're starting to get on my nerves.'

'You've got bigger problems, Benny. Five of your girls. *Five.*'

'Five. Of *my* girls. Right. Whatever that means.'

'One murdered, the other four missing. All of them visited your little studio. That's very unfortunate, wouldn't you say?'

Novacek laughed. 'Bartender! A Black Dahlia for my crazy new friend here.'

'I don't drink. Meredith Nichol. Geneviève Darlington. Why them?'

'You're trying to suggest I had something to do with a disappearance or a death.'

'*Murder*, Benny. Not a death. And "something to do with" is a broad brush, right?'

'You're talking front ways and back ways.'

'Then let me make it easy for you to understand. I have friends in the LAPD. I'd be happy to throw your name to them. I'm sure they'd be interested to work out exactly what kind of "something to do with" applies to a guy like you when it comes to murder.'

'I didn't kill anyone. And my work is all above board.'

'But if you tell a pig there's a truffle up the way, he's likely to root around. Don't you think?'

Novacek pushed an old cocktail umbrella to and fro on the bar top with his little finger as the Black Dahlia arrived. He kept his eyes on the cocktail and spoke quietly. 'Listen, I don't know what happened to your girls. I just took pictures. Posed them. Made recordings. That's what I do. That's all I do.'

'So talk to me.'

Novacek necked half the cocktail then looked around. 'How do I know you'll keep your word? How do I know the police won't turn up anyhow?'

'You don't. But it's a sure thing if you *don't* talk to me.' Iwata held up the catalogue. 'Meredith and Geneviève. Why them?'

'I dunno, man.' Novacek stared hatefully into the cloudy red liquid before gulping it down. 'I met them in a club, we got talking. They had the right look, I guess.'

'What's the right look?'

'Just *right*.'

'Right for who?'

'Me.'

'Not your clients?'

Novacek flinched, a gesture he tried to elongate into another sip of a drink he no longer had. 'Right is right.'

'Who are your clients?'

'We're not talking about that.'

'Who killed Meredith?'

'How the fuck should I know?'

'Where's Mara Zambrano?'

'I don't know anyone by that –'

'What about Geneviève? What about Ashley Nelligan? Patricia Hewer? Shari Goyer?'

'I don't fucking know!'

The barman caught the eye of security, his eyebrows telling him to be ready. Novacek cleared his throat and softened. 'Look. I'm telling you, I don't *know* anything about them. I just take their pictures, that's all.'

Iwata leaned in, close enough to smell the vodka on his breath. 'If you didn't kill them, then you know who did.'

A spindly blonde in a black dress approached. Relief washed over Novacek when she draped her thin arms around him. 'Ben-*nyyy*.' Her Russian accent dripped. 'I didn't know you vaunted to bring friend.'

'No friend, *khozyayka*.' He kissed her wrist. 'This gentleman was just leaving.'

With a wry smile, Iwata left. Outside, he approached the valet.

'What's your name?'

'Jorge.'

'Yeah, you've got a phone call.'

The valet hurried away. As soon as the doorman's back was turned Iwata opened the metal cabinet, plucked out the Jaguar keys and hurried over to the parking lot. Unlocking Novacek's car, he rushed back to the cabinet and returned the keys.

Sometime after 2 a.m. Iwata heard whistling: John Lennon's 'Jealous Guy'. The car door opened and Novacek dropped into the driver's seat. Before he could start the engine a belt had looped around his neck. Iwata snapped back hard. Immediately Novacek bucked and hacked against the leather, but Iwata's grip was resolute.

After a few seconds Iwata eased off the pressure and leaned forward to whisper. 'Now listen to me, Benny. I don't want to hurt you, but I need you to be honest.'

'You're crazy.'

'There's someone out there killing women. I'm going to find him. Do you understand me?'

'Nuh—'

Iwata pulled back hard again. After five seconds, he relented. Novacek choked, his spittle flecking the windscreen. 'You crazy bastard!'

'Benny, you're going to talk to me. Now, either you're the one killing these women or it's one of your clients.'

'Fuck you —'

Iwata punched him under the ear, then ripped the belt back again hard, the headrest creaking, the leather groaning.

When he let Novacek up for air, he was half sobbing. 'Plea— . . . please . . .'

'*Speak*. Where is Geneviève? Where is Mara?'

'I don't know. Pluh—'

'Then your clients. Give me a name.'

'I gahnt—'

Iwata pulled back again. In the mirror he could see blood coming out of Novacek's nose. His face was luminous pink. He counted to six, then loosened the belt a fraction. Another coughing fit which Iwata didn't have time for.

'Give me a name.'

'They'll kill me.'

'Who will?'

'I can't.'

Iwata let go of the belt, took the gun out of his pocket and put it against Novacek's temple. 'No more pronouns, Benny. I won't ask again.'

'He's a Mexican!' Novacek yelped.

'Go on.'

'Oh fuck. Okay. H-his name's Rivera. They call him Bebé.'

'Bebé Rivera?'

Weeping, Novacek yielded, whiffling the breath back into his lungs. 'He likes the trans girls . . . that's his thing. But he's in a different league. Buys a lot of my work. Pays like nobody else . . . If there's a girl he really likes, he'll want to meet them.'

'Where?'

'I don't *know* where, that's the point. I just know his private jet comes in for them when he's throwing a party.'

'And you send the girl down there for your cut.'

Novacek nodded.

'Where does he take them in his jet?'

'I don't know –'

Iwata jabbed the muzzle of the pistol into his ear.

'Ciudad Cabral! That's all I fucking know!'

'Ciudad Cabral . . .'

The doorman appeared in the parking lot and leaned against the wall. As he lit his cigarette, he squinted at them. Already, Iwata was out of the car. Novacek scrambled the locks down and opened one window a crack. 'I hope you go down there, you chink fuck! Go and see what happens to you!'

Iwata put his hands in his pockets and hurried away. Turning a corner, he stopped in an alleyway to vomit.

14. Flesh and Blood

Iwata was sitting on his mother's porch in the dark, looking at the street he'd half-grown up on. The lawns were perfect, the flowerbeds were mollycoddled, the driveways were clean. It was as if the people of Beech Avenue were forever preparing themselves for some regal procession that would never pass through.

Iwata wanted to go inside and look at the photos of Cleo, of Nina – he kept all his own in boxes – but he didn't want to risk waking his mother. Instead, he sat back in the porch chair and stroked his chin bitterly.

Benedict Novacek was many things. A shitty little man who exploited people and peddled flesh. But Iwata had looked into the eyes of killers before. He had seen power junkies, he had seen manipulators, he had seen animals that had learned to talk and walk on two legs. Novacek was none of them. He was just a weakling.

Bebé Rivera was an unknown quantity. But if the missing girls were all in Mexico, how had Meredith come to be murdered on some train tracks near Skid Row? And if she had been to Mexico, then she had certainly come back alive. Joyce Carbone had said as much. *Mr VIP dropped her and things changed.*

'Kosuke?' Nozomi Iwata stood at the door in her dressing gown. 'My god, what happened to you?'

'The other kid started it.'

'Come inside and leave the jokes out there.'

Iwata followed his mother indoors. She put the TV on so they wouldn't be alone, then busied herself in the kitchen. A minute later she came out with two cups of brown rice tea and handed one to her son.

Their eyes automatically drifted over to the screen. It was the shopping channel. An all-terrain folding wagon with divider in a range of colours was available for just $83.98 in three easy payments.

'Are you all right?' she asked.

'I'm fine.'

'You don't look fine.'

A Calista set of twelve hot rollers with clips and travel bag had a final price of $59, available for four easy payments. 'Mom, I need to talk to you.'

'You're leaving.' She glanced at him. It wasn't a question.

'For a short while.'

'Where will you go?'

A Joan Rivers jewelled oval pendant eighteen-inch necklace comprising antiqued gold tone and blue oval cabochon, framed by marquise-shaped beads in green, peach, pink and purple. The clearance price was $49.82 with $3.02 for shipping and handling.

Now this is not just about what you're wearing, how you're looking, or how you're being perceived by the world. It's about something more important than that. Something priceless. None of us can put a value on that, but if we were going to try, it wouldn't be fifty bucks, would it, Ken?

No, it most definitely would not, Marie. So what is *it about?*

Great question. I'll tell you. It's about how what you're wearing makes you feel.

'I have to go pay a debt,' Iwata said.

Nozomi took a breath and turned to face him. 'Before you go, I need to talk to you.'

Iwata looked up and saw photographs of his wife and daughter. He had wanted to see them earlier; now, they felt like shameful ornaments. 'I can't talk now, Mom.'

'Please, Kosuke. Please.'

Iwata stood and put his cup in the sink. He listened to the running water, keeping his back to his mother. 'I don't have anything to say.'

'Well, I do.' The loud desperation in her voice shocked him. 'We never talk. All this time goes by and goes by and we never say anything.'

'For what, Mom?'

'Because I have to, son.' Her old eyes were robin-egg blue in the moonlit kitchen. They were wet, and it was unbearable.

'When I needed you . . .' His voice stumbled. 'You left me. You left me in the middle of nowhere. *Years* pass and you come back for me with America, with words. How can I forgive that?'

'Kosuke, I'm not asking for forgiveness. I know you can't . . . Son, I'm just asking you to understand me. Maybe if you –'

Iwata walked past her and stopped at the door. 'I've already got my own regrets, Mother. I can't carry yours too.'

Nozomi closed her eyes, then nodded to herself. 'All right.'

Iwata left the kitchen and walked down the hall, ignoring the photographs. He opened the front door.

'Kosuke!' she called from the kitchen.

'What?'

'That box is for you.'

Iwata looked down at the white cardboard storage box by the door. For some reason it had a koi carp sticker on it. He picked it up and left.

Four a.m. Club Noir. Iwata was leaning against the wall, as far away from the bar as possible. He could not see Mara or Geneviève. His eyes kept returning to the bottles on the shelves above the bar. They gleamed in the neon like potions. For the first time in a long time, he craved them.

For years, he had not so much as considered a red-wine sauce but now he felt an angry thirst in his throat. He wanted to allow himself the fantasy of drinking. Of pills. The anti-gravity they promised. But allowing fantasy was the first step to relapse, and he could not accept that. Not while there was work to do.

Iwata closed his eyes. Even as a child he had been good at finding the truth. Ever since the bus station up in those mountains, he had been hypersensitive to it, waiting for reality to reveal itself again. The truth could not hurt him if he found it before it found him. And so he sought it constantly. At the orphanage he could see past why certain kids shouted and why others would hit out. When his best friend, Kei, disappeared a few months before they were due to leave, Iwata immediately deduced that the man responsible was the orphanage director.

But becoming police had not been down to some personal crusade. It was simply a logical career choice for a man with his natural inquisitiveness. From his first homicides on the cold banks of Lake Hinuma, through his years by the ocean in Chōshi PD, to his headline-grabbing apprehension of the Black Sun Killer in Tokyo, Iwata had always had a firm clarity. He always had the ability to see through other eyes, to imagine the angle, to see the logic in the lie. It was always there inside him.

But now Benedict Novacek was telling him that the truth would be found south of the border. He had implied there would be no coming back. After so long following cheating husbands and ensnaring perfunctory liars, at last Kosuke Iwata had a real case. He did not want it but he was absolutely bound to it, like a drinker's hand on the neck of a bottle. If the truth was in Mexico, then Iwata would go. This was not a momentous occasion, it was an underwhelming homecoming.

Iwata turned to go. He passed the private rooms on his way out. But something stopped him. There were thick drapes, translucent fabric partitions, plump couches. Before each one, women were dancing on poles. Little Dragon's 'Pretty Girls' was playing.

Iwata thought he'd seen something but now, in the red light, he was unsure. The only thing he felt with certainty was fatigue.

A hand emerged from behind a drape and beckoned. Iwata followed. He opened the drape to a loveseat. There was Mara enveloped in cushions and velvets, a dewdrop in a flower. She was leaning against the pole.

'Mara.'

'Who else?' She slid down the pole like a flag lowered in tragedy and sat across from him. She had a wig on, of vivid scarlet, and a simple black bikini.

'You disappeared.'

'Like a ghost?' She reached for Iwata's hand and placed it on her calf. It was smooth at first, then rumpled with goosebumps. 'See, flesh and blood.'

Leaning in this close to her, he could taste the spice in her perfume. Beneath olive skin and dark, small hairs on her arms, he could see the sea-green of her veins.

'Mara, I think you're in danger. There's someone out there —'

'Hush now,' she whispered. 'Lie back, relax.'

She eased him back on to the loveseat and folded his hands across his chest, a mother tucking in a restless child. Again he saw her tattoo, more clearly this time:

1:18 ISA—

A new song began and now Mara closed her lupine eyes in pleasure.

'Ohhh, I love this one. "Locos" by León Larregui. The lyrics are so beautiful, I wish you could understand. It's about how crazy we can be for love, how glad to have someone close to us.'

'Mara, listen to me, there's someone out there –'

She hopped back up to her pole and twirled. 'There's always someone out there, Inspector. We always have to watch out for *someone*.'

'You don't understand. He knows who you are –'

'Who?'

Iwata saw her, the shape of her, the mass, the volume – yet, like a man crawling towards a mirage, he did not quite understand the sight of her, he could not trust his eyes.

'Is Mara Zambrano your real name?'

'You're so good, aren't you?' She smiled gently, her whisper soothing. '*So good* at finding other people. But Inspector, tell me something. Have you ever searched for yourself?'

'Wait. Mara.'

She brushed away the drape and then she was gone. Iwata wanted to reach for her. Wanted to hold her back. Wanted to give her a reason not to run. But this was sympathy for a bolting fox. Gone was gone.

It was dawn by the time Iwata had packed a small bag and was ready to leave his apartment. The sky couldn't be called black and it couldn't be called purple. It was some ugly word that men and women of language hadn't yet bothered with.

Iwata took one last look at his mother's white box with the koi sticker then opened the door. Outside, the Bronco wouldn't start, the key drawing only wheezing coughs from the engine. Swearing, Iwata went back inside and called a taxi.

Half an hour later, he arrived at the Greyhound bus station. He bought pretzels, water and a ticket to Mexico. The bus opened its doors and Iwata got on along with passengers bound for home, bound for family. The driver honked his horn and pulled away. Iwata put his head on the window and closed his eyes. He would always be good at leaving.

A grey, rainy morning. Iwata leans against his Chōshi PD squad car. He has been called out early because of a fight between fishermen, which, in the end, has turned out to be nothing more than friends horsing around. Iwata smokes and watches the Tone River drift by. Tug-boats blow their horns, heading out to sea. Tall grass on the riverbanks flutters in the wind like baby hair. Heavy clouds rush past as though late.

Iwata was once thankful to Chōshi, the only place that had given him a break and the means with which to raise his family. But now, a few years on, he resents it.

He speaks languages, he crushes his competition in test scores, he even has international police training. Yet month after month Personnel politely ignores him. Initially, Tokyo had been a professional goal, somewhere his skills could be put to use. Given what he could bring to the table, Iwata had been confident it would be only a matter of time.

But by now the rejection is personal. After several years in the police force he has worked only a handful of murders. His day-to-day has more to do with floods or farming squabbles than anything else. His studies are decorations on a dead Christmas tree. And when, perhaps once a year, a dismembered body is found floating in the bay, it will be kept at arm's length by his superiors. Iwata will want to investigate, but the second tattoos are noted on the torso it will be dismissed as another difference of opinion between gangsters.

It starts to rain. Iwata crushes out the smoke and looks up and down the road. When he's sure there's no one, he reaches into his glovebox for the whisky. He rips open a sachet of honey, squeezes it into his mouth, then takes a long swig.

'*Kosuke?*'

Iwata turns to see his partner's wife. 'Hoshiko. What are you doing here?'

'I had some errands, then I felt like a drive. I thought I saw your squad car number . . .'

Iwata nods. He can't be bothered to think of a response. A scathing wind picks up and he wipes away cold, meaningless tears. He crushes the last of the honey into his mouth, then takes another swig, his voice deeper now. 'What do you want, Hoshiko?'

She looks around, her black hair flayed madly by the wind. She is wearing a stupid mauve puffa jacket, yellow rain boots and a rainbow umbrella, which for some reason he finds preposterous.

'I just wanted to check . . .' Hoshiko looks at the floor. 'That you're okay.'

He raises the bottle. 'Never better.'

She walks over uncertainly. 'Could I have some?'

Iwata frowns but hands over the bottle. She takes a

small, pathetic sip and wrinkles her turned-up nose as she swallows. 'I don't like that.'

'Yeah, well. This isn't the country club.'

'Do you mind if I stay a while?'

Iwata looks at her. They have shared dinners together, day trips, nights out. But they have never had a single conversation alone. For a while, he encouraged Cleo to socialize with Hoshiko, but she always pushed back. Watching her playing with the bottle, her plain eyes taking in the river, Iwata can see why.

'How is Taba?' he asks emptily.

'He's back at home. Things are better.'

'Hm.' Iwata cannot think of anything he wishes to discuss less than his partner's shitty marriage. He clears his throat, takes the bottle away from Hoshiko and twists on the cap. He returns it to the glovebox and zips up his coat. 'Well, I better go. Please tell him I'll see him soon.'

'Kosuke?'

'What?'

'Can you wait a second?'

He checks his watch. 'What is it?'

'I just need to talk to you.'

For the life of him, Iwata cannot envisage a single topic in this world that they would need to discuss. He feels saturated by her, almost as though her hollowness might envelop him.

'I really do need to head off. You know how it is.'

'Okay. But do you –'

'Do I what?'

'Do you think that I . . .'

'Hoshiko, what is it?'

She turns around, unbuckles her belt, then pulls her jeans down to her thighs. Her pale buttocks are rippled with goosebumps, a solitary mole on the right.

'Do you want me?'

'What are you doing?'

'Do you want it?' She juts her body out towards him. Her pubic hair is pitch black, her labia greyish. He does not want Hoshiko but before he can stop to consider the emptiness of it he is fucking his partner's wife against the police car.

Iwata is sick of being a good man. He is sick of his beautiful wife. He is sick of being a father. He is sick of the existence that everyone assumes he is happy in. Somehow the banality of Hoshiko's body feels natural. The wind carries the smell of her up to his nostrils and he turns his head away. He sees himself in the side mirror, the pointless bucking of his hips, the pointless emptying of his balls into this lonely woman, as though he were fucking the Tone River itself.

Iwata pulls out and rips up a wet clump of grass to clean himself. Hoshiko tries to kiss him, tries to tell him that she has always felt this way, but he pushes her away.

'You're crazy,' he laughs. 'Go home.'

Hoshiko's mouth drops opens but she just looks at her yellow boots, Iwata's semen dropping on to the dark concrete between them. She pulls up her jeans, picks up her umbrella and walks back to her car. As she opens the door Iwata calls after her.

'Hoshiko? Don't you fucking tell anyone. Understand?'

She begins to slam her face against the steering wheel, the horn resounding like clownish chuckles in the morning cold. Iwata gets in the squad car and drives away – a sick feeling in his stomach.

That night Cleo will ask him how he got grass in his underwear. Iwata makes up an excuse and swears to himself he'll never do something like that again. Within three days he's is back by the river, Hoshiko bent over and grunting as before.

PART TWO

15. Clean Work

Detective Valentín distantly puffed out cigarette smoke and swallowed coffee, tasting neither. This was her last case. That had no taste either. She listened to the hot rain drumming on the roof of her car and looked down at Ciudad Cabral, a city put together like a child in hand-me-downs. It was home to one million souls, living either in elegant old colonias in the centre, or in the sundry slums shoved up against the surrounding mountains.

And it was to these slums that Valentín had been called so often down the years. People lived on top of each other, voices carried. The smell of cooking mixed in with dog shit, laughter with fucking, birdsong with the screams of women. It was a city within a city, all colourful breeze blocks, crooked satellites, simple dirt floors. Murders here were rarely planned, customarily a moment of male jealousy erupting, like oil spitting from a hot pan. Those cases were solved in a day. But Valentín knew already: today's case would not be one of those.

As her eyes passed over the never-ending tin roofs tinkling in the morning rain, she realized she wouldn't be coming back here again.

At the end of the street a child schlepped a massive bundle of recyclables on his back. Across from him a chubby woman was opening up her salon for the day. Reggaetón poured out of a bakery's window. For Valentín, somehow seeing these little shacks for the last time was seeing them for the first time.

Today's dawn was colourless. In the distance, by the highway leading out of the city, she could make out words on a billboard:

NOS GUSTA HACER TRABAJO LIMPIO

We like to do clean work

Valentín didn't know what the slogan was referring to. Not that it mattered. There was nothing that could be sold to her anymore. She sighed and glanced at the passenger seat, half expecting to see Morel dozing. But of course the seat was empty. Morel would not be a passenger in this car again. With difficulty, she sipped her coffee and wondered how long it had been so hard to swallow liquids. Closing her eyes, she heard his voice.

Not a good sign, Vali. You need rest.

'And what about talking with my dead partner?' Her voice was stale with a slight lisp. 'Is that a good sign?'

You know what they say. To the dead the grave, to the living the pleasure.

She laughed. 'Always the pendejo, Morel. Even now.'

Pendejo or not, I'll be seeing you soon.

Valentín opened her eyes and forced some painkillers down with coffee. She had no answer for that.

Someone knocked at the window now. A young man in a grey raincoat stood there, shouting something over the downpour. Valentín wound down the window.

'Ma'am. I'm Sub-Inspector Velasco.'

She opened the door to Morel's side. 'My replacement.'

Velasco got in and swept the rain from his hair. 'I suppose so.'

'You want a bachita?'

'I don't smoke.'

She lit up. 'Where you from?'

He seemed surprised by the question. 'The south.'

'There's a lot of south.'

'Minatitlán.'

'You must know what they call this kind of rain, then.'

'No?'

'*Wives' rain. The kind that annoys you for the whole day.*'

Velasco forced laughter. 'That's a good one,' he mumbled down into his papers. He pretended to read them while Valentín listened to the rain.

'Tell me something, Velasco. Why are you here?'

He looked at her, puzzled. 'The homicide.'

'No, I mean in general. You could have been a lion tamer. You could have been a sailor.'

'Well.' He shrugged. 'Because of the insecurity. I wanted to help.'

That was the ubiquitous word for it: *la inseguridad*. The media used it for mass murders, mutilations, any imaginable human monstrosity. But that was like calling the Hanging Gardens of Babylon quaint. On TV the other night a controversial news panellist had used the phrase

'Our president's narcotheatre' – it felt right to Valentín. Everything was for show now, even murder.

At last, the door of the house on the corner opened and the Science Division guy emerged in white scrubs and a hairnet. Squinting through the rain, he gave Valentín the thumbs-up then ambled away. A murder like this might have been news in another city, another country. But here it would be just another shitty little footnote in the vastness of whatever this reality was being called now.

Valentín stubbed out her cigarette and slung her coffee out the window. 'Let's go.'

'Yes, ma'am.'

The rain was lashing down on this sloping street lined with stacks of human shoeboxes. Rubble, smashed furniture and syringes collected in alleyways. Cacti plumed out of empty lots and abandoned building sites. The only billboards here advertised Christian ministries or Coca-Cola.

'What's for breakfast, Velasco?'

'Victim is early seventies. No job listed.'

The crime scene itself was little more than a cement hutch. On the wall there were various Madonna icons and prints of Christ: the Agony in the Garden, the Temptation in the Desert. Velasco took Valentín through, noting little details, eager to impress. In the front room he delicately pointed to the corpse with the end of his pen. 'Cause of death is –'

'One too many holes. I can count, you know.' Valentín looked down at the dead sack of a man.

'I heard about you,' Velasco admitted. 'But I didn't think you'd be the joking type.'

She grunted her reply. Of course he had heard about her. *The woman.* Everybody had heard about her. There was no denying she was old school – police via the military. She was just moving up when President Zedillo passed the law to create the Policía Federal back in '99. For Valentín it had been throwing a lasso on a shooting star. Throughout, she'd suffered insults, slights and come-ons, but none of it got in her way. *They're just afraid of you, Chamaca.* That's what her father had said. *They don't like their geniuses to wear skirts.*

Valentín tried not to think too much about him anymore. She didn't do well with feelings. After all, a father like that had been a blessing and a curse – that much love and wisdom set a high bar. Long ago she had realized normal men were not compatible with high bars.

Valentín looked over at Velasco, who was gently lifting fingers with pencils and peering under tables with the delicacy of a proctologist on his first day. There was a time she would have treated him like the shit on her shoe just on principle. So obviously the collegiate type, so obviously from money.

In the last two decades she had met only one man who'd been more than shrugged shoulders – Morel. He had been a strange man, pudgy yet slender limbs, black hair but reddish whiskers, constant laughter despite having the darkest world view she'd ever encountered. Valentín hated him at first: his stupid jokes, his habit of spitting nails in the car. But years had passed and somewhere along the way she began to look forward to the jokes, even found herself shaking her head affectionately as she picked out little nail clippings from her car.

Morel had never saved her life. He'd never been much of a cop. But she had come to depend on him. Probably more than depend, despite their love affairs always fizzling out. Luis Morel had been a good man, whether or not anybody else saw it. Whether or not his ethics had wavered in the year before his murder. Now he was just a voice in her head.

Conscious of being observed, Velasco looked up at her. Valentín wondered what he saw. Her mental image was of herself at around thirty – a dark, buxom woman with perennially short hair, quick to wink, with green eyes thanks to a Scandinavian grandmother. But now her skin was pale, her eyes sunken. Her clothes hung off her. She probably wouldn't bother the scales at anything over fifty kilograms.

'A friend discovered him this morning,' Velasco offered. 'Landlord said it doesn't look like anything was taken. Not that there'd be much to take.'

'The killer was here for him.' She nodded at the old man. He was face down, his eyes half open. The last thing he would have seen before the bullets shattered through his brain was his own dirty floor. 'No witnesses, I'll wager.'

'No, ma'am. Which I find hard to believe. Two gunshots and somehow nobody hears anything through these walls?'

'Close-knit barrio doesn't want to talk to the chota. Big shock.'

Suddenly, Valentín was violently gasping for air, her collar sagging with sweat, her headache threatening to floor her. She staggered outside and gripped a road sign, grateful for the rain on her face.

It had started with vomiting. Trouble swallowing. White patches on her gums. She ignored it, of course, but the work medical had been unavoidable. The test results had no interest in her career. The old man would be her last case and Velasco's first. That was life: inauspicious beginnings, inauspicious endings.

Valentín took refuge under some stray metal sheeting and lit up, protecting the small flame against the wind. Her drag was deep but she registered no nicotine hit. Hers was a body which no longer experienced pleasures, a gum with the flavour chewed out.

Velasco sat next to her. 'You okay?'

'Fine.'

'I think there could be something out back. When you're ready.'

She followed him to a back lot sprinkled with chicken shit. The tyre tracks were clear – thick, unmissable impressions. Valentín hunched over them, running two fingers through the warm wet mud. They were losing their shape in the rain. *Same as me*, she thought.

The tyre tracks headed north. *The killer left the city.* Valentín didn't know his name but she could picture him. The designer T-shirt, the SUV, the cellphone – all of it would exhibit his standing. Especially here. In this place, his wealth would have told everyone that he was a man to be respectfully left alone. A man who was con-nected. A man who was just here to do a job. Maybe he winked at the younger boys who marvelled at his truck, one day hoping to be like him.

The socioeconomic theories modulated but, the way

Valentín saw it, wanting to get out was wanting to get out. And there would never be a Bible passage fiery enough, or a prison sentence long enough, to deter that. Politicians talked of the narco groups as though they were simple criminal gangs, using black-and-white language. But those groups were made up of brothers. Cousins. Childhood friends. Of course they committed atrocities. She saw those every other day in Ciudad Cabral. But the slums saw the other side of them too. Covering the cost of a funeral for a widow too poor to pay. Schools built on their money. Handing out rice and water after earthquakes. They even threw festivals.

So when situations like the dead old man arose threats were not required. The consequences were clear. Even so, Sicarios would openly kill in broad daylight, then turn to the crowd and say: 'Ladies and gentlemen, you know how this works. The closed mouth catches no flies.'

Valentín pulled her coat tighter around her body. She was cold all the time now, the chill deep in her bones. From here, she could see the corpse through the side door. Nobody would open their mouth for him. This was a city where nobody honked their horns. Most nights, the streets were empty. Every other door had a black ribbon tied to it. The sight of another one appearing overnight shocked nobody.

As for the old man, Valentín already knew nobody would pay for him. Nobody would demand justice. Certainly not her.

'Velasco!' she called. 'I'm heading back to the station now.'

He nodded, concern in his eyes. Valentín wanted to wish him good luck. She wanted to warn him about the whispers in his ear that would soon come. She wanted to tell him to only ever keep his hands in his own pockets. To steer clear of the path she had taken.

Instead, she just nodded at the body. 'Good luck with him.' She smiled wryly. 'And the rest of them.'

Outside, the first few state police officers had arrived on the scene and were reluctantly cordoning off the area. A small crowd had gathered at the police tape. Detective Valentín knew from experience they would not stay long.

16. Looking under Rocks

The bus journey was long and Iwata drifted in and out of sleep. He listened to the portable radio of the old woman in front of him. Somewhere in Arizona it started receiving Mexican frequencies. He enjoyed the frequent usage of the accordion and found the awkwardly translated government messages interesting.

An hour south of Tucson, the bus slowed. Iwata glanced at the billboard by the side of the road:

– US BORDER PATROL –
YOUR CAREER IN BORDERS. YOUR CAREER
WITHOUT BOUNDARIES.

The border fence came into view. It was of underwhelming height, no taller than two men, a rust-coloured vertebrae undulating over dry hills, repurposed Vietnam War landing mats.

Iwata entered Mexico just before midnight.

A few yards in, he got off the bus. Except for little shrouds of neon and streetlamps casting amber in convex, the city of Nogales was in darkness. Iwata could feel eyes following him, silent assessments being made. He had his gun, but it was still empty. Leaving the bus station, he stepped into the crisp desert night. At the nearest motel he paid for a single room, slipped his gun under his pillow and fell into a black slumber.

Iwata woke early and squinted out of the window. The buildings were of varying size, each one painted brightly; marigold, jade, celeste. The street was lined with hotels and bars, a few sleeping mendicants in the doorways of closed bordellos. People were sitting outside having coffee, sharing the banal in-jokes of their day-to-day.

In the dusty old courtyard Iwata ate spicy chilaquiles on a plastic plate and drank cold milk to calm the burn. Leaving the motel, he walked down the street and entered the pawn shop, where he asked for bullets. The man behind the counter rummaged around in the back and returned with two that were compatible with Iwata's gun. He quoted an exorbitant price. Iwata paid and left.

At the car dealership across the road he made an offer for an old Mazda sedan with a questionable past. Iwata was a foreigner paying cash but nobody was looking for long-term commitment here. In less than half an hour Iwata was, more or less, armed and mobile.

A few miles clear of Nogales he stopped at a gas station by an abandoned farm. The land was a goulash of rough-hewn hummocks and wild greens. Dirty argentite clouds pressed down low. Sipping coffee with ground cinnamon, Iwata watched an old weather vane creaking in the wind.

At 4.30 p.m. Ciudad Cabral appeared in the distance. The city crouched over a desert basin, a polluted river slicing through its centre and surrounded on all fronts by serrated mountains. On the largest mountain, a colossal message had been carved in lime, its white letters like a jagged Hollywood sign:

LA HIERBA SE SECA Y LA FLOR SE MARCHITA, PERO
LA PALABRA DE DIOS PERMANENCE PARA SIEMPRE

The grass wizens, the flower withers, but the word of God lasts for ever

Iwata entered the city from the south. On either side of the motorway ramshackle houses of sheet metal and plastic huddled together. He passed churches doubling as schools, hole-in-the-wall taquerias, a sprawling graveyard. The streets were practically empty, the only movement to draw the eye twines of black pigeons across the grey sky.

Just before his exit Iwata noticed an object up ahead – something hanging from the massive concrete flyover. Swaying gently in the breeze was a naked male body. It had no head and no testicles, as though a butcher had cut away the inedible portions. It hung from broken ankles, a thick caking of blood and shit everywhere. A cardboard sign had been attached to the torso:

Yo, José Velasco, follaperros, descuidé de las reglas. Con este gesto, quedo perdonado.

        – La Familia Cabral

I, José Velasco, the dog-fucker, failed to heed the rules. With this gesture, I am forgiven.

As the car passed underneath Iwata glanced up through the sunroof at the exposed stem of the man's neck. It looked like a cartoon shank steak, something Tom and Jerry would eat. Shocked, Iwata made his turning and tried not to wonder who José Velasco was or what he had done.

In a hotel near the old centre of the city Iwata hid his money under a loose floorboard and allowed himself a little rest in the hot gloom. Through the window he watched a rusty crane move, casting a dial of shadow over the square. From somewhere below he could hear Mexican ballads over lamenting guitar chords, and a football being kicked. As Iwata closed his eyes the building site's end-of-day klaxon went off and a flock of pigeons scattered. It sounded like insincere applause.

Cursing the universe, Detective Valentín slumped off the toilet without bothering to inspect the pink mess she had left behind. Between gritted teeth and tears she reached for the handle as though it would flush away what was happening inside her body. Every muscle ebbed between a constant ache and violent twists of suffering. Her breathing was feeble, her thighs and armpits were barnacled by a savage rash, her migraine was unrelenting.

Valentín ran her hand across her bony ribcage now, feeling the small, quivering life beneath. She was at peace with death – as much as anyone could be – yet she would lurch out of bed screaming every night. While her mind accepted the end, her body was still only made up of simple animal parts. It was easier to be here during the nights, surrounded, at least, by other people. Even if they were cops.

Valentín slipped her hand in her pocket and grasped the small knife Morel had given her. She had scolded him at the time: *Bad-luck gift.* But she loved its small solidness. It was real. He had given it to her. And it was still here. *Still here.*

Valentín commanded herself to stand up now, knowing that if she closed her eyes there would be no getting up again. She splashed her grey face, tried to gargle away the vomit taste and left the bathroom.

The precinct chief, a fat man with an agricultural face who addressed only men or tits directly, followed her with his eyes as she returned to her desk. It came as no great surprise when he shunted her on to the missing-persons desk. He might as well have tasked her with solving Fermat's Last Theorem using an abacus. And so the last few weeks had drifted by in a haze of painkillers and laughably hopeless cases. She tried to limit the amount of times per day she glanced over at Morel's empty desk.

Valentín thought back to how it began – a drunken send-off for a colleague somewhere, a year after being paired together. They had staggered back to the car. When he tried to kiss her on the back seat, she surprised herself by not rejecting him. Without considering the madness of it, she had thrust his head downwards and closed her eyes as she felt his beard scratch the inside of her thighs, the prickling and the tingling indistinguishable, the tongue of this unattractive man against her suddenly imperative. After she came, Morel rested his head on her hip and she fell asleep running her fingers over his scalp.

Nothing was said about it the next day. Externally, things carried on as normal but from then on the car itself was their own private chamber. Everything played out there. Exasperations, victories, laughter. Valentín loved being in that old car with him. Even silently sitting in traffic gave her pleasure. For a time, they were astronauts in orbit and Valentín had control of the stereo.

But Morel had kids to put through college. An angry ex-wife and lawyers to pay. Ends had to meet. Valentín never confronted him about his moonlighting with La Familia. After a while she had even come to help him on a few jobs. But Morel had been caught with his hand in the cookie jar – over sixty thousand American cookies, to be precise – and nobody was surprised when he didn't turn up for work one day. His rotting body was found a month later.

The graveyard shift was when Valentín would look at his file – a few sparse pages pertaining to an unsolved murder – signs of torture, plastic bag over the face, buried in the desert. It wasn't that she harboured any hope of his killer being brought to justice, that was beside the point for her; she just liked being able to see Morel's face.

Valentín looked out of the window, a dreary night stretching out. Little plats of streetlight, peach-coloured from the sodium vapour, twinkled against the swathes of darkness. Mist was crawling down from the mountains, swallowing what men had made.

Outside the police station a small group of Honduran women stood in quiet protest. One woman in her sixties, no taller than five feet, wore a sandwich board with the photograph of a young man on it.

ALIVE HE WAS TAKEN.
ALIVE I WANT HIM BACK.

The woman's eyes were hidden by the brim of her Nike cap but the tears on her cheeks shone in the streetlight. All the women wore these sandwich boards, as if their existence had been reduced only to finding those faces.

Valentín closed her eyes and thought of the beach cabin she'd grown up in. As a little girl, when she had nightmares she would creep out to the porch to look at the ocean. As night turned to dawn dove-grey cloud would roll in and the wind chimes would fuss. That was all she needed. In the mornings her father would wake her with a kiss on the forehead and a mug of chocolate.

But the cabin was long gone. Her father was gone. Morel was gone too. All she was left with was Ciudad Cabral and missing persons.

Her phone rang now. 'Valentín.'

'Front desk. There's a guy here asking to look at missing-persons records.'

In the waiting area of the central Ciudad Cabral police station Iwata was looking at the missing-persons posters that coated the walls. A large ceiling fan stirred the hot air. The Mexican flag hung limply behind the front desk.

A door opened and a short woman with a pale face emerged. The desk sergeant gestured to Iwata and she sized him up before approaching. 'You speak Spanish?'

Iwata nodded. 'I'm looking for some missing women. I think they came here.'

Valentín led him out to the parking lot behind the station. In the shadow of a cottonwood tree she lit up. 'I'm Detective Valentín. You a journalist?'

'Private investigator,' Iwata took out his ID.

'Well, this isn't America. You can't just walk in here and get access to our records. There are forms to fill out; it takes time. Even then I can't guarantee you'd get the relevant permissions.'

'How long?'

'A week. Maybe more.'

Iwata took out the pictures of the missing women and laid them on the brick wall. Valentín sighed but put on her spectacles.

'All American, I presume? If they were missing here, I'd know about it.' She looked at them in turn, but shook her head.

Then she came to Mara Zambrano's driver's licence. Valentín looked at it. She looked again and nodded.

'You know her?'

'She's not missing. Her name was Evelyn Olivera. She's dead.'

'That's not possible. I saw her two days ago.'

'Dead women make good aliases. This is fake. Evelyn had no driver's licence, let alone one from California.'

Iwata looked at the ID again. The cop was right. It

was a close likeness but it was not Mara Zambrano. Whoever he'd spoken to at Club Noir was not the person in the photograph. Why did she have a dead woman's ID?

'They found Evelyn's body a few hundred metres across the US border. She had been raped and shot.' Valentín shrugged. 'She was trying for a better life.'

Another connection. Another murder.

'So this is a fake name – you've never heard of Mara Zambrano?'

'Sure I have. Who hasn't? She was one of the most important actresses in the Golden Age of Mexican cinema. Hell, she was known in all of Latin America.'

Iwata scowled at the fake ID and pocketed it. 'Detective, where can I find Evelyn's family?'

'Thing is' – she blew out smoke – 'you're licensed to practise private investigations in the state of California, Mr Iwata. And that's a way away from here.'

'It would just be a few questions. It's very important.'

'To who? Your business?'

'The families of these women.'

Detective Valentín searched his eyes. Sighing, she stubbed out her cigarette. 'I'll give you the address, but you listen to me. You leave this city straight after, understand? The man that looks under rocks in Ciudad Cabral quickly finds the scorpion.'

Río Rosita was in the centre of Ciudad Cabral, on the south side of the eponymous river, so-called for its evening pink. But despite the delicate name, its banks had been concreted over long ago, hills of silt and trash now stacked up over the slow, putrid water. The night was tinted a sickly peach by the streetlight. Little makeshift bunkers, ñongos, had been burrowed in the concrete here, in the dirt, in the storm gates – a festering Xanadu for the marooned. Further along the river a sluice gate doubled as a shopfront for the dealers. A long line had formed.

At the bend in the river Iwata went up some rusted old stairs, as per the policewoman's instructions. This was Cuauhtémoc, a market since pre-Hispanic times, an open-air kermis of barter, bliss, bereavement. If Ciudad Cabral was a family, then this market was the problem child. The streets here were not so much streets, more little runnels of black-market life. The smell of grilled meat and the sound of cumbia music buffeted him. Everywhere Iwata looked he saw love, scuffed knuckles, scams. To him, it just looked like another version of Santee Alley.

Iwata weaved through bodies, the night crowd merry on cheap beer-margaritas. Never-ending stalls formed of rickety metal frames were clad in multicoloured tarpaulin – cloned DVDs, counterfeit sneakers, fake soccer jerseys, Real Madrid, Atlético and FC Barcelona. Though it was open air, the fairy lights overhead gave the market a feel of containment. Everywhere there was the sound of scooters and the bellowed mantra of Cuauhtémoc: *Ofertas! Ofertas! Ofertas!*

The market was heaving tonight; it was Holy Week, after all. Though the official saint of Ciudad Cabral was

Francis of Assisi, the patron saint of this quarter was La Flaca, the skinny one – Santa Muerte. Iwata saw her shrine in the middle of the market, festooned with flowers and offerings. The skeleton was dressed in white, her bones primped with pearls and flowers. At her feet, people had left apples, toys, money, tequila. There were cakes, bowls of chicken with mole, small clumps of marijuana. Her bony hands were outstretched, beseeching outsiders unto her – the outcasts, the wretched, the *non grata*. Those with illnesses, those with terrible secrets, those that lived with curses. The inhabitants of Río Rosita knew that, where other saints would not, Santa Muerte was willing to grant darker blessings.

At the end of the market Iwata saw his destination, a colourful tenement block one earthquake away from crumbling. Inside, it was a maze of cracked concrete and precarious narrow walkways, children playing in its corridors, plants spilling over balcony railings, clothes on the line like bunting.

The door to Evelyn's mother's apartment was ajar.

Iwata nudged it open. 'Mrs Olivera?'

Inside there were six beds, each one occupied with men and women at varying stages of deterioration. They were stick thin, their legs little more than bones wrapped in skin, their kneecaps wider than their thighs. All over they had track marks and ruined veins – at the joints, at the ankles, toes blackened. The tang of death hung in the air.

A man in a nappy at the end of the room had his face covered with a cloth, too weak to fend off the flies. In the next bed a gaunt young man with tattoos ignored his neighbour's death rattle and watched TV. The local team was playing. It was still o–o as the match entered its final throes.

A woman in a Mickey Mouse T-shirt wearing latex gloves came out of the bathroom holding a tray of syringes. 'Who are you?'

Iwata showed his card. 'I'm a private investigator. Are you the mother of Evelyn Olivera?'

'No, and she died a few months ago.'

'Are you a relative?'

'I live next door. She was my friend. But what does a man in your business want with Patricia Olivera?'

'I'm investigating missing women.'

The neighbour led him out to the balcony. Children were playing in the courtyard below. 'I don't know who you are, and I don't care to. If you want to ask about my friend, I'm willing to talk. But you should know that asking questions here will lead to bad things. You understand that?'

'I understand.'

She nodded. 'Evelyn left her mother's place to live with a relative. They had argued, I know that. But Patricia wouldn't go into detail. She only found out Evelyn had left the county later. She held on to the hope that maybe the girl would call or send a postcard. But it was the police that called. When Patricia found out her daughter had been killed, she lost the will to live. They even told her Evelyn was pregnant when she died. Can you imagine? It led my friend to the river, to drugs. She ended up with the same sickness as those people inside. I cared for her at the end. Before Patricia died, she asked me to look after others suffering from her sickness. Here I am.'

Iwata nodded respectfully. They both looked down at a little girl on the floor below them explaining to a Labrador how to tie shoelaces.

'Ma'am, did Evelyn know somebody called Mara Zambrano?'

'Like the film actress? I don't know. Did she cross the border too?'

'Possibly.'

'Then there is someone you could ask. They call him Lalo. He's the one that helped her cross over. Like everyone else in this city, he belongs to Bebé Rivera.'

'Where can I find him?'

'You'll find him in church.'

17. We Are Watching

Iwata was continually delayed by crowds and bad traffic. In the city's central plaza cars came to a standstill to catch a glimpse of a crucifixion reenactment, complete with Roman soldiers and wailing mothers. Over the road, the street vendors were doing good business. Children skipped along the packed sidewalks and licked at flavoured-ice cups.

The only lane that moved was for taxis so Iwata parked up and hailed one.

'Where to?'

'San Isaías.' Iwata reeled off the address the neighbour had given him.

'Ah, lovely church. My mother got married there.'

The driver turned out to be talkative and unhurried, the opposite of what was needed. At a red light a wave of euphoric children ran past. 'School's out and they go crazy, huh?'

'Mm.'

'When I was a kid the raspados were made with ice from the mountain and real hibiscus flowers. Now days these guys make them with syrup from Walmart.' He shrugged. 'Memories are just sandcastles built at low tide.'

Iwata cut through the philosophy with a five-hundred-peso note. 'I need to ask you something.'

He chuckled. 'If you're looking for a girl, then we shouldn't be heading for a church.'

'Bebé Rivera. Where can I find him?'

The driver eyed Iwata hard in the mirror before handing the money back. 'You don't need to pay for that. Everyone knows where he can be found.' He pointed at the mountain to the north. Squinting, Iwata saw a little cluster of lights overlooking the city and what looked like a white mansion.

'How do I meet him?'

The driver laughed. 'Just ring the bell and ask for tea with lemon.'

In the church of San Isaías Iwata took a seat in the back pew. The floor tiles were black and the walls were adorned only with hand-painted verse and dark wood Christ figurines. Evening Mass had just started.

To his surprise Iwata crossed himself with everyone else when the priest spoke. As he listened to the words of resurrection and victory over death he kept his eyes on the soft orange glow of the votive candles.

When it was over the priest, a tall man with a wild grey beard, chatted amiably with the faithful as they shuffled out. Finally, Iwata approached.

'Father Lalo?'

'That's me. But I haven't seen you before.'

'I'm not from around here.' Iwata wondered if there was any place in the world where he'd be able to refute such a statement. 'I need to discuss something with you.'

'Confession will be taken after Mass tomorrow.'

'I'm not confessing anything.'

Father Lalo's eyes lost their warmth. 'Then what can I do for you?'

'Do you know Mara Zambrano?'

'No, I do not. Now, if I'm not being rude –'

'Evelyn Olivera. I know she came to you for help. And I know you have answers.'

The priest tugged on his beard for a moment, then led Iwata to the confessional box and slipped past the drapes. 'Speak quietly.'

Iwata looked at the mahogany frame of the booth, almost blood red. Above the grille, a Bible verse had been etched:

Si vuestros pecados fueren como la grana, como la nieve serán emblanquecidos; si fueren rojos como el carmesí, vendrán a ser como blanca lana.

Though your sins are as scarlet, they shall be as white as snow; though they are red as crimson, they shall be white as wool.

Iwata moved his lips close to the grille and words almost tumbled out: 'Forgive me, Father, for I have sinned.'

Instead, it was Lalo who spoke. 'Look, it's true that I used to help people to cross, but that was a long time ago. I can't do the same for you –'

'I didn't come for that. I want to know who Mara Zambrano is.'

'I told you, I don't know any Mara Zambrano. As for

227

Evelyn, she was a good girl but she was living in sin. She cut herself off from the world, from her family. And all for that' – he struggled to say the word – 'homosexual.'

'A friend of hers?'

'No, her cousin. Adelmo Contreras.' Lalo winced at the name. 'They lived together in a cottage outside the city. It was . . . an abomination.'

'They wanted to leave this place?'

'Evelyn, God forgive her, came to me for help. Begged me. Said they couldn't live here any longer, that she wanted a new start for her and the baby. What could I do? I arranged for them to cross the border. She thanked me and went to the migrant shelter.'

'Where is this Adelmo Contreras?'

'They crossed together. That's all I know.'

'The migrant shelter, where is it?'

'The Diódoro Latapí Refuge is on the outskirts near the border. It's where they all go. The coyotes come at dusk to make their money.'

'And what about you, Father? How do you make yours?'

'Be sober, my son.' the priest spoke sadly. 'Be vigilant; for the devil, as a roaring lion, walketh about, seeking whom he may devour.'

Iwata left the booth.

Outside the church Iwata pulled his shirt tighter around his body. The nights were colder here. He stepped on to the sidewalk to hail a taxi when a car horn resounded behind him. It was Detective Valentín behind the wheel.

She rolled down the window. 'What did I tell you about poking your nose in?'

'A man can't pray?'

Laughing, she started the engine. 'Get in.'

It was nearing midnight in a packed dive bar near the river. Reggaetón jangled out of crappy speakers and green neon illuminated thick clouds of marijuana smoke. Valentín was drinking cheap mezcal, Iwata was drinking Mexican Coke, made with real sugar. Between them, there was a bowl of grasshopper salsa and tortilla chips.

'I like it here,' he offered.

'Me too.' Valentín smiled. 'No cops.'

'How did you find me?'

'A little birdie told me.' She held his eyes too long. 'You married, Iwata?'

'Used to be.' He looked at the dead grasshoppers in the sauce. 'You?'

'There was a guy once. But the prick went and got himself killed.' she toasted the river outside.

'What happened to him?'

'Just this place.'

'You ever think about leaving?'

'Where to?' Valentín smiled. Some smiles were shields. Others were wounds.

'I don't know, somewhere men aren't decapitated and slung over bridges.'

'Over here or over there.' She shrugged. 'Everybody dies, Iwata.'

'Some more than others.'

'You know' – Valentín drained the last of her mezcal – 'I could tell you were a cop the second you opened your mouth.'

'A lot of private investigators are former police. It's not much of a guess.'

'It wasn't your little ID card that told me. It was your tone. Even in another language I recognized it.'

'Okay, I'll bite. Why?'

'Most people live by some guiding principle – money, success, religion, whatever. And they use those principles to place themselves in the scheme of things, the world itself. Now all those principles will, in the end, be self-serving. Mother Teresa didn't wash feet for fun, right?'

'Go on.'

'Yet in you I see the detective's contradiction: your only guiding principle is the truth. It's why you're here. I mean, I know you didn't come to watch me drink mezcal because you like the shape of my ass.'

Iwata laughed. 'Maybe if we were standing at the bar I'd have a better view. But I haven't heard a contradiction in your theory yet.'

'The truth is your god. It's your everything. There's no self-serving in it. It just is.'

'Right.'

'But why? Why do you live by it?'

'I don't know.'

'*That's* the contradiction I'm talking about. See, Iwata, I never knew why, either. Yet we give our entire lives to it. We see things people aren't designed to see. We try to make sense of the senseless. We expose ourselves to things that ruin us. So how do we live with all that?'

'Learn to accept. Disassociate. Compartmentalize.'

'Exactly. And so we live in this strange no-man's-land where belief and feeling led us here to begin with. But then, in order to survive, we've learned to stop believing and feeling anything. You're like me – your heart is good but rotten.'

Iwata could only nod. He liked Valentín. It wasn't anything particularly to do with her, more just the fact that she inhabited the same world as him. There were lots of lonely people. But few lived in his particular brand of solitude.

'Valentín, I saw something this morning and I can't get it out of my head. Driving into the city, I saw a headless man hanging from a bridge.'

'La Familia Cabral.' She motioned for another glass. 'They're the reason you should leave this place.'

'I'm sorry, I'm not going anywhere.'

'Sooner or later they are going to notice you.'

'Then you might as well tell me what I'm dealing with.'

'Fine.' Valentín waited for the waitress to leave, then she spoke in a low voice. 'Fifteen years ago they were just a self-defence group, farmer vigilantes, sick of the kidnappings and murders by the dominant cartel at the time. They followed a strict code. No innocent blood to be spilled, the spoils to be given to charity. They managed to destroy the cartel and they evolved into an official peace-keeping force to ensure Ciudad Cabral remained free of drugs and murder. That was the plan.'

'So what happened?'

She swallowed her mezcal with great difficulty. 'Infil-trations from other cartels. Lines blurred. The families at the top got a taste for the good life. And so the narco-flow was reintroduced. A decade later, they're just a more savage mutation of what went before them. Today, La Familia Cabral controls a dozen major cities across two border states. It's become an aggressive corporate acqui-sitions unit. A paramilitary organization. A terror organization. The black trucks, the masks, the behead-ings on YouTube? They were doing this a decade before ISIS.'

'Why that name? La Familia?'

'In the beginning, members were all brothers, cous-ins, fathers. Everybody knew everybody. It was a community thing. But now they're sending several bil-lion dollars clean to Saint Lucia each year. They own copper-mining projects in South America. Gold, iron ore, wind farms. And what does this city get for it?' Valentín pointed at the river. Human shadows drifted over the dead water. 'Thousands living in ñongos, deported and hooked. Black ribbons on doors. Bodies hanging from bridges. Factories full of workers being paid one sixth of what an American makes. Children missing in the desert. And what do we do? We keep the public fooled into thinking they're unaffected by the people that live in those camps. Or the child prostitutes in the Cuauhtémoc basements. Or the fresh bodies that La Familia serve up every other week. The old ladies stabbing the earth all around this fucking city hoping to smell rotten flesh so they can find their sons, daughters, husbands.'

Iwata looked at his empty Coke bottle. 'Tell me about the coyotes that come to the immigrant shelters. They belong to La Familia?'

Valentín nodded. 'Iwata, there's a river of money running through that border and everybody's thirsty.'

'What about Bebé Rivera? Where does he fit into this?'

She looked at him for a moment before replying. 'How do you know that name?'

'A little birdie.'

'Every person in this city knows who he is. And not a single person will say a word about him, that much I can promise you.' She downed the last of mezcal, put money on the table and looked around. 'Not that I should be telling you any of this.'

'Where are you going?'

'To piss.' She stood gingerly and squeezed Iwata's arm. 'Then you're driving me home before I say something really stupid.'

When she returned from the toilet Valentín was ashen-faced. Iwata helped her to the car and laid her in the passenger seat. He drove slowly as she mumbled directions. Several times he stopped to let her vomit. In snatches of sleep she moaned a man's name. By the time they reached her apartment Valentín could barely move. He carried her up the stairs, shocked at how little she weighed. Her plush furnishings seemed at odds with her personality.

As he laid her down on her bed she whispered something.

'Iwata?'

'Yes.'

'Get out of here.'

'I'm leaving.'

'No. I mean this city. Leave tonight. Don't come back.'

He managed to convince her to drink some water before he left.

Outside, Iwata hailed a taxi and asked to be taken back to his hotel. At this hour the roads were empty. As they neared the motorway Iwata saw a long tunnel, its mouth grey like dead koi. On the concrete walls a message had been spray-painted in jagged black letters:

Recuerda. Te estamos observando.

Remember. We are watching you.

The next morning was grey and hot. Iwata was driving through the eastern outskirts of Ciudad Cabral. It was empty land, except for warehouses and manufacturing plants. A sign proudly proclaimed the city's designation as a Special Economic Zone following the NAFTA agreement. Underneath, graffiti had renamed the place:

SWEATSHOP ALLEY: WHERE LABOUR
IS ALWAYS COMPETITIVE!

El Diario Cabral, the city's only remaining newspaper, was hidden behind a sprawling dairy factory. There was no sign outside, no clue to its function. If what Valentín had said was true, nobody in this city was going to speak to Iwata about Bebé Rivera. He needed records, documentation, hard facts.

Iwata got out of the old Mazda and the distant stink of milk hit his nose. He took out his binoculars and surveyed the building. The entrance was covered by several armed security guards. Iwata could see he wouldn't be getting in without an invitation. Mulling it over, he got back in the car.

Iwata drove through the grand old boulevards near the university, ancient warped trees breaking through the concrete. At the red light a little girl juggled for change while her father did magic tricks with a white dove. Taxi drivers stared straight ahead, bored and hot, plastic virgins hanging from their rear-view mirrors.

In these beautifully decaying colonias, poetry had been painted on walls in white:

Que bonito detalle tuyo, ese de existir.

What a lovely detail of yours, that of existing.

Para soñar la vida, abre los ojos.

To dream life, open your eyes.

It was mid-morning by the time Iwata arrived back at Cuauhtémoc market. He approached the first Asian vendor he came to and bought an entire bin bag of cloned DVDs. He threw it in the trunk of the Mazda, then drove back to the newspaper.

Iwata changed into a faded T-shirt and cargo shorts. He left his gun in the glovebox. With the bag of DVDs on his back, Iwata approached the building. The first security guard immediately shook his head.

'Come on, pal. Hit the road.'

With a grin, Iwata put on his best broken accent. '*Ofertas! Ofertas! Ofertas!*'

'Hold on a sec.' The second security guard peered inside the bag. 'What have you got?'

'Very cheap! Very cheap!'

'Have you got *Jurassic World*?'

'All best film! All new!'

The first guard rolled his eyes. 'Come on, man. You'll drop us in the shit.'

'Relax, it's Holy Week.' The second security guard took out a handful of DVDs. 'I'll take these and you get ten minutes, okay?'

Once he was through Iwata ducked into the toilet, changed back into his shirt and took out one of his fake lanyards. He dumped the DVDs in the trash and made his way up the stairs, passing derelict dotcom companies from the early 2000s.

El Diario Cabral took up the top three floors. Iwata entered without incident and crossed the office like he belonged there. It was open plan with some sixty desks, only around a third of which were occupied. The floor tiles were white, the desk dividers red and there were Mexican flags everywhere. On the wall there was a framed photograph of a young man. There were flowers beneath it. Also in the frame there was an old front page:

President, we ask for justice for Roberto — for journalism —
for freedom of speech.

Iwata ignored the one or two glances he received and
made his way to the back of the office. There he found
what he was looking for: the records room. It was a glum
room that smelled of soggy paper, rows and rows of tall
shelves stealing all the light from a small window at the
end. Next to the microfiche machine was an old PC.
Iwata turned it on and was relieved to find that it had no
password; it had obviously been left out for the purposes
of basic reference searches. Iwata already knew *El Diario
Cabral* didn't have much of a website but even so he
searched for 'Mara Zambrano'. There were dozens of
returns and it took Iwata quite some time only to dis-
cover that every single one pertained to the film actress,
the last one being an article in memoriam.

Next he tried searching 'Bebé Rivera'. There were
only two returns. The first article was six years old, concerning the marriage of local business magnate Edgardo
'Bebé' Rivera to a well-known flamenco dancer from
Spain. In the grainy picture his lips were very full, his
face was plump and his apricot chin carried a prominent
beauty spot. He was half a head shorter than his wife,
despite his large perm.

The second article was more recent, concerning the
takeover of the local football team.

LOCAL BUSINESS TYCOON OVERJOYED AT OWNERSHIP OF BOYHOOD FOOTBALL CLUB

The takeover, agreed yesterday afternoon, will see Mr Edgardo 'Bebé' Rivera inject millions of pesos of his own money into the struggling team via his investment fund. He declined to answer questions but told media outlets: 'There will be money for new transfers, debt will be cleared and fans finally can look forward to a bright future for Club Deportivo Cabral.'

In this photograph, Bebé was posing with the club manager and the team captain. He had gained weight, his perm even bigger now. The club captain was wearing the kit, a deep red. And on it, the new sponsor: Grupo Valle Dorado.

There it was. A link. Hard and cold as a bathroom floor. Iwata didn't know what it proved but he knew now that there was, on some level, a connection between the surgeries that Meredith and Geneviève had undergone at Fox Hills Feminization and this football team. Both were being bankrolled by the same real-estate investment fund. And from the looks of things, that meant being bankrolled by Bebé Rivera.

Iwata span in his chair at the interconnectivity of it. It tantalized him. It meant everything. It meant nothing. It was a magic-eye picture that he was staring at; if only its true shape would reveal itself. Why would Rivera pay large sums of money for his girls to have surgery, then be flown out to Mexico, only to then have them disappear?

Iwata searched for Valle Dorado. There wasn't much. The fund had been started some five years ago. In the single article, Bebé Rivera was opening a new housing complex, named after the fund, just outside Ciudad Cabral with golden scissors, a crowd of jubilant people in suits behind him. 'I just want people to be housed and happy. Now that we can have the required funding, then Valle Dorado can be a dream home for families for decades to come.'

1975 – Tokyo

The Mannequins

That afternoon Yoko clock-watched grumpily. She was eager to get home to search the classifieds for a way to make extra cash. Perhaps it was the fatigue but today her debt weighed particularly heavily on her. She couldn't help but picture herself being dragged out of her front door by bailiffs, her neighbours gawping.

A man cleared his throat and Yoko snapped on her smile.

'Welcome to Department Store Q, sir.'

He was handsome, maybe forty years old, prominent eyebrows, a neat moustache. He wore an expensively cut suit and rested his hand on her counter, a gold ring on his little ringer tapping lightly on the glass like a conductor.

'I'm looking for a gift. Something with class.'

'Of course, sir.' Yoko beamed. 'Is this gift for any particular occasion?'

'No.'

'And who is the gift for?'

He smiled. 'I can't tell you that.'

To her surprise, Yoko laughed. But it was the laugh that belonged to her, not the customers. She lowered her voice now. 'Don't tell me you're having an affair.'

'You tell me something. Did you bring a jacket with you today?'

'Why do you ask?'

'They said it's going to rain later.'

'Please don't worry about me, sir. I have my jacket in the changing room.'

'Good. So. What about this one? Do you like this?' He tapped the glass counter. The gold necklace had a small jade pendant formed by two cranes, their wings and beaks touching. The price tag was well above a month's salary for Yoko. 'Sir, you're teasing me. You didn't need advice at all, you have wonderful taste.'

'I'm glad you think so. I'll take it. Please wrap the gift.'

Yoko placed the necklace in the most tasteful box she had and wrapped it with all the diligence she could muster. The colour of the ribbon complemented the paper and the handsome man seemed pleased with her work. He opened a large leather wallet and flipped through a selection of credit cards without any real consideration, a man picking a parking space in an empty lot.

That evening, as Yoko was closing up, she overheard the girls talking about her: 'Did you see the way Puppet Master was flirting with that customer?'

'I know! It was embarrassing. We all want to make a sale but there is such a thing as keeping your dignity, don't you think?'

'Notice she used a blue box. She only does that with the handsome men.'

Yoko waited until they were gone and then changed into

her own clothes, swearing to herself. As if any of those dumpy bitches would even be capable of flirting to make a sale! Not that she had been flirting. The man had clearly made up his mind by himself.

As she put on her jacket she felt something against her waist. A solid weight, familiar somehow. Yoko put her hand into her pocket and took out the same box she had wrapped that afternoon. Beneath the ribbon there was a business card.

Mr IMAI
Commercial Director
– 452 CORPORATION –

Yoko had never heard of the corporation, but she was impressed with Imai's title. On the back of the business card, something had been written in rich blue ink. It was the name of one of the finest restaurants in Osaka, with a date and time underneath.

'How presumptuous!'

It was a nice necklace, but Yoko didn't even know the man. The idea that he could set eyes on her, buy her the first thing he pointed at and secure a date with her three days later was almost offensive. Even though she was sorely tempted by the offer, Yoko made a point of making plans with a male friend on that night instead. Still, she thought about the handsome but presumptuous Mr Imai the whole time.

Some days later, while selling dainty peep-toe shoes to a customer with feet too wide for them, the telephone at

Yoko's counter rang. She excused herself, hoping it was one of the part-time jobs she had enquired about.

'Department Store Q, how may I –'

'You didn't come.'

'Excuse me?'

'I sat there alone like an idiot. Did you get my gift?'

Yoko lowered her voice and wrapped the telephone cord around her finger like a snake. 'Mr Imai, I presume.'

'Then you did get it. Are you wearing it?'

'No,' she lied. 'I only told you I liked it to make a sale.'

Imai laughed heartily. 'I'm going to wait for you outside the department store tonight. I insist on taking you to dinner. Just once. Consider it a one-off display of gratitude. After that, you have no obligations whatsoever to me.'

'Mr Imai, I'm serving a customer. Moreover, a gift that comes with obligations can hardly be called a gift.' She slipped two fingers inside her blouse to touch the jade cranes.

'Well.' He was flipping through some papers. 'You have me there.'

'You keep harassing me and I'll throw the necklace down the toilet.'

'Hang on.' She could hear him smiling. 'I thought you weren't wearing it?'

'Good afternoon, Mr Imai.'

That night Yoko closed up the store and fought her umbrella open against the driving rain. She was about to cross the road and hurry over to Nippombashi Station when a black Mitsubishi Debonair pulled up and the window wound down. It was Imai, grinning from ear to ear.

'Get in. Come on, you'll drown like a rat out here.'

The driver opened the door for her.

Yoko sighed. 'You better take me somewhere nice.'

'Remember what you said? I have excellent taste.'

Thud.

Yoko woke up. The darkness was warm. Gelatinous. She felt a great weight on her chest, as if a man were sitting on her. But when she opened her eyes there was nothing there. She was naked and still drunk. Neither of those facts troubled her particularly; she clearly remembered sleeping with Imai, and she wasn't going to worry about that now. Sitting up on her futon, Yoko felt the bruises on her breasts.

'Kentaro?' she called out in the dark.

Imai did not reply.

As Yoko stood up she felt pain in her vagina. This didn't worry her too much either. Imai had been a voracious lover. She had enjoyed it, but she had decided midway through never to see him again. She was sure that this would suit him too, as he was almost certainly married. Life would go on.

'Kentaro? Kentaro, are you there?'

Only a train clacking past in the distance answered her. She was about to get out of bed when something caught her eye across the room. The atlas had fallen on to the floor. She slipped her hand under the sheet and felt her vagina. It was hot and soaked.

In a panic, she ripped the sheet back. Between her legs there was a gushing puddle of blood. Yelping, Yoko struggled to her feet and staggered to the bathroom, dripping as she went. She had never seen so much blood, let alone from her own body. She got into the bathtub and filled it with cold water, trembling as it crept up around her, slowly turning pink.

The next morning, Yoko called her manager and told him she couldn't come in due to illness. As she had been such a good employee, he hardly said a word about it.

When she finally returned to Q five days later, she arrived late and dishevelled, her hair up in a hasty bun. She found it hard to engage the customers and made practically no money that day.

By the evening, many of her colleagues had left early, as it was Autumnal Equinox Day and the store was practically empty. Ordinarily, the temperature in the store was perfect but, for whatever reason, Yoko couldn't get warm. She had bundled herself up in scarves from the returned stock in the back room and was almost falling asleep when, a few minutes before closing time, a gaunt woman wearing sunglasses rapped her knuckles on the counter.

'Long day,' she said, her voice quiet. She was roughly Yoko's age, wearing the Q uniform.

'New?' Yoko replied.

The gaunt woman laughed. 'I've been here for a long time.'

'Explains the old uniform. But why haven't I seen you before?'

'I'm on a different level.'

Yoko scowled. 'Well, if you think you're just going to move

up here for the easy commission, you've got another think coming. I'm the senior employee around here, got it? Now beat it, I have to close up soon.'

The gaunt woman said nothing, she just left. Yoko finished her stock papers. It was only as she was locking up with the security guard that she realized how strange the encounter had been.

Dear Mr Kuroki,

I'm afraid this is all I have for now. I hope it wasn't too excruciating. If you're wondering how the story ends: Mr Imai has planted a cursed seed in Yoko that begins to turn her into plastic! When there's a big fire she tries to save the mannequins but she gets trapped in there by the strange woman who she encountered earlier (a ghost). When the fire is finally extinguished, her body is nowhere to be found. Yoko has ended up as the fifth mannequin, burnt and disfigured, shut away in the basement, with nobody to see her again for the rest of time. (Not exactly an upbeat ending, I know.) Well, that's it. Thank you again. And sorry for taking up so much of your time.

Yours sincerely,
Nozomi Iwata

Mr Kuroki leapt up from his desk and burst out of his office. Startled, the secretary looked up. He waved the envelope that had contained *The Mannequins* at her.

'Who delivered this?'

'A young woman, about an hour ago.'

'Did she leave her contact details?'

'Yes.'

'Call her right away. She's going to win us the Noma Prize.'

18. The Material

Dusk. The Mazda stopped outside a tall reinforced gate. A handsome sign proclaimed the Valle Dorado Luxury Complex. To look the part, Iwata had bought a suit from the tailor near the hotel. There was nothing he could do about the car. He had a spiel prepared but, to his shock, the gate quietly rumbled open. Beyond it, an enormous housing complex stretched out. Iwata hadn't expected to get in, and he certainly didn't know what he'd find. Only that what he'd discovered in Los Angeles and Ciudad Cabral seemed to knot together in this housing complex.

The security guard emerged from the sentry box, frowned at the Mazda and directed Iwata to visitor parking. A short man in a tan suit was waiting. He offered his hand eagerly.

'Mr Siew?'

'That's right.' Iwata smiled for all he was worth and shook it.

'You're a little early.'

'Sorry about that.'

'Oh no, please don't apologize.' His smile was toilet white. 'I'm Gustavo Garza. I'm the principal broker here. How was your flight?'

'Ah, fine.'

'Singapore is a long way to come. Can I get you anything?'

'That's very kind, but no, thank you.'

'You want to get straight down to it. I understand.' Garza gave a puzzled smile. 'We are ready to proceed but, Mr Siew, if you don't mind me asking, will your daughter be arriving soon?'

'I'm sorry?'

'Your daughter. She is with you, yes?'

'She's at the hotel.'

'Ah. Of course. It's a long flight.'

'She's very tired.'

'Completely understandable. Unfortunately, we are on a tight timeframe here. We want to care for her as soon as possible. She'll be able to come first thing tomorrow?'

'Absolutely. That's what I wanted to tell you.'

'Very good. Now, Mr Siew. Before we go any further, I want to assure you that your daughter will receive the best care. It's a solemn guarantee from my organization.'

Iwata placed his hand over his heart in appreciation and Garza nodded, as if their business was concluded. 'Very good, Mr Siew.'

'Has your organization been here a long time?' Iwata looked around the complex. The villas were all identical, large and modernistic. There were no people, no animals, no cars. Little parks were empty, swings were still.

'This particular facility is fairly recent but, yes, we've been doing this a long time.' Garza smiled. 'Since you're here, I imagine you'd like to view the material?'

'If possible, I'd appreciate that.'

'Of course. You've paid a lot of money. Unit 2234 isn't far, but you'll have to give me a moment. We don't usually do this.' Garza took out his phone and dialled. 'Listen, I'll need ten minutes, the client wants to see the merch—' He eyed Iwata now. '. . . But that's not possible, I'm looking at him . . . Are you sure? . . . All right, I'll be there in thirty seconds.'

'Everything all right?' Despite the churning in his stomach, Iwata kept his voice even.

Garza gave a strange grin. 'Seems there's been a misunderstanding. Please wait here.'

As soon as he was out of sight Iwata broke into a sprint. He turned left and right at random, his running stamina having seemingly abandoned him. There were voices now, small but angry on the night. He hid behind a tree, panting, fumbling for calm. *Which way is out?*

And then he saw it. Unit 2234. Iwata approached the front door and tried the handle. It fell open. Inside, it was dark and still. There was total silence; no dull buzz of a refrigerator. There was no refrigerator, no furniture. The kitchen too was empty. The dining room was completely bare, as were the study, the utility room and the garden.

In the downstairs bathroom Iwata found streaks of old blood in the sink, brown at the outer edges, pink near the drain. In the bin underneath there were latex gloves crumpled up and the faint smell of overripe meat.

Drawing his gun, Iwata crept upstairs. He smelled the next room before he saw it – an antiseptic stench. Switching on the light, he saw an operating table in the middle of the room, mobile lamps, metallic carts with drawers, a video tower. There were refrigerators containing various fluids and IV bags. A sideboard held rolls of paper towels, forceps, scalpels, boxes of anti-rejection medications.

Instinct told Iwata to get the hell out. It also told him there were answers in this place.

He returned to the corridor. The final door was closed. Taking a breath, Iwata swung it open. It stank of the same kind of antiseptic, but stronger, an intense mothball putrescence. And then his eyes adjusted. There was a young girl on a gurney, maybe nine years old. Her skin was dark, her eyes were closed. Several large straps had her tightly restrained. The man sitting in the seat next to her stood up, his newspaper dropping to the floor. He was wearing the same uniform as the security guard in the sentry box.

Iwata raised his gun. 'Don't move.'

Tentative compliance. 'The fuck are you?'

'The one holding the gun. What are you doing here?'

'I'm the babysitter.' He said this as if it were evident.

'Who's the girl?'

'The baby.'

Iwata's head was swimming. He didn't understand this place, its reason for existing, but he felt it. *Since you're here, I imagine you'd like to view the material?* Bile began to rise in his throat. And now there were voices downstairs.

Iwata turned to lock the door. Babysitter rushed him. Iwata span and snapped the butt of the gun into his nose. Babysitter dropped.

Boots thundered up the stairs, Garza's voice clear over the sound of them.

Iwata hurried over to the girl, his trembling hands fumbling with her restraints. 'Okay, honey. Let's get out of here.'

Her eyes lolled open but they had no focus. She moaned something small.

Outside, Garza barked orders and there was a shoulder smash at the door. Iwata had only one hand free, her other limbs were still secured. Another slam, the door convulsing in its frame. He looked hopelessly down at the girl. 'I'm sorry,' Iwata bleated. 'I'm so sorry.'

He picked up a metal stool, smashed the window and climbed into its frame. The door collapsed. Iwata jumped as the gunshots roared.

He landed badly and staggered out of sight. Dragging himself over the garden fence, Iwata was now in the alleyway between houses. Limping past five of them, he hefted himself over another fence. Landing in the soil with a yelp, he hunkered down in a bush and waited. Seconds later, there were boots on concrete. Iwata held his breath.

'See anything?'

'Don't see shit.'

'You take the south quadrant, I'll take this path.'

The footsteps thudded out of earshot. Iwata closed his eyes and tried to contain his panic. The pain in his ankle was bad but he knew he couldn't stay here.

Catching his breath as best he could, Iwata scrambled around the side of the house and saw Garza in the middle of the street, standing by a car. He was facing away, talking on the phone. Limping over, Iwata pistol-whipped him. Garza fell. But now Iwata was being wrenched away by a guard, locked in a chokehold from behind, almost lifting him off his feet. Planting both feet on the car, Iwata pushed backwards, sending them both to the tarmac. The gun went flying. But the guard still had the hold in place; Iwata's face was reddening, his struggle floundering. He saw a finger in his peripheral vision and bit down hard. The guard screamed and let go. Before Iwata could think he snatched up the gun from the floor.

'Get back!' His hand was shaking violently, his words wet with blood.

'What, you gonna shoot me, Chino?'

Iwata heard voices. At the end of the street, more guards were running towards them.

'See?' The man smiled. 'You're not shooting anyone.' With a snarl, he charged.

Iwata fired twice. Like make-believe, the guard span, a hefty ballerina falling to the ground. The sound was like a receding tide, then there was a throbbing silence. Blinking, Iwata got into the car. He spat out blood and smashed the car into reverse. There were two loud pops, then three, the glass of the rear windshield shattering.

In less than a minute Iwata was back on the road to Ciudad Cabral, the calm night wind whistling through the broken window.

Iwata parked the stolen car on the edge of Cuauhtémoc market. With his torn suit, bruises and limp, he cut an amusing figure to the night crowd, who figured him for a city sort who had come downmarket to cut loose.

He tossed his jacket in a gutter and stuck to the packed stalls, 'Gangnam Style' blaring out of the speakers. Young couples sat on a low brick wall above the river with fermented agave-sap drinks. Trios of mariachis passed through them, trying to agree romantic ballads for a fee. A group of young men wearing ranchero hats were leaning against a brand-new Escalade and drinking Herradura tequila. All of them had tattoos – secret numbers, clown markings, Santa Muerte symbols. They were arguing about the match earlier: Monarcas had lost at home o–1 to Santos Laguna. Iwata glanced at them and they stopped talking now.

Reaching the end of the market, Iwata entered the tenement block. He gripped the railing and dragged himself up the stairs, checking over his shoulder every few paces. He knocked on the same door he had come to before.

The neighbour opened up and death wafted out. It was familiar to Iwata by now.

The woman led him to the kitchen and poured him a glass of Coca-Cola. They both noticed his hands shaking and he put them under the table. From the next room, they could hear a throaty moaning. Iwata sipped his drink but tasted nothing. He tried not to dwell on the absurdity of reality, that he had shot a man, the weight of the gun recoiling in his hand as it fired.

'I don't have anything else to offer you,' the neighbour

254

said, as if life's own narrator. She nodded at the next room. 'They don't eat.'

'I'm not hungry.'

They sat in silence. The TV was on, the news on mute. Iwata spent a long time watching the shadows of cars passing across the wall like children's theatre. He was breathing hard. He needed to focus on something, on anything else. And as ever, his lifebelt was his case.

'I spoke to the priest,' he said. 'He told me about Evelyn. About Adelmo Contreras.'

The neighbour's face screwed up. 'That fucking boy is the reason Evelyn is dead.'

'They were cousins?'

She was going to say something more, but there was shouting in the courtyard outside. The neighbour went over to the window. Men in ranchero hats were hammering on doors, shouting for the Chinese man in the white shirt.

The neighbour turned to look at him. Without a word, Iwata stood up and walked past her. He slipped out of the tenement block by the back and headed for the river. He knew he had to get out of the city.

Late night. A desolate road cutting through dark, empty lots. Iwata was walking with his head down against the hard wind, his hand curled around his empty gun. It was cold in his pocket, as though it had never been fired before. Somewhere far away, Iwata could hear coyotes. Their howls seemed painful, as if stalking the desert night were a burden.

Nearing the old power station, he cut through a plot, empty except for rubble, dead batteries and plastic bottles. To the west, further out in the desert, he saw the floodlit car plant. Hulking freighters came and went, coming to give, coming to take.

Iwata wasn't sure where he was, but he knew this direction would take him back to the hotel. He had no choice: his passport was there. He passed an abandoned factory, then a closed gas station, emerging underneath a motorway flyover. He saw no one. Behind the slick sound of his footsteps a distant, slooshing drone of traffic could be heard in the wet night. Iwata scanned the parked cars for watchful passengers, or the glimmer of a gun barrel in the dark. There was nothing.

Winding through the old districts of the city, Iwata ignored the pain in his ankle, in his face. Though he had washed his mouth thoroughly, he could still taste the blood from the guard's finger. Iwata crossed the pedestrian walkway of a flyover, dark and wet as a whale. Each time a car passed, he tensed up.

At the other end of the flyover Ciudad Cabral became denser, apartment blocks and old restaurants glutted together on a once-grand boulevard. He cut through a filthy alley and recognized the street sign. The hotel was on the corner. Relief flooded through him.

Iwata glanced to the left and the right but saw nobody. Half expecting it not to be there, he felt the key in his pocket. Head lowered, he crossed the road. A dark BMW drifted quietly down the street towards him. He froze. The car stopped. There was a silent face-off until the driver's door opened. It was Detective Valentín who got out. She approached him, her smile lopsided. 'Iwata. Thank God you're all right.'

He stepped towards her, then stopped. There were three other figures inside the car. From the corner of his eye Iwata saw the dark blur of a rifle butt.

19. Amongst Friends and Colleagues

The announcement for the Sōbu Main Line train to Tokyo can be heard through the hotel window. Iwata sits hunched over the edge of the mattress, holding his head in his hands. He can smell the redolence of Hoshiko's body mixed in with his. He hates their joint smell. This week of October 2009 the hotel celebrates its sixtieth anniversary, and Iwata has booked the room at a greatly discounted rate. He hasn't planned the rendezvous, he never does, but he's glad for the discount – money is tight.

From the window, he can see Chōshi Station below. The Tone River in the distance. The convenience store where he bought the condoms. All three are now on the floor, shrivelled like dead animals.

'Kosuke, you know what I've learned about you?' Hoshiko runs a finger down his spine and he flinches.

'What?' His voice is low and thick.

'That you're very quiet. Whenever we would go out as couples, I always thought you were so fun and talkative. But the real you is actually very quiet.'

'Hm.'

'Does your wife mind that you're quiet?' Since they have started sleeping together, Hoshiko never refers to her by name.

'I guess not.'

'Do you believe in fate?'

'No.'

'Me neither, but sometimes I have this funny feeling' – her voice becomes a whisper – 'that maybe things are playing out in the present, even though they've happened in my dreams beforehand. I know that sounds a little crazy.' She laughs. 'But then I wonder if the whole world is just my imagination's handiwork.'

Iwata looks at the magazine on the bedside table. It's full of information about local attractions. The aquarium. The lighthouse. The old blue train. An exhibition showcasing the work of local artists. Iwata thinks he and Hoshiko in this room could be painted in grey, something that would make the viewer pensive and sad.

'Lately, I get that feeling more often. That my dreams are real.' Aware that she is losing him with her honesty, Hoshiko changes tack. 'Are you going to go to the party tonight?'

'Party?'

'The important new detective's birthday. Taba told me to dress up for it.'

Iwata is not listening to her. He has two layers of thought these days. The outer layer is thick, as though trying to experience the world through bathwater. The inner layer is fixated on death – thoughts of escape. Or starting again, like his mother. He thinks back to when she left him in the bus station. He remembers it clearly. The smell of the gas. The rip-rip of his backpack zip. His mother walking away briskly.

'Kosuke?'

'What?'

'The party?'

'No. It's hard to get babysitting.' Iwata has noticed that she never mentions her own little girl. He wonders if Hoshiko is mentally unwell.

'Well, maybe my sister could –'

'I need to shower.'

He gets up and goes to the bathroom. He hears Hoshiko singing to herself in bed, 'Farewell One Cedar', a song he has always hated. His mother hates it too. Iwata suspects Hoshiko fancies herself a good singer. There are so many things she is wrong about, he finds himself unable to resist feeding his silent contempt – as though it were a hungry pet and her shortcomings little meaty morsels.

For him, Hoshiko is emptiness itself. She is all the futility in his life crafted into a skin mirror. She is the richest indulgence of self-loathing he has ever known.

Iwata moves around the bathroom fluently. He knows the shower well by now, how to get just the right temperature. Showering off her smell is his favourite part of meeting Hoshiko.

Iwata returns home that afternoon. Cleo is singing in a whisper to the baby, Nina Simone to Nina, 'Do What You Gotta Do'. Iwata explains it's crucial he attend the birthday party to make a good impression on the new senior inspector. Cleo says she understands. Iwata asks if she wants to come, knowing she will say no. She says no.

*

That night, at the police station — a beige two-storey building that could just as easily have been the head-quarters of a fishing company— everyone is packed into the briefing room. The lights are off and the new senior inspector is blowing out his candles. The heating is on high and the air is thick with cigarette smoke. The cake is decorated with the Chiba Police mascot design — a blue dolphin wearing yellow boots, doing the V-sign with his fin.

As the senior inspector tells everyone how welcome he already feels Iwata's body begins to shake. He does not know the new man but he knows enough to dislike him. After all, his face fits; his career obviously will not end here in Chōshi.

Iwata backs out of the room unnoticed. The office is empty, the lights off. On the calendar someone has doo-dled little stars by today's date, the senior inspector's birthday. Iwata cannot stand bootlickers. His colleagues tease him as a contrarian, tell him it's his American side.

In the briefing room, they are all grinning: fellow inspectors, the badges, even the admin guys. *Apple-polishers*, Iwata thinks, *every single one*. He wonders what they would say if they knew about him and Hoshiko. It pleases him to imagine them so shocked, though the idea of them knowing he has touched her revolts him at the same time. Distantly, he realizes she has not showed up tonight. Nor has his partner, Taba, Hoshi-ko's husband.

Iwata sits at his desk in the corner and looks out of the window. Tiled roofs shine in the moonlight. In the distance pylons break through the forest canopy like migrating giants.

Iwata's desk holds very little beyond papers. He unlocks his desk drawer. Inside there is framed ticket stub for a Tokyo Verdy game from 1996, the year they won the Emperor's Cup. On the other side there is a photograph of Cleo holding a newborn Nina – her tiny lips making a bow, her eyes closed. Cleo's sweat makes the freckles on her cheeks shine. She looks to camera uncertainly.

Iwata shunts them to one side. He knows the Cipralex is finished but he thinks there must be some back-up Zoloft. At the very least, one or two vodka singles.

Someone has brought in a rudimentary karaoke machine and toneless singing is being clapped along to in the briefing room. Because there will be drinking for the birthday, nobody will question ruddy cheeks tonight. Nobody will question slurred speech. Tonight he is safe.

Iwata touches glass, the slim neck of a shōchō mini. He fumbles the cap off and swallows it in one.

'Nice night for a celebration.' A gruff voice at the other end of the room.

Iwata sees a large silhouette. As he approaches, moonlight ribbons across his face.

'Taba.'

'Did I miss the candles?'

Iwata frowns. Taba's tone is off, his twitching lips a tight line across his large, boorish face.

'What's up?'

'I think you know, partner.'

Instinctively, Iwata stands. They are a few feet apart.

The first people from the briefing room are spilling out, paper cups of beer in hand, smiles on their faces. They pass Iwata and Taba as if nothing were happening.

'Taba, why don't we go outside and –'

'Outside? No, no, no. It's too cold to go outside. I'm happy here in the warm amongst my friends and colleagues.'

'I'm going for a smoke.'

As Iwata tries to pass, Taba grabs him by the arm. 'You said you were going to quit.'

'Bad habits die hard.'

Taba punches Iwata in the eye and a wet smack echoes out through the office. There are gasps, and already the men are restraining Taba. He's a bear and it takes four of them, his face pink as a Christmas ham, spittle sparking from his mouth. 'Tell them, Iwata! Fucking tell them!'

Iwata drags himself up off the floor, one hand clutching his eye socket. He is terrified, but for some reason he is smiling.

Chief Morimoto emerges from his office. 'What the hell is this?'

Taba points a trembling finger at his partner. 'Ask him! Ask him what he's been doing with my wife!'

The entire police station is aghast at the unspoken obvious. The new senior inspector is still cradling a slice of cake. Morimoto is white with fury. 'I don't know what this is about, Iwata, but you're taking the night off. Taba, in my office. Now.'

Iwata picks up his jacket, his eye already closing up. He floats past his colleagues to the elevator. Grudgingly satisfied, Taba blows on his knuckles. At Morimoto's door he pauses. 'Hey, Iwata? Sorry I was late, I had to make a stop.'

'You told Cleo.'

Taba smiles a new moon until Morimoto barks at him to shut the door. The new senior inspector asks everyone to get back to work.

Iwata descends to the ground floor then steps out into the cold night. There is no traffic in either direction. Fuzzy drizzle is illuminated by the amber streetlight. Except for the low thrum of the power lines, there is only the sound of the wind. He crosses the parking lot and unlocks his car, a black 1979 Isuzu 117 Coupé. Crawling into the back seat, he concludes Hoshiko must have told Taba. *Not that it matters now.* Iwata wonders what he will say to Cleo. He decides that he will simply tell her the truth. He will say that she was right – she should leave – it will be best for her and for Nina.

And then I'll be alone, as it was always meant to be.

Iwata reaches under the passenger seat and lifts up the floor mat. He clutches the little tube of Solanax and shakes it. It rattles solidly – the sound of keys in the front door. He tosses two pills into a plastic evidence bag, bundles it up, then hammers the pills into a powder using the butt of his gun. It's not designed to be taken this way but he doesn't have time for digestion.

Rolling up a thousand-yen note, he snorts the Solanax. Immediately he is short of breath, dizzy, nauseous.

But already there is a tranquil warmth unfurling within him. The drug travels rapidly through the nasal cavity and past the mucus membrane, sailing across the blood–brain barrier like a hungry marlin. Iwata feels gently euphoric, the pain from Taba's blow already a strange memory.

He curls up into the foetal position. With tears in his eyes, he begins to laugh. 'What a day!'

20. Obligate Carnivores

When Iwata came to, he was being dragged. His blind-fold had come loose. With one bewildered eye, he saw a white mansion in the night like a mass of chalk swept off a blackboard. Far below and all around there was only dark, rocky desert.

He heard the crackle of a walkie-talkie. Then he was being lifted up on quivering legs and marched towards the mansion. Flaming torches led the way into gardens of ice sculptures and tiered fountains. Everywhere there were men in body armour carrying automatic rifles, scanning the distance. The mansion was surrounded by surveillance masts, infrared cameras, laser rangefinders.

Iwata was led to the side of the building, down an elevator and through two reinforced security doors. They clunked shut behind him and he was standing in some kind of bunker, music blaring. It was as if a large panic room had been dressed up as a karaoke booth. There were a dozen trans women in skimpy outfits and heavy make-up surrounding a table of champagne cool-ers and a sandcastle of cocaine.

On the stage Bebé Rivera was wearing a gold silk shirt, cowboy boots and a perm. He was singing 'Touch Me' by Samantha Fox, swinging the mic from his crotch as the women whooped. He caressed imaginary breasts, his forehead shiny with sweat, his diamond rings and hair sparkling in the disco lights.

The song finished to rapturous applause and Bebé returned triumphantly from the stage. As he took his seat a flute of champagne was poured for him, two raspberries dropped in. He sipped it and considered his new arrival at last. 'Girls, go stretch your legs.'

Pouting, the women shuffled out of the room.

'Except for you, Nayeli. You dance.' Automatically the lights dimmed and slow music began. She started to circle the pole on the stage. Except for her, Iwata was alone with Bebé.

'So,' he said, playing with one of his rings, 'here you are.'

Iwata didn't know what to say, so he said nothing.

'Sit.' The man patted the space next to him. 'You know who I am?'

'Bebé Rivera.'

'Then let's switch to English.' Bebé poured Iwata champagne. 'What do you think of Nayeli? She's an angel, isn't she?'

Iwata looked at the dancing woman on the pole, her muscles clearly defined in the purple.

'So strong.' Bebé grinned, his eyes glazing over.

'Why am I here?'

'Drink up.'

Iwata swallowed with difficulty, his head swimming with exhaustion. He presumed it was good champagne but his mouth registered only wetness.

The music finished and Bebé applauded. Nayeli smiled,

then excused herself. As she left Bebé kissed her on the mouth. Dropping back into his seat, Iwata caught a snatch of cologne. The man smelled good, somewhere between citrus and leather seats – the interior of a rental car.

'You're here because you're looking for missing women.'

'Yes.'

'Maybe if you had come to me as a friend, I could have helped you.' Bebé shrugged jovially. 'Then again, life isn't all about making friends. I mean, take your actions at my housing complex.'

Iwata put down his glass. 'I saw a young girl in that place. She was strapped to a bed.'

'We're discussing your business here, not mine.' He snorted a line then massaged the bridge of his nose. 'At first, nobody could figure you out. My people thought maybe you were CIA. Or you belonged to one of my competitors and you'd tricked the good Detective Valentín with a silly story. But you were looked into and it's as you say. Your business is the girls. And you've come a long way, you've taken risks. So, Mr Iwata, my only question is: *why?*'

'They're being killed.'

'So it's that simple, then. You think you're a hero and you thought you would find your dragon here.' Bebé snorted another line, leaned back and closed his eyes, his face pink. 'Well, sorry to disappoint you, friend. There's nobody like that on the loose in my city.'

'No? What about you? What about that little girl in the complex? What happens to her after the procedure?'

'That's my business.'

'And what about the missing women? You paid for Meredith. You paid for Geneviève. Benedict Novacek arranged the meetings. You paid for their surgeries. Then you flew them out here. That's the truth, isn't it?'

'Benedict has a good eye. What can I say? Existence is longing, every man has his needs.'

'What did you do with them? Are they in the desert?'

'You think I killed them?' Laughing, he toasted the quality of the joke. 'Mr Iwata, the zookeeper that loves his animals doesn't have specimens flown in just to see them die.' Bebé waved at the door. 'But this is all getting very serious.'

Immediately the women crowded back in. A white weasel loped into the room after them, snapping its small head around. It was so fast it seemed to undulate, letting out high-pitched chirps.

Bebé screeched with delight. 'He's free! He's free! Nobody touch him!'

'Aw, he's scared,' one of the women said.

'Diablo isn't scared of anything, he's a warrior. You know he has a war dance? It confuses prey. You'll see him do little backflips, frizz up his tail. Shit, I could watch him all day.' The weasel scurried under the booth and Bebé slapped the tabletop. 'Time for another song.' He turned to Iwata. 'Okay, Confucius, what's your favourite?'

'I don't know.'

'Bullshit, everybody has a favourite song.' He winked at the woman next to him. 'Anabel, my plum. Give us something with attitude.'

As she stood and headed towards the stage Iwata saw a bulge in the gusset of her tights. Bebé smiled at him wolfishly. 'You like what you see, don't you? Don't tell me you're not curious. Look at her, look at how perfect she is. I've been promising her money for the procedure for months but I just can't bring myself to lose it, you know what I mean? She's hung like a fucking donkey, after all!' Bebé slapped Iwata on the thigh and leaned in close. 'Not always, you understand, I'm no fucking maricón. But sometimes it just really gets me going. I don't know why. Best of both worlds, maybe. I like that I can see when she's turned on, you know? Anabel can't hide it from me. Not with the size of *her* fucking turnip.'

The woman on the stage started to sing Madonna's 'Lucky Star' in passable English. Bebé swigged his champagne, bopping his head, unable to take his eyes from the stage. 'She hates it, of course. Says having a cock disgusts her. She calls it *it*.' He sighed. 'I guess in the end I'll have to give in and make her happy.'

The room was clapping along. Bebé kissed the girl next to him on the shoulder and she scooped up a small mound of cocaine under her long pink nail. He devoured it then turned to Iwata, blinking. 'I was curious about you, Mr Iwata. You caused a bit of a stir in my town. But I see now you're nothing more than a Don Quixote with too many questions. Questions questions questions. My grandmother used to say, "The mouth is the gateway to catastrophe."' He laughed. 'Then again, so is shooting my men.'

Iwata felt a deep futility, a floating plastic bottle trying to reason with the tide itself. The weasel popped its head out from under the table now, then scurried into the corner of the room, baring its teeth.

Bebé beamed. 'Do you know what an obligate carnivore is? Diablo is one of those, you see. Another phrase I like is "true carnivore". But "obligate carnivore" has such a ring to it. If I ever write an autobiography, that's my title. *Obligate Carnivore* by Edgardo Rivera. Anyway' – he plucked out a raspberry and popped it in his mouth – 'I like to leave things on a high note. Heard this one the other day – see what you think. So. The world ends and all the people gather before God. The Russians speak first. They say, "God, we can only thank you. You gave us majestic mountains, you gave us oil, you gave us great literature, we were truly blessed by your gifts." And God says, "Well, yes, that's true. But I also gave you cold." The Americans are next up. They say, "God, we can only thank you. Not only did you give us incredible natural beauty and tremendous wealth, but you also gave us our precious freedom, the greatest gift of all." And God says, "Yes, that's all technically true. But I also gave you terrible inequality and discord." The Mexicans are last. When it's their turn, they kneel before God and say, "Dear God, of all the peoples that have come before you today, we can honestly say that we, the Mexicans, are the most blessed of all. Our lands have everything we need. We have natural resources, we have jungles, we have flowers. Our crops grow, our beaches sparkle, our animals are plentiful. All throughout the world, our food is treasured and our people are loved." God shrugs and says, "Yeah, but I also gave you Mexicans."'

Bebé laughed raucously and slapped the table. His women joined in on cue.

Iwata looked around the murky neon, the smoke, the sweat. It was as if the depth of the room were no longer a fixed concept, the confines of this space suddenly interchangeable with the black desert outside, the smiles surrounding him like coyotes'.

'Bebé.' The girl next to him nuzzled into his chest with a dreamy smile. 'It's unfair that your friend just gets to watch us without singing himself.'

'A wonderful idea! Choose something for him. Something oriental.'

She went up to the stage and programmed the song. 'Ready!'

Bebé turned to Iwata. 'Get up there and sing for us.'

'No.'

His jaw stiffened. 'Say no to me again in front of my friends, you chink fuck, and I will become unreasonable.'

On unsteady legs, Iwata drifted up to the stage. The music began, a jaunty eighties bass-line. He choked on the lyrics, a little yellow ball on the screen skipping across words like a happy frog.

'Fucking sing!' Bebé roared.

Iwata began to sing Aneka's 'Japanese Boy'.

'Yes! Louder!' Bebé started to dance, urging everyone to their feet. Surrounded by his women, he cycled his fists and moved his hips, a fat, permed Travolta. Panicking, the weasel ran from one corner of the room to the other. Iwata sang the song with his eyes closed, trying to grasp at memory instead of reality. He imagined he were somewhere else, somewhere safe. He imagined himself in the aisles of Mitsuwa, the music gentle in the background, the words not his own but those of Akiko Nakamura. He tried to imagine Cleo singing to the crying baby. He tried to imagine Callie humming to herself as she chopped garlic. He tried to imagine Van Morrison on his mother's porch. Anything to drown out his own voice in this room.

When the song ended the door opened and Valentín entered the room.

'Hello again, Detective,' Bebé said.

'Edgardo.' She nodded.

'It's like I say to my little boy. Make all the mess you want. So long as you do the tidying afterwards.' Bebé pointed at Iwata. 'That's your mess, Valentín.'

1975 – Tokyo

It was the first day of October and a lukewarm evening breeze was blowing through Yūrakuchō. The three drunks in the empty lot were discussing the upcoming Miss International pageant, the favourite a Yugoslav. On the radio in one of the bars the latest number-one hit was playing – Kenji Sawada's 'As Time Goes By'. The vendor across the street had two different newspapers in each hand. In his right, the *Yomiuri Shimbun*, its headline concerning President Ford's proposed visit to China and the dismay it was causing. In his left, the *Asahi Shimbun*, its lead article relating to the retrieval of the body of the last remaining tourist killed in the bus accident in Lake Aoki.

All around Yūrakuchō construction barriers were going up, development looming. Still, the salarymen looked on, ties loosened, beers in hand. If the ground split open and demons jumped out, Nozomi imagined another round would be ordered.

She had just taken an order of autumn beer when her father told her she had a call.

'Another day, another man,' he muttered.

'Ryoma? For God's sake, I've already agreed to meet him tomorrow.'

'No, some older guy.'

274

'Older?' Puffing her fringe out of her face, she answered. 'Hello?'

'Ms Nozomi Iwata? My name is Shinji Kuroki. Do you know who I am?'

'. . . Shinji Kuroki, the editor?'

'From Nichibotsu Ltd, that's right. Ms Iwata, forgive my directness, but I read *The Mannequins* and I have to say, I'm very excited. *Very*. I've already shared your work with my colleagues and we all agree you've really got something here. Would it be possible to meet tomorrow morning? I'd really like to discuss where we go with this . . . Ms Iwata, are you there?'

'Yes,' she bleated.

'Wonderful. Ten a.m., then? You'll be expected at the office.'

'Ten a.m. Thank you. Thank you.'

The man finished the call and Nozomi remembered to breathe.

'Who was it?' her father asked.

'I'm expected,' she whispered.

'Yeah?' He lit a cigarette. 'And you're expected at table twelve with those autumn beers.'

In the end, Nozomi's meeting at Nichibotsu had taken all day. Even so, it felt like time was roaring past her, as though she were standing between two passing trains. She was introduced to an entire cast of people she could not hope to remember, all of them smiling at her like she was the sun after a long season of rains. It was beyond strange for her to hear other people discussing the fate of Yoko and her mannequins as though they were real, Nozomi's pen strokes like iron bars imprisoning her characters into existence.

By 5 p.m. she had a cheque for a little under half a million yen, a publishing contract for *The Mannequins* as a stand-alone novel and a numb elation in the pit of her stomach. She stopped by the bank, where she deposited the money to the congratulations of the manager, then drifted over to Kimura's club; he was now working as muscle at a Kabukichō yakuza drinking den.

Seeing her, he lost his customary work scowl and lit up. When Nozomi told him her news he whirled her around like a carousel horse and insisted on asking for the evening off. 'Dinner,' he announced with a grin. 'The best in town.'

'Are you sure?'

'Of course. But come with me so they'll see I'm not making you up.'

Kimura asked his colleague to cover for him and led Nozomi inside. The bar itself was normal enough, nothing out of the ordinary beyond the eye-watering prices and the topless girls on the podiums. Keeping her eyes on the floor, Nozomi followed Kimura down the stairs until they reached the private room. Cigarette smoke crept up from beneath the sliding *shoji* doors and thick guffaws made the paper screens tremble. Taking off his shoes, Kimura timidly slid one open, bowed deeply and apologized unreservedly for the interruption. He approached an old man in a black *yukata* who was midway through downing a whiskey highball and whispered something in his ear.

'Hm? Where is she?'

Kimura gestured behind him. The old man smiled grey teeth and waved Nozomi over. She took off her shoes and approached. He squinted at her through his cigarette smoke. Up close, she could see the tar in his skin, the hunger in his eyes.

'Kimura's girl, huh?' He looked her up and down. The others did too. Not taking her eyes from her, the old man addressed Kimura. 'Normally, I'd have your balls for this, boy. You've taken an oath, you don't get to drop in and out when it suits you.'

Kimura bowed, seemingly physically hurt by the words.

'But, I suppose given the calibre of this particular filly' – the man squeezed Nozomi's left buttock as if testing it for firmness – 'we can make an exception. Gentlemen?'

The old men leered their approval.

'Well, there you have it, Kimura.'

'Thank you, sir. Thank you.'

Open-mouthed, Nozomi glared at her boyfriend.

'Now get the fuck out of here.' The old man punctuated his order with a smack on the back of Nozomi's thigh. She flinched, swallowed her fury and marched out.

In the street Kimura begged her forgiveness, pleaded with her, tried to explain he had no choice but to accept the old man's shit – that was what paid the bills now. Nozomi was furious; she wanted to stay angry too. But after a few minutes she began to see she couldn't really blame him. Though Kimura was built like a bull, he was still a little boy next to those men. And it wasn't as if she hadn't known what he did for a living from the beginning.

'I shouldn't have taken you in there, I know, I know. But I had to ask the old man a favour. After all, I want to take you somewhere special tonight.'

Remembering her promise to Ryoma Hisakawa, she shrugged. 'Well, I can't. I just came by to tell you the news. I've already got plans tonight.'

Kimura's face shifted. 'With who?'

'An old friend, you don't know him.'

'Who is he?'

'Just a friend from university.'

'You never talk about him.'

'He's just a friend.'

Kimura took Nozomi by the wrist. 'Cancel.'

'. . . what?'

'You heard me.'

'Kimura, I don't like the way –'

'I'm sorry, I'm sorry, I'm not telling you what to do. I just love you, I love you more than anything that's ever been in my life before and, tonight of all nights, I just want to take my beautiful genius girlfriend for dinner.'

She searched his eyes, staring at him hard. Nozomi had never heard anyone say such a thing out loud to their girlfriend, much less in public and much less *Kimura*. Shaking her head, she held out her hand. 'Coin.'

'What?'

'*Coin.*'

Kimura fished one out for her. Nozomi went to the

phone box, called Hisakawa and told him that she was feeling unwell and would have to cancel.

'Again?' There was music playing in the background and she could hear the ice cubes in his drink. 'Nozomi, I'm starting you worry about you.'

'I'm fine.'

'But I haven't seen you in weeks.'

'I'm sorry, Ryoma. I've been busy.' She brightened. 'But hey, I have some good news. I got a publisher!'

'Oh.'

'You don't sound very happy.'

'I am, I'm just surprised.'

'I see.'

'Come on, don't take it like that, Nozomi. I just – I don't know. It *is* surprising.'

'Look, I have to finish up a manuscript by the end of the autumn. Let me call you when I'm on the other side of it, okay? Then my mind won't be wandering.'

'But that's weeks away.'

'I know, Ryoma. But . . . well, I don't know what to say.'

'Nozomi, I've always been kind to you. Bought you things. Done you favours.'

'I know, you've been very kind –'

'I just want to feel like you *want* to be my friend. That's all.'

Feeling a shank of guilt, she shook her head. 'Ryoma. I swear, once I'm finished, I'll call you. We'll hang out like before. Okay?'

'. . . Okay.'

'Good. Look, my money is running out.'

'You're in a phone box? I thought you were sick.'

'I am, I'm just heading home now.'

'Oh.'

'Bye, Ryoma.'

'Nozomi?'

'Yes?'

'Congratulations.'

When she emerged, Kimura was beaming. He crushed her with his massive hug, which he had never done before in public, then hailed a taxi. Getting in, he gave the driver an address she did not recognize.

The helicopter was owned by Kimura's boss. The old man was, it turned out, a lieutenant in a notorious yakuza family. Nozomi felt unsure about getting in – for a number of reasons – but as soon as they took off and the electric effulgence of Tokyo spread out like a giant deep-water squid, she forgot her worries.

The helicopter banked this way and that and she kept having little flashbacks to signing her contract. Hard as it was to believe, she kept telling herself: *This is all real. Life can be this beautiful.* Kimura nudged her and handed her a foil package. Nozomi unwrapped it to find two chocolate bananas.

'I told you,' Kimura shouted over the noise. 'Finest dinner in Tokyo!'

Long after they had landed and gorged themselves at a chankonabe restaurant, they found themselves walking through the leafy campus of the Marine Sciences University, not far from Tokyo Bay. It was late but there were still students sitting out drinking wine on the grass. Nozomi could hear a radio blaring from one of the dorm windows, Muhammad Ali had beaten Joe Frazier earlier that day in Manila. Kimura suggested buying a few cans and sitting out, but Nozomi shook her head.

'I can't, I have to go home and write.'

'It's *midnight.*'

'I always write late, you know that.'

'Well, I've got paper at my place.' He smiled wolfishly.

'All my notes are in my room. I have to finish this, I've signed a contract now.'

'I *know*, but come on. You've got plenty of time. Two months is ages.'

Irritated, Nozomi checked her watch. 'No, it really isn't.'

'Fine, don't stay. Just come round for a bit. We'll get a cab.'

Nozomi was doing the mental calculations as he slid an arm around her waist and tried to kiss her neck under the shadows of the flowering dogwood trees. Had he not done that, she might have relented.

'Kimura, get off.' She shoved him away and, off balance, he stumbled a little.

There was an odd silence, as if they had both ruined something.

Then Kimura's face changed, an ugly metamorphosis, even in the half-dark. 'You know, most girlfriends don't hold out like this, Nozomi. All I want is a screw. If you hadn't noticed, I treat you pretty fucking well.'

Face burning, she shook her head. 'Then why don't you go back to Hedonia. I'm sure you can find someone more obliging.'

'Finding someone isn't the problem.'

'No, especially when you tell them about your diamond trade.'

'Fuck off.' He took a step forward, almost squaring up to her.

Shocked, Nozomi began to walk away, Kimura pawing at her shoulder.

'Hey, come on.'

'Get lost.'

'Look, I'm sorry. All right?'

'I told you from the day we first met. I didn't want to . . .'

'Want to what?' He was using his doorman tone. He stopped in his tracks, his face hidden in the shadow of a stone war memorial.

'Nothing.' She carried on walking.

'It's just a fucking *book*, Nozomi.'

She turned, open-mouthed. 'Is that how you feel?'

'Have I ever said something I didn't mean?'

Fighting back her tears and furious at herself for producing them, she reached the main road and hailed a cab. Just as the door closed, Kimura was at the window, at once embarrassed and incensed. His words were muffled through the glass. 'Get out of the car, Nozomi, for fuck's sake.'

'Drive, please.'

The cabbie looked over at her. 'I don't want any problems.'

Kimura slapped the window now. 'Nozomi, get out! I told you I was sorry, now stop acting like I'm some —'

'Just drive!'

The cab lurched away. After a few trembling seconds Nozomi looked back through the rear window and saw Kimura standing there in the road, his beautiful suit dishevelled, fury distorting his face. Sitting back low in her seat, she ignored the driver's glances and closed her eyes. She didn't know if it was fear or regret she felt in amongst the helpless love, but she knew she didn't want it anymore.

Nozomi got out in Jinbōchō and decided to walk the rest of the way. By the time she arrived home it would probably be too late for writing, but it wasn't as if she would be able to think straight now. The argument with Kimura had shaken her, brought so many things into question. Either Kimura had been changed by his job, or she was merely seeing the side to him that had always been there. Nozomi never really bought his shy, gentlemanly approach but it had never particularly mattered.

Now, however, the lies were beginning to add up. Reservations that had been there since the beginning were now meeting new doubts forming in her mind.

Nozomi passed Nichibotsu Ltd. Only a few hours ago she had emerged feeling joyous. It angered her that something as simple as Kimura could have any effect on that, the single achievement in her life, the potential of *doing* something in this world. She promised herself that, from now on, nothing would do that ever again.

It was gone 2 a.m. when she reached her street. It was deserted, even the homeless trio gone. She cut through the empty lot and could hear a blaring radio from somewhere, Hachiro Kasuga's 'Farewell One Cedar' – one of her father's favourites. The song was about a man parting with his love at the end of his village by the cedar tree, the mountain jay crying for their sorrow.

Nozomi was mouthing along with the lyrics. As she looked up at the moon, her breathing was stopped. It took her a moment to realize she was being strangled, those little squeaks coming from her own throat. Panic carved through her. Nozomi felt her face tightening, as if the blood in her head were expanding. If she didn't do something, she would die.

Nozomi mule-kicked the shin of her attacker. There was a hissing and his grip loosened. She staggered away, through the jagged concrete, weeping for air. She could hear the song, Hachiro Kasuga singing of the village girl still unmarried, years passing, waiting for her lover's return. Nozomi lost her balance and fell.

There was a strange silence and then rubble crunching under footsteps. Terrified, Nozomi flipped on to her front to crawl away. But there was a weight on her back now, an inarguable weight. She felt her mouth being forced open and something being shoved in, something rough and greasy, something that smelled of leather.

And now she was being dragged through the lot by her hair.

'Come on, doggie.' The man spoke playfully.

Exposed iron-mesh wire from fallen concrete slabs slashed at her, broken glass cracked beneath her knees. She tried to scream out, but her throat betrayed her, as if complicit.

The man flung her into a corner of what was once a room. Part of the ceiling was gone. She could see the moon through a crack. *This must be a dream. I'm still flying over Tokyo with Kimura. Or maybe I never woke up today at all. I'm late for my meeting with Mr Kuroki.*

The man stood over her now, his face blotted out, the moonlight silver on his shoulders. 'Hello, Nozomi.'

'. . . No.' She croaked.

'I was waiting for you.' He unbuckled his belt. 'But I think I've waited enough.'

Nozomi realized they were only metres from her house. She could hear her father's TV blaring, the tinny quality of the audio so familiar.

The man looped the belt around her and punched her in the face. She had never been hit in the face before; there was a dreadful detachment from it, like nodding along with something you did not understand. Nozomi counted five punches and wondered if she ought to close her eyes.

Then he was tugging off her clothes and flinging them around the rubble. She could hear Detective K's flying car. There he went, saving the world all over again.

Nozomi imagined it was next October, or last

October, or any other October that ever was. She imagined herself on a hill all alone, with nothing for a thousand miles, watching the Tears of Saint Lawrence. She imagined her fictional mannequins smiling quixotically. She imagined her ashes placed into a tiny capsule and shot into space to circle the Earth for evermore.

21. Sleep with the Angels

Río Limbo ran through the highest of the Sierra Cabral mountains then plunged four hundred metres into the gorge below. In winter months, thick mist would descend on these narrow mountain roads, rasping rains sweeping them away like bad ideas. But it was a calm blue afternoon and Valentín knew the way by heart.

The jungle canopy kept out the day, only little jewels of light visible in the interstices. Valentín's mind was swimming as she drove, her head a cumbersome weight. She was coughing continually now, swallowing down blood. There was a strange release of pressure and distantly she thought she might be wetting herself.

In the back seat the two men wearing ranchero hats had said nothing the entire time. One was tall and stocky. The other was short and skinny.

'There it is,' said Skinny.

Up ahead, the structure came into view. The dummy airport had been built years ago for special police-response drills but spending had ballooned and governments had changed. The building had been left to the elements ever since.

When the road ran out Valentín stopped the car. Weeds had broken through the concrete of the runway. The jungle clutched the terminal greedily, its windows cracked, wind howling through. Lakes of rainwater had collected, green with makeshift life. The simulation airport had only been abandoned some fifteen years yet now looked like an ancient Mayan ruin – wildly overgrown and heaving with the richness of human absence.

Valentín got out of the car, the two men behind her.

'Ready?' said Stocky.

'First things first,' she replied. Sitting on the bonnet of the car, Valentín lit up and tried not to cough up blood. In the distance, she could hear the quiet, constant roar of the falls. The jungle was screaming and whirring and ticking as it always did. Beyond the waterfall colossal, flossy clouds were turning pink in the late afternoon. She recalled what she had said to Iwata. *Over here or over there. Everybody dies.* She hadn't been wrong.

Valentín finished her smoke and nodded. The men opened up the trunk and dragged Iwata out. He was blindfolded, his face bloodied. A large cardboard sign hung around his neck, a message scrawled on it:

La boca es la puerta a la catástrofe.

– La Familia Cabral

The mouth is the gateway to catastrophe.

Skinny and Stocky had worked Iwata over before putting him in the car. There hadn't been any anger in the beating; they were just two plumbers polishing their tools.

Valentín spat and took out her gun. 'Might as well get this over with.'

'Where do you want him?' asked Stocky.

She pointed to a large tree at the edge of the jungle. The two men dragged Iwata over to it and propped him up. His head lolled and Stocky patted him on the cheek.

'Sleep with the angels.'

Valentín fired and the bullet hit Stocky in the forehead, his eye socket withering. She swung her aim to Skinny and pulled the trigger once more. And again. She was firing, but there were no shots. With her gun raised overhead, Valentín bellowed and charged.

Skinny reached for his own gun now but Iwata booted his wrist hard and the gun flew into the undergrowth. He responded with a savage left hook to the temple and Iwata slumped. Skinny span in time to block Valentín's blow. Then he was on top of her, hammering down blows with her jammed gun, the jungle screaming like schoolboys egging them on.

It was over quickly.

Skinny rolled off her. They were both panting in the sweltering dusk. Valentín began to laugh. Her mouth was cartoon gore, all missing teeth and strings of gum, her nose caved in.

'I fucking knew it.' He shook his head. 'Once a pig.'

Valentín whispered something.

'What?'

She repeated herself.

'What are you saying?' Skinny lowered his head to her mouth.

With the last of her strength, she grabbed him by the hair and stabbed him in the jugular with Morel's knife.

Skinny's eyes bulged as he tried to pull the knife out, thrashing for the life spurting out of him. He fell on her, spasming. Then there was stillness.

Iwata opened his eyes. He crawled over to Valentín and dragged the body off her. 'Valentín. You're hurt. You need a hospital.'

'I need a smoke. Help me.'

Iwata lit a cigarette for her and perched it between her ruined lips, holding it in place while she sucked feebly. 'Is that a waterfall I can hear?' he asked.

'The most beautiful one you'll ever see.' She gurgled blood.

'I'll get you water.'

'No, just stay.'

'Okay.' He took her hand.

'Iwata, I know what you're thinking,'

'What am I thinking?'

'You're thinking, how could I work for them?'

'That's not what I'm thinking.'

Valentín's breathing became wet and abraded. Her pain had been replaced by a soft dizziness. It was as though she were not lying in the wet mud but instead running – running flat out in someone else's body, about to make a leap of uncertain distance.

'Iwata . . . the knife. Please bring it to me.'

Iwata cleaned the blood off before placing it in Valentín's hand. She smiled at the feel of it, the slight weight of it. She wanted to close her eyes but couldn't. Not yet.

'Iwata, listen to me. It won't take them long to realize

what I've done. They know who you are. The border roads are controlled. The US Consulate will be watched. There's only one way out. You'll have to try and cross with the migrants.'

'Valentín.' He squeezed her hand. 'Stay with me, don't close your eyes.'

'Let me be.' She squeezed back weakly. 'And it's Astrid. My name is Astrid.'

With nothing else to say, Iwata closed his eyes. After a while there was the distant crack of thunder. Far above, the clouds lit up like foxfire.

When he spoke again Valentín didn't reply. Though she was warm, Iwata felt no pulse. He folded her hands in her lap as though she were waiting patiently for a late train. For the second time, he carried her. He didn't know why but it felt right to sit her up by the tree.

Iwata got into the car and took a last look at the jungle clearing, three dead bodies in its long grass. Then he started the engine and descended the mountain road. Out of the window he saw the pearl thunder of the waterfalls. The escarpments around it were like islands in a vertical sea, the water evaporating before hitting the rocks below, falling for ever.

Eight miles outside of Ciudad Cabral Iwata turned on to a dirt track for hunters and got out of the car. In the distance the city stacked up like some forgotten game of mahjong. The brittle grass scratched his shins and the yipping wind was cold, but Iwata was numb – nothing more than footsteps in the desert.

Finding an abandoned hunter's cabin, he hunkered down under some old rags. He had no thoughts; he'd reached his limit.

At 1 a.m. Iwata emerged from the cabin wearing a poncho he had fashioned from an old blanket using a piece of glass. He used rainwater to clean the blood from his face. The cold enraged his injuries, now indistinguishable from one another, but he knew he couldn't afford to stand out any more than he already did.

Shivering, he started walking.

The northern side of Ciudad Cabral was a city of trucks and depots, the final link in the supply chain to the United States. Millions of tons of product, declared or clandestine, passed through this place every year. Machinery, food, livestock, fuel, lubricants, heroin, marijuana, humans – nothing stayed for long.

Massive rigs rumbled in and out of compounds. The roads were too wide here, too well lit, too many people working in the night. Iwata stuck to shadows like a goldfish hopping from puddle to puddle.

At 4 a.m. he reached his hotel. Someone had celebrated their quinceañera during the night. Paper cups rolled through the empty plaza, sounding like impish laughter. Iwata imagined the celebrated girl asleep in her bed, her dreams whirling with the infinite possibilities of her future. She'd be warm and safe and loved.

But thoughts like these always led to Cleo. Always led to Nina. She'd be going on six now. Not that she would ever be going anywhere. Her ashes were contained beneath a stone monument on the other side of the planet. Cleo's name was etched next to Nina's. Iwata's name was there too, his characters painted red. One day the paint would be washed away and they would be together again. *Maybe one day soon.*

Iwata slipped into the shadowy doorway just in time. The large black SUV was moving slowly through the barrio, creeping through the narrow streets, orange street-light washing over it. Iwata didn't move, he just watched. It looped around the boarding houses, a flashlight flicking on and cutting through the shadows. The engine sounded like a languid tiger.

When it finally drifted away Iwata headed over to his hotel. He entered through the back and climbed the stairs. The door to his room was wide open, the room ransacked. His things were gone. His passport too. Iwata lifted the loose floorboard and found that the money was still there. He snatched it up and hurried out of the hotel. As he crossed the street, he saw an A3 poster stuck to the streetlight. It was his own face blown up, copied from his passport. Beneath it there was a phone number and a single word:

BUSCADO

SOUGHT

The poster had been plastered on every other street-light he passed. Head down, Iwata hurried through the empty blue-grey streets of Ciudad Cabral. He frequently hid in doorways, alleys and telephone booths.

The north-east of the city was the closest point to the border. The stalls here were all open, catering exclusively to migrant needs, their prices extortionate. Backpacks. T-shirts. Hats. Coats. All of them black or camouflage-print. There were also playing cards, sunblock, snakebite kits, condoms, writing paper, sanitary pads doubling as insoles for shoes. Contraceptive pills were advertised on a piece of cardboard:

ATTENTION FEMALE MIGRANTS – 80% OF YOU WILL BE RAPED DURING YOUR CROSSING. PROTECT YOURSELVES

Iwata bought a hat and some plastic sunglasses, then continued north, staying on the backstreets.

22. A Free Country

The Diódoro Latapí Refuge was a large breeze-block structure on a street of shabby homes, arenose ruins and lemon trees. It was not yet dawn but this place was teeming with bodies, hope and fear. A handful of exhausted-looking men sat outside, cross-legged, smoking roll-ups and sipping coffee.

Iwata arrived just as a truck creaked to a halt outside the shelter. Slinking back into the shadow, he watched at least thirty people spill out of it. Two men in orange polo shirts had white words emblazoned on their backs:

REPATRIACIÓN HUMANA

The deportees were mostly male, all of them carrying belongings in large plastic sacks. Their cheeks were reddened by the sun, their eyes dulled and accepting. Many of them wore knock-off sports merchandise in support of American teams. Others wore clothes with patriotic eagles and star-spangled banners, the word 'USA' all over them, as if trying to convince the beholder of their legitimacy.

One of the repatriation agents stepped forward. 'Two lines, please! The sick or elderly on this side, the rest over there.'

The lines formed quickly and without comment. Pulling

the blanket tighter around his body, Iwata joined them. Apart from his ethnicity, he didn't particularly stand out.

Inside the shelter there was the wet, doggish smell of recent mopping. Daybreak sunlight glared on the wooden crucifix above the door. It took an hour to reach the front desk. Iwata gave his nationality as Taiwanese and the name Lia Xia was entered into the database – the first name he could think of – that of a young Chinese woman who was murdered years ago in Japan: his first case.

He was given a small bar of soap, a rough blanket and a breakfast ticket. Not wanting to risk being recognized, Iwata went straight to his bunk and closed his eyes. Evelyn Olivera had been through here. Her cousin Adelmo Contreras too. And now it was Iwata's turn. He knew it would only be so long until La Familia Cabral came looking here.

Iwata closed his eyes and pictured Bebé Rivera. Valentín. The accidental confluence of their lives. The drug lord, the dying policewoman, the lost detective – an unintended ecosystem.

In the busy courtyard outside a quiet hubbub drew him out of his thoughts. A single coyote had arrived. A small man climbed the soapbox usually reserved for the priest. His hair was a thick clump of grey, a single gold chain around his neck.

'Ladies and gentlemen, I won't talk for long. I know most of you have come a very long way just to get here.' He had the demeanour of a manager who did not enjoy giving his employees bad news but business was business.

'They call me Cookie and I'm here to offer my services. I can help you cross the line into America and through the desert. The path will be long and hard. You will suffer. There is great risk. There must be no illusions. In return, I won't discriminate. If you're sick, if you're old, I'll still lead you. My price is $3,000 a head.'

'Why should we trust you?' someone called out from the back.

'Who you trust is up to you. Those who want to go should be ready by midnight.' Cookie hopped off the soapbox.

When he had left, the migrants began murmuring amongst themselves. Some were keen. Many simply didn't have the money. Others wanted to see if there would be a price reduction later from the other coyotes. But most said nothing and just stared at the ground, exhausted from the disappointment and degradations.

Over the course of that day Iwata listened to the coyotes that came and went. Sooner or later, he would have to deal with one of them; his passport was gone and there was no going to the US Consulate, as Valentín had said.

The dorm filled up steadily, forty men in wooden cots stinking and snoring. Iwata was back in the orphanage again. There was a familiarity to dormitories, the unbefriended isolation, the pathetic intimacy. The boys back then had been used to ignoring sobs and covering their ears. Iwata had quickly become one of them. He realized now, thirty years later, he always would be.

The room dreamed in unison of wives and children.

And in a few hours they would wake to the dolorous reality of not knowing when they would see them again.

At dusk, several white vans pulled up outside. Men and women in pale blue scrubs and high-vis volunteer bibs entered the courtyard and erected a medical tent. They set about handing out bottles of water, first-aid kits, protein bars.

When a large crowd had formed a female volunteer took to the soapbox. She explained that they had come to provide free medical examinations to every single person at the refuge but that those who wished to donate blood would be offered a discount towards their crossing the following evening. The hundred or so migrants were weighed, their blood was drawn for testing, their urine collected, their hearts were listened to, they were given wristbands according to blood type.

Iwata took advantage of the emptied dorm and slipped out to the canteen. He devoured three bread rolls and drank five cups of tamarind juice before returning to his bunk.

The refuge was like a station with no tracks, no trains, and the midnight service was provided by the man who called himself Cookie. Five men, one woman and a child stood in the courtyard wearing camouflage clothes and holding water containers painted black. Except for them, the courtyard was empty. They resembled a ragtag platoon that had deserted a long time ago. Iwata woke to their whispers.

Cookie came ambling up the road, dressed much the same. One by one, he took their money and counted it with expert fingers. When he reached the woman, he looked down at the little boy, no more than five years old. 'The desert isn't for him.'

'He's my son. What choice do I have?'

Cookie shrugged and took her money. He removed his cap as Father Lalo appeared now. He took to the soapbox and looked at the small group.

'Most sacred heart of Jesus, on the eve of your great resurrection, we accept from your hands whatever death may please you to send us this night. With all its pains, penalties and sorrows, in reparation for all our sins, for the souls in Purgatory and your greater glory.

'Yet, despite our willingness, Holy Father, we ask that you look over our immigrant brothers and sisters as they head into wilderness and uncertainty. Lead them not into danger and humiliation. If it please you, keep them on a righteous path. May your love warm them in the night when they become stricken with doubt and cold. May your love cool their hearts when the desert sun oppresses them. Amen.'

Father Lalo nodded at the goodness in it, then stepped off the soapbox. One by one, he touched his thumb to the forehead of each crosser in blessing. 'Always remember. Come to Him and you shall be purified. For through Him, though your sins are as scarlet, they shall be as white as snow; though they are red as crimson, they shall be white as wool.'

Iwata bolted up in his bunk. He felt a swelling of

unintelligible realization in his belly. It rumbled like a hunger he could not feed. Jumping out of his bunk, he rushed to the front desk and snatched up the Bible.

'Ezra...Nehemiah...Esther...Job...the Psalms... Proverbs ... Ecclesiastes ... Song of Songs ... *There*.' Instincts churning, he stabbed his finger down on four words: The Book of Isaiah.

Iwata closed his eyes and saw Mara smiling in the laser light, her lips cartoonish in their beauty. He pictured the delicate cursive running along her collarbone. *Yes, it has to be.* He ran his finger down the pages of Isaiah and stopped at verse 1:18.

Though your sins are as scarlet, they shall be as white as snow; though they are red as crimson, they shall be white as wool.

'That's what your tattoo is, isn't it?' Iwata whispered. 'Isaiah 1:18.'

Yet even as he felt the rare swelling of a development, he realized it meant nothing. The tattoo proved nothing of value. This was mere trivia. Or maybe it meant something. Father Lalo's church was San Isaías. The words from his confessional lived in the very skin of Mara Zambrano. Evelyn Olivera had been through there. She had come here too. Her ID card had been repurposed by Mara. And Mara was connected to his missing girls.

Iwata rushed out into the courtyard. Cookie and the group looked at him.

'Where's the priest?'

'He just left. Are you coming?'

'Yes.'

'You have $3,000?'

Iwata counted out the money and handed it over. Cookie recounted the money, then nodded once. 'Then follow me.'

Outside, an old Ford pickup was waiting for them. The bed had been customized to twice its original size with handrails soldered on to the frame and standing space for at least twenty people. One by one, the group clambered on to the back of the pickup. The engine started. Then they were away.

Holding on to the metal bar, Iwata watched Ciudad Cabral shrink into the dusty distance, the smell of diesel thick in his throat. It did not feel at all odd to be smuggled across the border with these strangers. His ability to process now boiled down simply to what hurt and what did not.

The road to the border was little more than a dirt track running north. The truck bounced hard through the desert terrain. Ramshackle restaurants sprouted up: Super Coyote and Viva México. Makeshift gas stations were being run out of small sheds, their prices eclipsing those in the more affluent neighbourhoods of Los Angeles.

After forty stomach-churning minutes the border fence came into view. Iwata had seen it only a few days ago, but now it seemed changed somehow, undulating across the horizon as though it had grown there. America beyond it looked no different, a grubby mirror.

The truck finally shuddered to a halt. Cookie got out,

unlocked the safety bar and the group climbed off. Everyone was shivering. Iwata helped the woman off, then her little boy, who threw up as soon as his sneakers touched the earth. Cookie glanced at the mother but said nothing.

The pickup drove off and the group watched the red lights dwindle into the darkness. They were left alone by the border fence in the cold wind. Cookie led the group a hundred yards east. Hidden under sticks and leaves was a pile of old pushbikes.

'Listen up. Tonight will be simple. Do as I say: watch your step and stay completely silent. The hard part begins when the sun rises. Whatever you do, do not take off your clothes. Everything must be covered. Believe me when I tell you the sun can kill you.'

The group nodded. Cookie checked his watch and hopped on to his bike. The group followed, single file. With their hefty backpacks, black clothes and cheap knick-knacks, they looked like a clan of destitute ninjas.

They followed Cookie east for thirty minutes. By now, the border fence had run out and had been replaced by thick metal anti-vehicle barriers, just a few feet high. After another half an hour it had petered out into a single strand of barbed wire. Beyond it, the empty land was cracked, a lunar expanse. It didn't look like another country but another world.

'Hold it!' Cookie shouted.

He waited for a few seconds, then veered off the path into the bush. The group scurried for cover too. Iwata followed the woman and her boy under a crooked tree.

They were both panting, the whites of their eyes pale blue in the dark.

'Spaceship,' the boy whispered. His little eyebrows were sparse, his spiky dark hair growing back from a buzz cut.

A small black object drifted serenely over them, forty feet in the air, quiet as a ladybird. It hovered there for some time, then flitted away.

Cookie called out that it was safe to go. The group returned to the path. Soon the barbed wire all but ran out. Cookie hopped off his bike and pushed it into the bush. The group followed suit.

'Ladies and gentlemen, this is it. Take a look at that desert, because she wants to kill you. But she's the only chance you have. And, if you follow my instructions absolutely, you're going to make it. Understand?'

There was a fearful murmur.

'Now make sure these are tight on your feet.' From his bag, he handed out squares of old carpet along with a few rolls of duct tape. 'We need to hide our footprints.'

Cookie was the first to scurry through the gap in the barbed wire. Then the woman with her boy in her arms. Then the rest.

Keeping low, Iwata followed them into America. It was a strange sight: a small detachment of terrified and exhilarated people casting long shadows over the pale badlands. The group trekked through the cold dark, leaned forward into the bitter wind, looking down at their carpeted feet.

After a few miles Cookie held up his hand and the group halted. 'Nobody has come for us yet so the sensors must have taken us for animals passing through. The carpet did its job.'

'How long do we get to stop?' someone asked.

'Two minutes. Anyone needs the bathroom, now's the time.'

Cookie wandered over to a towering bank of cacti. The men in the group followed him and somebody made a timid joke about bar toilets as the steam from the piss drifted up. Cookie glanced at Iwata. 'Where you from, friend?'

'Far away.'

'Don't want to tell me? Well, it's a free country.' Cookie's teeth were white in the gloom. 'Listen, the group needs a sheepdog to bring up the rear. You look like you've got the lungs for it. Don't let anyone dawdle.'

Iwata nodded and gritted his teeth against a brisk wind.

'That's the spirit. You'll fit right in here.' He shook himself off and walked away.

When Iwata returned to the group, he took up the rear. Once again, the small, pathetic shuffle of feet over rocks, feet over rocks. A sad, quiet rhythm.

23. Good News

A few hours before dawn, somewhere in the dark hills of the Tohono O'odham Nation, Cookie whistled and the group groaned to a halt. He pointed to a cluster of tall mesquites and they laid out what blankets they had, using backpacks as pillows. The boy crawled into his mother's jacket and she buttoned it over him.

'It feels bad, Mami.'

'I know it does, my love. Close your eyes.'

The cold wind surged around them, sounding like a coming train. At Cookie's invitation some of the men climbed to the top of a hill. Besides Iwata, there was a cheerful Honduran named Edwin, and a Guatemalan, Diego, who hid his youth under a cap. They looked out across the desert in silence, smoking knock-off Fiestas. A bottle of mezcal was produced and three of them took trembly sips, their wet lips freezing but their bellies burning contentedly. They made hushed small talk about what their new lives would be like. When the mezcal was gone, they went back down the hill.

Iwata laid his things down and Diego settled nearby. Both men looked up at the sky, the cold stinging their eyes.

'Where are you headed?' the younger man asked.

'LA.'

'You got family waiting for you?'

'Not really.'

'I have a cousin in Phoenix. My mother is at home with my little brother . . .' Diego lost his words now, the mezcal stirring his emotions. Iwata remained silent. When the young man spoke again, he was brighter. 'My little asshole brother is glad I'm doing this so that I can buy him a PlayStation.'

Iwata laughed, his eyes closed.

'I was expecting a big wall – weren't you?' Diego shrugged in his sleeping bag. 'Maybe I'll be able to get him that PlayStation after all.'

Nobody replied. The desert wind sounded like a raging sea.

A rare morning of winter sun in Chōshi. The sky is an empty blue, the ocean gabbles and chatters peacefully against the cliffs. A bell buoy can be heard in the distance, its single note clanging.

Iwata wearily climbs the stairs to his apartment, seagulls cawing above him. He hopes Cleo does not want to talk today; he needs sleep. Iwata opens the door and hangs up his keys. He's glad they won't have to live here much longer, in this box at the end of the world.

Iwata realizes his wife is laughing. It's a beautiful laugh and he's relieved to hear it; it's been a long time. Then he sees her.

Cleo is in the kitchen, standing on tiptoes by the window, flashing her breasts to the street below. Iwata looks out of the window and sees three confused fishermen looking back up at him. 'Cleo, what the fuck are you doing? Have you lost it?'

'Oh, relax. I'm just bored.'

Iwata considers his wife. She is thinner. Paler. Pink around the eyes. Normally so blue, they seem glazed these days.

'Clee, if this is about me and Hoshiko –'

'No, it's really not. I forgave you, you should too. Anyway, I'm in a good mood today. Why don't you shut up and come give your wife a kiss?'

Iwata puts down his bag, which is heavy with case papers. He takes off his shoes in the *genkan* and pads over to Cleo. He kisses her on the lips lightly but she clamps her arms around him and pushes her tongue into his mouth. It's been so long since he's felt this that it's like a new sensation.

She pulls back, her lips pursed, her eyes dreamily removed. 'When you kiss me, I feel like I'm standing on top of a mountain.'

'Are you sure you're –'

Cleo lifts herself into the sink and leans back against the window sending plates clattering. She spreads her legs and pulls her knickers to one side. 'Come on.'

'I need to shower,' he says.

'I don't care about that. I like it when you smell.'

'I care.' Iwata turns away and struggles out of his tie-knot. Then he flicks on the radio and begins to boil water. 'Do you want tea?'

'No.' Cleo hops sourly off the sink and sits at the table. She begins to scratch her scalp. 'How was your night?'

'Fine.'

'Only fine?'

'Only fine.' His attention is snagged by the radio.

. . . confirm that convicted cult leader Takashi Anzai, leader of the Children of the Black Sun, was executed this morning at 5 a.m. Masatake Kuramoto, director of Tokyo Detention House, said the condemned made no statement and rejected his last meal. Despite the unusual length of Anzai's incarceration before his execution, Mr Kuramoto declared the hanging to be 'a textbook application of justice' . . . Sport now, and the Chiba Lotte Marines threw away the lead last night against the Fukuoka SoftBank Hawks, going on to lose the best-of-three first stage of the Pacific League Climax Series . . .

'Kosuke, if you won't touch me, talk to me at least. I want to know how your day went. And don't say it was fine.'

'Now that I think of it, I do have some good news.'

'Ohh, tell me!'

He realizes something. 'Where's the baby?'

Cleo's mouth twitches. 'Asleep.'

Iwata checks his watch. 'It's 11 a.m.'

'She was tired. I put her down.'

'At 11 a.m.?'

'Yes, at eleven-fucking-a.m., Kosuke.' Cleo's face hardens for a second, then she smiles. 'Now, come on! What's the good news?'

He takes his *techou* out of his pocket and tosses it to her. She opens the leather pocketbook. 'This doesn't say "Assistant Inspector".'

'I know.'

Cleo shrieks, leaps up and embraces her husband. 'This is amazing!'

'We'll be out of here soon enough.'

'But how, you said they hated you –'

'The new senior inspector? He left. Tokyo called. Morimoto asked me if I would fill in.' Iwata extricates himself from his wife's embrace and pours water into a cup. The aroma of the brown rice tea is soothing.

'We should go out and celebrate.'

'I have to work again tonight.'

'I mean *now*.' She is scratching her scalp again, violently now.

'Now?' He laughs. 'Where?'

'I don't know, let's drink a fucking beer. Or I know! Karaoke! We can sing our song.'

Iwata puts down the tea, an odd cold twisting through his gut.

'Cleo, what's going on?'

She smiles flimsily. 'What do you mean?'

Iwata goes into the bedroom to check on Nina. She is sleeping; no sign of anything wrong with her. Iwata returns to the kitchen. 'I come home to find you flashing strangers from the window. Then you want to have sex, even though you're on and you hate that. Now you want to go drinking in the middle of the morning and you know I've worked through the night. That's what I mean, Cleo.'

She puts her head in her hands, her fingertips wet with the oily blood from her scalp, and mumbles, 'I can't, Kos.'

'You can't what?' Iwata sits next to her and places a gentle hand on the small of her back. Her whole body is trembling.

'I'm having thoughts,' she whispers.

'What thoughts?' Iwata does not know what this means but it terrifies him all the same.

'Of dropping her on purpose. I can't help it.' Cleo peeks at Iwata through her fingers like a scared child. 'She keeps on *saying* things to me.'

'. . . Who?'

'Who else? Nina.' She looks over her shoulder with wide, manic eyes. 'Keep your voice down; she'll hear you.'

Iwata feels something give out in his chest. He knows there is no way back from this. 'But Clee, Nina doesn't speak. Her brain isn't . . . You know this. I don't understand.'

'That's what we *thought*,' Cleo whispers into his ear. 'But they lied to us. She does speak, she does. She says things to me when you're not here. She knows when you're gone.'

Iwata grasps his wife by the shoulders and embraces her, as if proximity will shake her out of it. 'Cleo, the baby can't speak. Nina won't ever speak. I don't – I don't know what this is. Why are you saying this stuff?'

Cleo runs to the front door. 'I can't be here anymore!' she wails.

Iwata catches her on the stairs. Terrified, he clamps her arms by her sides in a bear hug. 'It's okay, baby. It's okay. Stop now. It's okay.'

'She fucking speaks! She asks me to hurt her!'

Iwata puts all his weight on her to contain her.

She can only grunt now, her skin scarlet. 'Don't you understand? There's something inside that child. Something wrong.'

The bell buoy clanging is like Mass. Beneath him, his wife is hyperventilating. Iwata curses himself for having ignored the signs, for telling himself she was just unhappy.

'We're going to get you help, Cleo. We're going to get you help right now.' He knows there is no *we*. He knows they are alone.

At 7.30 a.m. the group were on the move. Though the sun had not long risen, they were already sweating. Nobody spoke; there was only the crunch of footsteps, a sluggish ambling across a sea of baked sand, the uneven sloshing of the water jugs.

Edwin made a joke about spotting a scorpion at which nobody laughed. Later, the woman with the boy began to lag behind, their faces pale. Iwata encouraged her to keep the pace. She looked at him and nodded with a smile but did not speed up. Without saying anything, he took the boy from her and put him on his shoulders. He expected it to feel like agony but there was only a distant pain. The boy dug his little hands into Iwata's hair to steady himself. Freed from the weight, the woman thanked Iwata and walked a little faster.

When the sun was high in the sky and the entire group was panting Cookie led them to the shade of some whitethorn acacias. The blossoms were vibrant in the sun, and all around them there were quail brush, mormon tea and mountain mahogany. The dead scrub on the scorched gold hillocks looked like horse hair. The group ate their provisions robotically, their bodies aching, their feet burning beyond sensation.

'Hey.' Edwin turned to Diego. 'Why do Guatemalans laugh three times when you tell them a joke?'

Before he could reply there was a distant crackle of automatic gunfire. Three quick, short bursts, then a loud crump of an explosion.

'What is that?' Iwata asked.

Cookie shrugged. 'Finish up, friends. Time to go.'

At dusk they passed a massive boulder marked with spray paint:

TO THE SONS OF BITCHES WHO WORK THIS ROUTE WITHOUT PERMISSION – WHAT IS OWED WILL BE PAID. IN BILLS OR IN MEAT, YOUR CHOICE.

Cookie said nothing as he led them past the rocks into a narrow gully. At the other end of it there was just another desert expanse. The group bowed as they exited the gully, hands on their thighs, exhausted by the relentless endlessness of it.

The little camp huddled under the freezing moon in another circle, this one smaller than the one before. The night sky was brighter than the day, an infinite arc enplumed with green blackness and rhinestone stars. Half of the group was already asleep before they had even eaten.

Iwata chewed on oatcakes, which he shared with the boy and his mother.

'Mami,' the boy asked, his mouth dusty with crumbs, 'tomorrow I want to ride on the man's shoulders again.'

'No, Santi. It's not up to you.'

Iwata smiled at the woman. 'How old is he?'

She smiled down at her son. 'Five.'

'He's very brave.'

'He just doesn't say much.'

'I can respect that. Where's his father?'

'He died three years ago.'

'I'm sorry.'

The woman looked up at him. There were scars on her cheek, one of her teeth was missing. 'Do you have a son?'

Iwata shook his head.

'You're good with kids. You should find an American lady.'

'I'll let you know when I meet one.' He gestured around the empty desert and she laughed.

She wrapped Santi, who had fallen asleep in her jacket, and said goodnight.

Iwata laid down and felt the cold beneath him. He smelled apache plume and turpentine bush; he could hear the distant wailing of coyotes.

Closing his eyes, Iwata thought about Evelyn Olivera. Her cousin Adelmo Contreras. Mara Zambrano. He recalled the body hanging from the bridge. He recalled the sound of Detective Valentín's final breath. He recalled the dazed eyes of the girl strapped to the bed. Iwata knew these things belonged to him now.

24. Scorpion

At sunrise the group were trooping through the heart of a desert too barren for a name. Despite all the precautions, some had angry sunburns, others were vomiting every few hours. Iwata was now hounding half the group not to lag behind, Santi clinging to his back.

When the early afternoon sun was at its most brutal, the group took refuge under a walnut tree. Provisions that had been intended to last five nights were running low already. Cookie went behind some ocotillo to piss, and Iwata followed.

'They're not doing well.'

'Nobody does out here,' Cookie replied.

'How far to Tucson?'

'We have to circle around the mountain and approach from the north. Maybe two days.'

'They won't make that. They need rest.'

'They're resting.'

'More than five minutes. They're exhausted.'

'This isn't my first rodeo, brother. The quicker we get out of the desert, the longer these people live. You want to hang around and admire the scenery, that's up to –'

Between their heads an ocotillo stem exploded. In the empty desert the shot sounded like a space shuttle lifting off. Iwata hit the ground. Cookie fumbled out a gun from his pack. There was another shot, a zipping noise and then a loud splat. He fell backwards, his forehead blooming open.

'Everyone down!' Iwata shouted. But the group had already bolted.

Iwata crawled behind Cookie's body, prised the gun away and squinted into the distance. The next gunshot gave him the location. High up on a hill, two men in front of a white truck.

Iwata fired twice. The shooter took cover. Then Iwata was up and running after the group, two hundred yards ahead. 'To the right! Get to that rock!'

Nobody was listening. The next bullet shattered the kneecap of an old man. He buckled and started screaming. Up ahead, Diego made it behind the massive bluff. Then Edwin. A final shot twanged off the rock a few inches from Iwata's head as he rounded it and fell to the floor.

'Where's the woman? The boy?' Iwata gasped.

Diego pointed back to their walnut tree. 'They ran into the cactus field. Where's Cookie?'

'He's dead.'

'Who's shooting at us? La Familia?'

'Doesn't matter who,' Edwin spat. 'We wait him out until nightfall, then we walk away.'

'And if he comes in the dark?'

'I've got this.' Iwata held up the gun. 'But we can't wait until nightfall.'

Edwin shook his head. 'Speak for yourself. You think I'm leaving this cover?'

'The woman and the boy are back there. The water as well.'

'For all you know, they're dead too. We can last until nightfall without water.'

'And after that?'

Diego held his head in his hands. 'Cookie had the map and the compass anyway.'

Edwin shrugged. 'I'll take my chances without them.'

They fell quiet and heard the groaning of the old injured man. Iwata held up the pistol. 'Do either of you know guns?'

Diego and Edwin shook their heads.

'Then I'll need a runner.'

'Forget it. I told you.' Edwin sat down against the rock.

Diego nodded. 'I'll do it.'

'No, you fire the gun. I can outrun you.'

Edwin snorted. 'Let the kid go, man. He's fast, I can vouch for –'

'Shut the fuck up.' Iwata glared at him, then turned back to Diego. 'Now, look. It's easy. You just hold it like this –'

'See you in LA.' He broke into a sprint.

'*Diego!*'

His head was down, his arms were pumping, zig-zagging across the desert.

'Son of a bitch.' Iwata wheeled out from behind the bluff and fired in the direction of the shooter. He gave it three seconds then fired again, but the barrel slid open. He was empty. In the adrenaline, he had forgotten to check his rounds. Diego was halfway across.

'*Diego!*'

His face was red with determination, he was running as hard as he could. The bullet hit him in the cheek. Diego staggered, then foundered, then fell. His body quivered. And he was still.

Iwata screamed, hammering the empty pistol against the rock. It made *snack snack snack* sounds in the silent desert afternoon.

A little after nightfall Iwata slipped out behind the bluff and braced himself for the shot. Nothing came except a cold, buffeting wind. The old man was silent, the smell of flesh already notable in the air. Iwata hurried past him and reached Diego. Through the bullet hole in the side of his face, he could see fillings. Iwata put his hand on Diego's face and shut his eyes, his eyelids cold as pebbles.

Returning to the walnut tree where they had taken refuge earlier, Iwata desperately gorged on water. He saw the cactus field off to the left.

'Hello?'

No answer.

Iwata got closer. 'Hello?'

'We're here.' The woman's voice was small.

Iwata waded into the cacti, the thick spines ribboning through his flesh. He reached into the prickly chaos for the boy. Santi began to scream as the movement cut him, but he was soon out. Iwata washed the boy of blood and filth, then applied disinfectant and plasters.

'It hurts!' Santi wailed.

'I know, son.' Iwata wrapped him in blankets and set him by the tree. 'Now I'm going to go after your mami, okay? Stay right here.'

Breathing deeply, Iwata again waded into the cactus field, the cuts worse than before, fresh ones ripping into old. He reached the woman. There was foam around her mouth. She was convulsing.

'Are you hit?'

'I don't know,' she whispered. 'I can't breathe.'

Iwata knelt down and ran his hands over her but felt no wound. 'You need to drink.' He eased the woman up and saw a crushed bark scorpion beneath her. Kicking it away, he laid her back down. She bucked for a few seconds and then seemed to ease. He washed away the froth from her mouth and tried to grasp for some solution.

'*San*— . . . *Santi* . . .' The woman grunted.

'He's fine. He's going to be fine.'

'You . . . plea— . . . plea— . . . He's fi— . . . five. Don't leave . . . him. Don't . . .'

'All right.' Iwata looked at the horizon. 'I'll take him.'

The woman grabbed his hand and nodded furiously, her eyes fixed hard on him. Then the nodding stopped and her grip slackened. Iwata whispered a prayer and closed her eyelids.

In her pockets he found the boy's ID card. His name was Santiago Buendía. Taking Cookie's digital compass, Iwata noted the coordinates down. They would be needed one day.

Then, checking the horizon for any sign of the white truck, he picked Santi up. 'Come on, son. We have to go.'

For miles and miles, the boy cried for his mother. The wind sang through the cacti, their stems bobbing in delight.

Iwata carried a sleeping Santi on his shoulders through the darkness, trembling, bleeding but adamant that the boy would get out of this place. The saltgrass danced with the wind. The cold hurt and smelled of sweet four o'clocks. The towering saguaro cacti loomed. A pocket mouse scurried over some rocks. Santi laid his head on Iwata's crown and he held him tight by the ankles, as though a lifebuoy. Every so often, he would check over his shoulder for the men in the white truck. There was no sign of them; as if they had been imagined.

Iwata's body was a wreck, but he felt something strange inside, something unfamiliar – an intense warmth, a determination. And in that moment Iwata realized he had a new reason to go on. To protect this boy.

At midday they stopped under a rocky outcropping for shade and water. Iwata gave the boy the last of the tuna flakes. The water was almost gone.

'I'm tired.' Santi spoke with a full mouth.

'How about a story?'

'What kind of story?'

'Which do you like?'

'It depends on my mood.' Santi cocked his head. 'What's that over there?'

Iwata followed the boy's gaze. In the distance, there was a strange crucifix. Then another. Then another. They had been in the desert for four days and three nights. They had been burned. They had been shot at. Between the hunger and a throbbing headache it took Iwata a moment to realize what he was looking at. *Telephone poles.*

They ran out from beneath the outcropping, across the salty moonscape and over the crest of a scraggy slope. Below them, the telephone poles flanked an old back road.

Whooping with joy, Iwata and Santi rushed down the slope. Across the road, there was an old service phone. Without stopping to thank the stars, Iwata dialled Callie Mendoza's number.

'Hello?'

The relief of that single word demolished him. 'Callie . . . It's me.'

'Kosuke? My god, where are you?'

Iwata began to sob.

Callie Mendoza pulled up outside 3375 Descanso Drive a little after 6 a.m. She carried a sleeping Santi up the stairs to the apartment, then went back down for Iwata, who could barely stand. She put the boy to sleep in the bedroom, leaving the door open. Then she sat next to Iwata on the sofa and held his hand.

'What now?' she asked. 'Do you even know?'

'No.'

Callie put her head on his shoulder. He was already asleep.

Over the next few days Iwata searched for Mara Zambrano. She was tangled up with John Smith, one way or another. And she was in danger, whether she understood it or not. But Mara was nowhere to be found.

Iwata returned to Club Noir, but nobody there had heard the name. He tried other trans bars, then hostels, shelters, emergency housing resources. He looked under bridges, in abandoned trains, old water towers. He searched storm drains, Skid Row, the mountain forests. Sometimes, through the window of a restaurant, Iwata would see a shoulder or a strand of blonde hair that would make his chest swell. Sitting at level crossings, as a train thundered past, he would swear he had seen her face in the blur. He walked into hotel lobbies with the feeling she had just been there. In empty crack dens, he traced the walls with his hands and his fingers would come back rich with the scent of her.

In the evenings Iwata returned home to Descanso Drive and spent time with Callie Mendoza and little Santiago Buendía. They played games, practised English, watched TV. Happy families from the outside looking in – absurd bliss.

But Callie's mood changed. One week after she had saved Iwata from the desert she left with Santi to stay with her sister. Iwata understood. There was no sense in getting comfortable in their bubble. Bubbles popped.

When they were gone he tidied the apartment and felt their absence. The open window let in the distant hum of city life. He saw his Spanish CDs on the table, the newspaper ad for the Japanese singles night his mother had sent him, the sweet bay plant in the corner.

But after groping through the darkness for John Smith, blundering through Ciudad Cabral and surviving the desert, those domestic mementos felt like the version of Iwata that never was, the Iwata that had fooled himself into happiness.

Iwata realized now that he only ever was, and only ever would be, a cutting tool, an instrument of discovery. *I'm sorry, but you're a born cop.* McCrae had been right.

As if seizing on his return to solitude, the phone rang. Lost in thought, Iwata answered.

'Hello again, Inspector.'

'. . . Mara?'

'Who else.'

His heart thudded. 'Where are you?'

'Don't ask me anything, just answer one question. Do you want to know the truth?'

'Yes.'

'Then write down these coordinates.'

Iwata fumbled for a pen and scribbled them down. 'Mara, we need to talk.'

'Once you've reached those coordinates, you'll need to head back to the Tucson–Ajo Highway heading east. When you come to San Humberto, make the turning and you'll reach a place called Cactus Café. Get there by tomorrow afternoon. Oh, and if I were you? I'd be ready.'

'Ready for what?'

'Goodbye, Inspector.'

'Mara, wait –'

The line was already dead. Iwata looked at the

coordinates and hastily scribbled directions. Hanging up the phone, he dialled another number.

'Mingo, it's me.'

'Hey, Yojimbo. How's –'

'Listen, I need a gun. And I need it today.'

25. Huxley, Arizona

The sun was rising and Iwata was back in the desert. After renting a Toyota 4Runner and collecting the gun from Mingo, he had left Los Angeles and driven through the night. The road this far out was old, its cracked yellow centre lines running far into the horizon. On either side, there was nothing more than empty, benign scenery. But Iwata saw the desert differently now, like looking at a calm sea and knowing it could swallow you whole.

Following the coordinates Mara had given him, Iwata turned off-road and rumbled into the desert in low gear. He didn't know what he was driving into, answers or a trap – though Mara had promised him the truth, both seemed equally plausible.

A few miles later Iwata came to a small stream. There was a figure lying next to the water. Getting out of the truck, Iwata looked around then knelt down to examine the body. The man had been young, probably no more than twenty, wearing camouflage clothes and an LA Dodgers hat that had fallen off. No belongings, nothing to identify him.

There were two bullet holes. The first was much larger, clean through the shoulder blade. The second was at the nape of the neck, a black, powdery, circular, burning stain around the wound.

Contact shot. An execution.

Iwata stood and surveyed the land. He saw tyre tracks that led down from a hillock to the east, then carried on south past the body.

'They shot you from up there . . . With something high-powered . . .' He swept his finger along the tracks and stopped at the stream. 'Then came down to finish you off.'

Iwata thought about the two men with the white truck that had attacked his own group. Were they responsible for this body also? And if so, why? Familia Cabral snipers protecting their trafficking routes? Bandits? Border vigilantes 'defending' their country?

Iwata got back into the 4Runner and tapped the wheel. Mara had given him specific coordinates, and the tyre tracks that ran past the body seemed to be heading in the same direction.

A quarter of an hour later he stopped again. He had arrived at a small scrub forest too dense to drive through. The sound of the engine sent a volt of vultures screeching up into the air. Iwata got out and checked his location against the coordinates. He was close.

Gun in hand, Iwata fought his way through the branches and came to a clearing awash with colour. Bright T-shirts, jeans, orphaned shoes and hundreds of empty bottles: Sunkist, grape soda, Squirt, Jarritos, Tamarindo Sol, Coca-Cola, Pepsi. But between the foliage the most prominent colour was red. Blood. Bodies. Spent shells glinting gold in the sunlight. Now there was the smell; somehow it was cold, an unholy mix of putrid meat and shit.

Covering his face, Iwata stepped deeper into the scrub. There was a sound, strange and restless. It became a loud roaring, like a freeway. In the next clearing he saw a mass of black flies buzzing angrily around the massacre – open wounds, open mouths, open eyes. The bodies had all fallen face forward, hands at their sides. The backpacks had been heaped in a corner, pockets hanging open. Money had been taken.

In the madness, Iwata realized he recognized some of the victims from the migrant refuge. They were all wearing the wristbands according to blood type that had been given out by the medical team. All of them were the same colour – red.

Iwata forced his vomit back down and staggered back to the 4Runner. He checked the coordinates Mara had given him again. This was the place. She had promised him the truth, yet he had found only death. Perhaps she would explain at the meeting place.

The Cactus Café turned out to be a dusty little roadside diner with a neon sign that declared it open twenty-four hours a day. A sandwich board outside had been adorned in colourful chalk flowers and a phrase in cursive:

THERE IS NO O'ODHAM WORD FOR WALL

Iwata parked in the lot. Getting out, he squinted up at the sun. The midday heat was brutal. In the little phone box at the back of the gas station, he found the number for the local police department and called anonymously. He reported multiple homicides in a shrub forest, gave the coordinates and hung up.

Iwata turned towards the diner, looking for Mara already. He was early but she was unpredictable. He almost missed the white Ford Raptor with the green stripe. But there it was. It was instantly familiar, gleaming white in the sunlight. This was the vehicle he had seen up on the hill the other night, the one belonging to the snipers. What Iwata had not seen was the blue eagle symbol and the words beneath it:

BORDER PATROL

Glancing around, Iwata circled the truck. The registration plate had the seal of the Department of Homeland Security. Crouching down, he saw the dirt on the tyres was fresh, the same rich orange as on his own. On tiptoes, he peered into the bed of the truck. Inside, there were spent shell casings. Blood smudges.

'Shit.'

Iwata chewed his lips for a moment. Mara had promised the truth. She had not said she would meet him. First, she had given the coordinates. Second, the diner. Was she saying the first led directly to the second?

Iwata approached the diner and peered through the window. He pretended to read the menu board as he scanned the room. The place was busy: families, workers at lunch. Mara was nowhere to be seen. At the back there were two men in dark green Border Patrol uniforms. The larger one was blond, blue-eyed and large-chinned. The patch on his shirt read: COUSINS. The smaller man had dark hair, his eyes hidden behind aviators. He was ignoring his partner as he tugged on a thin moustache. His patch read: ORTEGA.

Iwata slunk out of view. *There's blood and bullets in their truck and they stop for cherry pie and ice tea?* It all felt off. Still, Iwata had seen their faces now. He knew their vehicle. It was just a question of waiting.

Iwata watched Ortega and Cousins for six hours. They drank coffee, smoked and checked out the waitresses. They obviously weren't there for each other's company. Iwata figured they were waiting for something or some-one. He floated the idea they were waiting for Mara.

At 4 p.m., however, the smaller man got a call. They hurried to the truck and screeched out of the lot, hit-ting the freeway at speed. Iwata followed. The rented 4Runner was generic and these men weren't the sort to be checking behind them.

They drove north for half an hour until they made a turning.

Iwata overshot, gave it two miles then turned around. He took the same turning as the border-patrol truck. It was a small, uphill road without any kind of signage. At first dusty and full of holes, after half a mile the tarmac sud-denly became liquorice-smooth as it dipped downwards.

Out of nowhere, a town appeared. It was in a desert basin unseen from the freeway, wedged in between mountains. The town-limits sign had no slogan, no motto, no information beyond its founding year of 2010 and a population of just a few hundred. It read:

HUXLEY, ARIZONA

26. Nightlight

Iwata drove slowly on to the main strip and stopped the car. Huxley was spread thin, the desert visible through gaps between houses and buildings. He scanned the street but saw no one. Nobody jogging. Nobody walking a dog. Nobody sitting on their porch enjoying the sunset. Windows were dark. Drapes were closed. Businesses shut.

Yet the streetlamps were on. The gas station at the end of the strip was illuminated. Although, looking around now, he realized there were no cars whatsoever. It seemed as if Huxley had been abandoned, yet the buildings looked new.

Iwata circled the town twice in search of an explanation, some trace of normality. He found none. On the south side of the town the houses seemed less new. What Iwata noticed first were the faux balconies, little wooden artifices. Then he considered the houses themselves. On closer inspection, they seemed like flimsy, nonsense houses. The lawns were overgrown, the driveways were cracked, the roads too. It was as if Iwata had stumbled on to a movie set that nobody had remembered to dismantle. All the windows on this street were dark. There was no noise, no movement; no signs of day-to-day life.

Iwata got back in the car and pulled a U-turn, heading back towards the main strip. He would start knocking on doors if he had to, but he wasn't leaving Huxley without an explanation. As he made a left the border-patrol truck squealed up behind him.

Iwata stopped the car. There was an uncertain silence now, only the sound of his breathing and running engines.

The one Iwata recognized as Cousins got out and approached the window. Up close, he was clean-shaven and muscular. His eyes roved through the 4Runner before finally settling on Iwata himself.

'Evening.' There was a warm drawl to his voice.

'There a problem, Officer?'

'No problem. Only you look a little turned about.'

Iwata smiled sheepishly. 'I'm kind of lost.'

'Okay.' Cousins circled the SUV, his eyes flicking down to the tyres. 'But, uh, how come you're lost here?'

'Thought there might be gas.'

'Down an unmarked service road?' Cousins looked at the fuel gauge. 'And you must be a careful driver. You're plum two-thirds full.'

'It's a big desert. Anything could happen.'

'Well, I guess that's about true.' Cousins smiled acridly then stood up straight. 'But there ain't no gas here, sir. So please go on back the way you came now.'

'What is this place?'

'Training facility – private property.'

'I didn't see any signs.'

'You have a nice night.' Cousins patted the bonnet and returned to the patrol truck. It didn't move. This only left Iwata with one path, the main strip out of town. He drove slowly, keeping his eyes on the rear-view mirror.

At the end of Huxley, Iwata made the turning. But the second he was out of sight of the patrol truck, he turned again, sharply, into an alleyway. Before he could think about it Iwata opened the door. The cold was nettles.

Sticking to the shadows, he skirted between homes and non-existent businesses. The alleyways were littered with empty cardboard boxes and discarded building materials, but there was no rubbish beyond this, no food, no piss, no broken glass. In the distance he could hear the patrol truck grumbling through the empty town.

Iwata leaned back against the wall, his heart beating hard. The wind ruffled his hair, cooling the sweat on his forehead. There were other noises now, more engines. Hiding behind a plastic drain pipe, he glanced around the corner.

Three flatbed trucks were rolling into Huxley, each one crammed with people. They were immigrants, all of them sporting coloured wristbands, their hands bound with plastic zip ties. Men with tattoos, ranchero hats and assault rifles gripped on to the roll cages of the trucks and kept their eyes on their cargo. Then they were gone, roaring south.

Taking two deep breaths, Iwata pushed off from the wall and went in the direction of the trucks. He zig-zagged through Huxley's backstreets and followed the distant sound of the engines.

At the fringes of the city, close to the foot of the mountain, he stopped. There were voices, footsteps close together. There was scared weeping, some laughter above it, radios crackling.

Iwata emerged into a dark cul-de-sac. A hundred yards behind him, the flatbed trucks were being unloaded, people being sorted into wristband colour.

The houses on the cul-de-sac were half constructed, just wooden frames. Iwata looked up at the upstairs windows and saw faces. Scared faces. Little grey smudges in the shadow. For a moment, he wondered if they were mannequins. But they were blinking. At the other end of the road, one of these houses had its door open.

Iwata checked behind him. The flatbed trucks were still being unloaded, people being shouted at to jump down quicker. The men with rifles worked dispassionately, two of them watching a video on a phone. Iwata scurried out of his cover. He braced for a shout but he felt only the wind. Reaching the house, he slipped inside and shut the door behind him.

Iwata was in an empty, unlit room painted ashen blue by the moon. There were faint noises coming from upstairs. He drew his gun as he passed a table with what looked like large playing cards on it. Peering closer, he saw they were passports. On the table, there was an ashtray with two recently crushed cigarettes in it. It smelled of sweat here, it smelled of men. Iwata knew he should leave this place, and yet he moved forward with a nauseous conviction. He climbed the stairs slowly, praying for silence in his steps.

Reaching the top, somebody coughed. Iwata froze. When his eyes adjusted he saw he was in a large attic space. He recognized the antiseptic smell from the housing complex he had fled from. There were twelve small cubicles separated by plastic sheeting hanging from hooks – a small abattoir. The stink was overwhelming.

Gun raised, Iwata inched forward. Another cough resounded, making him flinch. It came from the first cubicle. Taking a breath, Iwata peered inside. He saw a thin naked woman lying face down on a bed, her wrists and ankles bound, her eyes wide. Her anus was dark with blood. On the floor there were a dozen discarded condoms. In this gloom they looked like little sherbet UFOs. On the end of the bed there was a clipboard. It showed the woman's age, blood type and her 'match'. There was also a date underneath.

Iwata thought back to the housing complex. *Since you're here, I imagine you'd like to view the material?* He recalled the face of the little girl tied to the bed, the man babysitting her.

Iwata's stomach lurched, nausea and realization kicking in at the same moment. He gripped the bed frame to stop himself from falling and the woman began to scream against her gag. Staggering away, Iwata ripped back the sheet to the next cubicle. The next one. And the next one. He found men, he found women – all ages, all colours, all of them bound and terrified. On every clipboard there was a date and an organ underlined:

Cornea
Kidneys
Liver
Fat
Blood

*

At the end of the attic, there was a closed door. Light seeped out beneath it. Iwata found himself wading towards it. He opened the door and stepped into soft lamplight. The nightlight projected Dora the Explorer warmly across the ceiling. The room was filled with small grey Formica tables. On them, there were cardboard boxes. Inside them, squirming little figures. Some of the babies were crying. Some looked sick. Blood types had also been written on the side of these boxes.

Dora the Explorer was swinging from a vine, a smile on her face. A shadow crossed over her. Iwata turned. There was a flash, then a heavy weight on his temple.

Iwata slumped against the wall and dropped his gun. The wood was rough against his cheek. Warm blood tickled his ear as he looked up.

'I told you to get the fuck outta here, didn't I?' Cousins picked up the gun, then crouched down as though admonishing a badly behaved puppy. 'But you had to take a piss on my leg and tell me it was raining, huh?'

Iwata punched him in the windpipe – instant, brutal. Cousins frowned, hacked, then fell forward. Iwata grabbed his gun back. A gunshot erupted. Iwata looked down at himself. The bullet had gone through his upper arm. The gun dropped from his hand, as though suddenly commanded. Ortega was in the doorway, his pistol raised, face illuminated pink and blue from the nightlight. He stepped forward and lined up the shot. Iwata closed his eyes and thought of Cleo and Nina.

No shot came. Iwata opened his eyes. Something had happened to Ortega's face. It was a plastic, crinkly outline, sucked in at the mouth. Hands appeared at either side of his head. Mara Zambrano was behind him, suffocating him with a plastic bag.

Ortega bucked hard but Mara did not waver. Her poise was perfect, the distribution of weight incontrovertible. Ortega had no foothold; he could only claw at the plastic.

Then, just as his struggle was fading away, she dropped the bag. Ortega fell against the wall, his skin purple, his eyes pink, choking for his own existence.

Mara Zambrano looked down at him with no expression. 'You don't remember me, do you?'

Ortega looked up at her, in terror, in disbelief.

'Then let me remind you.'

With an open palm she smashed his nose in. Then, fast, before he could understand it, she had him around the neck from behind, forcing him to keep his head up – as if a mother holding a child above water. She held him as he thrashed and gargled on his own blood.

When Ortega had drowned to death Mara dropped him. She peered at her hands in the moonlight, front and back, as if they had been lent to her.

Iwata's consciousness bled out.

27. Sins as Scarlet

Cold and warm currents meet in Chōshi's waters. Every morning at Wholesale Fish Market Number 1 boat after boat unloads a hearty catch and the tuna auctions go nosebleed high. Large bays open on to the sea where trawlers unload directly for maximum freshness. Fishing is the lifeblood of Chōshi so when a man is stabbed over swordfish Iwata is not surprised that Morimoto calls on him, despite the time off he has been granted. *Can't have bad blood at the fish market, Iwata. I'm sorry, I know your wife is, uh, unwell, but you'll be done in a few hours.* With little choice, Iwata responds to the call.

He parks the squad car behind a warehouse, preferring, as always, to arrive unseen. This draws less attention and minimizes time for people to think up excuses. Skirting old forklifts, Iwata squints as the cold morning sun catches the glistening, dismembered fish in the ice boxes. Wooden pallets are laid out on the wet concrete. They hold countless neat rows of tuna fish, their expressions in death identical. Men in caps and rubber boots crouch down to inspect the carcasses. Wholesalers and private bidders are covering their mouths as they speak into their phones. The oily stench of guts is thick on the ocean air. And then, just as Iwata spots the uniformed officer talking with the stabbing victim in the first-aid room, his phone rings.

'. . . Where are you, Kosuke?' Cleo sounds distant, sleepy.

'I'm at work. Are you okay?'

'It's a beautiful day today.'

'Yes. How is Nina?'

'We're going for some air.'

'Okay. I'll be back soon, I promise.'

'I love you, Kosuke. Goodbye.'

'Me too.'

Iwata hangs up, then stops still. He calls Cleo back but she doesn't pick up.

'Oh no.'

Iwata sprints back to the car. He backs out of the wharf and screeches along the oceanfront road. Telephone poles, fluttering grass banks and warehouses blur by. He swerves around lorries and powers through intersections until he reaches the road leading to the lighthouse. Iwata makes the turning at the old seafood stalls, then speeds over the paving stones towards his apartment. He screams to a halt outside his apartment and is running up his stairs when he sees it. A police cordon has been set up around the lighthouse. Already, a pack of journalists are jostling with each other, craning their necks to catch a glimpse. A busload of tourists has just arrived.

In the scrum, Iwata identifies himself and a paramedic leads him to the ambulance. His shoulders are covered with a shock blanket and the paramedic asks inane questions. *What's your date of birth? Who is the prime minister?* Iwata answers numbly and just looks out over the Pacific. Today it is a vitric blue. The blanket crinkles in the wind, its silver surface sparkling in the afternoon sun.

Taba and Morimoto are off to one side. Iwata supposes the chief is trying to convince his old partner to come and comfort him. Iwata hopes Taba does not come. There is no point. The paramedic instructs Iwata to lie back and lift his feet over his head. He feels empty and clammy.

'What have you been doing this morning?' the paramedic asks.

'What?'

'Well, what do you remember?'

It has been a normal morning, or whatever passes for normal these days. Cleo seemed in a good mood. They ate slices of orange before he had to leave.

Iwata will not remember, for a long time, slipping under the police cordon. He will not remember, for a long time, the sight of his wife on the rocks below the lighthouse, her legs broken at horrific angles. He will not remember, for a long time, the way Nina looks next to her mother, wrapped in a yellow blanket, her head like a little garlic bulb torn in half. He will not remember, for a long time, the airlift helicopter coming for the loves of his life, nor the seagulls inquisitively circling above.

Iwata feels a thick hand on his shoulder and Taba appears next to him.

'I just got off the phone. The helicopter arrived at the hospital and it's good news, Cleo's still fighting.'

Iwata doesn't respond. He looks at the witness, who is being questioned off to one side. He looks like a fisherman, his rubber boots bright yellow. He looks upset and embarrassed all at once.

'Look, Kosuke.' Taba sits down next to him and the ambulance creaks. 'I wanted to let you know, what happened with us is over. And I just want to say I'm sorry. For all of it, I know you love Cleo and Nina.'

Iwata puts his head between his thighs and throws up. A few cameras flash. Taba pats his back like it'll all be okay. Iwata blinks tears out of his eyes. 'What about Nina? Where is my baby?'

Taba says nothing. They both listen to the policeman off to one side questioning the fisherman. 'And can you remember anything else?' he asks. 'Anything at all?'

'Just what I told you,' the fisherman says. 'She was telling the baby it would be over soon.'

Iwata woke up in a mobile home. It was small and neat except for a stack of cardboard boxes filled with papers in the corner. Iwata was tied to the bed, his head distantly pulsing with pain. He couldn't tell how tightly he was bound, not that he had the strength to test his restraints. His right arm, where he had been shot, had been elevated, the wound dressed. There was a small bedside table. On it he saw a blood-splattered Top Cat wallet. Next to it there was a framed photograph of Evelyn Olivera hugging Adelmo Contreras. Iwata finally understood. It felt as simple as just waking up.

'You were lucky.' It was a woman's voice. 'The bullet only grazed you. When the painkillers wear off it'll hurt, but you'll be okay.'

Lifting his head, Iwata saw that it was Mara, sitting before a mirror, two lamps duct-taped to it. She was doing her make-up, her movements, quick yet precise, almost like incisions. Her vanity was heaving with products, an altar to cosmetic perfection. Ben Nye Creme Stick in soft beige. Mehron CreamBlend in Cocoa No. 3. Honey-chocolate hues for the cheekbones, temples and hairlines. Pigment for delicate application to the eyelid. Extra Dimension Eye Shadow in Dark Dare to line the eyes with feline essence. On and on it went.

'Mara.' Iwata's voice was sluggish.

'I'm working.' She blinked her eyes gently as the bristles tickled. Her movements were meticulous, her words clear. But her voice and her gaze seemed to come from somewhere else. There was a veiled distance there, as if she were programmed.

In this light Iwata could see Mara clearly for the first time. His mental image of her, one always rooted in glances, in darkness, in cloudy deliriums, was now gone. In its place, he saw her, at last, in truth. And there was the tattoo along her collarbone.

'Isaiah 1:18,' he whispered.

Mara paused her brush and looked at him in the mirror. '*Si vuestros pecados fueren como la grana, como la nieve serán emblanquecidos.* You know what that means, don't you, Inspector.'

'Though your sins are as scarlet, they shall be as white as snow.'

'Those words matter.' She considered him in the mirror for a moment. Then she carried on with her routine

340

as if someone had pressed Play on a tape. 'The look must be absolute.'

'It's you. You were Adelmo Contreras.'

Mara put down the brush, turned, and looked at him. Her eyes held his at first, then seemed to fade, as though drifting away. 'Yes.'

'Those women aren't missing, are they? You killed them. You killed Meredith. You killed Talky. You killed Geneviève. You killed them all.'

Mara walked over to the little window. She looked out at the desert and gave a slight shrug, as if it was water under the bridge. 'I did what I had to do.'

'But why?'

She snapped her head round, her gums revealed, the rage beneath the make-up impossible to mask. 'You think *I* wanted this? You think *I* started this?' Her glare fell on the photograph of Evelyn and Adelmo on the bedside table and she softened. 'No, Inspector. I just wanted a life.'

'Then why Meredith?'

Mara's eyes were glazed now; she still hadn't blinked. A single tear fell and immediately she wiped it off, like disinfecting a wound. The name 'Meredith' was nothing to her; Mara's tears were for herself.

'We lived in an old cottage. When I was sick, Evelyn would boil lemons so that our whole apartment smelled like' – she closed her eyes – 'beauty itself. We had nothing, you understand. But we cooked stews on an open fire. Jackrabbit meat tasted smoky in a way I wouldn't know how to begin describing. We had an old school projector and we'd watch movies on the wall while we ate. *His Girl Friday*; *Dr Jekyll and Mr Hyde*; *A Farewell to Arms*; *Mambo*; *Le Notti Bianche*. When I think of happiness, it's the smell of lemons, the taste of smoke, the sound of dialogue from old movies . . .' Mara's chin trembled. 'Evelyn knew who I wanted to be. Who I *was*. We were cousins but, even from an early age, we knew it was something more. We understood each other more than we understood ourselves. And the closer we got, the clearer it was that there would be nobody more perfect than Evelyn for me. It didn't matter that we wanted different things. It didn't matter that I'm a woman. That I want men. We were never lonely, we had each other. We loved each other.'

'But she came to the priest and asked for his help. She wanted to escape. It was the baby, wasn't it?'

Mara closed the window and looked at him like it was obvious. 'Evelyn wanted to be a mother and I loved her. Of course I was going to look after her. But we knew we had to get out of Ciudad Cabral. Leave for ever.'

'You went to the refuge.'

'We took the medical tests like everyone else. The price was much better that way. You must already know what happened to us after that.'

'Yes. You were double-crossed.'

'You got my coordinates, you know how they operate by now.'

'They get the migrants across the border in the normal way. Somewhere in the desert they're intercepted by Border Patrol. They've already done the tests to determine who's valuable and who's expendable. Those carrying the right colour wristbands are loaded on to trucks; those who aren't are killed.'

'Huxley is the same as Valle Dorado. They look like small towns but they're operating theatres for black-market body parts. There are countless others just like it. Rich people with sick children come and they leave with a brand-new kidney. The rich take the very last thing the poor have left to give, their own blood, their own organs. The First World *eats* the Third World and La Familia turns a profit.'

Iwata felt like a telephone operator who had accidentally patched into a hundred conversations at once.

'For the first few metres, we were free. I just remember Evelyn's smile in the moonlight. I'd never seen her so happy. And then Border Patrol arrived. They told us to get down on the ground. They started shooting. We managed to get away, but it was dark . . .'

Mara Zambrano returned to her vanity. Her gown hung open. It was a hard body, an obvious power beneath the skin, each curve, each plateau. All over it there were tattoos, her symbols, her folklore – the stifled language of a woman living in shadows.

'But I didn't bring you here to talk. I need to finish.'

'Mara, I understand what happened to you. But what you've done? You murdered Meredith. You murdered Geneviève.'

'I told you, I didn't *want* to. But none of them would help me. I couldn't let them live once I had confided in them.'

'And what about the others? The missing?'

343

'Don't you see? Everybody knows what Bebé Rivera likes. I *had* to kill them. To eliminate the competition. That was the only way I knew that, eventually, Bebé would call on Mara Zambrano. He had to choose me. And finally the call has come. In the end it was you that led me to Benedict Novacek. He was worried at first, but I talked him round.'

Iwata shook his head. 'You feel nothing after what you've done?'

'"Feeling". What does that word mean to me?'

'How can all these lives be worth it to you? Just for revenge.'

'You think that's what this is about? I watched Evelyn die and there was nothing I could do. Revenge won't change that. Do you think, when I killed Ortega, I felt happiness? No, I felt nothing. But I didn't come to Huxley tonight for revenge, Iwata. I came for you.'

'Why?'

'You wanted to know the truth. And now you do. But you're weak and I knew you would get yourself killed.'

'So why save me? I'm nothing to you, like everyone else.'

'Because you can make a difference.' She pointed to the stacked boxes in the corner. 'I saved you for them.'

'What are they?'

'Financial papers. Deeds. Medical records. Evidence. It'll take you a while to get out of those ropes. And when you do I know you're not going to follow me. You'll take my findings to the right places. You're going to talk to the prosecutor. She'll know where to take this. You've seen what La Familia do. This is a chance to stop them. To hurt them. To protect those who will be victimized by them. But if you don't, it will all have been for nothing.'

'*It?* Mara, you murdered people.'

'I know there can be no forgiveness for me, Inspector. I'm beyond that.' She leaned her head to one side and put on a large gold hoop earring. 'You remember what my name means, don't you?'

'Bitterness.'

She smiled sadly. 'I am Mara. It's all I am.'

Looking at each other in the mirror, Iwata recalled seeing her at Club Noir. They had glanced at each other in reflections there too. 'Mara, untie me.'

'I wasn't sure about you at first. I knew you liked me. But I also thought you were one of them, maybe hired by La Familia. How else you could have found me in Geneviève's apartment? I had to defend myself. But after that I watched you. I followed you. I saw your eyes. And I know now that I can trust you.'

'Like Meredith trusted you? Like Geneviève trusted you? You betrayed them.'

'Bebé liked them. But they wouldn't give me an introduction. When I explained my background, they said I was crazy. I never wanted to hurt them. Yes, what happened was sad. But it's a sad world.'

'Why Meredith? Why by the train tracks?'

'We were in her room. She ran out down the fire escape. There was an old piano. A wire was hanging out. I didn't plan for it to be that way.'

Iwata closed his eyes. He remembered the piano,

running his finger along the keys, something missing in the sour notes. He'd been inches from the murder weapon.

'Right and wrong is for those who want to exist, Inspector. When I saw Evelyn die I didn't care about living anymore. I made up my mind to stay in that desert and wait for death. But then I thought about Bebé Rivera. I realized that, although he was miles away, safe in his black silk sheets surrounded by his whores, that really, *he* was the one who killed Evelyn. He was the one stealing those kidneys. He was all of it.' She applied her lip gloss surgically. 'That's when I knew I would become whatever I had to become to get close to him. I survived the desert. I learned how to fight. How to steal. How to falsify. How to kill. I whored myself to anyone who would pay. All through Arizona. Texas. Nevada. California. On and on it went. Raymondville, Reno, Coolidge, Modesto. Ten, fifteen minutes. Anything the man wanted. Anywhere he wanted it. I'd stay a day or two, then move on.' Mara picked up some car keys and tossed them into a black clutch. 'That's how this began. But as I said to you, Inspector. It wasn't me who started this. It was Bebé Rivera.'

'This is really who you are?'

'I'm more myself than anyone I ever met. I was always going to be Mara Zambrano. I just wish it had been happier.' She sprayed herself with perfume. 'But that doesn't matter. I'm close now. And nothing on this earth is going to stop me.'

'Mara, don't go.'

'What would I stay for? Killing Bebé Rivera is the only reason I'm still alive.'

'Mara, there are other things. I know there are. You're lost. I am too. But maybe that means we're in the same place. There are others like us –'

She took a rolled-up pair of socks and stuffed them into Iwata's mouth then checked he could breathe. 'You know, Bebé Rivera took everything from me. But after some time I realized he had also *given* me something – a great gift. Do you know what it is?' She clenched her fist in front of Iwata's face, the tightening skin sounding like rope. 'The tremendous richness of rage, Inspector. The *richness*. Like pure gold stuffed deep in your pockets. And nobody knows about it but you.'

Mara Zambrano, who had been Adelmo Contreras before that, who had contorted and recast herself across countries, across characters, across seven seas of suffering, stood up now. Iwata saw she was no longer a person but intention itself, agency embodied – a masterpiece of vengeance. She gently brushed the hair from Iwata's brow. For a moment it looked like she would kiss him. 'You're wrong about me, Inspector. I'm not like you. I'm an asteroid. And sooner or later asteroids have to collide.'

At the door of the trailer. Mara stopped. 'Maybe in the next life.' She smiled and the night breeze gorged on her hair. 'Seems like we move in the same circles.'

Then she was gone.

28. Night Flight

Mara Zambrano got out of the stolen car. Checking over both shoulders, she headed for the exit, her heels clicking through the subterranean parking lot. Planes moaned in and out of LAX nearby. There was sea fog tonight and Mara hoped there would be no delays. She hurried along the sidewalk, hugging herself against the chill.

Across the concrete lanes of Imperial Highway there were mail-sorting offices, warehouses, aviation companies. The freeway rose up and Mara welcomed the shadows beneath it. Traffic on the flyover above sounded like birthday candles being blown out.

She cut across the road, through a FedEx truck stop and past the Korean Air cargo terminal. Men in high-vis jackets rubbernecked.

'Nice night for a walk,' one called, eyeing her legs.

Mara ignored them. Next door to the cargo terminal, she came to a modern building that gave out to the runways. The sign read:

ELITE SKIES

Inside, the plush lobby was empty except for the man behind the counter.

'Here for the pleasure cruise?'

Mara nodded.

'I'll need to see some ID.'

She handed over her fake driver's licence and the man consulted a list. Checking her off, he nodded. 'You can go through now. Your friends are already on board.'

Mara stepped through the secure doors, trying to control her nerves. She was now standing in an enormous hangar, deafened by the hydraulic whine of engines. The Gulfstream private jet was black, its airstairs illuminated by LED lights. As she walked towards the open door she heard 'Don't Look Any Further' by Dennis Edwards and Siedah Garrett.

A well-built man met her at the plug door, his aviators gleaming, his ranchero hat white. He patted her down unapologetically thoroughly, then shone a torch in her handbag. Satisfied, he shouted over the noise in Spanish. 'You took your sweet time.'

She smiled. 'I got here as soon as I could.'

'Just get on the fucking plane.'

Mara climbed the stairs, the music louder now. Her heart was racing, though not through fear. It was the anticipated knock at the door. It was the glimpse over the edge before leaping into water. It was everything she had been living for. She could barely breathe.

The cabin was dark, only two strips of purple neon illuminating writhing figures. The air was pungent with sweat and perfume. Mara heard the cabin door clunk shut behind her as she made her way down the aisle. There were only thirty seats. She could not see Bebé Rivera.

Someone slapped her left buttock. The plane began to taxi out of the hangar as another song began – 'All Night Long' by the Mary Jane Girls. Some people were dancing, others were snorting lines from the duty-free trolley being pushed up the aisle. There was shrieking, laughter, bass. Splotches of whipped cream and fragments of fruit hit Mara as she made her way towards the black glass screen at the rear. She ignored these people; she ignored everything that wasn't Bebé.

Cabin crew, seats for take-off.

A hand reached out and clutched Mara by the wrist. 'Better buckle up, sweetie.'

She let herself be dragged down into the chair next to Benedict Novacek. She let him clip her belt on. She let his hand slide over her bare shoulders, the hair on his arms scratching her skin. 'You glad I got you in here?' His voice was low, his eyes glazed.

'Very.'

'Just very?'

'Very very very.' She used her playful voice, like everything was a game. She could see that they were in the line for take-off, the land outside dead grey. Soon the plane would head out over the Pacific before looping back over the glittering dreck of Los Angeles, an amber organ, never-ending, beautiful, rotten.

Soon they would be airborne and Mara realized she wouldn't touch foot on this earth again. That provoked no feelings in her, the same as knowing you'd never return to a roadside service station in a country you didn't particularly like.

'Drink some champagne,' Novacek goaded with a grin.

'Aren't you going to pour for me?'

'Drink from the bottle. Friends share.' He unzipped his pants. 'And you and I are friends, aren't we, Mara?' He wiggled his cock like a puppet.

Mara did not want to ruin her make-up, she did not want to be touched. For the longest time she wouldn't have cared, but things were different now.

'Don't be shy, sweetie.'

Mara had counted eleven men in the cabin, only one of whom she figured for muscle – the man who had frisked her. There was no telling what was behind the dark glass at the back of the plane but it had to be where Bebé Rivera was.

Mara closed her eyes. Her odds for getting it done were slim. Her odds for getting back down again alive were neither here nor there. But she could not risk being sidetracked by Novacek.

'We're friends, Benny,' she purred. 'This will be my pleasure.'

Mara lowered her head slowly. Novacek closed his eyes in anticipation. Then she snapped her head upwards at speed, her skull crunching into his jaw. She drove an elbow into his temple and he flopped backwards. As Novacek's eyes closed he groaned the word 'oh', and a tear of precum dropped out of his urethra, lit up purple.

Mara planted a kiss on his cheek to brand him with lipstick and unbuckled her belt. She slipped the sharpened nail file out of the pouch she had fashioned in the strap of handbag.

Ladies and gentlemen – reprobates too, quick update: the fog means we're a little backed up, but I've just been told by Control that we should be underway in a few minutes. Find some way to entertain yourselves until then. We have some great in-flight magazines.

Mara was the only one standing now; everybody else had taken their seats. She could feel the stares but these people didn't matter. She reached the black glass screen and knocked. The door opened. A tattooed man with a scowl stood there.

'Wait your fucking turn, sister –'

Mara punched the file hard into his neck then raked it through his jugular. She snatched the gun out of his holster and fired blind three times.

Return fire roared back and she used the dead man's body as a shield. The shots splattered into his body. From the trolley next to her Mara picked up a litre bottle of vodka and threw it into the private room. It smashed. She fired at where it had landed. There was the whooshing sound of fire catching, then screaming. Mara closed the door on the flames just as an alarm went off. In the same moment, at the other end of the plane, the cockpit door opened and a laughing Bebé Rivera wearing a captain's hat emerged.

Mara saw him, at last, with her own eyes. She had not hesitated once to get here, she had not once given into pity or mercy down the years. Yet now that she was looking at him, she was dumbfounded.

Bebé saw the gun in her hand, he heard the screams in the cabin. He understood. The man in the ranchero hat came out of the toilet. Bebé screamed at him to fire. He didn't hesitate. The shot jangled past Mara's face, air

352

fluttering her fringe. She returned fire and hit the frisker in the chest. Something inside her snapped. In the alarm, in the screaming, in the purple neon, Mara fired over and over, hitting baggage bins and the backs of heads.

There was a second of stillness in the chaos. Then Bebé disarmed the cabin door and jumped out into the night.

Mara screamed.

Tossing the empty gun, she ran after him, shunting people aside. The frisker grabbed her ankle. Mara picked up a metal tray, lodged it in his mouth and slammed her shoe down. There was a wet crack and a puff of cocaine.

Mara unhooked her heels and leapt out of the plane. The concrete was cold on her feet, the noise of planes taking off tremendous. In the swirling fog all around her, there were lights of every colour, a line of planes inching forward, fuselages gleaming. Mara ran fast, pumping her arms, her breathing even. For the first time in a long time she felt alive. She felt true. For once she was not hiding. Not anymore. Mara Zambrano was here.

Three hundred metres ahead, Bebé checked over his shoulder. His face was white, his pudgy little frame not built for running for its own life.

Mara had cut the distance in half by the time he reached the terminal and bolted into the passage beneath Gate 68. She reached it just as the service elevator doors slid shut on Bebé. Mara hammered the call button and the twin elevator arrived. She went up two levels. After a few interminable seconds she stepped into a boarding corridor. At the other end of it the door hung open.

Mara emerged into the departures area, which, despite the late hour, was busy.

Hello. This is Mayor Garcetti. I would like to take this opportunity to give special thanks to our nation's servicemen and women for the incredible work they do. I'd also like to remind all members of the military about the Bob Hope USO right across from Arrivals – bringing that 'touch of home' we all need sometimes.

Mara saw Bebé now. He was on the level above, talking on his phone and looking around wildly. Plucking out a newspaper from the bin, she casually walked along the concourse towards the escalator. Hiding her face behind the newspaper, she reached the upper level. He had his back to her. Mara was close enough to hear his voice. She dropped the newspaper.

A businessman bent down and picked it up. 'You dropped this, honey.'

Mara tried to dodge him.

'Now come on, in this country we don't just litter –'

She drove her knee into his stomach and shunted him out of the way. There were some gasps. Someone was calling the police. Bebé span around and saw her. He glared at her, then ran for the VIP lounge. Mara broke into another sprint and was quickly behind him. But as she reached the lounge, the receptionist came out from behind the counter.

'Excuse me, ma'am. Do you –' Mara floored him with a punch to the face and ran through the lounge doors.

She heard a loud thud. Then the same sound again, a pitchfork in hay. Now she felt a cold wooziness. Looking down, Mara saw the steak knife sticking out of her side. All that training and she had fallen for a child's trick.

Not yet.

As Bebé tried to rip the knife out again, she punched him deep in the gut – a perfect delivery. With unfeeling hands, she tore it out. Bebé was staggering away from her, desperate to get air into his lungs. Mara was bleeding profusely but she wasn't going to be stopped. Not now.

'Bebé, you know why I'm here.' She spoke the wet words in Spanish.

'She's crazy!' he squealed in English. 'She's trying to kill me!'

Exhausted, Bebé clambered on to the buffet, planting a bloody hand in the beef burgers, his sweat illuminated by the heat lamps. The VIP lounge was mostly empty, elderly white men dozing in front of twenty-four-hour rolling news. Now they were trying to blink away the dream.

Mara climbed on to the buffet counter then straddled Bebé, her thighs across his chest. His hands fumbled for weapons but all they found were meat, potatoes, fresh fruit.

'Edgardo Rivera.' She coughed on her own blood. 'May God illuminate you.'

Mara gripped him by the perm and cut his throat slowly, fending off his frantic blows with ease. She felt the silent spray of his windpipe. It tasted of glory. Then Bebé was still, his torn gullet sounding like an old sink.

Her head was spinning. Mixed blood was dripping on the buffet. There was shouting behind her, though. She could tell that much. It felt like she was either side of a dream.

Don't fucking move!
Drop the shit! Right now!

Mara hopped off the body, the knife still in her hand. Blood and tears blurred her vision, but she could make out the shapes before her. The shapes of threatening men looked the same everywhere. Their poise, their eyes, their snarls. Carnivores didn't care what you called them.

In broken glass, Mara could see her reflection. She closed her eyes and thought of Iwata. She hoped he would do what was right. She hoped he would grant her the full revenge she had spent so long cultivating. Not for her, but for all the others.

Easy now, we don't want to put you down.
Drop. The. Knife.

These final seconds didn't make any sense; they fit no narrative. The thoughts in her head were inane, paralysed by the thought that she should reach for some stoicism or great, redemptive philosophy at the end. Instead, she couldn't think of anything beyond fear and relief at onrushing death.

Mara glanced over at Bebé's dead body. Urine was dripping out of his pant leg, mixing on the floor with the burger grease. In death, his round face looked scared. Mara Zambrano drank in the image, savoured it as though she could take it with her.

'Evelyn,' she whispered. 'I'm coming.'

Then Mara raised the knife and ran at the men. In the next second her cranium was a flesh piñata, blood and brain slapping the departures board – Zurich, London, Honolulu, Tel Aviv, Tokyo – every city dripping blood.

29. Beside You

POLICE SMASH ORGAN-HARVESTING RING IN DESERT RAID

Wesley Kwang & Iverna Mejía | Reporting from Huxley, Arizona

Doctors, lawyers and fugitives with links to organized crime were among the fourteen suspects arrested over the weekend, the Phoenix District Attorney Office says. Investigators descended on the small unincorporated desert community of Huxley in the early hours of Saturday morning following an anonymous tip-off. They were expecting to find evidence of a black market in organs and human tissues. What they discovered instead was a scene of imprisonment, carnage and death – including the bodies of two Border Patrol officers suspected of corruption.

Law enforcement officials say the first officers on the scene were 'shocked' by the extent of the operation, describing the uninhabited town as 'one big kidney motel'. Documentation allegedly shows healthy organs being sold for as much as $100,000. For those 'supplying' the organs, many of whom are undocumented and facing severe financial difficulty, the promise of high-value recompense is 'a dream come true', according to Katherine Floccari of the Los Angeles District Attorney's Office, who is collaborating on the case. However, it seems as if many of the foreign nationals found at Huxley were being held against their will. Investigators found evidence of murder,

357

sexual assault, large-scale forgery of documents and money laundering in an operation that already seems to stretch across state lines and international borders. Early indications seem to implicate several hospitals across Arizona, Southern California and the Los Angeles area. The investigation is ongoing.

Iwata was sitting at his mother's bedside in the Torrance Memorial Medical Center. The news of his hospitalization for a gunshot wound had provoked a massive heart attack in Nozomi Iwata. Though he'd avoided infection and left hospital after just a few days, the damage had been done. Nozomi hadn't opened her eyes in days.

Iwata sat by her side, holding her small, limp hand. Decisions would have to be made, bills would have to be paid. He knew he needed to take action, at the very least to gather himself. But Iwata had nothing. Nothing but guilt and woe. Like a poor man expected to foot a bill, he turned his empty pockets out.

Out of the window, far beyond the hospital grounds he saw two young girls putting up clothes on a line. From the way they were moving it looked as if music might be playing there. The pegs looked like little dead birds.

'Mom?' Iwata's voice sounded strange, childlike. The bleeping from her life-support machine was steady, as if she were agreeing.

Yes. Yes. Yes.

'The nurse said I should talk to you.'

Yes. Yes. Yes.

'But I guess we never say much, do we?'

Yes. Yes. Yes.

Iwata switched to Japanese, speaking more furtively, as though it were a secret. 'You wanted to talk and I kept on saying no. I – I shouldn't have done that. I'm very sorry. I'm always sorry.'

Yes. Yes. Yes.

Morning became afternoon and the city outside slowly turned a bronzy brown, as though baked with butter. Iwata opened the koi carp box that his mother had wanted him to see. Inside, bound with coloured ribbons, was a stack of notebooks.

Carefully, Iwata took one out. It smelled of his mother. He opened it and saw her delicate pen strokes. *Every year on my birthday there is a meteor shower called the Perseid Meteor, or the Tears of St Lawrence to Christians.*

Slowly, frequently taking breaks to breathe, Iwata consumed his mother's past, her history, her stories. And in them, it was as if he was meeting someone that he had always known for the first time.

Against all prognoses, Nozomi regained consciousness for a single sunny afternoon a few days before her death. Iwata described the blueness of the sky, as her eyes were no longer functioning. He described how the ocean sparkled in the distance, though he could not see it from where he sat. Nozomi, her voice now so different and small, made only one request. To be taken to Hibiya Park. Struggling to speak, Iwata told her that maybe the next day, when it would be less hot.

'Is it warm outside, then?'

'Yes.'

'. . . Where is outside?'

'Torrance, Mother. Your home.'

'Oh. Are there flowers here?'

'Yes, they're very beautiful. Snapdragons, I think.'

'It's my birthday soon.'

'Yes,' Iwata lied. 'We'll have cake. I'll go to Mitsuwa.'

'You always buy too much. Go with your girl.'

'Yes.' Iwata laughed, desperate tears dropping into his lap. 'I will. She's Japanese. You're really going to love her.'

Nozomi reached out her one exposed finger and Iwata kissed it.

The funeral was on a day of perfect blue sky and temperate sun. A soft breeze passed through the lone arroyo willow outside. Above the Toyota Meeting Hall, tall palms swayed gladly. A yellow kingbird sang somewhere nearby, its high-pitched call sounding like *chi-bear, chi-bear.*

Nozomi's instructions had been clear. The funeral was a heavily choreographed procedure; everything was accounted for. The people arrived with their *kōden* envelopes swathed in satin – the amounts contained within depending on their closeness to Nozomi. The envelopes varied in aspect but they followed minute rules relating to ribbon placement, where names were written, whether the flap ought to be up or down, and so on. They were accepted by two teenage volunteers from the arts centre who then handed over a bag in return containing a thank-you card and personalized tea, to be enjoyed while remembering Nozomi.

When everyone had arrived and taken their seats the process began. The nōkanshi, an elderly man who had been flown in from Japan, took great care to ensure that nobody present saw the bare skin of the deceased. He cleaned Nozomi Iwata's body underneath the quilt with a sterilized cloth, the weariness, the cares and the pains of this world washed away. He worked tenderly, as if he had felt a great love for this woman all his life.

When the cleaning was finished the nōkanshi dressed her in her final clothes – a white-and-purple kimono – wrapped right over left, in contrast to the living. He applied her make-up with the gentlest of brush strokes and used Nozomi's favourite colours, the pallidness of death replaced by a faint, human blush. Throughout the process the nōkanshi worked with absolutely serenity, his old face serious yet sympathetic, his movements unhurried, like he had no audience. Iwata had never witnessed such dignity.

When the work was complete Iwata could barely look at his mother, she was so beautiful.

'I will now affix the lid,' the nōkanshi said in Japanese. Iwata and Earnell McCrae helped him lift Nozomi's small body into the casket, made of fine hinoki cypress.

'She is ready for viewing,' the nōkanshi announced.

Nozomi's face was visible through a little window, as though she were in a cuckoo clock. Iwata bowed behind the coffin as the guests passed by to say their final good-byes. The priest began to chant a sutra and, one by one, the guests offered incense to Nozomi. Lastly, flowers were placed around her shoulders. In death, she received

361

a new Buddhist name, the kaimyō – given in order to prevent the return of the deceased if their name were called.

When it was over Iwata travelled to the crematorium. Alone, he stood next to his mother's coffin for a long time. He wanted to say something but could find no words to convey his love. He kissed the coffin, then nodded. As Nozomi Iwata slid slowly into the cremator, her favourite song played – Van Morrison's 'Beside You'.

Afterwards Iwata picked her bones from the ashes using large chopsticks. He started with the feet bones and worked his way upwards to ensure that Nozomi would not be upside down in the urn.

In the parking lot of the crematorium Iwata stood alone. The sun had almost set. On the other side of the street Callie and Santi were sitting outside the frozen-yoghurt place, chattering about something or other. Iwata did not know what they could have in common, yet they never ran out of things to say to each other. He smiled and put his hands in his pockets, feeling bereft and peaceful all at once.

'You look like you could use a smoke.'

Iwata turned to see an old man in a black suit and heavy spectacles walking towards him. He had a white beard, liver spots on his cheeks and fluffy silver eyebrows.

'No. Thank you.'

'That was a tentative rejection. Quitter?'

'More than once.' Iwata considered the man. 'I spoke to you on the phone?'

He nodded. 'I'm Kimura. You're Nozomi's son.'

'I am.'

'You grew up here?'

'Partly.'

'You're like gaijin, huh?' The old man laughed. 'American gaijin, that's you.'

'I guess so.'

'I knew it was you the moment I saw you.' Kimura's smile faded. '. . . What a shame.'

'Excuse me?'

'Nothing, it just would have been easier the other way. Anyway, ignore me. It was a wonderful afternoon.' He took out a trembling cigarette and lit up. 'Your mother would have approved. We were friends.'

'I know, I've read about you.'

Kimura seemed surprised by this. 'Read?'

'She kept journals.'

'Ah. That explains it. I probably don't come off too well.'

'No, not really.'

'We should talk.' He puffed out smoke and pointed to his car. Iwata helped him into the driver's seat, then sat on the little concrete lip of the parking lot.

'My mother's journals just stop. They're full of blanks. I want to know why she left me, I want to know why she just disappeared.'

Kimura bowed his head, then nodded. 'You already know I was close to your mother. Truth is, I loved her.

One day she just disappeared on me too. I searched all over for her, but nothing. It was like I had imagined her. Then years later, she sends me a letter out of the blue. Says she loved me very much but she's started a new life with someone else in America. Imagine my shock – little Nozomi on the other side of the world. I always figured I would love again like that, but I never did . . .' He sighed the sigh of regretful old men and smiled distantly, a long-held bittersweetness. 'Only recently I was thinking of calling her, saying to her, "Nozomi, how did we let forty years slide without seeing each other?"'

Kimura looked over at the crematorium and fell quiet for a time. 'I only saw Nozomi once again. I was in Los Angeles with work and we met for coffee. It was just a single hour. But we had entire lives to catch up on. You see Nozomi told me the truth, what really happened.' He looked up at Iwata. 'Tell me something, did she ever talk to you about your father?'

Iwata felt a chill in the pit of his stomach. 'No. Never.'

'All right, the truth is' – Kimura closed his leathery eyelids and sighed – 'I came here because I thought there was a chance it would be me. Your mother never told me explicitly, only that she had a son and the timeframes matched up. But looking at you, I know now that you're not mine.' Opening his eyes, he shook his head. 'Kid, I'm sorry, but your mother was raped. The man who attacked your mother is Ryoma Hisakawa. Your father.'

'Hisakawa . . .'

The name hit Iwata hard. Dormant memories erupted from deep within him, the truth of his childhood returning with force. He remembered the early years his mind had protected him from for so long: the beatings, the hunger, the muffled shrieks from the other room as his mother was tortured. Iwata remembered the pills his mother would escape into, her vacant eyes and grinding teeth. He remembered the smile the blank man gave when he whipped him, spreading out the lashes, long enough for the burning on his buttocks to subside, only to rip into them again. And now, as if stepping out from behind some drapes, Iwata remembered the face of his father, Ryoma Hisakawa. He had always known the name, burrowed deep within him like a botfly, the name he himself had been born into – Kosuke Hisakawa.

Iwata considered what he was being told. That this man, this rapist, had created him. That his entire existence had been born out of an act of filth. Iwata's throat constricted, not at this knowledge but at the thought of what his mother suffered. His face burned with the shame of all the things he had thrown at her, all the poison that had dripped from his tongue.

Iwata put his head between his legs. Tears stung his eyes, his eardrums pounded, the panic surged. After a few seconds he laid his cold palms on the warm, cracked Californian concrete and exhaled. Iwata felt a tentative hand on his shoulder.

'I'm sorry, kid. But you deserved to know.'

'Finish it,' Iwata said thickly.

Kimura sighed. 'Hisakawa's father was Somebody, a powerful man. He was buying up all the land in Yūrakuchō. After Hisakawa attacked your mother, he gave her a choice. Marry him, or her father's business would be crushed. She had no choice. She left me and married Hisakawa. Tolerated him for as long as possible. But then one day she couldn't. She just ran. I suppose she met your stepfather a while after that. Never came back to Japan again. Your grandfather's bar burned down shortly after your mother left. He died a few years later.'

'Hisakawa . . . is he still alive?'

'Yes. And now he's a Somebody too.'

There was a long silence between them, only the far-off drone of the freeway mixing in with the breeze through the trees.

'I was thinking on the way over here' – Kimura licked his lips – 'maybe there could be a way for you to . . . confront him. I'm not suggesting anything untoward. Just that you would be able to give him a piece of your mind. Maybe I could help arrange a meeting. We'd give you a good cover story, change your name, of course. I used to know some people. With some luck I think I could get you a sit-down with the bastard.'

Iwata pictured an old, fat man grinning – a grotesque version of himself. The revenge would be perfunctory; there would be no sanguine luxuriation. He would simply pluck Ryoma Hisakawa from this life – lint on a cuff. It made perfect sense to Iwata, this simple act. Even if he hanged for it, it wouldn't matter. That, at least, would be the end of it, the sad little circle finally broken.

'A sit-down . . .' Iwata echoed.

'Kid, I'm old, but you? Well, look at you. You're strong.'

Look at me, Iwata thought. He looked nothing like his mother. That left one alternative.

But now he heard a child's laughter. Iwata looked over the road at Santi. He was smiling, picking sleep out of his eye. This tiny artless gesture was all it took for Iwata to feel it: there were better things in this world to live for. To love. To fight. To do good things.

Otherwise, he would be his father's son. Otherwise, he would be like Mara – an asteroid.

'Mr Kimura, why did you come here?' Iwata asked.

The old man frowned. 'To pay my respects, of course.'

'I think an old man came here today to tempt a younger man into vengeance.'

'I came here to tell you who raped your mother and burned down your family business. That's all. I'm just saying, you know, that it wouldn't be too late to talk to him. Make him see.'

Iwata nodded. 'Maybe another time.'

'Now hold on –'

'Safe journey home, Mr Kimura.'

Iwata crossed the road. Santi had frozen yoghurt all over his face. Callie squeezed Iwata's hand under the table and it felt like life itself. From where they were sitting, he could see the palm trees against coming night, their fronds like spiders in dark windowpanes.

'Thank you for helping me today, Cal.'

'You know I love being with him.' She smiled sadly. 'Will you be okay?'

'We'll be fine.'

'I'm going to miss my two guys.' She buried her face

in Santi's wild mop. When she looked back up at Iwata there was a crumpled smile on her lips and tears in her eyes. 'But this is best for all of us.'

'I know it is.'

Callie passed Santi over to Iwata and kissed him on the cheek. 'Santiago' – she spoke in Spanish – 'look after your uncle – deal?'

'Deal.'

'Goodbye, Kosuke.'

She hugged them both in the same motion. Then she walked away.

Iwata put his face on the crown of Santi's head, smelling kid shampoo and Callie's perfume. He watched her get into her car and drive back to her old life – a place where both of them knew he never belonged.

'Shall we go home, Santiago?'

'Sure,' he answered.

Iwata smiled. The boy's English was getting better.

30. Sunset

The sky above Los Angeles was shockingly blue. Front gardens were stippled with succulents, monarch butterflies bobbed about milkweed. In the Starbucks on North Vermont Avenue a woman in a Joy Division T-shirt was writing a screenplay about a gay magician whose life was turned upside down when implicated in a murder at the Magic Castle involving his trademark trick.

A mile to the south, on Virgil, in a repurposed butcher shop, a Nicaraguan man spoke of heaven and the redemptive power of financial contributions. At the hipster café next door two young women from podunk towns were discussing their idea for a meditation-retreat business over almond-milk lattes. Across the road two policemen gave a homeless man a ticket for sleeping in the street. Fly-guy inflatables danced outside the second-hand car dealership on the corner.

All over this city the eye took in slogans and messages:

COLLATERAL NOT NEEDED – WORLD-
FAMOUS PASTRAMI – LIQUOR – EGGS ANY
STYLE – FREE REFILLS – HELP WANTED –
BUT WAIT THERE'S MORE– JESUS
SAVES – END

In the doorway of an abandoned psychic parlour a homeless woman had made a bed of newspapers. Beneath her, Donald Trump was smiling, his campaign announced, his catchphrase in white letters. The headlines were mocking him.

And on Sunset Boulevard Kosuke Iwata was sitting at his desk. The new office was half the size of the old one, but it was cheaper and there was a coffee shop next door. When a breeze blew it carried the smell of roasting beans and snippets of conversation.

Iwata had set up the Astrid Valentín Humanitarian Foundation a month ago, offering investigative services pro bono for the families of those missing while attempting to cross the southern deserts, for the families of missing trans persons, anyone unaccounted for, anyone lost. Nobody was turned away. Kate Floccari, partner in the charity, helped with the paperwork. There would be no more unfaithful spouses for Iwata.

On his desk there were missing-persons files and thick textbooks on US immigration law. They were his daily bread now: the lost, the abused, the murdered in the borderlands, those swallowed by the dream of a better life.

This, for many, was a mirage seen through America's vast deserts – deserts that could kill with tremendous heat, hateful cold. But for the men and women who dragged themselves through the emptiness the dangers were not only those that occurred naturally – not all wolves walked on four legs.

There were men who came to collect, men who came

to rape, men who came to claim territory. Others came in search of blood, to make statements, to strike fear. And, like little ants over a chessboard, the migrants were clueless to the moving pieces around them, the stratagems that swirled above them. Iwata was not in the business of protecting them, but he tried to give them names, at least. To their families, some semblance of closure.

Given a murder case with finite players, secure crime scenes and investigative resources, Iwata was a first-rate inspector. It wasn't something that he thought much about, nor did he take much pride in it, it was merely as evident as the greys in his hair. But the desert had no interest in his abilities, the shrewdness of his lines of enquiry. In the desert there was no cooperation with any kind of force beyond death.

Week after week Iwata would take on a case and head out in search of missing fathers, missing mothers, missing children. He was meticulous in his work, using all the tools and information available to him. He questioned those who could or would be, combed for clues. Sometimes Lily Trimble would even come with him. Earnell McCrae would help surreptitiously from his desk when he could.

Yet almost always Iwata's searching resulted only in empty plastic bottles, a torn jacket, the hint of a footprint. Perhaps a student ID card one time, perhaps a clavicle the next, a child's pencil case, a cellphone – sad little tokens of lives relinquished.

The local deputies all came to know Iwata. Some

appreciated his work, others rolled their eyes at yet another John Doe, as though Iwata were a cat bringing dead mice to an owner. But that was what he did now, that was his function in this world. For hours and hours he would shout out names to the desert, names that had lost their owners, names echoing out over the scorched hillocks in absolute futility. And so Iwata's days were spent in a stack of cases, forty-four missing persons in the desert. He lived in them like his own secret chamber in a tower of nameless bones.

The hopelessness of it might have slowly poisoned a normal man. But Iwata knew little beyond existing in well-intentioned futility. His little patchwork of contradictions. The guilt of his cowardice. It followed him like a large black trunk, his own sneering memories an attentive porter who only coughed for tips at night. Bleakness would always pump through Iwata's veins.

And yet he looked forward to his evenings. The evenings meant Santi. The evenings meant peace.

Not once since the desert had the boy asked about his mother. Iwata wondered what he would say when that day came. He wondered how Santi would grow up, how he would raise him. Santi was a US citizen now; Mingo Palacio's contacts had seen to that. But would he become American, this country replacing the one in his blood, the one in his past? Iwata had no clue; he was sure only that he would love him. Somehow, the boy had become his anchor in the uncertain blue of life itself.

The door opened now and a warm and mellow dusk seeped in. Somewhere not too far away Iwata could hear

Arthur Russell's 'What It's Like'. Charlotte Nichol walked in. She didn't smile, she merely sat across from Iwata at his desk.

'I got your report,' she said flatly. 'I came to thank you.'

'Please, don't thank me.'

'It doesn't make it any easier. But I do appreciate knowing who hurt Meredith.'

'Well' – Iwata managed to meet her eyes – 'then I'm glad.'

She nodded at his arm. 'How's it coming along?'

'The physical therapy is slow but I'm getting there.'

There was a long silence as Charlotte looked around the office. She noticed the photographs of Cleo and Nina on his desk. The photo of Nozomi. The photo of Santi on a pedalo in Echo Park.

'Kosuke, what you're doing here . . . It's a good thing. Cleo would be proud.'

'Thank you.'

Charlotte didn't smile, but her mouth might have softened. 'Well.' She stood. 'I should go.'

Iwata accompanied her to the door and they stepped into the warm thrum of traffic. The sun was setting. The smell of coffee and hot concrete was strong in the air.

They looked at each other for a moment, but neither of them could fathom the proper goodbye. Charlotte nodded once then headed for her waiting car.

Iwata decided to call it a night. He locked up, then gave himself a few moments to watch Los Angeles play out. There were thousands of cases out there, endless questions to be answered, truths to be discovered. Iwata could feel them like mosquitos in the dark, hungry for his blood. There would always be murders. There would always be betrayals. And there would always be sins – of all colours.

Iwata put his tea-shade sunglasses on and started home.

The owner of the coffee shop next door waved. 'Didn't catch you today!' she called.

'I was pretty busy. Maybe tomorrow.'

'Tomorrow is another day.' She smiled. 'That's what they say, anyway.'

'Yeah.' He returned the smile. 'That's what they say.'

Looking up, Iwata saw the last of the sun setting over the boulevard, a sunset on Sunset, an infinite circle.

Acknowledgements

As ever, to my parents and family; however far I am from you today, I keep you close inside and think of you each day. *Y como no, para Lela, hasta el cielo de la calle*. To my love, Camille, the coolest person I've ever known. Without you, I wouldn't be where I am now, in more ways than one. To Moira, my unofficial PR guru, whose home is my own corner of England here in California, I will always be grateful. To my Los Angeles friends Aliyah and Jay, thank you for helping to make this strange city feel like something akin to home.

To Saoirse, without whom this book would not have come to be. Never have I known someone so lion-heartedly open so quickly. I'll always be indebted to you for your truths and insights. The meaning of your name is *freedom* and nobody deserves it more – may you have it all of your days.

Para mi compañero, Stewart, the Geoff Horsfield of undiscovered storytelling genius: Inspector Iwata will never not owe you a cheeky pint. And to my brothers in Team KR: all your mums. To my friend cut from the same cloth, the council flat Gorky: Chris, thank you for your letters, in every sense of the word.

Professionally, it's an honour to once again pay grateful tribute to my editorial dream team: Maxine Hitchcock,

Eve Hall and Rebecca Hilsdon—Michael Joseph for ever. Thanks also to Penguin legends George Foster, Gaby Young and Isabelle Everington. (Is this a good point to say any errors in this book are absolutely my own?) And to my agent and numero uno, Gordon Wise. With each day that passes, my understanding and appreciation of your support only grows.

To all the booksellers, reviewers and book folk who helped my novel along; there are no words I know to sufficiently convey my esteem. And of course, to the readers themselves, you are the very lifeblood of this dreamworld you let me live in. I thank you from my nethermost.

And finally, to all the nameless people who died in the US Borderlands in search of a better tomorrow. This book is beneath every single one of them, but it is both for them, and of them. May the dream they died for live on for ever.

Author's Note

Sunsets and Hummingbirds – The Story of the
Story of Sins as Scarlet

This book began life in death. Specifically, a dead hummingbird in the pocket of a dead man, his remains found near the US–Mexico border in 2009. A common indigenous symbol of safe passage, hummingbirds are considered a messenger between the living and the dead. I wondered if the man, presumably a Mexican or Central American migrant, had brought it for luck, to keep him safe during the crossing.

But I'm getting ahead of myself. I'll step back by moving forwards in time.

In late spring of 2016 I was sitting in a café near the corner of Sunset Boulevard and Hyperion Avenue, nursing my jet lag and an over-conceptualized coffee. I had just moved to Los Angeles and was scratching my head, trying to decide what to do next. My first novel, *Blue Light Yokohama*, wasn't even out yet, but here I was, trying to decide which direction to take Inspector Iwata in.

Even in his earliest conception, he was always going to have more than one story to tell. Before I had shown anyone a single word, Iwata was already swamped in sequels and prequels and short-story ideas. But then I got an agent and, even more miraculously, a book deal for two Iwata novels. Somehow, I was now beginning work on what would become *Sins as Scarlet*.

The only thing I was certain about was that I wanted to take Iwata out of his 'comfort zone' – I had no interest in him riding the wave of his success, in having power, in commanding respect. Iwata would not be Iwata if doors opened for him.

By moving him to Los Angeles, he'd be a nobody overnight. If I took away his badge, no doors would open for him; he'd have to blag or bribe his way in. Besides, the City of Angels had kindled my love of detective fiction. I grew up with my imagination submersed in its filthy kingdom of noir – the seediness, the scores, the snobbery. Through the eyes of everyone from Marlowe to Rick Deckard, I wolfed LA down, dreaming of one day writing about a detective stalking through her streets, doffing his cap to the ghosts of his predecessors as he went. Now I had my chance.

Thematically, I knew I wanted to explore two things in *Sins as Scarlet*: the past and identity. Iwata's mother, Nozomi, appears briefly in *Blue Light Yokohama* but, after so many drafts, her voice fell largely silent. Now I could burrow into who she was, where she came from, what led her to abandon her son. And by delving into *her* past, we would also understand Iwata more thoroughly.

Iwata is bicultural, with a talent for languages. Like me, he's from two places and no places all at once. These were all things alluded to in *Blue Light Yokohama*. Now I wanted to dive into them headfirst. His upbringing has straddled two countries, two cultures, two languages. On the one hand, he is Japanese; on the other, he grew up in the United States. How would that affect him now, approaching forty, living alone in Los Angeles? Who would he be?

Of course, I'd mapped out Iwata's backstory long before I got a book deal. I'd told myself then that, if I ever made it this far, my second Iwata book would take him back to Los Angeles and, in the undertones beneath the framework of a crime-fiction book, it would attempt to explore biculturality, alienation, generational gaps. After all, following on from the events of *Blue Light Yokohama*, it was logical that Iwata would want to leave Japan behind, certainly the Tokyo Metropolitan Police. Moving him to LA would bring him closer to his mother, while turning him into a private investigator would also drag him down the rabbit hole again.

As a crime writer, I see setting as its own character. I believe the landscape dictates the mood of a story just as much as its events or the characters that drive it. Like Tokyo, there is an idea of Los Angeles, fed by a million movies. People believe that Angelenos live in either Bel Air mansions or in South Central gang territory. Angelenos are either the über-wealthy drinking Mai Tais up in the Hollywood Hills, or they're far below, pimps and hustlers squabbling behind squalid motels on the Strip.

Indubitably, I wanted to attempt to bring these contrasts to the page. But at the same time, this city's profound disparity constitutes just a single mask: Los Angeles wears many.

While I wanted my detective to navigate the upper crust and delve into the underworld, I also wanted him to pass through the Every Day of this city: open-air markets, the industrial landscapes, people going to work, people having coffee, sitting in traffic.

In trying to find a way into *Sins as Scarlet*, I scoured newspapers, a list of John and Jane Does, and the LA County Coroner's unclaimed-persons page. That's when I came across the website for the Colibrí Center[*] and read the story of the man with the hummingbird in his pocket.

It was such a striking image, omen-like, a dead man with a dead bird, without a name, lost in the desert. Immediately I knew I wanted Iwata to be investigating a case similar to this, to be investigating a world of nameless migrants, rackets and trespasses. I wanted him to be on the case of a man found dead in the desert with a hummingbird in his pocket.

And like a tap turning on, the heart of the book gushed out. *Sins as Scarlet* would be a world of the vulnerable, the abused, the homeless, the addicted, the marginalized, the transgender, the undocumented, those dying in the street. I walled myself in with books about Los Angeles, the Borderlands, Mexico, the narco war. I spent days traipsing around Skid Row. I spoke to people living in tents under flyovers. I walked hundreds and hundreds of miles through the streets of LA. I visited Mexico and researched the migrant crossings into America. I made friendships with migrants who had started new lives in East LA and we spoke at length about being far away

[*] www.colibricenter.org

from home, starting again in America. I spoke with transgender women about their lives, their experiences. I did research on postpartum psychosis. I read California's Private Investigator Act and interviewed private investigators, asked them about the reality of a gumshoe's day-to-day. As my research developed, *Sins as Scarlet* began to take shape. I also began to learn about the reality facing migrants crossing into this country,[*] the homeless population of Los Angeles[†] and transgender women of America.[‡] The data was fragmented, the true picture buried beneath, somewhere in those lost: the shamed, the misgendered, the transient, the decomposing. *Sins as Scarlet* is a work of fiction but, ultimately, I wanted it to be driven by the stark realities facing the vulnerable, the abused, the oppressed.

As for the dead hummingbird, it never did make it into the novel. Originally, I wanted it to be the great denouement for Inspector Iwata, a moment of chilling epiphany

---

[*] US Border Patrol recorded more than 7,216 deaths in the south-west border sectors of assumed migrants between 1998 and 2017 (https://www.cbp.gov/document/stats/us-border-patrol-fiscal-year-southwest-border-sector-deaths-fy-1998-fy-2017); Colibrí currently has records for more than 2,400 missing people last seen crossing the US–México border (https://www.iom.int/news/migrant-deaths-remain-high-despite-sharp-fall-us-mexico-border-crossings-2017)

[†] LA's homelessness surges in six years by 75 per cent (http://www.latimes.com/local/lanow/la-me-homeless-how-we-got-here-20180201-story.html)

[‡] https://www.hrc.org/resources/violence-against-the-transgender-community-in-2017; https://www.nytimes.com/2017/11/09/us/transgender-women-killed.html

at death's door. (I even toyed with the idea of including 'hummingbird' in the title somehow.) They say good writers borrow and great writers steal, but I just couldn't bring myself to take it out of that dead man's pocket. So I leave it there, beyond the greedy gaze of my imagination, and pray (if it can be called praying) for his positive identification one day. That's what Iwata now spends his days doing.

I'm writing this on Sunset Boulevard, drinking another over-conceptualized coffee at the same café where I first started plotting *Sins as Scarlet* two years ago – just a few blocks away from where we bid farewell to Iwata at the end of the book.

It's a beautiful afternoon, the sky triumphantly blue. I sent my final draft to my editor a few days ago. I'm both overjoyed and heartbroken for it to be over, at once hopeful and hopeless, drunk on its absence. Above me there are street signs, Sunset intersecting with Hyperion – the father of the dawn and sunset, the death of each day.

I've always been an over-thinker, and my imagination runs away with me, but in this moment, writing the final words for the very end of this book, it feels like there's a supertemporal circularity to things, as though years have passed and no time at all.

But like Kosuke Iwata, I know it's time to put on my sunglasses and walk out of this joint. After all, tomorrow is another day, another case.

Nicolás Obregón
Los Angeles
April 2018

Inspector Iwata will return in . . .

BLACK SUIT CITY

Tokyo. 2020.

As Japan prepares to host the Olympic Games, an English
exchange student is bludgeoned to death in a love hotel. She lies
in an empty room with a dead spider for morbid company. Could
this be a calling card from her killer?

The world's eyes are on the Japanese police, and Commissioner
Isao Shindo is desperate for a lead. But before his department
descends into disarray, he hears of the return of his old protégé,
Kosuke Iwata.

Iwata wants no part in an investigation that means stepping back
into a past he had no intention of revisiting. Until he is given an
offer he can't refuse.

As Iwata attempts to uncover a city's darkest secrets,
he gets caught up in its tangled web of lies, power and
conspiracy, encountering old ghosts and new, whispering from
its hidden corners.

READ ON FOR THE GRIPPING FIRST CHAPTER . . .

Tokyo, somewhere

Mr Sato glanced around the carriage as he nibbled off the nail from his little finger. Confident that nobody had seen him, he plucked it out from between his lips and dropped it into his jacket pocket to be with the rest. Keeping them was his little habit, his little secret.

The train was heading south, past the airport, out towards the fringes of the city. Not that Mr Sato knew where Tokyo's limits were. He wondered if anybody did any more. The carriage jolted in the warm evening, packed so tightly all the passengers swayed as one. Unlike the others, however, Mr Sato did not crane his neck for a view out of the window or a glimpse of newspaper. He simply looked at his shoes and accepted the journey, occasionally closing his eyes. That was the way in which he took this train every day, the way he lived.

Mr Sato was of medium build, of middle age. His hair was neatly cropped and his shirt impeccably pressed. Tie: seasonal. Watch: classy, not flashy. Suit: from a respectable department store. Everything about him said *mid-range*. He had no birthmarks, no scars, no distinguishing attributes. His face was ordinary. His only jarring feature was his eyebrows, at once sparse and long, like the hair on a spider's legs. It called to attention his habit of blinking too much; his irises two flies trapped in a web.

Mr Sato worked in the corporate headquarters of a confectionery manufacturer that specialized in chocolate bars, dairy products, ice creams, and, lately, dietary supplements. Its slogan was: *healthy, tasty, happy*.

He had joined the company straight out of university and had never worked a single day outside of those office walls. For the first ten years, each spring, an innocuous little slip of paper would arrive on his desk notifying him of a raise in salary without any kind of explanation. When Mr Sato's wife became pregnant, he swore he would redouble his efforts and aim for top management.

But in the following years, the pay rises diminished, and while his 'classmates' were promoted, Mr Sato was quietly farmed out to the comfort of his current dead-end position. He quickly found himself lost in a quagmire of sleepless nights and angst. His wife told him not to worry, things would work out, they would be okay. Hard times were just part of life. After all, *stress* was the most common English loanword in Japan.

Mr Sato tried everything. He went to 'mind gyms' to relax with special light goggles and music. He visited stress-relief salons for aromatherapy sessions in vibrating cubicles. He had even tried IV drips at a special clinic. When the newfangled failed, he fell back on the more traditional methods: massage, hostesses, drinking with old university friends. Once in a while, he would visit a bar at lunchtime where he could pay a small fee to smash plates. Nothing helped. At his lowest, Mr Sato considered ending things.

And then one day, as if by magic, the stress vanished. By then, he had been working at the company for over twenty years. If they had forgotten about him, then he would respond in kind. They paid his salary. He fed his kid. Looked after his wife. Put gas in his car. He refused to worry about needing anything more. For the first time in his life, Mr Sato swore to be his own man.

The train gave off a low moan as it trundled over narrow tracks, a tiny ventricle in a never-ending Tokyo heart. It ran past the backs of apartment buildings, dirty billboards, and offices now operating on the unpaid hours of the devoted.

Wishing the window would open wider, Mr Sato undid his top button. There was a brief stop at an elevated station and a few relieved commuters hopped off. Along the sagging telephone wire above, an unkindness of ravens huddled, throwing up their throaty *kraa kraa* calls at the deepening dusk. Mr Sato remembered the boutique nearby that his wife loved. It would probably still be open. He gauged the amount of bodies in his way; the amount of shoving and apologizing it would take while juggling thoughts of what kind of present he would even begin to look for. But as he wondered whether a voucher would make for an anticlimactic gift, there was a small hiss and the doors shut. *Tomorrow maybe*, he thought.

The little train rose high over the streets, then down through level crossings where flocks of homebound bicycles gathered. Not a single person in the carriage knew another; not a word was spoken. The sky was a soupy orange, the last of the sun flaring green through the apertures in the cityscape.

The thoughts in Mr Sato's head were unremarkable – his work, his dinner, his son. His son was a good boy. A little quiet, a little wide-eyed, but a good boy. Thinking about him made Mr Sato's chest feel like a cuckoo clock, as though at any moment his secret pride could burst out. He inhaled deeply, his nostrils drinking in the sweat hanging in the gaps between bodies, the stench trying to hide in perfume like an elephant behind a lamppost. But Mr Sato didn't mind smells.

He spent the rest of the journey focusing on agreeable thoughts, ultimately wondering what sort of a man his boy would grow up to be.

Mr Sato arrived home a little after 8 p.m. He ate a pleasant dinner with his wife and son then helped out with the homework. After bedtime, he sat with his wife in front of the television watching the news while she read her book.

At 11:30 p.m, Mr Sato tried to kiss her but she turned him down.

'I'm sorry, I just don't want to shower again.'

'It's okay.'

'If you want, I can use my hand?' She marked the page in her book.

'It's okay,' he smiled. 'Another time.'

Mr Sato got up and went into the kitchen. He climbed a stool and took out a maroon-coloured thermos from the highest cupboard. Looking over his shoulder, he opened it. A viscous pork smell escaped. He slipped his hand inside his jacket pocket, dropped in his nail clippings then quickly fastened the lid again. Wafting the smell away, Mr Sato washed his hands and returned to the living room.

'I'm going back in,' he said apologetically.

His wife looked up from her book with a sympathetic pout. 'You have to?'

'Afraid so. Deadline approaching.'

'Please try to rest a little during the day, then.'

'I will.'

She checked her watch. 'Will you make the last train?'

'I still have time.'

'Good.' She nodded at the thermos under his arm. 'What have you got there?'

'Just some tea.'

'You get through so much these days!'

'We all have our vices.' Mr Sato said goodnight and left.

Outside, instead of turning right for the train station, he turned left towards the small parking lot. Getting into the family car, he flipped through digital albums on the dashboard before settling on Céline Dion's 'The Power of Love'.

It took Mr Sato ninety minutes to reach the dark Ibaraki mountain roads, his car looking like a stray firefly in the dark.

By the time he was snaking through the narrow country lanes north of Lake Hinuma, it was a strain to contain his excitement. He was debating whether to pull over to masturbate when he spotted the familiar sequence of chinquapin trees followed by the unmarked turning.

Mr Sato loved the crackling, popping sound of his tyres slow over the twigs and dead leaves. It made him imagine himself as a giant worm, slithering through the warm earth.

Mr Sato parked in the usual dense grove and got out. He took the tarp sheet he'd hidden in the nearby tree and covered the car. Then he texted his wife to tell her he hoped he didn't wake her but that he was making good progress at work.

Mr Sato set off. With his keyring torch, he found the old path. The low buzz of crickets was constant, its throbbing pitch like a triggered burglar alarm. There was a chilly current through the trees, their branches screeching gently. Beneath it, there was the sound of little animals bolting away in the blackness. The woody tang of the forest smelled like life. Mr Sato filled his lungs with gusto.

After a short while, the path gave out on to a secluded lake, the water a still mauve. Mr Sato made his way along the muddy shore to a rickety jetty. He walked slowly over it, his footsteps creaking on the wood then lowered himself into an old rowboat, his intrusion rippling out across the lake.

The islet was four hundred metres away. There was nothing special about it to the eye, simply a patch of inaccessible trees in the middle of the lake. But Mr Sato knew what lay beyond them. His heart hammered for the knowing.

He was sweating by the time the boat scraped on to the shore of the islet, steam rising off his shivering shoulders. Carefully climbing out, he steadied his breathing and luxuriated over the exquisite commingling of nerves and anticipation for a moment. Then he raised his torch and made his way through the thick knot of trees.

On the other side of them, Mr Sato saw what he had come for at last. It was a simple A-frame cabin, little more than two telephone boxes in size, but it was *his*. The country air was strikingly fresh on his eyelids, his lips. He licked them, distantly smelling animal shit.

A twig snapped beneath his plain black size-eight Oxfords. Sleeping birds flapped out of the low branches, grazing the surface of the lake. It was misty, as though boiling. A single peach tree leaf fluttered down to the water and spun slowly, anti-clockwise, as if in a slow waltz to the cricket song.

Feeling the key in his pocket, the grass rustling underfoot, he recalled what his father would say whenever he asked him for chocolate as a child: *look at you, your hand is reaching out of your throat for it.*

Mr Sato worked the locks briskly and the chain fell to the grass. The soundproofed door opened. From the darkness inside, a woman screamed.

'Good evening,' Mr Sato said jovially. He kicked the door shut behind him.

He just wanted a decent book to read ...

Not too much to ask, is it? It was in 1935 when Allen Lane, Managing Director of Bodley Head Publishers, stood on a platform at Exeter railway station looking for something good to read on his journey back to London. His choice was limited to popular magazines and poor-quality paperbacks – the same choice faced every day by the vast majority of readers, few of whom could afford hardbacks. Lane's disappointment and subsequent anger at the range of books generally available led him to found a company – and change the world.

'We believed in the existence in this country of a vast reading public for intelligent books at a low price, and staked everything on it'
Sir Allen Lane, 1902–1970, founder of Penguin Books

The quality paperback had arrived – and not just in bookshops. Lane was adamant that his Penguins should appear in chain stores and tobacconists, and should cost no more than a packet of cigarettes.

Reading habits (and cigarette prices) have changed since 1935, but Penguin still believes in publishing the best books for everybody to enjoy. We still believe that good design costs no more than bad design, and we still believe that quality books published passionately and responsibly make the world a better place.

So wherever you see the little bird – whether it's on a piece of prize-winning literary fiction or a celebrity autobiography, political tour de force or historical masterpiece, a serial-killer thriller, reference book, world classic or a piece of pure escapism – you can bet that it represents the very best that the genre has to offer.

Whatever you like to read – trust Penguin.